SONS OF THE SHENANDOAH

KATHLEEN L. MAHER

Endorsements

Kathleen L. Maher brings her story to life with characters you fall in love with and become family. Her knowledge of the Civil War era draws you in, allowing you to experience the sadness, fear, and uncertainty of a nation torn apart. Her ability to write a CW novel from both the North and South perspectives without bias sets a new bar for Civil War stories. This is one novel you won't want to miss--a true page turner you can't put down.
Debbie Lynne Costello, author of *Sword of Forgiveness*
an Amazon's #1 Best Seller

Ms. Maher's exquisite skill in storytelling is evident throughout this tale of two brothers on opposite sides of a devastating war that tore both a nation and their family apart. I felt like I was in the middle of a civil war battle one minute and the next dancing my way through a fancy ball. Feelings are raw, emotions are high, and romance is strong in this epic story of love, loss, faith and family that I will not soon forget.
MaryLu Tyndall, best-selling author of the Surrender to Destiny series

The Abolitionist's Daughter by Kathleen L. Maher is a Civil War Novel that will draw you in from page one, and for me, it was almost as if I read the first fifty pages in one breath. Maher's skill as a novelist as well as an editor shine here in a kind of glory with scenes that cause you to think you are actually there, opening your eyes to passion, romance, truth, and a glimpse of history in a new and inspiring way. This is a long novel that I believe will make you want to learn more about history, and more about God.
Molly Noble Bull, award winning author.

The Abolitionist's Daughter is a sweeping story set in a time of national turmoil – the Civil War. Yet, it is also an intensely personal one, well-researched and with strong characters that will cause you to cheer and to weep as they make their choices and live out their destinies within the historical framework of their time. Freedom, self-will, duty and faith are themes that span the length of human existence and you will find them here, in Kathleen L. Maher's novel, replete with heart, history and hope.

Grace Greene, USA Today Bestselling author, and national bestselling author of *The Memory of Butterflies*

Dedication

To John, who holds my world together like Atlas, allowing me to write.

Mom, to whom I owe everything. May your heaven have a beautiful piano for you to play.

The Abolitionist's Daughter
SONS OF THE SHENANDOAH

ISBN: 9781718026247

All Scripture is taken from the King James Version of the Bible.

Cover Design by The Killion Group, Inc
www.TheKillionGroupInc.com

Acknowledgments

Many seasons, people, and resources went into the writing of this novel. First, my longtime critique partner and best friend Debbie Lynne Costello, thank you for absolutely everything. You remember the words when I've forgotten the song of my heart. You were the first to slog through this story in its roughest form, and your eagle eye saw the potential it could be. Thank you for believing.

Carrie Fancett Pagels, your help and friendship came along at a time when I really needed it. From southernisms to dialect, to word flow and countless other things, your advice and guidance always rings true. Thank you for opening doors for me!

Mark Woodhouse, archivist for the Gannet-Tripp Library, was very generous with his time and knowledge as I researched the early years of Elmira Female College. I am deeply grateful for his direction and resources.

The archivists at the Steel Memorial Library were particularly kind and helpful as I researched John W. Jones, the Langdons, and other Elmira history. A special thank you for your time and expertise.

I owe Professor Michael Horigan, author of *Elmira: Death Camp of the North,* a debt of gratitude for having the courage to tell this history as it really happened. Without your commitment to research and truth, the real story may have remained buried. You shall know the truth and the truth shall set you free.

Diane Kalas, Chris Granville, and Linda Marie Finn, my Beta readers—thank you for your excellent insights and help. Ditto to my old Civil War Yahoo group. Your commitment to historical accuracy has been an inspiration.

To the various ACFW Genesis judges—thank you for your advice, your encouragement, and your prayer. I have learned much through your example and mentoring.

How I weep for you, my brother. Oh, how much I loved you! And your love for me was deep, deeper than the love of women.
2 Samuel 1:26

Prologue

Charles Town, Virginia
December 2, 1859

The wrong ideas could get a head—and a body—into a heap of trouble.

Ethan Sharpe craned his neck, staring up thirteen plank steps at the gallows. His breath stopped as John Brown's body plunged, thrashed for a few seconds, and then went limp. A creak of rope marked the radical's only requiem among the silent attendants from Virginia Military Institute.

Ethan exhaled a dizzying breath and curled his toes in his boots to test the ground's firmness beneath him. Counting slow and even draws of air, he stole a glance at the cadet next to him—his identical twin. Devon's stance was straight as an Enfield ramrod.

"Reckon that snapped his neck?"

Devon tucked his chin to his chest. "Shh! Colonel Jackson'll hear you."

Ethan swallowed against his constricting collar, wishing he could tug at it without breaking rank. Brown's noose bore in on him with more than contemplation.

Devon's cheek muscle twitched. "An eye for an eye."

Ethan weighed those words. The abolitionist had waged a holy war through Kansas the previous year, murdering slave owners in their beds. Attempts to dole out the federal arsenal to contraband had secured John Brown's hempen necktie. A chill snaked down Ethan's spine. If successful, no telling how quickly they'd have stormed the Shenandoah Valley, or overrun the Sharpe family farm.

New York newspapers hailed Brown a hero, his death sentence martyrdom, particularly their Senator Seward. But the abolitionist hadn't cut into Yankee sleep at every rumor of slave revolt like a machete to the throat. Devon had the right of it. Brown had earned his fate.

Ethan shot another glance at Devon, who rolled his shoulder as though tossing off a fly. Then he let his gaze wander to the scene of Brown's crime, imagining clues to the man's actions could be cut from the topography.

Harper's Ferry loomed eight miles in the distance. The Blue Ridge Mountains forged a chasm where the Shenandoah and the Potomac rivers converged—one channel flowing from the north, the other from the south. Maryland Heights crested a long way up from the churning water, suggesting a breathtaking drop. Like the one Brown had just taken through the floor.

Ethan gasped a pent-up breath and blinked back swirling colors in the pool of his vision. Surely the man's soul had slipped its fleshly shell by now and fled to the waiting judgment. Would God be more merciful to him than the jury of his peers? Each draw of air grew thicker until a wheeze rattled deep in his chest. *Not now.*

A trickle of cold sweat scrolled down his brow. Asthma compressed his chest, while tiny white bombs burst behind his eyes. He clutched his brother's arm.

Devon elbowed him in the ribs. "Heads up, E!"

Ethan gasped for air. If only he could loosen the band around his ribs, cast off the strange thoughts brewing, and be strong like Devon. If only….

Chapter 1

Maryland, ten miles from Washington D. C.
Summer 1860

Mari Hamilton crept on her hands and knees into her bedroom hearth. The stone lay swept clean with disuse, the Potomac bringing refreshing cool to the house even in summer months. The conversation a floor below drew her there like a pauper gathering charcoal, to pick up words.

Her parents' conversation took on hushed tones, but if she flung her long dark braid over her back and stuck her head through the flue, she could make out enough of what they said. She must prepare herself. They would decide her fate without her.

"Levi, I implore you to consider her future. A young lady of delicate sensibilities shouldn't…."

"Now Cora darling, she's still young. There is time."

Mari's nose itched, but she dared not move a finger to scratch it, lest a trail of soot come loose in the chimney and reveal her perch.

"Marietta should have been to the salons, made her debut this spring!"

"She will in due time, dear." Papa's voice held the tenderness she so loved him for—even against the determination in Mama's tone. Mari's heart thrilled at the way her father defended her against such silly impositions. Why would she want to be locked away in some stuffy salon with corsets strung so tight they'd pop her eyeballs out of her head? Sipping tea and speaking French with a bunch of pampered brats would have to wait. God needed her right here in Maryland. People's lives were at stake.

"In the meanwhile," her father continued, "we must prepare her for the world in which she lives. To value our dedication to freedom."

Dear Papa. He might have read her heart the way he articulated it. Mari held her breath and waited for her mother's answer. The silence told Mari that Mama was either considering Papa's words or calculating leverage. The anticipation was dizzying.

"You're taking her on your mission, then, Levi?" Resignation loosened the starch in Mama's voice, and Mari expelled a breath. She should have felt sorry for Mama, but the matriarch's assent left her reeling with elation.

Her father's tread moved over the hardwood floor, and a ruffle of material summoned the image of him taking Mama in his strong arms. His voice, perhaps passing through Mama's hair, came out muffled. "She will be safe. She will be with me. I promise you, Cora, no harm will come to her—or to her 'delicate sensibilities.'

Mari stifled a giggle.

"Very well then, Levi. She may go. But if you must expose her to the evils of this world, I insist that I accompany you both."

A soft chuckle preceded Papa's consent. "I would expect nothing less, my dear."

Mari withdrew from the hearth and rose to her feet, slapping imagined ashes from her skirts. No sooner had she made herself presentable than her mother's footfalls ascended the stairs. Mari flounced upon her bed, propping a book in her lap. The door creaked open and Mama strode in.

"I suppose you heard every word, didn't you, young lady?"

Mari prepared to argue but her mother raised her brows at an angle, silencing her.

"Your delight gives you away. Not to mention the soot on your nose." Mama huffed. "You and your father win. You may go with him on his rescue mission."

"Oh, truly? Thank you, Mama!" She hopped down from the bed and sashayed to her.

Mama shook out a silk handkerchief and dabbed Mari's nose before receiving the embrace. "Now, mind you, we are acquiring your new maid if anyone asks."

"Yes, Ma'am." Mari smiled as demurely as she could. "When do we leave?"

"Tomorrow."

ଓଷ୍ଠ

Harrisonburg, Virginia
Rockingham County Fairgrounds

With a commanding tug on leather lead, Ethan led the last of Sharpe's thoroughbreds into its stall. Satisfied with the thick cushion of straw he'd just laid, he leaned against the plank wall to rest a moment. He lifted his black felt hat and mopped his forehead with a sleeve. Breathing in the pungent mix of manure, hay, and perspiration, he surveyed both the men and livestock packed into the surrounding barns and corrals for the annual auction.

"Betcha sales'll double now that we're home to help," Devon spoke from the next stall.

Across the aisle their father stroked a curry comb over a sleek flank. His shoulders bunched under an invisible load. The pressure to outsell the year's expenses bore down as tangibly as the oppressive heat.

Heedless, Devon lit in on the topic again.

"School didn't teach nothin' useful anyhow. Reciting Roman history won't split seconds off Cinder's mile. He's still doing two minutes, sixteen, and change."

Ethan smirked at his brother over the partition. Devon had been his only rival academically, so why did he dismiss the importance of a classical education now? "Book learning may not inflate a mediocre horse's value, but it might improve your grammar."

"Mediocre?" Devon huffed, and tilted his chin in their father's direction. "Pa did all his learning in the saddle. He don't seem no worse for it, does he?"

Ethan glanced across the aisle where the old man bent at the waist, a hock pressed between his knees. After picking the hoof clean of dirt, he released the horse's leg with a pat. With an exhale he stretched and raked straight, black hair away from his swarthy face. He cast a scrutinizing look in succession at each of the boys—Ethan, Devon, and their younger brother, Ben.

"Besides," Devon continued, his back turned to their father. "Apprenticing sets better with me than Thom Fool's lectures."

Ethan couldn't resist. "Professor Jackson holds high standards for his cadets. Pity you couldn't meet them."

Pulling himself up to their twin six-foot height, Devon glared over the stall partition at him. "Me?"

"Yeah, you. Who else got suspended for calling Jackson an old woman in soldier's pants?"

"What about you, swooning at John Brown's hanging?"

A loud guffaw burst from the last stall in the row. Ben's sport at Ethan's expense sent heat prickling over his ears.

"I did *not swoon*."

"Did too, just like a school girl!" Devon thrust a finger in his face. "You convinced Pa to send us home, calling the trip a 'misappropriation of authority.' So, getting expelled weren't all my doing."

"Take that back!" Ethan stopped short of scaling the barrier, one leg up, when his father appeared in the entryway, his eyes a sparking fuse lit by their devilry.

"The horses ain't gonna groom themselves." The old man held their silent attention just long enough to make his point. He turned on his spurred heel with a low growl, stomping to the end of the barn. After a moment, a puff of tobacco smoke trailed from the same direction.

Ethan waved it away until the tickle in his throat settled, joining his brothers in the open entryway of the barn. He furrowed his brows at Devon. “Now we’ve done it.”

Devon laughed and offered him a pinch of chew.

Ethan waved it away. “You don’t reckon he’s mad?”

“You kidding?” Devon spat and wiped his mouth. “You saved him from payin’ all that tuition. He’ll likely name you secretary of his treasury.”

Jangling like an ox bell rose over Devon’s prattle. Metallic and chilling, it lured Ethan out to the edge of the road to investigate.

A chained centipede of men snaked around the row of barns and came toward him and his brothers. Individual forms took shape through the heat haze, beginning with dark-skinned men showing the first signs of gray curling at temples. Following them were the broad shoulders and stout chests of men in their prime. Then boys about Ethan and Devon’s age of sixteen shuffled near the end of the line. Finally, a few women and children of various ages brought up the tail of the iron insect. The fettered group two abreast and a dozen long turned down the dirt path toward the grandstand. To the auction block.

Ethan cringed. Slaves had been a fixture his entire life, but this shackled spectacle seared into his conscience like . . . like a public execution.

A fair-skinned woman and child brought up the rear, clutching hands. The pair passed so close the hem of the woman’s muslin dress brushed the top of Ethan’s boots. Her vacant stare unseeing, she moved in shrouded silence. The boy locked gazes with Ethan, and a charge passed between them. Ethan stared on as the group moved down the road until the heat waves rising from the ground swallowed them.

Devon muttered something in his cavalier way, but the words didn’t register. A shaft of sunlight streaked through the overcast sky, creating an image in the cloud break like a white hangman’s mask. The sunbeam traveled over the road with the shifting clouds, moving steadily toward him. Then it lit over Ethan, the fiery finger of God.

He scuttled back within the dark interior of the barn.

Waving his wide-brimmed hat, he fanned his flaming face. Devon sidled up beside him, studying him curiously. Ethan set his jaw and slapped the hat back on his head. Their father returned just then through the double doorway, arms laden with coffee and apple fritters. Whether from the prospect of full pockets with the afternoon sales, or a full stomach from the offerings at hand, the old man's expression had mellowed. But the hot dough promised no comfort for Ethan. Instead the heavy aroma of cinnamon and grease roiled his stomach.

Chains on a child? He struggled to process the image.

Devon and Ben dug into the food, and their father shared a tidbit about a horse breeder from Kentucky looking to add to his stock. Once the food was gone, the old man turned to Ethan. "I was thinking about what you said earlier, about the value of a classical education. If you were freed up from some of your chores, you might take up your books again."

Ethan braced for a wallop. Devon wouldn't cotton to resuming studies, but neither would he have Ethan besting him in any arena. He flashed his twin a sheepish grin.

His father continued. "Adding another stable boy might be just the thing."

Devon swung about to face their father. "You're buying a boy?"

The old man nodded. "You and Ethan go. I'm too busy here."

"Yessir!" Devon strutted like a courting fowl.

Ethan gaped. Even their eldest brother Gideon had never been assigned such a task.

"Get one young enough to train, but big enough to work. And mind you, don't spend all my money."

Devon grabbed Ethan's arm and tugged him toward the grandstand.

ଓଃ

Marietta followed her parents through the swarming crowd. Though Mama had drilled in her that a young lady's comportment be modest and retiring, Mari couldn't help but push her bonnet back and stare. Even a scolding couldn't dull her curiosity or stem the excitement rising within her. Her heart was like to burst through her stays, attending her first slave auction rescue mission.

She'd attended meetinghouses with Mama and Papa where orators the likes of Frederick Douglass and Lucretia Mott had delivered horrific accounts of human chattel markets. She'd drank in their words until she could swear she tasted the sulfur of hell. But the company here seemed less nefarious, comprised of gentleman farmers and hawkers of wares. Her brow quirked. This wasn't what slavers looked like, was it? And here sharp-bladed, shiny new plows, the latest well pumps, and innovations in harvesters and reapers sat on display at the side of the main stage. Such ordinary—even amenable—surroundings could surely not be the underbelly of humankind. But there, just beyond stood a group of slaves huddled in the sweltering August sun. They turned stooped backs to the crowd, denying an evaluation of muscle or willing expression. She puzzled at their quiet composure, imagining what she'd feel, about to be sold to strangers. Occasionally one of the womenfolk peeked beneath turban or kerchief, and the whites of her eyes shone in stark contrast to her deep complexion. Silence fixed each face like carved ebony.

One woman stood out from the group. Her skin pale as ginger, with features more angular, she piqued Mari's curiosity. A boy stood by her side, his arms folded over his chest and his feet planted square. She guessed his age to be ten years. Despite his youth, he seemed more sentinel than ward. He mirrored the woman's fair coloring, and Mari felt sure the boy was her son.

The woman's pinched gaze flitted up to the crowd and connected with Mari's. Compassion swelled within Mari's breast, staggering her breath. She moved in closer to her mother. "That's the one, Mama. I want to help her."

Proceedings began. Wealthy gentlemen in broadcloth suits congregated at the platform. They bid as though wagering on a game of cards. They chatted and joked with one another, stealing salacious glances at the womenfolk in chains. Mari shuddered. Could no one else see the plight of these unfortunate souls? Mari seemed to be all that stood between them and perdition.

But wasn't she purchasing one of them today, too? Were these men no different than she? *No.* She rehearsed her intended purpose. She and her family were there to ransom, not enslave. She swallowed down her qualms and sought again the young mother and child among the chained commodities. The young mother was led to the block. Mari's heart pounded, and she raised her chin in defiance of the whirlwind inside her. *Lord, grant us thine favor.*

Chapter 2

Ethan and Devon settled on a vacant patch of grass on the county racetrack's infield. Handbills advertising the order of the sale already underway circulated amid the pressing crowd, and Devon grabbed one, holding it out between them. Ethan glanced between the leaflet and the platform to match words with their human counterparts. The page listed a brief description of twenty-three people, noting gender, age, and occupation. Among those offered to the highest bidder were field hands, domestic help, a cook, even a blacksmith. Devon pointed to item number ten on the page, a young male whose specialty read "farm help."

Ethan browsed the list and then the crowd, seeking item number ten in flesh and blood. Not catching sight of their objective in the lee of the stage, he nodded in silent communication with Devon, and they waited for their prospect to come up for bid.

Ethan rubbed the cuff of his sleeve between his fingers. "D'you suppose the chains are really necessary?"

"Can't be too careful since John Brown's raid."

From the shadow of the grandstand, a portly slave woman emerged and approached the platform. The furrowed brow of age bunched at her kerchief, and her legs teetered as the wooden plank bowed beneath her weight. The auctioneer's steward pushed her up the incline, reminding Ethan of a recalcitrant cow.

"That one looks like trouble, all right," Ethan muttered. He consulted the bill in his hand. *Cook*. "She's probably got a ladle hidden in her skirts just waiting to incite a riot."

Devon shushed him. "I don't make the rules. Now, be quiet. Ours is next."

The cook shuffled down the steps to her new owner, and the auction steward replaced her with the young boy Ethan had seen at the barn, this time without his mother. The boy paused mid-stride and bent to touch his ankle where the shackle had grooved his flesh. The handler thrust him forward, and the boy stumbled, catching himself on splayed hands in the middle of the stage. The man cursed and jerked him to his feet.

The auctioneer introduced item number ten. "This healthy thirteen-year buck has been working Jones's farm for several seasons." The handler lifted the boy's homespun shirt and turned him in a slow circle, showing a smooth back. "He's a right-smart, obliging young'un, as you can see. No evidence of hard treatment. He'll work your farm and give you no trouble." The assistant snapped the boy's muslin tunic down again. Ethan wondered if they'd inflated the boy's age. He looked rather small to be that old.

"Who'll start the bidding on Jonesy's boy?"

Devon raised two fingers to the auctioneer, sending a jolt through Ethan. Surely *this* wasn't the boy they'd agreed to buy? His heartbeat bucked in his chest. The boy's mother, where had she gone? They'd missed a few opening bids. Had she already been auctioned off? Ethan rued the thought of separating them, but maybe the deed had already been done.

The auctioneer squinted over the distance, and then smiled in recognition. "Master Sharpe starts us off with two hundred. Make a nice stable boy, wouldn't he? Who'll raise the bid before Sharpe's sons steal this likely prospect?"

A gentleman across the infield offered a counter-bid. Devon squared his stance and waved a finger at the auctioneer again. Disaster loomed on their plans as the man raised Devon's bid by twenty-five more. Ethan clenched his jaw, examining their competition. The man wore a fine overcoat, and a fob trailed from his vest pocket, catching the sun in glittering gold. His dark, collar-length hair gave way to salt-and-pepper at his temples and a hint of frost on his trimmed beard.

Ethan's collar cinched, heat broiling inside his cotton shirt. Sure, buying time for studying was tempting. An extra hand would afford him that. But at what expense? Nothing was worth tearing a child from his mother. A wheeze rattled in his chest, just forming, tightening. Ethan coughed and tried to press past the tension constricting his breath.

The bid jumped to three-hundred, and the auctioneer looked their way. Devon yawned, stretched, and tipped an indolent finger forward, raising the price by another twenty-five. Ethan gazed at the man across the infield. A young lady stood with him, young enough to be the man's daughter. She tugged at the gentleman's arm and pointed at the stage.

Devon scoffed. "Jehoshaphat! Look at those deep pockets. We're done for."

The young lady's daddy waved at the auctioneer and topped the bid again.

Devon exchanged a look of desperation with Ethan and upped the ante one last time.

The gentleman's daughter turned in their direction and stuck her pert little nose in the air with a huff. Then she took her daddy's arm and looked up at him beseechingly. Ethan read her lips. "Papa, please."

The man bowed his head, shaking it side to side with finality.

A pout rounded her full lips, and she released his arm, folding her hands over her skirts. She flung a glare across the infield, and Ethan flinched as though stuck with a fiery dagger.

The gavel banged, and the auctioneer shouted. "Item number ten. Sold to Sharpe Stables for three-hundred, seventy-five dollars!"

Devon strode forward to claim their prize while Ethan tripped over his own feet in numb pursuit. Halfway there, the lament of the slave mother rang in Ethan's ears as she choked out a sorrowful goodbye to her child.

"Be good and brave. Maybe the good Lord bring you back to me someday." She no sooner embraced her child when rough hands thrust her into the back of a wagon. Screaming, she fought her captor's hold, and broke free.

The boy reached toward his mother, and just as his grasp connected with hers, a man's hand clamped over the child's wrist like an iron band. The auction steward dragged the boy back toward Ethan and Devon while the wagon carried his mother away.

The slave woman's wailing ripped the air like hail on tobacco leaves. Ethan wanted to shutter his ears with his hands. Before he could react, that fiery young lady bustled through the crowd, her wealthy Mama and Papa scrambling to keep up with her. The girl dashed into the road, her molasses curls spilling from her bonnet as she flagged down the wagon, the slave woman tossing about in the back like a sack of produce until the conveyance slid to a halt. For an instant, the girl's glare burned into Ethan, scorching him from twenty yards away. Her well-formed lips, her upturned brows, her impassioned features held more threat than her Daddy's bidding. Ethan's breath staggered, and a grin tugged at his lips. She was the prettiest thing he'd ever seen, even if she *was* fiercer than a feral cat.

Her Mama caught up to her and seized her by the arm. "Marietta Hamilton! Come away from there at once. You're making a spectacle."

The girl covered her mouth, and her angst pained Ethan. She raised a gesturing hand between the weeping slave mother and the Sharpe's new stable boy. Then her father stepped up to the wagon's driver and withdrew his wallet. The girl—Miss Hamilton—seemed to gather her composure as she gathered the folds of her skirt. In the next moment, the driver swung down from the rig and released the slave woman into the Hamilton's custody.

Ethan sought his brother, but their new stable boy stood between them. The boy's round cheeks glistened with two equal tracks, and his Adam's apple slid in a swallow, but he stood his ground. Was it courage or defiance smoldering in those umber eyes?

Ethan blinked. The girl would've purchased both mother and child, but Devon's efficient procurement of their new servant had crushed her hopes. He opened his mouth to cancel the deal, but it was too late. Crisp bills exchanged between avaricious fists, and the steward released the boy and his papers into Devon's custody.

Ethan's pulse thrummed a dull throb in his cavernous chest. He felt eyes on him. Glancing up from his boots, he came face to face with that wildcat, Marietta Hamilton. His mouth parched. Silent pleading lit her beautiful eyes.

"Please, couldn't we come to some sort of arrangement?"

Before he could answer, her mother led her away with a firm tug of her arm.

Had Devon noticed? No, Devon was too busy evaluating their purchase with a pinch of shoulder muscle. When Devon reached to inspect his mouth, the boy swung out of Devon's hold, his solid shoulder ramming Ethan's chest.

"Oomph!" Ethan staggered a pace away and rubbed his ribs. "Watch where you're going!"

Devon laughed and clapped a hand over the boy's shoulder. "You know, colts back home can sure pitch a row at weaning. Reckon you're no different. By and by you'll forget your mammy—just like them weanlings. Come along now."

Ethan hung several paces back, searching for the Hamilton girl and her family. But they had disappeared in the crowd.

☙❧

On the Valley Turnpike toward Maryland
Later that day

The auction wasn't the gallant rescue mission Mari had dreamed. In fact, it had been one of the worst disappointments of her life. How could things have gone so wrong? The poor creature sitting next to her shook and sobbed over most of the trip home, once so violently Papa had to pull off the road to calm the horses. Mari's heart ached as she imagined the young mother's pain, watching her son sold before her eyes, able to do nothing to stop it. But none of her imaginings offered the consolation she longed to give. She had failed to secure the boy's safety. *Failed*! A tapestry of grief shrouded the carriage.

Mama's posture straight and her demeanor unruffled, she looked the forlorn woman in the eye. "What is your name, dear?"

Drawing a shuddering breath, the slave woman replied, "My name's Matilda, ma'am. Folks call me Tilly."

"Have faith, my dear Matilda. The Good Lord will bring your son to safe harbor." The soft tones of Mama's voice soothed Mari's heartache. How could they fail to reassure the bereaved young mother?

Wiping her nose with the sleeve of her gingham dress, Tilly replied. "My boy half a world away by now. Mos' likely I never see him again." Puffy eyelids only half-concealed the glaze of defeat over her deep brown eyes.

"I have an inkling you'll see him again, and soon. Mr. Hamilton is a clever man. Leave it to him."

Mari's words blurted out ahead of better sense. "If Papa'd only bought the boy now, then we wouldn't—"

"Young lady." Her mother's chin rose until she looked down her sharp nose at her. "We might have secured both for the price we paid for one. If you had held your composure and refrained from challenging those young men, we would have. Mind you appreciate what your father has done."

Mari studied the stitches in her embroidered pelisse, cringing under the deserved rebuke. By and by she braved a glance up, to observe her mother's serene countenance, infused with an inner light, gazing on Papa. A knowing smile lifted her mother's expression, restoring a youthful glow about her lovely features.

Mari sighed. How wonderful it would be to remain forever under the wise counsel of her parents, or at least until she met the Godly man intended for her. What could the salons an ocean away impart to her that her dear Mama and Papa could not? With all her heart, she wanted a marriage like her parents' someday. But did she have to do the silly things Mama insisted upon to catch a husband? Couldn't she just follow her Mama's example, and practice being noble, sincere and good? Did she have to enunciate her syllables and walk with mincing steps, and be like those ridiculous girls at finishing school? Sudden movement next to her interrupted her thoughts.

Tilly knelt down, folds of calico dress sinking to the bottom of the carriage as she clasped Mama's hand. "He a good boy, Ma'am. He a hard worker!" she sobbed. "If you fetch him back, he sho' to earn his keep—"

"Matilda, I want you to listen to me. You have not been purchased to serve as a slave in our household. We paid your price to rescue you from the evils of slavery. You will never be anyone's property again, do you hear? And neither will your son, once we secure him. God willing, you and your son will live as free people, working for wages, and getting an education. We want you to serve the Lord and live honest and good lives to glorify Him who purchased your eternal freedom. Do you understand?"

"Yes, Ma'am." Tilly nodded, but bewilderment still troubled her expression.

"What Mama means is we would like you to stay with us at our home. You could help me with my chores, and we'll pay you money for your work. Would you like that?"

Tilly lifted her dewy gaze for a second to Mari and dropped it to her hands. "I'll work hard to buy my boy back." Her brows pinched together, but her tone had sunk low, whether in peace or resignation, Mari couldn't say. All she could think to do was to pat the woman's arm, words failing her.

Her own tears brimming, Mari turned to her mother. "Does Papa truly have a plan?"

ꕥ

Bridgewater, Virginia
Late October 1860

Ethan scooted in next to Devon and Ben, already seated at the dinner table. With a cautious appraisal, he studied his father. Coffee and a racing sheet seemed to sate him while their house servant Ezra carved the roast. Ethan smiled to himself. Thank goodness, his tardiness hadn't ruffled any feathers.

Devon pilfered two biscuits and set them in his lap, casting a dubious look at Ethan. The warm aroma set his mouth to watering. One nudge and Devon obliged him, passing half his cache under the table. With one last quick look at the old man, they popped simultaneous bites into their mouths.

Their father sat back from the table, but instead of commencing with the meal, he reached up and fished in his waistcoat. "Got a telegram today."

Ethan focused on the note his father held. Must have been pressing if the old man missed biscuit thieving right under his nose.

Reaching across the table and taking a serving of beef, Sam Sharpe signaled the boys to fill their plates at last. "A certain gentleman from Washington came to the auction last month looking for a saddle horse. Apparently, due to other 'pressing business', he claims he missed his chance. He writes his regrets, and has prevailed upon us to deliver a horse to him right away."

"That's a good thing, isn't it?" Ben asked through a mouthful of peas.

Ethan elbowed him. No sense in letting the youngest catch the censure he and Devon deserved for speaking out of turn, or with one's mouth full.

Their father's dark eyes roved over each one until even their chewing stilled. "I'm not fond of being pressed upon for the convenience of others."

Devon shrugged. “What’s the man's hurry?”

“Not his hurry, Devon. Mine. The sooner I settle accounts *with those people*, the better.”

Devon nodded, but Ethan cocked his head to the side, wondering what he’d missed.

“Business is hard enough without sectionalist politics thrown in.” The old man tore a considerable bite out of a biscuit, washing it down with a swallow of coffee. Clearing his throat, he added, more to himself, “And they want me to send one of my boys, besides. Can’t they handle their own horseflesh?”

Ethan’s curiosity got the better of him. “If they missed the auction, doesn’t that mean they’re paying top dollar?”

“Oh, *they’re paying*, all right, especially if I have to deliver. We’d better conclude this business in short order before this election fixes to lance the boil of the country’s sectionalist politics.”

The approaching presidential election had seemed little more than idle talk at neighbor’s fences and hitching posts. Washington was surely too remote to affect his world for long.

“Reckon you’ll want the sale dispatched as soon as possible, then,” Ethan replied.

“I hope to send you boys first thing next week,” the old man gave Ethan and Devon a lingering look. “If you think you’re capable.”

Devon threw down his napkin. “Of course, we are, Daddy.”

“Yes, sir” Ethan agreed.

“Easy, now. You’re not catching any train tonight. I’ll purchase the tickets tomorrow and telegraph the man with your expected arrival time.”

Ethan grinned at Devon. First the auction, and now this. What would Gideon say? Visiting relatives in Charleston, Gideon would be plumb green-eyed at their liberty.

Devon clapped Ethan’s shoulder. “This apprenticeship beats school by a mile. Admit it.”

A chuckle rose in Ethan's throat at his brother's smug told-you-so, but then he sobered. His father was looking directly at him.

"That new stable boy."

"Yes, sir?"

"How's he coming along?"

Devon had taken on the boy's orientation, and answered. "Reckon he only hitched up plow nags before, but he seems to know which ends kicks and which end bites."

His father's gaze traveled over the rim of his cup before he set his coffee down. "Good. Because the man offered me twice what I paid for him."

Startled at the news, Ethan turned to Devon. His twin replied wryly, "So much for getting us back to our books."

Ethan wanted to shrink under the table. He *knew* he'd never hear the end.

The old man settled back into his chair until it creaked. "Seems you both have fine racing prospects this year. Which one of you is selling their horse to pay for the boy?"

Neither moved.

"What? No takers?"

Ethan kicked Devon's foot under the table.

"Good." The old man lit his pipe, waving out the Lucifer match while its sulfurous smell wafted in curls over their supper plates.

Ethan swallowed before a coughing spasm erupted, holding his breath as the smoke thinned. He wasn't about to make trouble over any slave, even if this one had been promised to benefit him.

Chapter 3

Maryland
First week of November 1860

"Tilly, let's say a prayer that Mama permits me to go."

Matilda clenched hairpins in her teeth as she wove a ribbon into the last of Mari's braids, waiting to up-sweep and pin them in a crown about her head. She paused and grasped the hairpins in nimble fingers to reply. "You think that best, Miss Mari?"

"I do. Now that Papa's back from his business trip, he should be able to convince Mama. Perhaps if I employ the proper charm, those boys will forget all about the auction and that unfortunate bidding war."

Tilly secured the top crowning pieces above cascading layers of curls and held a hand mirror to reflect her handiwork in Mari's dressing mirror.

"Lovely, Tilly. As always. Thank you."

"Yes'm." Tilly set down the ivory mirror. "I was wondering, Miss Mari…"

Mari smiled to ease the poor young woman, still not entirely assured Tilly knew she was free to speak, free to question, free….

"Yes?"

"If you needs me to go with you, I-I could—"

Mari took the woman's hand in hers. She considered for a moment how to reply. "I'm concerned that if those slaveholders suspect our purpose is to free you both, they'll be far less likely to cooperate." She squeezed the maid's hand ever so gently. "You understand, don't you? It will be best for you and your son to keep a low profile while Papa conducts negotiations."

Tilly's shoulders sagged a bit, and she bit her lip. "Yes, Ma'am."

"Oh, Tilly, let's say a prayer. We're so close!"

The maid exhaled and nodded, swiping at her eyes. "Yes, Miss Mari. I'll be prayin' the whole time you gone."

ঙ্ଛ

Sun pierced the wooden slats at the window, illuminating the dial of Ethan's pocket watch. The livestock car in which they traveled slowed on a curve. Even now the outline of buildings appeared above the tree line as they neared Washington City.

Devon roused from the corner and dusted the hay from his trousers. "Almost there. Figures the old man was too cheap to buy us passenger tickets." Pressing a pocket pomade and comb into service, Devon swept his straight, dark hair from his face.

Ethan shook his head at his twin's conceit and gathered their belongings. "Jonesy, you take the bags. I'll handle the horse."

While the stable boy obliged, the jolt of brakes threw them forward, and the gelding sent up a whinny lost to the sound of grinding metal and hissing steam. A water bucket sloshed its contents over Devon's satchel. Ethan snorted in laughter while Jonesy ducked out of Devon's reach, drawing the sliding door.

A cloud of soot and smoke billowed in. Through the haze, Ethan's attention tangled on a comely sight—a young lady standing at the gate no more than ten yards away, her hand raised above the brim of her hat to shield her searching eyes. She turned her head his way, and an angelic smile brightened her face. The look of this petite beauty reminded him of that feisty young lady from the auction last month, only a sweeter, kinder version. Ethan stood taller, straightening his rumpled clothes. The horse took advantage in his distraction and jerked the leather lead almost out of his hand in its haste to leave the compartment. Ethan scrambled to regain control, but the spell was broken. The girl's gaze had shifted from him to Jonesy, who had hoisted the bags from the car and stepped to his side. Something lit her expression, a spark in her eye akin to a cat's focusing on prey within striking distance.

Just then, Devon joined them on the platform, smoothing his hair back and offering a rakish smile as he surveyed the Washington depot. The girl's pleasant expression vanished, and her eyes narrowed. Ethan squinted. Her bonnet concealed all but the outline of her features, but that glare, he recognized in an instant. *Couldn't be.*

Devon walked out free-handed, swaggering toward the older gentleman at the girl's side. The man doffed his hat. Ethan drew up beside Devon.

"You must be Sam Sharpe's sons." He held out a hand. "Levi Hamilton."

Ethan couldn't believe it. It was indeed the same father and daughter from the Rockingham County auction. He shook the man's hand. "Mr. Hamilton? Pleased to make proper acquaintance this time around."

Devon's expression belied more than casual interest, appraising the girl the way he would a pawn shop trinket. Ethan elbowed his twin.

Gathering the young lady to his side, Mr. Hamilton chuckled. "Indeed. This is my daughter, Marietta. I'm afraid you'll have to tell us which of you is which."

Ethan captured Miss Marietta's hand in his and bowed. Straightening, he batted a playful wink. "I'm Ethan Sharpe. You may distinguish me as the better-looking twin."

Marietta fluttered her long lashes but couldn't conceal the amusement dancing in her hazel eyes. "It seems you are identical, except for your mouths."

Devon's laughter rose over the clang of the engine bell. Ethan released her hand, and his brother rushed in. "I'm Devon, Miss Mari. The older and wiser twin."

Mr. Hamilton chuckled, and grasped the horse's lead, looking over the liver bay's conformation. "Fine animal." The man peered around the wall created by Ethan and Devon's side-by-side stance to where Jonesy stood with the bags. The man's mouth twisted, seeming to hold back from saying something.

Ethan took Marietta's available arm, and the three of them—Devon, Miss Hamilton and he—walked to her father's waiting carriage. Ethan helped her into her seat and hopped in next to her, casting a triumphant look back at his brother, who settled beside Jonesy on the baggage platform, grumbling under his breath.

After tying off the horse's lead, Mr. Hamilton climbed the driver's pedestal and picked up the reins. Soon the brougham clipped away from the station. Across the street a brass band struck up a tune, and a passerby waved the patriotic colors of a campaign banner.

"What's that?" Ethan gestured toward the assembly.

Mr. Hamilton turned to face them, his booming voice carrying over the street din. "That, boys, is the Democratic process on display. One of the candidates arrives on the twelve-thirty train."

Outside the city, river sounds accompanied them over several miles of wooded road interspersed with sprawling lawns and walled estates. By and by, a brick structure with tall chimneys and symmetrical dormers appeared over the crest. A manicured garden surrounded the circular drive and at the center was a double-columned entry. Behind the main house lay the carriage house, stables, and boat house leading back to the banks of the Potomac.

Mr. Hamilton slowed the horses onto the cobbled drive. Jonesy hopped down from the back of the carriage and hustled to hold the reins. Devon untied their thoroughbred from the back, giving Ethan opportunity to help Miss Hamilton alight.

He offered his arm and she grasped it in small, gloved hands, and the weight of her seemed barely more than dandelion fluff floating down from the platform. Ethan reached about her to help with her trailing skirts, and she raised her pert nose in the air with a compulsory "thank you" before gathering them herself and flitting up to the house. Left standing there, Ethan tucked his chin and shrugged.

"You gonna help us, E?" Devon called.

Ethan nodded and jogged down the sloping lawn to where the men worked putting away the carriage and horses. Once Jonesy had been instructed on where to bed down the new animal, Mr. Hamilton invited Ethan and Devon up to the house. Inhaling a measure of ballast, Ethan prepared for round three with the tempestuous Miss Hamilton.

Mrs. Hamilton, the starchy woman Ethan recalled from the auction, met them the door. After a quick peck on his wife's cheek, Mr. Hamilton entered ahead of the boys. The woman's curious gaze appraised Ethan and his brother in turn before she beckoned them inside. "Welcome. Do come in."

The air hung in a savory aroma, and Ethan thought it polite to comment. "Something sure smells good."

Devon nodded. "I'm fit to starve after that train ride."

"I would be pleased to have you stay for dinner." The matron held a practiced smile. "Please wipe your boots before you tread on the Persian rugs."

ᘓ೫ᘐ

"Tilly, come quickly!" Mari called from the back hallway. Her low voice barely contained her urgency.

Breathless, Mari waited outside the maid's chamber door.

She had excused herself from the visitors and hastened to find the maid. Mari had advised the girl to lay low, but she hadn't expected to have to search for her.

"Yes'm?" The young woman emerged in a fresh serving dress and pressed apron.

Marietta grasped her hand, and instantly the contours of the dear maid's face lifted into a sublime expression of hope. A soft gasp caught in her throat.

Mari's voice resumed evenness, but with effort. "Papa's plan was successful. Your son is here."

The corners of Tilly's eyes crinkled, and Mari could only guess her maid's emotions. Marietta cleared her throat and maintained a straight posture, though she longed to spring down the corridor.

Tilly squeezed Mari's fingers. "My boy? Where's he now?"

Marietta led the way toward the back door. "I'll take you to him, but only for a short moment for now. After dinner has been served and cleared, then you two may have the evening to yourselves." She turned abruptly. "We must attract no attention. You understand, don't you?"

"Yes'm."

ଔଓ

The sumptuous meal should have smoothed Ethan's ruffled feathers as the light of the chandelier cast an amber glow, bathing the table in a mellow light, and contentment spread over him with the warmth of the fireside. It would be perfect, in fact, except for a small trifle. Devon had secured the seat next to Miss Hamilton.

An inspired thought struck. "Devon, fetch the pedigree father sent. Our lines trace back to the legendary foundation sires Matchem, Herod, and Eclipse."

Devon obliged with a lingering look while Ethan assumed the vacated seat beside Miss Marietta. Long lashes fluttered over her hazel eyes, and he suddenly found himself bereft of anything clever to say. Instead, he grinned and fiddled with the buttons at his collar. At last, Devon returned and took Ethan's chair with a barely audible grunt. Pedigree in hand, he'd also retrieved small parcels for Mr. Hamilton and his wife, also sent by their father.

Mr. Hamilton opened his first. The wrapped box concealed a bottle of cognac. The man motioned to pour for his guests until his wife's prim wave stopped him.

He lifted the bottle. "My thanks to our new friends, the Sharpes. May the Lord bless and prosper you all."

The ladies' box revealed a French-scripted label, containing petit fours. Delighted cooing assured Ethan that his father had hit the mark. Miss Marietta lifted the paper and offered Ethan and his brother a sample of the tiny chocolate covered cakes. Though tempting, Ethan refused. He could not as easily refuse a lingering study of Marietta's hands, now uncovered, small and pale beneath her gloves. The tips of his own fingers tingled as he imagined the soft feel of them. He'd be sure to investigate at the first opportunity.

Mrs. Hamilton stood. "Would you entertain our guests with a song on the piano, Marietta? I'll be along shortly after Tilly and I get everyone—everything, that is—settled."

"Yes, Mama." She rose and led the gathering to the parlor. Past a wide entry with cherry pocket doors, a gracious room opened to them, furnished with a grand piano and carved fruitwood chairs. His brother plopped down into one, and Ethan settled in another beside him. Marietta took her place on the piano bench, while Mr. Hamilton chose a sofa in the corner.

Marietta's hands lifted, ready to awaken the instrument. Then, a flurry of precision strokes graced the keys with trilling waves of sound. Molasses curls spilled over ivory shoulders as the young lady swept those delicate hands over the keyboard, every movement arched and alluring. Ethan wrestled with the notion that this was the same fiery creature glaring daggers at the auction. She'd been transformed, and in her presence, so had he. She finished the recital in a lingering chord, and one glance consummated the moment for him. Her hazel eyes met his. She flashed her perfect white teeth in an arresting smile at him, and he melted like one of her chocolates left too close to the fire.

Ethan's pulse still thrummed, his breath kept rhythm with the meter of the music. The soft glow of her skin in the lantern light sent flame through his veins. He pictured cupping her pretty face in his hands and….

Devon rammed an elbow into his ribs. "It's getting late." He stood and bowed to his hosts, and then turned back to Ethan, quirking his brow. "Shouldn't we be settling our accounts?"

Mr. Hamilton consulted his pocket watch. "It *is* getting late.

I'll tell you what. If you stay, I'll show you boys the capital tomorrow. We'll discuss business over a fine meal in town. What say you?"

Devon looked down at his boots, his lips curled. Ethan's hopes inflated. A rare occasion indeed, Devon deferring to him to make the decision. Mr. Hamilton awaited reply.

"I'm sure Father won't mind if we stay another day. By then you'll be satisfied that the horse is to your liking."

Devon gave Ethan a perceptive nod. "I reckon one more day would be all right."

Mrs. Hamilton entered the room, flushed from her activities. Mr. Hamilton turned to her. "Is everything in order, dear?"

"Yes, I believe all is settled now."

"Very good. Would you mind showing our guests their accommodations for the night? They must be tired after their long journey."

"Of course. Won't you come with me, gentlemen?"

Devon went ahead but Ethan hesitated, casting a lingering glance at Miss Mari.

She slipped from the piano bench and treaded softly toward him. Face to face with her now, Ethan found his tongue.

"Mozart would be proud."

Her smile struck Ethan as too shy for a girl of such privilege. Surely, better compliments had been paid her, and by gentlemen possessed of greater charm than a boy with a Tidewater accent and unrehearsed delivery. Before she could respond to him they were interrupted.

"You recognize the composer?" The genteel tone belonged to Mrs. Hamilton, who still stood in the threshold. Devon halted in the hallway and returned to Ethan's side.

"Yes, ma'am. Our mother played."

"Oh? Do tell us more about yourselves and your fascinating family." The lady's inflection made the invitation sound more like a command.

Ethan obliged. "Devon and I recently left Virginia Military

Institute to apprentice at home."

"Is that right? Our son Aaron graduated Washington College two years past." Her honeyed tone belied the calculation in her eye. "Your prospects must be great indeed to return home from such a prestigious placement."

"Yes, ma'am. Ours is among the finest horseflesh in Virginia. We hold almost a thousand acres, with a herd of four hundred."

Mr. Hamilton stepped forward to join the discourse. "Sounds like a great deal of work. I imagine you've invested in quite a labor force?"

"My brothers, father and I oversee most everything from foaling to training. But it helps to have a few hands."

"By hands, you mean slaves?"

Devon cleared his throat. "I reckon that's our father's affair, sir. With all due respect."

"Yes, son. Of course. I only ask, because I hope we can come to a gentlemen's agreement on the stable boy you've brought with you."

The stable boy. The very one that started the bidding war. No doubt the real reason this sale had been arranged. *But why?* The loop of Ethan's memory circled back to the Rockingham County auction again. He'd been mesmerized by a pretty distraction at the time, but he suddenly had a clearer view of the events. The slave woman and the boy, their chains. The omen in the clouds. The hangman's mask. The finger of God. And the scorching heat, now climbing up his neck once again.

Ethan's breath hitched. Managing a deep, even inhale through his nose and out through pursed lips, he still couldn't mitigate the tightness cinching his chest. He suppressed a cough and willed himself to pull deep draws of air. It wouldn't do to have an episode here, so far from home.

Devon placed a bracing hand at his shoulder and whispered, "Are we holding up?"

Ethan rued his weakness, but he didn't trust his voice yet.

Devon always had to handle things because of him and this blasted infirmity. He nodded.

Devon assumed a disarming grin and addressed their hosts. "We'll take you up on that room now."

"Of course." Mrs. Hamilton gestured toward the staircase. "Please, right this way."

Ethan caught a glimpse of Marietta just before they turned up the stairs. Her narrowed eyes and piqued brows burned an image into his mind of displeasure. Or concern.

He would know her disposition toward him in the morning.

Chapter 4

They're not selling!

She had been close enough to hear the brothers' whispering. It didn't sound promising. Good thing they'd hurried to their room before her emotions got the better of her. Retreating to hers shortly after, she would try to quiet the pounding in her head. She'd placed so much faith in this plan, and now it looked as though it would unravel.

But Lord, this must succeed. Marietta crouched beside her bed, adjusting her nightdress beneath her knees. She tried to bow her head but the urgency inside her kept drawing her gaze to the window, as though a sign might be written in the sky. The gibbous moon nodded between clouds and bare branches, and its cold, stern face reminded her of how distant her answers loomed from grasp.

"My prayers don't seem to be reaching, Lord."

Marietta looked down at her folded hands and wiggled her fingers to keep them from going numb. She'd been bent in prayer for nigh on half an hour, silent, waiting for an answer. But the hard floor grew colder and her patience waned thinner the longer she knelt.

She reflected on the evening with some satisfaction. Her charm seemed to be working on one of the brothers, an encouraging sign if she hoped to influence his decision. But the other twin stood aloof, as though on guard. That one, the more calculating one, would be more difficult to persuade.

"Heavenly Father, Papa said they'd bring the boy with them, and he was right about that. But what if he was wrong about them being willing to sell? I couldn't bear it if Tilly had to say goodbye to her son again."

Her Bible lay on her bed, opened to Proverbs, the 24th chapter. But before she read, she turned her gaze skyward again. "If they leave with the boy, how will his poor mother ever trust you?"

The very idea of failure, and crushing Tilly's newfound faith and hope, churned through her. "Please, show me your plan."

The Bible returned to her focus. She read aloud.

"If thou faint in the day of adversity, thy strength is small. If thou forbear to deliver them that are drawn unto death, and those that are ready to be slain; If thou sayest, Behold, we knew it not; doth not He that pondereth the heart consider it? and He that keepeth thy soul, doth not He know it? and shall not He render to every man according to his works?"

The words on the page grew blurry beneath hot tears. She wanted to deliver this mother and son from this attack on the natural order, the severing of family ties, the killing of hopes—the murder of personhood itself that was slavery.

She must not faint or shrink from helping in any way the Lord would have her to. But help how? Do what?

Oh, Lord, speak.

To mark the scripture's place, she'd tucked a leaflet into her Bible. She'd saved it from one of the many abolitionist rallies she'd attended with her parents. The words on the leaflet, attributed to Matthew Henry's *Concise Commentary on the Whole Bible*, read:

If a man know that his neighbour is in danger by any unjust proceeding, he is bound to do all in his power to deliver him. And what is it to suffer immortal souls to perish, when our persuasions and example may be the means of preventing it?

The words stoked a fire within, compelling her to a course of action. Her unique position to do good for this mother and child could be no coincidence. Her "persuasion and example" might be the only means left of preventing these souls from suffering the injustice of slavery. "Lord, if tomorrow brings no resolution, I am prepared take matters into my own hands."

She pulled herself up on tired legs and climbed into bed. After trimming the wick of her lantern, she leaned over and blew it out. Drawing the covers up over her shoulder and snuggling into bed, she entertained visions of a ginger-skinned Moses and Jochebed embracing by the Nile. She smiled a sleepy smile and whispered into the darkness, "Amen."

଼

Ethan followed Devon down to breakfast, the sound of Miss Marietta's voice quickening his pace.

"Has Papa left for work already?"

Mrs. Hamilton appeared in the doorway, her back to the boys as she faced the adjoining kitchen. "Senator Seward summoned your father early this morning by courier. He requires your father's immediate assistance."

Devon wedged himself into a seat at the table and craned his neck toward the direction of the food. Ethan cringed at his brother's deportment and sat at the table beside him.

Miss Marietta emerged, followed by a fair-skinned servant, each balancing a platter. Tea and toast, poached eggs, and sectioned citrus fruits were among the fare. The servant girl was Jonesy's mammy, all right. Ethan remembered her well from that pitiable procession in chains. But she seemed a different person. Here, she hummed as she worked, and something in her smile infused him with warmth. Perhaps it was the simple joy of reuniting with her son.

A weight settled in his stomach, robbing his appetite. It would be a shame to tear these two apart again. He'd speak to Devon about the Hamilton's purchase offer.

Before he had the chance to pursue the thought, the graceful Miss Hamilton settled her dishes over an embroidered tablecloth and took her place at the table. She offered both Ethan and Devon a smile and "good morning" before bowing her head over her plate. Ethan studied her, wondering if she'd be pleased once her father made the servant's acquisition. It seemed to be terribly important to her at the auction. He'd like nothing better than to make her happy.

Her mother took a seat at the table and blessed the meal. Ethan had just lowered his head to pray, when Devon swung about.

"What's this?" Devon seized a newspaper left open on the table.

Ethan skimmed the headline over his brother's shoulder.

SPLIT CONSTITUENCY: LINCOLN LIKELY WINNER

He'd all but forgotten about the election.

His father had spelled out the implications of a Lincoln White House. Lincoln, who had vowed not to enforce slavery in all territories, would generate a thousand John Browns—fanatics who swore a sacred duty to arm slaves and murder their captors. Violent uprising might overtake the land under such leadership soft on upholding the law.

Equally worrisome, Devon had no compunction about spewing his politics over the serene table the same way he'd just spurted his coffee. Ethan locked gazes with his brother. He winced, hoping that his silent plea would restrain the brewing storm.

After a brief, tense meal, Mrs. Hamilton rose from the table. "I regret to tell you gentlemen that Marietta and I have a prior commitment to the ladies' auxiliary today. Mr. Hamilton will return as soon as he can to entertain you. Please make yourselves at home in the meanwhile, and our maid Tilly will see to your needs until Mr. Hamilton returns."

As soon as the ladies departed, Devon rose and paced the floor.

"They've stranded us! No payment, no terms… They've made fools of us."

Ethan followed a few paces and stopped. "Surely not. They'll keep their word."

"Don't you find it suspicious? I mean, the least they could do is settle accounts and give us the option to stay or go."

Nodding, he had to concede Devon's point. "Reckon we ought to gather our horse and our stable boy and cut our losses?"

Devon burst out the back door and led the way out to the stable and carriage house. Arriving at an empty building, Ethan stood beside Devon, mouth agape. No horse, and no boy, either. If Ethan had been about to ask Devon to sell the boy to the Hamiltons, he found no incentive to now. He fished in his pocket and produced their train tickets. "What do we do now? We can't leave without payment."

Devon commandeered one of the tickets. "We should'a demanded our money last night. We've been hoodwinked!"

"No, they're bound to return home sooner or later."

Devon ceased pacing, as if too furious to go on. "I need a smoke." Exiting the barn, and sagging against the top fence rail, he procured a small leather pouch from his breast pocket. Folding a pinch of tobacco into a paper wrapping, and sealing the stick with a twist, Devon looked about before lighting a Lucifer match.

Ethan stood sentinel with him. "Figure the old man's wondering where we are?"

"No doubt! These people wouldn't understand what this election means to us." Devon shook out his match and discarded it on the cobble.

"It's not the Hamilton's fault." Ethan stooped to pick up the spent stick. "They're not the devil."

"No. But they voted for him, I'll warrant."

"Their interests are different from ours," Ethan reasoned.

Devon took a deep drag and expelled a blue cloud. "We could take that wench as earnest until we get our payment."

Ethan sucked a breath. "No, Devon. We won't disgrace Daddy like that."

"What's he got to do with it?"

"He wouldn't stoop to common thievery."

With another puff, Devon's volatility ebbed a measure. "I suppose you're right. He'd know how to turn this around without losing his shirt or his head, so that's what we'll do."

Ethan clapped his brother's shoulder. "We'll make the best of it."

"Yep. Have to."

ଔ

Wheels ground on the stone drive, signaling the Hamilton carriage's return. Ethan jumped to his feet, but Devon already led the way out to meet it.

Levi Hamilton emerged first, and then Jonesy, serving as footman, helped the ladies alight. Ethan stopped short, watching as the boy scampered off to take charge of the horses. So, they *had* taken Jonesy with them. But where was the thoroughbred?

While Ethan tried to conjure words, Miss Marietta slipped away and followed her mother straight into the house.

Devon stood beside him, taut as a drum skin. "Are you going to say something, or should I?"

Ethan grit his teeth. If Devon spoke in this state, there would be no salvaging the damage.

Before he could open his mouth, Mr. Hamilton apologized. "I'm sorry I had to leave you this morning so abruptly, but urgent business called. I suppose you've heard the results of the election?"

Mindful of his mother's good breeding, or at least his father's business sense, Ethan reined in his reply. "We've heard."

Levi led them both up to the house. "I hope the country will keep an open mind about Mr. Lincoln."

Devon sucked his teeth. "We've been practicing an open mind all morning, sir, while it appears that not only has the election been stolen from us, but our horse and our servant, as well."

Mr. Hamilton waved his hand in an ameliorating gesture. "On your advice, I have taken the opportunity to attest the horse and boy are to my liking. The young man has proven most useful looking after my wife and daughter on their sojourns through town. And my eldest son Aaron has the gelding as we speak—a very fine animal. I am prepared to offer you a handsome sum for both."

"The price just went up for our time and inconvenience."

The man's brows raised, but then a chuckle transformed his features. "A skilled agent, I see. I'll save the blood-sport for my real adversaries up on the Hill. I promised you gentlemen a night on the town, and I would hate to spoil anyone's appetite."

Devon folded his arms and refused to follow him into the house. "On the contrary, sir. I find debate only whets the appetite."

Mr. Hamilton's tongue moved in his cheek as if tasting something unpleasant. In the next moment, though, the corners of his mouth lifted into a cordial smile again.

"After dinner in town, I wonder if you boys might join us for our mid-week church service? Marietta plays the accompaniment for the choir, and I know she'd appreciate your support."

Ethan hadn't expected this. Neither had he the will to say no to Miss Mari. "We'd be pleased." A sudden spike drove into his back—Devon poking him with all the ferocity one finger could muster. Despite the savage spearing, Ethan maintained a polite facade.

Devon snorted. "We ought to prepare for the outing, then, oughtn't we, brother?" His successive jabs commanded mobility at last. Ethan led the way into the house, and upstairs, toward their guest room.

Once out of the Hamilton's sight, Ethan thundered. "*What?*"

"We need to get home!" Devon ground out through clenched teeth. "What are you doing, agreeing to stay another night?"

"Well, we've come this far." He turned into the bedroom and Devon followed. "Reckon we might see Washington for our trouble. And get to know Miss Mari a bit better…."

His brother leaned against the closed door and scrubbed a palm over his face. "So, this is about a girl?"

Ethan raised his arms in surrender, grinning. "Maybe."

Devon shook his head, but after a moment his grin broke the tension. "Fine. But it'll cost you. What're you willing to trade?"

Ethan sighed. Asking Devon to stay another night did warrant a good turn. "I'll let you make the final decision on Jonesy. Just as soon be rid of him so we don't have to sell our horses."

"What about your studies? He was supposed to help you."

Ethan's face burned. "I don't need a boy to do my work. I can manage both."

Devon didn't need to remind him of his infirmity. He didn't need special treatment and he would prove he could pull his own weight around the farm.

Chapter 5

As promised, Mr. Hamilton entertained them with a fine dinner. Ethan noted that even his brother had become so distracted by the courses of oyster bisque, crab cakes, the roast leg of mutton, and mincemeat pie that all talk of business was forgotten. And gaining Miss Marietta's approval by their attendance at church promised to be worth staying an extra day, no matter what he'd had to promise Devon. Besides, there'd be plenty of time to talk trade on the carriage ride home.

As the Hamilton's cream-colored brougham approached the church, Ethan gawked at the overwhelming size of the building. Back home their churches were rustic affairs with plank benches. Women sat on one side, and men on the other. The scale of this cathedral told another story entirely. Ethan followed Devon and their hosts through the vestibule and into the sanctuary.

Vaulted ceilings, flying buttresses and scrolled pews filled the expanse, and jewel-toned glass colored each window, depicting scenes from the gospels. What would make the people, whose names were inscribed at the bottom of each stained-glass display, compelled to donate such extravagant gifts to a building only used once a week? Ambition came in many forms. Like the lengths some folks would go to impress his father with their version of horseflesh. Sam Sharpe had set a high bar, and anyone who fancied the sport in the valley had to measure up to it. Must be like that.

Only the currency here wasn't horsemanship. It was holiness.

He and his brother swaggered in, necks craning to see the details of architecture and statuary. Ethan then turned his attention to the parishioners, initiating curious exchanges with waxy, expressionless faces. Devon's laughter echoed to the vaulted ceiling as he made imbecilic faces at a dour old woman seated on the aisle. Ethan caught him in the act and shoved him into a pew. The heads of a dozen saints whipped around to determine the source of the disruption, but Levi smiled and greeted them by name, smoothing away offense. Being guests of the esteemed Hamiltons could excuse a hobgoblin, Ethan noted with delight. He consulted his twin for conspiracy.

But where was Miss Hamilton? Ethan turned front and center, scouring the platform for her. Then she appeared, seating herself at an upright grand piano. Before she could play a note, a wave of organ music flooded up the pipes behind the pulpit, belching out sound like factory smoke, and drowning out the delicate sound of her playing. The congregation arose to their feet.

Devon whispered provocations in his ear, doubtless hoping to make him squirm or laugh. But the music countered with a sobering effect. The melody awakened some forgotten place, resurrected from over a decade of dormancy. Deep-seated emotions welled, conjuring the smell of French perfume, another piano, and Mother's hands caressing the keys between cajoling twin boys. Ethan's cravat pressed at the lump forming in his throat, every throb of his pulse tightening at his neck.

The congregation sat in a fluid ripple, and Ethan sank down with it, thankful for the opportunity to regulate his breathing. The robed man at the pulpit addressed them in a broken-voiced call to prayer. Heat spread over Ethan's face at the clergyman's impassioned entreaty. What was it about invoking blessing on a new president that would cause a grown man to cry? No one at home would be weeping in public no matter how bad they felt about the election.

Devon happened to catch his eye, making a rueful face. A

snort of laughter erupted before he could stifle it. The sound reverberated over the perfect acoustics, rising above the genteel prayer, mingling with the murmurs of intercession, until in that improbable moment a transformation of intent occurred. Ethan's mockery resounded over the flying buttresses like… a sob.

Horror wrapped Ethan's chest in claw-like fingers as scores of the sympathetic fixed their approving gazes upon him. Hands reached out from across the aisles to affirm the Lord's touch upon him. Devon shook with muffled hilarity while Ethan received the fawning of many zealots. The stir had attracted attention all the way to the pulpit.

"Young man!" The prophet's blue eyes blazed twenty rows back, to where Ethan sat, and their light kindled terror upon him. "The hand of the Lord is upon you. Have you been chosen for such a time as this? I see you, swayed beneath the weight of conviction as though the death of the hangman was for you! There is one who died on a tree, yea, for the sin of the world, for the sin of this generation! Look, all ye lukewarm, and repent of your cold religion! A hard rain is beginning to fall. I see a rain of fire! A fiery baptism is beginning to fall upon this generation. Do you not see it? Fall upon the rock before the rock falls upon you, and crushes you, you empty chalices, you whitewashed sepulchers, you cold and dead religious. The blood-guilt of a people has made a stench to heaven, and it is time to pay for the wages of sin!"

All breath had fled from Ethan, as well as blood, prickling as it drained from his face.

"A thousand may fall, young man. Yea, ten thousand at thy right hand, but it shall not come nigh thee. You will only look and see the destruction of the wicked."

The preacher called for backsliders to come forward and renew their salvation. Ethan ducked his head into his folded arms in a pretense of prayer to muffle his asthmatic gasping. Neither he nor his brother moved until the benediction called them to their feet. Then Devon grabbed his elbow and spirited him out of the church ahead of their hosts, rushing all the way to the carriage. Ethan slumped against the brougham, his ribs rising and falling with every strained breath. The Hamiltons soon emerged from the church, making their slow way through the parishioners toward them. Devon hid Ethan in the back seat, propping him up in a posture to draw sufficient air. Devon remained outside, standing sentinel, his eyes glittering a warning to the Hamiltons not to ask questions.

ଔ

All the way home Marietta stole curious glances at their silent guests. Each time they passed a street lantern, the gas light cast a pall over the twin seated by the window. He looked positively ill. A twinge of caution tempered her eagerness to have the matter of Tilly's son settled. It almost seemed Ethan Sharpe struggled for breath sitting there beside his brother.

She turned aside to watch the buildings go by her own carriage window, rehearsing in her mind the delightful rebuke Reverend Sterling had given. Serves a slaveholder right to be publicly censured like that. But at the same time, concern pressed in on her ribs as though Tilly had laced her corsets too tight. Over the sound of the horses' hooves and the rattle of wheels on brick, she could almost be certain she heard wheezing….

ଔ

The hour was late when they arrived, and Devon used it as an excuse to retire.

Once behind closed doors, Ethan collapsed onto the bed, and Devon fell in beside him, holding a cold flask of brandied coffee to his lips, prepared for such an occasion. Ethan didn't resist and swallowed the medicine liberally.

Finally confident he could summon his voice, he gave a weak laugh. "Don't that beat all?" He knitted his fingers behind his head to hide their jittering.

"Reckon this's my fault, E." Devon's eyes belied any teasing.

His brother's concern prickled him. He cuffed Devon in the

upper arm. "You weren't any help, that's for sure."

Devon shook with laughter. "I must confess, though, brother. That was rather spectacular."

Ethan slapped at his shirt to dispel the skittering sensation creeping over him. "A spectacle, you mean."

Devon sat up and glowered down at him. "I see the fires of hell, son! Repent! Repent of your card playing! Repent of your horse-betting, your slave-holding." Devon's straight face cracked, and hooting laughter erupted. "God's gonna burn the South right out' a you, boy, until you're as yella and Yankee as the rest of them!"

Devon's mockery eased Ethan's humiliation. His twin could always find a way to make him feel better. "Hallelujah, brother. I see the light. Prez'dint Abraham done showed me the way!"

ଔଷ

The moon pouring in through the beveled glass windowpanes sought out Ethan's wide-awake eyes. After Devon's charade, they'd talked little, and he rested content that no tension lingered between them. Devon slept beside him like a colt in clover, but Ethan tapped his fingers over his nightshirt and stared up at the shadows on the ceiling. At least if his brother were awake he'd have someone to talk to.

The rich foods consumed earlier in the evening returned to haunt him. Ethan's stomach lurched at every thought of the strange church service. Of course, Devon could laugh anything off and be done with it. Maybe he'd feel different if *he'd* been the one singled out. The audacity of that preacher! As if he deserved rebuke. He wished he could be more like Devon, who seemed blissfully ignorant of his own wickedness.

Wickedness? His heart slammed against his ribs as though he'd just fallen into an icy water trough. Sitting bolt upright in bed, he breathed slow and deep, but couldn't settle his sudden panic.

Was he wicked?

An image invaded his mind—that of a child, restrained in

shackles, as his mother endured the examination of strange men. The precocious brown eyes of the boy bored into Ethan's.

Could I have intervened?

No. His brother had been pretty determined, and there was no crossing a determined Devon.

Could I intervene now?

Possibly. But he'd left the matter in Devon's hands.

An invisible noose pressed at his Adam's apple and he saw again the floor dropping out from underneath John Brown's feet. He rolled out of bed and sought solid ground.

The moon's shadows lent an uncertain quality about the room. Light-headed, Ethan clutched the foot board. The air in the room felt heavier than wet fleece. His stomach roiled, his dinner setting like a stone in his gut. He slipped into a pair of trousers and spirited out the bedroom door and down the steps.

The drafty foyer greeted him, cool and fresh. He donned his boots, set by the door, and imagined being back home, the morning mist hovering over the ground on his trek out to the stable. Surely this was just a bout of homesickness. But just in case his stomach rebelled, he'd best be out-of-doors.

He wandered out into the shadowy yard beyond the house, seeking refuge where the comforting aromas of old barn wood, leather and horse beckoned. The carriage house and stable drew him under its dark cover, and the steady, deep breathing of the animals infused the space with a comforting cadence.

Inside, the moonlight diffused, falling softer on his eyes. He moved slowly into the interior, and had wandered around a high stack of hay, when tall figures stirred. He nearly overturned a bucket of water in his backward stumble.

A voice sounded from the dark corner. "Ethan? Is that you? It's me, Marietta."

His eyes adjusted and now he could see her—a silhouette in a hoop-less skirt standing outside the thoroughbred's stall.

"What're you doing out here?"

"I should ask you the same thing."

He reckoned he ought to leave for propriety, for dignity, for a thousand other reasons, but the contours of her form drew his captivated study against his better judgment.

"I was praying for you, Ethan. I feel awful about what happened at church. How uncomfortable that must have been for you."

He set his jaw. He didn't want her pity, but he didn't mind her attention. His silence was more awkward than he intended, but he supposed it easier on her ears than voicing his thoughts about that preacher.

"Do you often pray in the barn, alone, after midnight?"

She cleared her throat and shuffled her feet, the straw rustling under her skirts. "I was praying that you wouldn't be offended by the message. I'm so sorry. The wrong delivery can spoil the truth."

"The *truth*?"

"Well, yes." Her voice sounded tight.

He moved toward her, but she held her ground. Her pale face reflected the silvery light, her mouth set, her lashes batting. She drew a breath.

"I believe God does have his hand on you, and that he has something special in store for you." Though she faced him, her hands remained behind her back. She lifted her chin, and every muscle in her neck and jaw—even her partly bared shoulders—articulated in tense lines.

"God had something *in store* for me, all right. I mean, fire from the sky, apocalypse, and judgment?" He whistled. "If sin can dawn on a Dixie heathen like me, then there ain't no excuse for you republicans, right?"

There. He'd spoiled all chances of endearing himself to her now. But he wasn't about to pass up the chance to set the record straight.

Her laughter provoked him.

"You find that funny?"

She toned down her amusement with a smile that showed

those perfect, white teeth. "If only you knew God's will."

He groaned. "*God's* will?"

"If the preacher's right, you have a great call on your life, Ethan. God knows that you're in a unique position to impact systems and people as very few can."

"Me and Devon, you mean."

She bowed her head. "Perhaps."

A movement behind her drew Ethan's attention over the braided crown of her hair, into the darker shadows of the stall. The horse bobbed its head, and a hand reached over the horse's muzzle to quiet it.

"That you, Jonesy?"

Her eyes rounded, the whites gleaming in the moonlight. Her breath rose and fell with her flounced neckline, and she shrank back against the stall door. "We should probably let the poor boy sleep now."

Whispering from behind the stall partition alerted him. Something was amiss. "What's going on here?" He strode forward, and with a firm grasp, he pulled her hands from behind her skirts.

A wad of bills fell from her fist, landing next to a small satchel at her back. The form in the stall behind her divided into three distinct shapes—one bridled horse, the servant woman, and Jonesy.

Miss Hamilton tried to slip past him, but Ethan tightened his hold on her.

"You were out here praying, huh? Praying no one would catch you horse thieving and—and what? What were you planning to do, Marietta?"

With a small grunt she twisted in his hold, her eyes smoldering like that feral cat he recalled from the auction. "Accuse me if you want, but I think you sense the truth. Otherwise, why would you be out here in the middle of the night?"

He narrowed his eyes. "Good thing I am, with you up to no good!"

"I imagine after a public rebuke from God it would be very

hard to sleep—" She yelped as he grabbed her by the waist. He pressed her to him for a brief moment, warring between throttling her and kissing her.

She squirmed in his hold, bracing herself as if to launch a counter strike. "It's no coincidence, you know. While I prayed for you tonight, God called you—like the prophet Samuel. God told him of a judgment coming, just like the preacher tonight."

"God wasn't calling me," he ground out through clenched teeth, "and I *don't* need any what-for from some abolitionist preacher." He slackened his hold on her. "So *that's* what you were doing at that slave auction? *You're freedom shrieking abolitionists!*"

Chapter 6

Defiance smoldered from her in short, hot breaths. “We prefer the term *emancipators.* As I'm sure you prefer ‘slaveholders’ to *heartless chattel mongers.* After all, dividing a mother and child. For shame!”

Her words pierced him. “I never intended to break up that family.” Ethan clamped his mouth shut. He’d said too much.

Her wide-eyed expression registered all as she turned to face him. “So, it *does* trouble you.”

He released her completely and took a step away, running a hand through his hair. “So what if it does?”

Instead of running, or even gathering the loose bills on the ground, she stood and faced him, her comportment entirely changing. Gentling. “Ethan, is that what's troubling you tonight?”

How had the conversation gotten this far off-track? He lowered his gaze. “It’s unfair. The boy should have stayed with his mammy.”

She reached out and took his hand. “It’s not too late to do something about it.” Her small fingers lacing through his felt warm and exhilarating. “Help me.”

He snorted, shaking off even such a small indulgence. He would not be suckered in by feminine wiles. “My mama was taken when I was far younger than him. He'll adjust.”

Gentle reproach sounded low in her throat and she shook her head. “There’s a world of difference between the two. Death is

God's doing; the other is man's. Things can change, Ethan, and it all starts with one willing person."

"So, I should turn a blind eye while you *steal* from us?"

"*No.* No, it's different than that."

He snorted a laugh. "Thou shalt not steal. Except under certain conditions?"

She smiled as though his sarcasm hadn't stung her. "Of course, God's Word still stands, even when property laws are unjust. Still, God speaks personally to His people. But that's the question, isn't it? *Are* you one of his people, Ethan?"

"So now I'm a heathen." He laughed, but with no humor. "Maybe folks'd figure my father the devil's first cousin with his drinking, smoking, and gambling, but my mother was a good woman. She played piano for church, just like you."

The angles about her eyes softened. "I don't mean to insult you or your upbringing. I'm sure your mother was a saint, but her faith can't substitute for your own. Have you made a personal profession of faith, Ethan Sharpe?"

"Of course, I believe in God."

She patted his hand with an air that he registered as patronizing.

He clenched his fist into a ball and withdrew from her touch.

"Nicodemus was a high priest. Wouldn't you think that his years of training in the Torah and his religious service in the temple would have qualified him? Jesus told him he had to be born again. Are you born again, Ethan? Jesus wants to be that friend that sticks closer to you than a brother."

He found that an odd concept. No one could ever be closer than Devon to him. Not even his mother, God rest her soul. It had been Devon ever since she had passed who had looked out for him, been his constant companion.

And yet, when he looked into her tear-glistened eyes, a quality beyond her obvious beauty took hold of him. His middle pulled with an urge that needed no explanation—like the need to draw breath. Yearning for the tenderness of a girl's touch, and maybe even that of the divine.

"Do you know the Lord like that?"

She looked so earnest he figured she deserved an equally honest answer. He shook his head. "No, I reckon I don't."

"You can!" The corners of her mouth lifted, and her eyes sparkled with luminous joy. "Pray with me."

The moonlit carriage house grew hushed like a candlelit chapel. The slave mother and child embraced one another, and whispered prayers *for him*. In that solemn moment, he lost all cynicism. His mind filled with hope that he could resolve his guilt over the slave auction once and for all, and perhaps make a difference in the lives of this hapless family.

He bowed his head but refused to close his eyes. He wouldn't broker a deal going in blind. It felt right, what was happening, but if this was to be an invocation of the Almighty, he wanted to have all faculties intact for the meeting. His father had taught him to conduct business nothing short.

"If you agree with this prayer, Ethan, say 'Amen'. Dear Father, I repent of all my sins. Thank you for taking my punishment on the cross for them. I receive your justification of my soul by faith. I invite you to be Lord of my life. Amen."

"Amen," he repeated.

So, this was it? The prayer seemed foolishly simple for such a momentous occasion as the regeneration of one's eternal soul. And he hadn't seen any blinding flashes of light or felt the earth shake. His brows pinched. "I don't feel any different. Isn't faith something you just convince yourself of, like courage, or talent?"

She gazed heavenward, her countenance angelic. "Faith is the assurance of things hoped for, the evidence of things unseen. I think in the days and weeks ahead, you'll just know."

"I'm not ready for any big changes. I like my life the way it is."

"Do you feel better than when you came out here tonight?" she asked.

He shrugged. He had to admit he was no longer queasy or haunted by images in his head. He could breathe better, too. "I reckon so."

"Isn't that a welcome change?" Her smile was teasing and delightful.

He grinned. "All right. I confess, it is."

"Old things have passed, behold all things have become new. You may not feel it, but everything *is* different. You'll get back to sleep now, for one thing." Her eyelashes fluttered in the pale light with a hint of teasing. "So will I."

"Wait a minute. What about them?" He cast a hard look toward Jonesy and his mother. Nothing had been resolved concerning them.

She sighed a soft little breath that made him want to promise her anything she asked. "I'm sorry. I know now I should have waited for you to tell Papa your decision. Will you let us purchase the young man's freedom?"

When she put it that way, her beguiling spell over him was broken. "I'll have to talk to Devon. I promised him that if he'd agree to stay an extra day, I'd let him decide Jonesy's fate."

"Oh." The hollow sound of her reply riddled him with remorse. Her lashes fluttered faster, and she swiped at her cheeks.

He rallied a defense against her tears. "But I'll try."

"Please do try, Ethan. I'll be praying for you." She reached up and kissed him so quickly he didn't have time to respond. He stood there stunned as she called a shy "Goodnight."

ঔ৩

Ethan dressed in silence while Devon rolled over and buried his face in a pillow. The eastern sky seemed unusually bright for a November morning as he poured water into the wash basin. Taking up his straight razor and shaving brush, he lathered soap over his chin.

The blade made a melodic tone against the edge of the porcelain bowl. He breathed in the clean aroma of the lavender soap and exhaled a full, deep breath. No trace of last night's asthma. *Thank God.* Ethan tilted his head and listened to the chatter of chickadees declaring the start of a new day.

"Wake up, Dev!"

His twin grunted.

Ethan sloshed a handful of water at him.

"Hey!" Devon launched his pillow through the air, which bounced off Ethan's chest. Then he growled and, holding a hand over his eyes, hauled himself up to sit at the edge of the bed. "What're you so all-fired happy about?"

"Nothin'." Ethan replied with a grin.

"To be getting home, I suppose."

He shrugged. "Maybe."

Devon shuffled around the bed to retrieve his bag, all the while rubbing the night out of his eyes. "I get it. You're happy 'cause you're sweet on the Hamilton girl." He groaned and stretched. "Too bad it's your last day with her."

The thought struck like a hoof to his gut.

Devon put a patronizing arm across Ethan's shoulder. "A word of advice? Don't make yourself a fool for no Yankee gal. Next thing you know, she'll be getting in your head with her high-minded ideas."

Ethan shrugged out of his hold, inadvertently ramming Devon's ribs with his elbow. "I'm nobody's fool."

Devon picked up the razor and began his own ablutions. "What about that new preacher back in Staunton? Heard he's got two daughters about our age."

Ethan straightened his collar, grinning at his reflection in the mirror. "Don't worry, I haven't made any declarations."

"Good." Devon wagged a finger in his face. "'Cause there ain't no future for you and Marietta Hamilton."

Ethan would've liked to twist that wagging finger backward until Devon yelped, but for thought of the previous night, and the prayer he'd prayed. He'd press past his brother's provocation if it killed him. As his rendezvous with Miss Mari filled his thoughts, vibrancy returned to the room. The passion in her eyes, her conviction, all came back in vivid colors and tones. He smiled, hearing her words again as if she were right there speaking them. *Behold, all things have become new.*

Devon interrupted his thoughts. "I'm giving Mr. Hamilton my answer about Jonesy. He isn't for sale."

Ethan's smile dropped. "Wait—what? Right now? But he probably isn't even home…."

"We'll see." Devon set the razor at the side of the basin and wiped his face clean with the towel. Snapping the bed sheets together and assembling his belongings, he prepared for the departure. It didn't take long.

Pausing in the doorway, Devon asked, "Shall I wait, or meet you downstairs?"

Ethan fiddled with his shirt button and muttered, "Don't suppose my opinion matters either way." By the determined look on Devon's face, he knew it was true.

ઌ

Footfalls on the stairs drew Mari from the kitchen. She'd been waiting for Ethan and his brother to come down to breakfast. She'd prayed most of the night that he'd been able to convince his brother to let Tilly's son go.

She entered the dining room in silent, slippered feet where Papa sat at the table, his hooded eyes reflecting the heavy burden they both wore. Devon sat first, and Ethan fell in beside him, opposite from Papa. She tried to connect gazes with the young man, but he turned to the side.

Mari's smile fell. Packed bags waited by the door. She sunk into a seat and let her mother serve breakfast without her help.

Devon spoke. "Thank you for your hospitality, Mr. and Mrs. Hamilton. But under the circumstances, I feel it best we return home at once." He commanded Ethan's united front with a nod in his direction.

Mari pleaded silently, but Ethan refused to look her way.

Instead, he studied his hands, folded on the table.

"Father must be anxious for our return," Ethan agreed, resignation darkening his voice.

Papa sighed. "If you must go, I feel it is my responsibility to see that you go safely."

Marietta's heartbeat crowded her throat. This couldn't be the way things ended. She'd prayed! She'd pleaded. Surely there would be an eleventh-hour miracle. She offered Ethan another imploring look. He finally met her gaze, but with an inscrutable expression. Even if he spoke up, would it change Devon's decision? Would he challenge his brother? The weight bearing down on her heart sank into her stomach.

Ethan found his tongue. "No, sir. Don't trouble yourself. We'll see ourselves home."

Papa tossed the morning paper toward them, and the sharp whiff of ink overrode the warm aroma of coffee, turning Mari's appetite to ash. "Emotions on both sides could ignite a powder keg."

Devon waved in dismissal. "Unlike you, we're of no consequence to the government. We'll have no trouble crossing into Virginia."

"I see." Papa's pride surely ruffled, he tried to hide it by straightening his cravat. "I wouldn't want to be a detriment to your safe passage." Ever the gracious gentleman. Her heart swelled with a glimmer of hope that he might make things right even now.

Devon blew a forced breath. "No Lincoln supporter would be safe where we come from."

Ethan jabbed his brother's arm with a look that suggested he'd rather it had been his mouth.

It took every ounce of her strength to refrain from speaking, and her mother's silent censure doubled down on her. She folded her hands together so tightly her nails dug into her tender knuckles.

Papa extended an ameliorating hand. "May I see you to the train, at least?"

Ethan clasped it and shook. "We'd be obliged, sir."

Devon folded his arms across his chest. "We'll need payment for the horse first, of course."

"And the boy?"

Devon shook his head. "The stable boy has suddenly become invaluable to us."

Papa sighed deeply and withdrew his watch from a breast pocket. "If you're resolved, then so be it. The next train leaves in half an hour." He rose from his seat. "I'll get my bill fold and bring the carriage around."

Crushed, she withdrew to hide the tears that sprang to her eyes. Thank goodness Mama had given Tilly the morning off to spend with her son. Her sweet maid didn't have to hear the horrible news just yet. But how would she break it to her? Hopes raised, only to be dashed again. *Oh, merciful Father.*

Papa retreated out the back door, and Mama followed him to the threshold. Commenting on the drizzle that had begun to fall, Mama called for him to come back for his overcoat. When he didn't, she fetched it herself.

With her parents' departure, Mari grew so still, she wished she could disappear into her seat. She bit back the disappointment trying to spill from her eyes.

As though her wish had come true, Devon turned on his brother, completely blind to her presence. "What'd you encourage him for? We're capable of seeing ourselves off."

Marietta sniffled, and both boys startled as though just seeing her. She took a deep breath. She had nothing to lose at this point.

"I'm sorry you must leave. I was so enjoying your company." Her voice struggled for polite tones devoid of too much emotion. "Now Heaven knows if I shall see you both again."

Devon waved off her sentimentality. "Perhaps in the spring you could come visit us at the farm."

"Lord willing. But one never knows what the future holds. That is why we must make the most of opportunity when first it strikes."

Ethan swallowed. He gave his brother a hard look.

Too late to settle the obvious conflict smoldering between them, his searching eyes sought her now, and more boldly than was prudent. Heat simmered into her cheeks.

Devon stood to his feet. “I'll bring the bags to the carriage.” He slipped through the screened door, and his tread became lost to the pattern of falling rain.

Ethan mopped back the roguish hair that had fallen over his face. “How’d you manage to do this to me?”

She pressed a hand to her bosom. “Me? Do you think I single-handedly elected a president? Impressive, since women can’t even vote.” Her smile invited him to laugh, but he apparently found no humor in the situation. Heartache chased hard on the heels of her mirth, and she swallowed.

“That’s not what I meant. You've got me all tied in a knot.” He pressed fingertips to his temple seemingly to order his disheveled thoughts.

Her resolve to use charm returned in a last act of desperation. “Are you trying to say you’ve become fond of me?” She smiled, full of wit and sparkle like those silly debutantes, though she rued the turmoil behind his eyes.

He paused and took her hand, gazing at her with earnest. “What if I am?”

Her heart skipped an unexpected beat. The warmth of his hand, the intensity of his smoldering dark eyes captivated her until she almost lost focus. But she employed the only wiles that occurred to her, for Tilly's sake, though her heart preferred to stay in this delightful, spontaneous moment. She wet her lips, offering a smile intending to get him to promise anything. Though she recoiled from such conniving, the mission demanded every available weapon in her arsenal.

And yet, the longer she looked into his eyes, the more her own heart betrayed her. She longed for him to make her stop smiling like that at him, but the only way that came to mind was for him to kiss it away—a kiss he initiated, and not some quick little gesture like hers had been the night before.

He cleared his throat. “I'm sorry I can't leave the boy.”

She reached with her other hand, inviting him to meet her half-way across the table with his. He refrained for the moment. She left the invitation there and tilted her head. “Perhaps it’s part of God’s design, to connect our families.”

He gave in and took her fingers in his, caressing them with his thumb. “I hope so.”

“Will you continue what we’ve started?”

“I promise to say my prayers and study my Bible like a good boy,” he teased.

“Will you write to me?” Her pout, complete with fluttering eyelashes, came all too naturally. “At least to tell me if Tilly’s son is doing well, to give me hope that they won’t be separated forever.”

He rose and stepped around the table, and the determination in his expression made her certain he would make good on that kiss. But Devon's voice called from the front of the house. He pulled her to her feet and drew her to him, his height and physical bearing stealing her breath.

“I'll write,” he promised.

She leaned into him in a farewell embrace. When they parted, her heart carried on her gaze following him out to where he joined his brother in Papa's waiting carriage. As the conveyance slipped over the rainy road, she whispered a prayer that somehow they'd meet again. That they would finish what they had started. That Tilly's tenuous trust would not be crushed. And despite the threat of political unrest, she believed God would answer her prayers.

Chapter 7

Sharpe Homestead,
Bridgewater, Virginia
Late November 1860

Devon covered the worn path between the house and the paddocks in search of his brother. The sound of the farrier's hammer echoed from one barn to another as the sunrise fought its way through the fog. A gaggle of geese in migratory form passed over the mountains, heading deeper south for the fast-coming winter. Ethan's commands carried on the air indicating he was already at work in the training paddock. Rounding the end of the barn, Devon spotted him.

Ethan stood beside a saddled horse and the short figure of the stable boy. He bent to give Jonesy a leg-up onto the iron-colored filly's back. "You ready?"

"Yassuh. Ready as ever."

"I'll turn her loose, then."

Ethan released the leathers and backed away from the moving horse until he bumped the gate. Devon unlatched it, and Ethan slipped through. Standing side by side at the fence, the brothers watched.

"Reckon she'll be fast once she gets straightened out." Devon nodded.

"She's fast all right. Be a small miracle if he stays on her back."

Devon laughed and rubbed the dirt from his palms onto the back of his work trousers. “Better him than me. I got bruises where the sun don't shine from that filly.”

Sure was nice having someone else risk his neck for a change. He cocked his head back and stuck a boot on the bottom rung of the split rail fence. “What about you? Still miss Lexington?”

Ethan shrugged. “No, I reckon not.”

“Probably too love struck to think about school.”

“Whatever do you mean, Devon?”

Ethan’s pretense didn’t fool him. “You’ll have your newlywed cabin built before long, what with collecting race winnings like you did last weekend.” They'd worked out a way to satisfy their father's loss on the stable boy by arranging back-road race meets. “I underestimated your shrewdness, brother.”

After a moment, Jonesy brought Tempest around the perimeter well in hand. She had her head down and seemed to be concentrating on her rider's commands. Jonesy turned in the saddle toward them. “What you want for me to do now, Marse Ethan?”

The filly’s ears flicked a second before she turned her head and swung about. She sidestepped, while Jonesy clung to her like a four-legged tick. “Whoa, horse! Who-o-o-a!”

Devon lunged halfway over the fence before Ethan stopped him. “Wait, Devon. He's got this. Jonesy, rein her in!”

“Yassuh, Marse Ethan.” The boy regained his seat and drew up the slack with both hands. The filly responded.

Ethan gripped the top rail and leaned forward. "Good. Now bring her around."

“I still don’t know about this, E. You’re taking a risk that he’ll run off with one of our fastest horses.”

Ethan raised his brow. “More likely she'll run off with him.”

Devon didn't laugh.

“Aw, c'mon, Dev. That was funny.”

“I just don't like it. It's a risk either way.”

Ethan threw up his hands. “I thought the whole reason you

wanted to keep the boy was to relieve our workload. You have a better idea how?"

Devon folded his arms across his chest. He knew how much Ethan needed the boy, so he bit his tongue. If Jonesy's help meant less trouble with his health, then he supposed Ethan could work the boy however he pleased. "No. Reckon not."

"All right, Dev. Let's talk about something else, then. What did you think of the new preacher's sermon yesterday?"

It had been his own idea, going to church, to introduce Ethan to Reverend White's daughter Ellen. "It was fine." The two had certainly gotten along sportingly. Ellen's lighthearted flirtation seemed to engage Ethan. Maybe enough to ground his interests closer to home.

"Reckon we ought to make church a regular habit." Ethan stared off, adopting a puppy-dog look that could only mean one thing. A girl.

Devon smiled. Seemed his plan was working. "Sure, why not?" They were quiet for a bit, and the gaiting horse, the fence side, and the scenery faded. Devon was taken back to a time when their mother's singing filled the church. Her voice wrapped like velvet over his heart, even if the words had all but faded.

Melodies played upon him as fragrances did others, stirring memories. He and Ethan had made the dining table a Spanish galleon that day, mother's china trunk a pirate's chest, filled with six-year-old boys' idea of booty. Daddy's silver flask, mother's sewing sheers and a few baubles from the top drawer of her dresser, Gideon's spy glass, two stick swords, and a chicken from the barn, since they didn't have a talking parrot. Mother had sat at her piano, oblivious to their pillaging, her arpeggios rising like an angel's harp until the shattering of Limoges abruptly ended the sounds of heaven. Ethan and he had dashed out the back door, but not before Devon spied her slumped over, hands covering her lovely face while large teardrops splashed the ivory keys....

Devon shook the hair out of his eyes to rid himself of the scene. His low voice barely registered. "Still, it's not the same without Mama."

Ethan leaned into Devon's shoulder. "Yeah, I know what you mean. But for a moment, while we sang *Rock of Ages,* it was almost like God gave her back."

Time had tried to drag him back, but Devon shook from its grip. He wasn't six years old anymore, looking down at his mother's funereal face. Still his promise to her remained. He'd always look after his brothers. Someone had to watch out for his gullible twin, or he'd buy any bill of goods coming down the Valley Turnpike.

"Reckon if God took Mama, He's not giving her back. He's a shrewder horse trader than the old man."

"Ever consider that God's love is different? It's not the jealous kind, but puts the needs of others first."

"Oh, that's right." Devon winked. "You're the expert on love now."

Ethan twisted one side of his mouth and it looked like he would broach the subject again. Plunging hooves approached a few feet away, mercifully ending the exchange.

Devon snapped his fingers at the slave. "Bring her to the gate and dismount." He darted away before Ethan could foist any more doctrine on him. Leading the horse, Ethan dogged him to the tack barn. Devon turned around for a second and noted that a flush burned in his brother's cheeks and his breath blew with force. Devon slowed his stride. A surge of protectiveness coursed through him. He needed to fix whatever troubled Ethan. Something told him it traced directly back to that Hamilton girl. Only one remedy for that. He'd arrange another outing with the Reverend's daughter, and soon.

ଔ

Marietta set down the silver tea carafe she'd been polishing at the kitchen work table. She looked up as her maid scrubbed a pan in the nearby washbasin, sending water sloshing this way and that under her intense movements. It had been almost a month since

Tilly's son had gone away with the twins, and this was the first it seemed that a thaw had begun to melt the young woman's ice-packed heart.

"Tilly, take a break and come sit with me."

The young woman ceased from her toils and bowed her head but didn't move another muscle for a full minute. And then, small spasms shook her shoulders. Restrained sounds of weeping reached Mari's ears. Her heart swelled. Nothing seemed to be able to comfort the young mother, though Mari had tried very hard. She rose and stepped over the distance to the maid's side.

"I know you miss him. And I know I've failed to keep my promise to you. I wouldn't blame you if you hated me."

Tilly turned to face her, her umber eyes large and glistening with suspended tears. "No, ma'am. I'd never disrespect you, Miz Mari."

"Please, don't be afraid." Mari placed a reassuring hand on her shoulder. "I'm not accusing you or trying to trick you. It's just—well, I know the good Lord hasn't given up on us. Even though I feel to blame."

Tilly wiped her hands on her apron and dabbed her eyes with the same. "No, Miz Mari. You has a good heart, an' I know you done all you could do. I do thank you." Her steady voice belied the tear that slipped down her ginger-colored cheek. "The Lord just don't seem interested in a slave woman's prayers."

Mari couldn't counter the lie directly, so she came at it indirectly. "What if we were to write a letter together, and inquire about your son?"

The woman's heaviness lifted, and something lit her eyes apart from the sparkle of tears.

"Mr. Ethan said he would welcome my correspondence. Asking after your boy would only be natural. Would you like that?"

Tilly winced, hope at war with her obvious pain. Cascades poured from the corners of her eyes. She nodded and sniffled.

Mari handed her a handkerchief. "There, now. Even in the

seeming silence, God has a plan. But in the meanwhile, we must keep praying, and send our care in letters."

Mari led Tilly to the bench beside her mother's secretary desk and seated herself in the chair. She swung the door down to set the writing surface in place, and prepared a bottle of India ink, a nib, and a sheet of ivory parchment. With a stroke of the pen, she addressed the missive to Mr. Ethan Sharpe.

☙

Ethan drew in the crisp night air. A few feet away, Devon's cigarette spun a thin blue ribbon straight up into the heavens. When his brother exhaled, a fouling cloud invaded the clean scent of pine and earth. Ethan waved it away with a slight cough. They'd escaped the house after Devon pilfered the old man's tobacco stash, and had settled in their favorite hiding spot, the hollowed-out stump of an old oak. The December night showcased a veil of stars in twinkling clarity, and Ethan drew a contented sigh.

Devon stretched beside him in the frost-tinged litter. "One of these days this will all be ours—lock, stock, and tobacco pouch."

Ethan t'sked. "In the meantime, you'd better sleep with one eye open. When the old man finds out you stole from him, there'll be the 'wages of sin' to pay."

Devon laughed. "I see the fires of hell, son."

Ethan gave up a grudging laugh. "Repent of your tobacco smokin', your pouch stealin'!"

"Father Samuel gon' show me the way."

"Seriously, you really shouldn't steal."

"Yassuh, Marse Ethan. Don't tell ol' massah."

It was a high ambition, indeed, running this farm. Their father's cunning and hard work had brought it to considerable success. With their oldest brother Gideon teaching artillery at The Citadel now, and courting Uncle Marcel's daughter, it seemed unlikely he'd settle here. It appeared the farm would indeed be theirs.

Ethan looked forward to the day he and his twin would settle down in neighboring homes here along the Valley Turnpike, while their kids played in the same meadows and creaks where he and his brothers had played. He loved the farm, lock, stock, and tobacco pouch—just as much as Devon.

Still, it was an empire with flaws. The horses that filled the acreage paid their living mostly through gambling of one sort or another. And almost every timber that constituted the frame house, barns, and fences had been hewn and hoisted by African backs.

Ethan gazed across the expanse at slave shanties, silhouetted against the rising moon. Rough-beamed walls bore gaping holes, patched with mud or plaster. Dirt floors permitted drafts and harbored pestilence. Sagging roofs couldn't insulate from summer's searing heat or winter's numbing chill. Babies had died in these shacks, like little Jim, the last one born on the farm. Their father had sold off the women of childbearing age after that. All the rest were men or boys old enough to work.

Sunup to sundown, the feeding, grooming, haying, shoeing, and schooling posed a far greater task than the four Sharpe men could manage alone. The Hamiltons had been right—they needed a workforce. Even with Gideon's help there would never be a way to do it without slave labor. Though he wished it weren't so, ever since that conversation with Marietta in her carriage house, his eyes were opened about the plight of Jonesy and his mother. And Ezra, Colby, Jim, and the rest.

"Once this is all ours, do you think we should keep the status quo?"

Devon puffed on his cigarette. "Mm-hmm. If it ain't broke, why fix it?"

More fouled air drifted into Ethan's space at Devon's exhale. He turned away, gazing on the winter gardens surrounding each shanty, meagre defense against Sam Sharpe's thrift.

Yet, many evenings, hymns and spiritual songs filled the quarters. Ethan marveled that these people found anything good to sing about. But sing they did, rain or shine, in good times or bad. Resilience, and this perplexing gratitude were qualities to be admired.

Devon's exhale intruded again. "Let's go over to Walt's."

Their closest neighbor, both in proximity and age, had returned from school. Rumor had it that Old Man Thompson sent for him after the election. His homecoming was as good an excuse as any for a party, now that the days were shorter, and the slower winter pace had settled in.

"Heard that your Miss Ellen and her sister'll be there. She's been asking about you, E."

Heat spiked through him. Devon never missed an opportunity to mention the Reverend's daughters. "I owe a letter to Miss Mari."

Devon's grin broadened. "Ah-ha, what's this? Two fish on one line?"

He thrust away Devon's poking finger. "You've got me figured for a rake."

"Only one way to know for sure if Miss Ellen's sweet on you. Come with me." Devon stood and chafed the backside of his pants, chattering from chill. "There'll be a bonfire, maybe some dancing. Eh?" He took Ethan's arm and spun him around in a do-si-do.

Ethan laughed, but his feet dragged. "Sorry." He shook his head. "Seems I'm out of step."

"Oh, come on, E! It'll be fun."

"No thanks. I'm not giving Miss White any encouragement." Not when Mari's face was the only one in his sights.

Devon's brows pinched. "Ever since we got back from Washington you haven't wanted to do anything together. What's wrong? Are you mad at me?"

"No, Dev." He blinked in surprise. He hadn't expected his refusal to hurt his brother's feelings. "We still have fun together."

"Pffft. Just church."

Ethan stood askance. "What? That was *your* idea."

"You're hiding in your books. Come out with me." His grin had the look of a puppy who'd stolen a sock and invited chase.

"Well, the Bible's more than a book, Dev."

Taking a last draw on his cigarette, Devon cast it into the grass, snubbing it out with his boot. His gaze had already fixed across the pastures toward Walt's property line.

Ethan lowered his head. He couldn't expect him to understand. He'd wait for a better time to explain his new-found faith. When he had Devon's undivided attention.

"It might be a little about Marietta." He smiled, filling with warmth at thought of her latest letter.

"Well, you're beating me two girls to nothing. I'm goin' on over to Walt's to score one for myself."

Ethan wrestled the urge to jump up and follow him. But something held him there. Devon couldn't be allowed to call the shots anymore. Greater things were at stake.

Chapter 8

Maryland on the Potomac
Winter Solstice 1860

Marietta stroked the gelding's neck and drew in a deep breath. The smell of leather and hay surrounded her with the essence of *him*. The memory of Ethan's visit lingered everywhere she looked lately—at the dining table, at church, seated beside her in the carriage. She hadn't expected to feel such sensations, but yearning came flooding over her with every thought of the Virginian. She felt especially close to him in the carriage house, recalling the night he had prayed with her. The night he'd held her in his arms and professed his faith.

A delicious shiver tingled down her body that had nothing to do with the winter chill. If being near the one thing he'd left behind could substitute for Ethan Sharpe's nearness, she'd live out here in the stable beside this beautiful horse. The fact that her mother would never think to find her out here only sweetened the escape.

The liver bay head nuzzled her, and she pressed her cheek against the cool silk of the gelding's face. He lipped the fringe on her coat and she pushed him away playfully.

"Thought I'd find you out here."

She started. "Aaron! Gracious, I didn't hear you come in."

Her older brother strode over and grasped the horse's halter and held its head. She smiled at him, and he returned the gesture, his brown eyes twinkling with mischief. "Hiding from Ma?"

She shrugged. "Maybe." A giggle escaped her lips.

"Which reminds me." He cocked his head to the side. "I didn't expect you'd be here when I arrived. Thought they'd have made you a Prissy girl by now."

"Very funny. You mean Paris." The chill in the air returned, and she rubbed her upper arms. "Mama would have." Her thoughts returned to the auction, to her failed mission, and to the ache that had buried itself in her chest. "With the political unrest, Papa thought I should stay at home for now. But the social season will come all too soon, and Mama will be after him again."

Aaron patted her shoulder in a commiserating way. "It can't be so bad."

"It's not like school is for you." She frowned, the tension between her brows creating a slight pinch. "At least you get to come home from Georgetown for Christmas."

"Looks like I'm home for more than Christmas." He quirked his brow, drawing her curiosity.

"Really? Has Papa sent for you to work with him?"

Half his grin turned down. "No, not exactly." He leaned over the stall partition to stroke the gelding's nose. "I... I figure I'll be ready when war comes. South Carolina has made it certain, now."

"Oh, Aaron, no! You wouldn't, would you?"

Now both sides of his lips turned down and he faced her. "Blast it, Mari. Do you take me for a lily-livered coward?"

She cringed. Aaron had never raised his voice at her before.

"I'm sorry." He traced the horse's white blaze with his fingertips and cast an apologetic look at her. "I was just hoping that I'd find some support from you, of all people."

She stood on her tip-toes and reached up to give him a quick hug. "Of course, you have my support. It's just that I'd worry awful about you, and…."

He cocked his head to the side. "And?"

And if war comes, we'd be Ethan's enemy. "Nothing, Aaron.

It's nothing." She shrugged off the burst of sentimentality that radiated from that familiar ache in her bosom and offered a brave smile. "Just pray about it first. Promise?"

"You sound like your mother." His easy-going grin tugged at his mouth again. That same smile set more than a few of her friends' hearts aflutter. "All right, Mari. I'll pray before I run off and sign my life away. What about you, though? What are you planning to do about finishing school?"

She worried her lip for a moment, but then she squared her shoulders and strode to the carriage house door. "You leave that to me. I'll think of something."

ଓଃ

Ethan couldn't escape talk of South Carolina's secession. It dominated every gathering from the moment it made news on Thursday, December 20th right on through to Sunday church service. Fiery dissertation from the Secession Delegation echoed from every neighbor and visitor, while talk of local militias drummed. Any one of the county boys would have given their eye teeth for a report of gunpowder as an early Christmas gift. Any one, that is, except Ethan.

Reverend White had hung the Virginia flag in a prominent place in the sanctuary while he, too, sermonized on states' rights. He waxed poetic in his rhetoric about a heavenly litigator who existed to affirm political views. But in quieter moments, where Ethan immersed himself in study, God refused sides in partisan affairs.

The cock-surity of his friends and neighbors left him a bit off balance. What if they knew something he didn't? Maybe a tyrannical government skewed against southern interests justified full-scale rebellion. If good men like Colonel Jackson, Reverend White, and his own father deemed it a worthy fight, then he'd pledge his life, too. But protecting slavery? He couldn't escape the catalyzing issue, no matter who flavored the debate in honeyed terms.

A good many southerners felt the "necessary evil" would just die out on its own. He ought to rest in their confidence.

Hooting *amen*s presently filled the sanctuary, interrupting his thoughts. He couldn't concentrate on the sermon, so he slipped out to the foyer to wait for service to end. Gentle stirring revealed he had company. The clear blue eyes of the reverend's daughter studied him from where she sat on a small pew against the wall. She smiled at him.

"Miss White. How long have you been sitting there?"

"Since I saw you leave." Ellen blushed and bowed her head, an appealing smile catching his eye along with a golden ringlet peeking beneath her azure bonnet. "I wanted to ask if you were coming to the Christmas party. Daddy is hosting a celebration. He says there will be no more itinerant preaching, since the board has agreed to keep us on permanently in Staunton."

She seemed to seek his approval, and he obliged her with a nod. "That's grand."

Her eyes shone with pleasure. An intoxicating curiosity flashed through him. Had Devon been right? *Was* she dangling on his line, waiting for him to reel her in?

"So, will you celebrate Christmas with us?" Ellen's cheeks pinked.

Tempted to explore the possibilities, but not entirely trusting his motives, he was still obliged to answer her.

"We'd be pleased to come."

She clasped her hands over her blue velvet skirt. Her smile told him the pleasure was all hers.

Unexpected emotions stirred. In light of the way he felt lately, out of step with church, the community, even with Devon, it sure felt nice to belong.

"We used to have the most festive Christmases when mother—" He stopped abruptly. He rued it as soon as the words left his tongue.

She crossed over to Ethan and stood beside him. "It took father time, too, after our mother passed. But a reverend can't avoid Christmas forever, and he found his spirit again."

He nodded. "How old were you?"

She looked down at her gloved hands, worrying a bit of lace at the cuff. "I was eleven. It was scarlet fever. The hardest part was the quarantine. I never got to say goodbye." Pools brimmed over her lashes and she blinked, letting them fall.

He stilled her fretting hands in his, offering a measure of comfort.

She lifted his right hand to her cheek and leaned into his touch, her lashes dewy and alluring.

"You gonna kiss her?" Devon stood in the doorway next to Walt Thompson, a crooked smile passing between them.

Walt hooted, the sound resonating over the perfect silence.

More than a few heads turned, including Reverend White's. Ethan's arm seemed to go numb, and all defense fled from his mind. Ellen's cheeks blossomed into bright roses, and she slid out from beside him.

White walked in. "Seems your boys move faster than your horses, eh Sam?"

Ethan's father joined them, pushing past the cluster that had formed in the doorway. He raised his brow, apparently posing the same question at Ethan. "That's the nature of the beast, I suppose."

"No *beast* is getting near my lambs." White's smile belied his warning. Ethan stood, and collected his coat and hat from the hanger.

ଓଃ

A dozen overtures from Devon had not cooled Ethan's wrath. From the minute they'd left the church until now, past supper and almost bedtime, Ethan refused to even look Devon's way. He'd taken his leave from the table and retreated to his room. Devon could have corrected the misunderstanding, but he stood there silent while White scolded him. Because he thought it funny? Because he resented him studying instead of doing chores? Because he was jealous of him and Marietta? Whatever the reason, it stung.

And why hadn't Mari responded to his last letter? He'd written and rewritten the draft so many times he could recite it from memory, though it had been several weeks since he'd sent it out.

Dear Marietta,

I am well, as is Tilly's son. I have spoken to him of your letters, and he sends his affectionate greetings to his mother. He is a fast learner, and good with the horses. He makes himself very useful, and I for one prize his help, though I am sure that is poor consolation to one who must miss him greatly.

I think often of your words concerning my being in a unique position to impact systems and people, but I have found no opportunity as yet to bring about any changes here. I just seem to find trouble.

Despite my honest search, it seems that even God can't make up his mind on the matter of slavery. Paul tells Onesimus to remain in service to his master, but Moses set the enslaved Israelites free. Which is it? Are there definitive answers?

I hope you and your family have an enjoyable Christmas. Send regards to your parents from all of us.

Fondly,

Ethan Sharpe

The evening whiled away into the quiet of night as he immersed himself in Greek texts. Snow falling outside lent a serene hush, and the words of scripture practically spoke themselves aloud. A chill brushed his skin in the drafty room, and his page fluttered.

"So, have you finished yet?"

Ethan blinked. "Finished what?"

Devon strode in, apparently emboldened since he hadn't been ordered out. He came to sit on the edge of Ethan's desk and flipped the Bible back to its cover. "Your book, here."

Ethan scowled, nursing his grudge. "The Bible isn't the kind of book you finish, Devon."

"What's taking you so all-fired long if it ain't plodding through a thousand pages from cover to cover?" Good-natured teasing chiseled away the tension between them.

"Maybe it's finding the exact passage that tells me I have to forgive the likes of you." He folded his arms and leaned back in his chair.

"Oh, it's in there. Keep looking. Better yet, take my word for it, 'cause your search is takin' too long."

"You better be glad that this is how I've chosen to cool off, otherwise you'd be gumming your dinner through the New Year." The intensity in his tone was meant to make Devon guess whether-or-not he was kidding.

"Big talk, Bible boy. Show me your goods." Devon shoved him in the chest.

Ethan grabbed his arm and twisted it behind his back, lowering his tone to a growl. "You make sport of me again to the pastor, and I'll forget I am a Bible boy."

After a minute of struggle, unable to escape his lock, Devon yelped "All right! I'm sorry! The joke went too far. It's a bad habit of mine."

"Yeah, well you watch I don't deliver you from your habits the hard way." Ethan twisted a bit more and released.

Devon laughed as he shook out his arm. "All that page flippin' done gave you some fearsome muscle."

Ethan lifted his chin. "Don't forget it."

"So, I've been dying to know. What's with you and Ellen?"

"Nothin'."

"That wasn't nothin'."

"Was *too* nothing. A mistake." Ethan narrowed his eyes.

"Whose? Yours, or hers?"

He turned and paced a few steps. "Both. The whole situation. You misunderstood what you think you saw."

Devon rubbed his jaw, a grin peeking through his fingers. "Then why is she telling everyone that you're her escort for the

Christmas dance?"

"What?"

Devon shrugged. "Something must have given her the impression that you were going with her."

"Well doesn't that just beat all! She didn't say anything about a dance."

Devon whistled, taking a seat on Ethan's bed. "Looks like you're in deeper than you figured. But don't worry, I'll help you."

"You'll help me?"

"Sure. After all, I'm partly to blame, right?"

Ethan scowled. "It didn't help none, calling everyone's attention on us the way you did."

"You can let Ellen off easy over time, no hard feelings. Leave it to me. I'll walk you through it. We'll go to that party together, and if things get uncomfortable, I'll ask her to dance. I've got your back, brother."

"Thanks, Dev. I'm obliged."

Devon's eyes held an inscrutable glint. "What're brothers for?"

Chapter 9

The chords of a Christmas carol rolled from Mari's fingertips, seated at her piano. She played at her mother's request for a small gathering of her brother's friends—all of them eligible young bachelors attending Georgetown and Howard—who apparently had nowhere else to go for the holiday. Mari took a deep breath and launched into the chorus.

"Oh, come let us adore hi-im! Chri-ist the Lord."

Mama sat with Papa on the settee, looking quite pleased. Three young men in broadcloth and tweed surrounded her, lifting their voices along with hers. Aaron hung back by the doorway sipping punch and chatting with another of his chums.

She played the last chord and let her voice fade with the young men, feigning enjoyment in their company. Two of the young men nearly tripped over one another fetching her a glass of refreshment.

She bit her bottom lip and tried to stop her mind from seeing the image of Ethan's handsome, tanned face in place of any one of these pale bookish gents. She could almost sense him in the rugged hint of horseflesh when they'd first come in, now long lost to the essence of book binding leather and parchment glue, and the increasing saturation of nutmeg from the kitchen.

Tilly brought in a tray of cookies still soft and warm from the oven. Marietta met the maid's eyes. She looked tired, braving a sadness Mari could only imagine this first Christmas away from her son. Her heart cinched, and she suddenly noticed the gentleman standing next to her, holding out a glass to her. His spectacles reflected the candelabra, and she couldn't see the color of his eyes.

"Thank you, Mr. Hastings. How kind." She sipped, turning her lips in a prim smile.

"Would you do me the honor of a duet?" He gestured to the keyboard.

"Oh, do you play?"

He leveled her with a downward gaze through his wire rimmed lenses. "I'm told I am quite good, actually. Perhaps we'd make a fashionable match. In music." He smiled, his incisors a bit pronounced. She couldn't decide if the effect was predatory or gawky.

She forced her own smile, but her thoughts tumbled about for an excuse not to have to share her bench with this overly assured young man.

Aaron came to her rescue, clapping his big hand over Hasting's narrow shoulder. "I hear you'll be on the first ship bound for Cambridge if this mess in South Carolina erupts."

The man turned to her brother and shrugged. "No man with real prospects is going to waste his future over any war. Unless of course he's a true patriot like you."

Marietta huffed. Mr. Hastings's insincerity lit a conflagration inside her. "A pity you feel that way. I'm sure the country could use an accomplished *musician* if it comes to war."

Aaron stifled a guffaw, and a gasp sounded behind her from the vicinity of her mother.

Marietta assuaged Mama with a curtsy and scooted over on the bench to accommodate the man's entirely too narrow frame. She considered playing a rousing *Yankee Doodle*, but then considered the man was too vain to comprehend the insult to his honor. And then, there was her poor mother's sensibilities. She began a reflective version of *Auld Lang Syne* instead. Hastings joined her with flourishes worthy of a music hall, but all the while she thought only of a young Virginian who had come into her life last fall and galloped away with her heart.

☙❧

December 24th swept over the Shenandoah Valley with a blanket of snow and yuletide cheer. Devon had gone with Ben and their father into town, leaving Ethan to attend chores. He trudged out through the snow to the brood barn, clutching his collar in gauntleted fists against the biting air. As he neared the barn, the chatter of horse boys arose to the cadence of their morning chores. He gave a stout pull on the door and blustered in with a swirl of white.

Ethan paused and shook the snow off his hat. Adjusting to the tempered light, he focused on the first object he met. One of the stable boys, Colby, attended a mare in cross-ties.

Her mahogany belly had swelled, due to foal within the week. She chewed her hay from a muzzle bag while Colby examined her rear hoof.

The boy, born on the farm a year after Ben, had grown to a comparable height to he and Devon, and his coppery complexion marking a startling resemblance to their own Cherokee persuasion. Ethan ignored the rumors that had circulated about the boy. He was a hard worker, and that was all that should matter to him. At least that's what he'd been told.

"Thrush clearing up?" Ethan asked.

The servant stopped what he was doing. "Yassuh. She let me pick her hoof today with no trouble."

Ethan nodded, and he moved on to Jack, who spread fresh straw in the mare's box stall. The old hand tucked an extra depth into the corners in case the mare's time came. Ethan leaned in to assure that the sandy loam beneath the bedding appeared raked and dry, then he passed with the same nod. After a few more inspections he came to Jonesy.

"Morning, suh." The boy flicked a dandy brush over the shining withers of another brood mare with one hand, while clutching a saddle blanket around his shoulders with the other.

"Where's your coat?"

The boy lowered his head. "I don't have one, suh."

"Don't have one? Weren't you given one?"

"Yes, suh. Marse Sam give me one, but I give it to Hiram at the church meetin' 'cause he say his folkses cain't give none to they people."

The little farm bordering theirs to the southwest was a small affair growing subsistence potatoes and a small cash crop of tobacco. They were the talk of the county the way they had sold off property acre by acre and took such scandalous care over their remaining holdings. The rage his old man would fly into could curl a person's hair, seeing their neglected horses, hips showing, rain rot matting their coats. Neglect was worse than greed in his father's eyes.

"Why'd you give away your coat, knowing you'd go cold all winter? You can't afford to get sick."

"Yes, suh. But the Good Lord, He know my need."

Jonesy shivered in the few seconds he paused his work. Ethan drew an exasperated sigh. His father was strict about provision, but how could he ignore this?

"Follow me to the house, and I'll see if we can't scare up another one for you." He led the way down the aisle, ducking the ties, and paused midway. "Mind you come and ask next time you feel generous. If you see a need, tell me, and *I'll* arrange something. Hear?"

Addressing them all, a chorus of agreement answered him.

Jonesy shivered through the open area near the door, pulling his horse blanket tighter. Ethan motioned for him to take another one on their way out. Jonesy swung the wool weave over his shoulders, and the dusty barn aroma wafted on the air as they departed together.

Laughter from the servants rose as they passed. "Look like Christmas done come a day early."

Once out of earshot, Ethan turned aside. "That was quite a

gesture you made for your friend."

"Oh, he not my friend, suh. But the Good Book tell us to bless our enemies."

"Then he's your enemy?"

"He say I'm high an' mighty, ridin' horses like white folk." Jonesy shook his head so disgustedly that Ethan laughed.

"So Hiram's wagging his jaws about you, and you turn around and help him?"

Jonesy shrugged. "I'm just reapin' hot coals, suh, like the Good Book say."

"Hot coals and warm coats. I don't know if I would'a done the same if that was my only coat."

"Reckon you would, suh." The boy's eyes scrutinized him. "You's a good Christian, suh."

Conviction lanced through him. If he were a good Christian, he wouldn't have separated the boy from his mammy. He studied the boy walking beside him, wearing his horse blanket like a royal robe. Such dignity and conviction. This was no common young man. And then it occurred to him. Perhaps he'd found someone who shared his faith. Devon cared nothing for the good book, but Jonesy did.

"So, these church meetings you attend. Who reads the word?"

"Nobody knows how to read, but we each knows scriptures, an' we shares 'em from week to week."

They arrived at the big house. A wall of warmth and the fragrance of wood smoke met them as Ethan swung open the door. Jonesy left the dirty blankets on the front porch, and they stepped in. The house was empty, except for an old spotted hound that raised her head at their entrance but sank down again to pursue rabbits in interrupted dreams. Ethan led Jonesy to a wardrobe where sundries lay packed into its depth, among them blankets and provisions for the winter. Ethan doled out a pile of items to the young man beside him. "Are there any other needs I should know about?"

"Colby's feet grown a mite big fo' his old shoes, suh. He goin' barefoot in the cold."

"I'll see he gets what he needs."

Ethan closed the closet door. Jonesy had already shrugged into the wool coat, looking himself over with a grin.

"How's it fit?"

"Right fine. Don't know how to thank you, suh."

Ethan led the way outdoors. "Well, there is something."

"Yassuh?"

Ethan could just hear Devon scolding him for what he was about to propose, but he ignored the voice in his head. "I'd like to teach you to read the Bible for your church meetings."

Jonesy's eyes grew wide, and he clamped his lips shut, tightening the consternation in Ethan's gut. Perhaps he should have heeded Devon's imagined scolding. "Would that be all right with you? Or will Hiram think you've gone completely pale?"

Jonesy swiped at the air. "Aw, Marse Ethan, I don't care what he think."

Still feeling the heat of Devon's breath down his neck, Ethan concluded. "I've got my own Hirams to worry about, so I'll work out the particulars and get back to you."

A few hours passed, and Ethan hung the muck rake on its peg, chores finished at last. He took his gauntlets off and blew on his hands, watching his breath frost on the frigid air. He'd just decided to head back to the house when the double doors slid open. Ben entered.

"Back from town already?"

"Got an early Christmas gift—something from your *girlfriend*." Ben hid his hands behind his back, a quirking grin daring pursuit.

"All right, let's have it." He reached for Ben, but the impish boy dodged.

"Give it up."

"Which ha-a-and?"

"I'll let you know after I wring both, now hand it here!" He lunged forward and grabbed one shoulder, twisting Ben's wriggling body around to see what he concealed—a letter. Ben's hooting filled the barn, alighting pigeons in the rafters. He evaded Ethan's grasp, his auburn hair flopping as he escalated the struggle into a merry chase.

"Hand it over!" Ethan tackled the boy and pinned him to the hard-packed dirt floor. "You're gonna tear it."

"Ouch! All right, here, take your stupid letter." Ben rolled away, rubbing his shoulder. His laughter hitched on moans.

Ethan claimed his prize and retreated to the tack room. Once behind closed doors, he sat down on a bale of hay and, muttering annoyance, smoothed the wrinkled envelope over his knee. He held it up to behold the penmanship. Something about the way Marietta wrote his name sent a small thrill through him. His lips stretched into a grin, but as he read the letter, his rush of excitement quieted.

Dear Ethan,

I confess lately my heart has been occupied with thoughts of you. I think often about your visit, the way you and Devon made me laugh, and the sincerity of your prayer with me. I 'm so pleased that you haven't forgotten the commitment you made. Your dedication fills me with hope. I pray what I write will not rend the friendship I've come to hold so dear.

I could articulate my thoughts on that dreaded subject of slavery, but instead, I have enclosed a memento in hopes that it explains my position. I pray it helps you on your faith journey. No matter which side of this debate we land, above all I hope you know that I still remain,

Your devoted friend,

Marietta

Ethan lifted the page to discover an accompanying leaflet. It was a printed quote by some man named Matthew Henry. The bottom bore the imprint *The North Star.* That abolitionist rag. Ethan recoiled.

"If a man know that his neighbour is in danger by any unjust proceeding, he is bound to do all in his power to deliver him. And what is it to suffer immortal souls to perish, when our persuasions and example may be the means of preventing it?"

Vivid images invaded his thoughts. Two different boys reaching out for their mothers, as stronger hands bore her away. One was Jonesy. The other, Devon.

He and Devon had been so young when mother had died. And like Jonesy, Devon had tried to cling to her when it was time for their final goodbye. Gideon had to hold Devon back, as the pall bearers lifted her coffin and carried her away.

His stomach constricted considering the one thing that stood in the way of Jonesy's reunion with his mother—fear. He'd been so afraid of offending Devon that he hadn't considered what it cost Jonesy.

Ethan bowed his head.

"Lord, I ask your forgiveness for remaining neutral in a war of good and evil. Give me the strength and the courage to do what's right—to do your will. Amen."

A shuffle of straw drew his attention. Ben's inquisitive stare met him from the doorway.

"Hey!" Ethan clutched the letter against his coat.

"Did she dab it with perfume?"

Ethan stood up, sending Ben scampering out of the barn. His heart hammered against his ribs, but he rationalized that he hadn't been caught at anything more incriminating than prayer. His nerves dispelled with a long, cleansing exhale, and he tucked the letter into his breast pocket. Walking back to the house, he watched Ben frolic with a cluster of foals in the far pasture. Thank God, he'd escaped scrutiny for now.

Chapter 10

Ethan reported to his father that the graining and haying were done, the herds were secured, and the water troughs chipped free of ice. Anticipation hummed in the air. The servants were all given small gifts and the promise of light work and a turkey dinner on the morrow.

Ethan and his brothers were finally free to prepare for the Christmas party. Presently, he stood in Devon's doorway.

"What're you wearin'?"

His brother bent into his wardrobe, rummaging through haberdashery for the occasion. The way he preened reminded Ethan of a gamecock flashing his plumage.

"I'm thinkin' about this hunter green jacket. You should wear yours, too."

Ethan scoffed at the suggestion of matching attire.

"Okay. What about your burgundy?"

"Red and green? Surely you jest."

Devon was steadfast. "I'm not. Tan riding breeches and black waistcoat. Now go—you're wasting time."

Devon gave the orders and Ethan marched. But a few seconds later, Ethan made an about-face and poked his head back in.

"My ties Devon? I can't seem to find any of my cravats for some reason." He knew why. Devon had borrowed them all.

Devon shook his head. "You're hopeless. Here."

He tossed a silk ascot and Ethan scooped it out of midair. "Thanks."

"And E?"

"What?"

"Relax. They're only girls."

Ethan grunted and turned back to his room. As fun as the evening promised, he couldn't help wishing he were spending it with a certain molasses-haired wildcat. He wondered what Marietta was doing for Christmas.

After dressing, Devon started downstairs, and Ethan and Ben followed close behind, thundering like driven cattle in their haste.

Donning woolen overcoats, the three dapper young men stepped out into the swirling snow. A smolder reflected off the clouds in the western sky, coloring the world in amber sunset and blue shadow. Climbing into the sleigh that Ezra had brought around, Ethan watched the sun sink behind the wintry landscape. Every tree sagged beneath a burden of white, every fence post and rail lay capped with glitter. Even the Shire pulling the sleigh sported large downy clusters over harness and bells and thick, flaxen mane.

Devon reached under his coat to retrieve a pair of wrapped boxes. Extending one to Ethan, he winked.

"What's this?"

"Don't reckon we ought to show up empty handed, so I took the liberty of selecting a token for the girls."

Ethan contemplated the little box in the palm of his hand. "What is it?"

"Just a trifle. Nothing much."

"Thanks, Dev. Looks like my debts are amassing."

Devon's smile broadened. "I'm sure you'll find a way to make up for it."

The horse's harness jingled as he trotted along, the sounds muted in the falling snow. Soon, a white spire rose into the squall, the cross at the top hardly visible. Framed by tall, swaying pines, the church and adjoining parsonage marked their destination. At the end of the swept walkway, the open door beckoned.

Blanketed horses stood sentinel with parked sledges outside the old country church, and Ezra pulled the Sharpe's sleigh into alignment. Devon hopped down, and Ethan followed, both tucking their gift boxes into pockets. Ben scampered up to the door ahead of them.

Reverend White stood in the vestibule, and beyond him, his daughters.

"Good to see the Sharpe family in attendance this evening." He extended a handshake to each. "Merry Christmas Benjamin, Devon, Ethan."

Ethan managed to return his greeting, haste and distraction dividing his interest between the aroma of food and the sight of the sisters preening beyond the doorway. White stepped aside, allowing his girls to receive their guests.

Ethan took the arm of the young lady presented to him. He passed Reverend White with a nod. "Thanks for having us, sir."

A servant took their overcoats before they left the foyer, and the conversation between Devon and Adelaide waxed flirtatious already. The church hall opened to them at the end of the passageway, cleared of pews. Rows of tables and chairs rippled back from the fireplace on the far side of the room. The county's faithful were there and offered deferential greetings to Sam Sharpe's sons. From the far corner, a trio of musicians livened the gathering with fiddle, piano, and a mellow tenor voice.

Ben joined a cluster of friends near the refreshments, leaving Ethan alone with Ellen. Self-aware and bereft of any further distractions, Ethan met Miss White's shimmering smile. She wore her golden hair swept up with little platinum ringlets cascading from red tartan ribbons the exact match of her taffeta skirt. She could have been a porcelain doll in a shop window. His nerves thrummed to the rhythm of the music. With the white starched lace frothing up from her bodice, contrasting a waistline the envy of any belle, and the bright hues in the plaid of her dress reflecting the blush at her cheeks, she was the most fetching thing in the room. He wasn't aware of his immediate words to her, they just spilled out.

"You look fine, Miss Ellen."

"Why, thank you, Ethan. I must say, you're quite dashing yourself. And look! Our colors—they match."

"How 'bout that." His mouth went dry, and he escaped from her hold for a second. "Why don't I fetch us drinks?"

He fled for the punch bowl and found his head again as the cool concoction brought his temperature down. From across the room Devon waved, Walt Thompson at his side. Thompson muttered something in Devon's ear, and his brother nodded, raising his glass, reminding Ethan to fetch Miss Ellen's drink. He nodded back, and returned to her, promised refreshment in hand.

She took the opportunity of the exchange to slip her hand into his. "Come and see our tree."

He followed her like a tethered steer. The scent of roses trailed behind her, skimming his awareness. They passed the candle-lit tables where many of the guests were already seated. She led him toward a cozy corner of the room and a stately fir, bedecked in colors of the season. A few blown glass ornaments flickered in the light of the fireside, spiraling in undulating contours, not unlike feminine curves. Ethan stepped away, running his hand through his hair.

"What's the matter?"

Her fawning made his temperature rise, and he tried to think of an excuse to escape the prickling heat. "Pine trees make me itch."

"Oh, why didn't you say so? Come, take a seat over by the fire and you'll feel better."

She held his arm, pressing it to her side. They drew up to the table where her sister and Devon had settled. Ethan nudged Devon's arm, but he turned his back to him. He'd be no help, despite the promise he'd made. As the realization dawned, Ethan ground his teeth and exhaled a heated breath. He would have to navigate this battlefield alone.

Ellen moved in closer, and he cautioned himself to be careful where his eyes fell. Her shorter stature gave him an intimate perspective beneath the garnet pendant at her neckline. He was no saint yet, and decidedly no martyr.

"Lord," he muttered under his breath. "Help."

Coffee and dessert were served, and during this interlude Devon took the opportunity to present his gift to Adelaide. Ellen compelled Ethan to watch her sister peel the ribbon away and open the small parcel, revealing a gold locket. Adelaide asked him to fasten it about her neck and gathered her long tresses, exposing her bared shoulders to him. Devon raised his brows, obviously relishing the task. Ideas of Cain slaying Abel brought a wicked smile to Ethan's lips for a moment before his conscience straightened him out. He couldn't imagine his brother would actually fulfill the unspoken promise of the gift. Such a lavish gift surely meant devotion of which his impetuous brother was incapable.

And then he remembered. Devon had handed a box to him. For Ellen. He swallowed as his throat seemed to swell.

Right on cue, Devon turned to him with a smile that would charm a bee from a blossom. "Guess who's birthday falls on Christmas, Ethan? Good thing you got Miss Ellen something extra special, eh?"

"I did? I mean, I hope she thinks I did, but she'll have to open it to find out." He produced the trinket box with apprehension, kicking himself for not peeking inside first. At last, he held it out to her.

"Why Ethan Sharpe! You're a subtle thing, keeping a secret like this." Her slender fingers worked on the wrapping, and when the box popped open on its hinge, both her jaw and his dropped in unison. Inside, beneath a thin velvet layer, was a ring.

Reverend White rose from his seat across the aisle and thanked the congregation for taking him on from his itinerant preaching circuit. The people clapped, and Devon slipped Adelaide away amid the commotion, leaving Ethan gaping at the bauble on Ellen's finger.

She sipped from her drink, her full lips pressed and slightly opened, peering up at him through hooded eyes over her fluted glass. His head swam, and his tongue had gone numb. She set her glass down and smiled, well-rehearsed in the art of coquetry. He swallowed again as all the air in the room fled. He sent up another silent prayer.

He couldn't blame her for the predicament in which he found himself. She was as much a casualty to Devon's prank as he. Like one of those ornaments on the tree, she hung suspended, looking for a safe place to land. But there was no way he intended to perpetuate the misunderstanding.

After a nervous chuckle, he cleared his throat and found his voice. "Of course, it's not intended as *the* ring. It's just a token. For a friend. Merry Christmas, Ellen. Oh, and happy birthday, too." He pulled at his ascot.

Her lashes fluttered for a second.

"Thank you, but you really shouldn't have." She withdrew her hand from his and her crystal-blue eyes iced over. "I can't accept such an extravagant *token*. It raises too many questions." She slid the box with a bit more force than necessary into his empty hand.

She stood and gathered her taffeta skirt, leaving him sitting there, torn between strangling chagrin and breathtaking relief.

ꕥ

New Year's Eve had come and gone, and Marietta's spirits hovered somewhere between the festivities of the season and a subtle melancholy. Papa had scarcely been home at all since Christmas. She had so looked forward to celebrating with the whole family now that Aaron had returned home, but Papa's absence started before she arose in the morning, and sometimes he wouldn't return until after she'd gone to bed.

Serving as one of Senator Seward's chief aides explained his absence. Her father had been a strong Seward supporter from the beginning, having joined the Republican party in its early days. After Seward's failed bid for president, her father secured stronger ties to the Senator when they campaigned together for Mr. Lincoln in the early fall. Papa had hinted that he and his esteemed colleague shared much more than politics. With common associations on the Underground Railroad, they also shared a cause.

Mama couldn't be happier with the appointment. Seward had been favored to win the nomination at the Republican National Convention and might have been president, but for his stance on the moral evils of slavery. Still, the man was a rising star on the political scene, and Mama felt that the advancement could only further their family's causes.

Mari agreed with Mama here. All the while she'd wrapped her hopes and prayers on a single concern, the Lord had been working to elevate Papa to one of the highest offices in the land. Perhaps through Papa's new associations, someone might champion the plight of Tilly's son—maybe even Lincoln himself.

For the afternoon, Mari, Tilly and Mama had been hard at work preparing dinner, hoping Papa would join them. To Mari's surprise, not only did Papa's carriage ascend the drive, but another's as well. She hastened to make ready.

Papa led the way through the door, a bearded man in an overcoat following. Tilly took the men's hats and coats and once they stepped from the foyer to the parlor, Mama received their guest, while Mari stood alongside. She didn't recognize the man, and curiously, Papa didn't introduce him. Might he be a new political acquaintance from Lincoln's forming cabinet? Everyone expected Senator Seward to become the next Secretary of State, but no official announcements had been made yet. Perhaps they hoped to maintain secrecy in their negotiations.

"We'll take refreshment in my office, Cora." Papa kissed Mama on the cheek, and Mari thought she heard him whisper something in Mama's ear. In a clear voice, he asked, "Would you mind summoning Aaron for me?" Then they disappeared behind closed doors.

Mama's expression never dimmed, but she went dutifully to gathering her preparations onto a cart for entertaining Papa's guest. Mari stood blinking, apparently a moment too long.

Mama raised her brows and peered down her long, thin nose at her. "What are you waiting for, young lady? Any guest of this house, no matter who they are, deserves better than cold coffee."

Mari set to work, taking after her mother's example, though she couldn't bring herself to smile. Whoever this guest was, his arrival meant she wouldn't have the intimate family dinner that she'd hoped.

Presently, Mama directed her to the cart. "Please bring this in to your father while I find your brother."

"Yes, ma'am." Managing the cart with one hand, Mari knocked twice and opened the door. The room smelled of beeswax and pine, and the gas sconces shone brightly over the polished surfaces. Aaron approached briskly from the hallway and followed her in. His eyes expressed a certain animation, and she paused for him to gather a few of the preparations on her tray, just long enough to read his lips.

Bounty hunter.

A chill coursed through her. It had been a long spell since slave catchers had come around. Mama and Papa were careful, but all it took was one person to report suspicious activity. They hadn't directly assisted any fugitives in many months. These days, Papa mostly financed those that did, rather than place his family in jeopardy. She studied Aaron's expression. Caution and something else lingered there. "Thank you, sister. Why don't you see if Mother needs help with the wash?"

She understood immediately. The false washroom. Mama would need help sliding the washtub to conceal the back passageway beneath the floor.

The casual intonation of Papa's voice making small talk accompanied her to the door. "Mr. Hamlin is most eager for

Seward's confirmation of Lincoln's offer. The Vice President-elect would have the matter of the new cabinet settled sooner than later."

"There are many in the South eager to know what position Mr. Lincoln will take on the Fugitive Slave Law."

It seemed an eternity passed while Marietta copied Mama's calm domestic routines, waiting for the door to open to Papa's study. At last, the click of hardware and the deep timbre of men's voices drifted to her ears. Footsteps.

"Cora, dear, would you please find Mr. Silsby's coat?" Papa asked from the parlor.

Tilly emerged from the washroom and set down a compote and the drying rag onto the dining table as she passed. "I'll fetch it, Mr. Hamilton, suh."

"Thank you, Matilda."

"I'll see papers on your gal." The man pointed an accusing finger at Tilly.

Mari pressed her folded fingers together so tightly in her lap, she feared they'd make an audible crack. Tilly never broke stride but continued with her head held high to the cloak closet in the foyer.

"Of course," Mama replied to the man. "We purchased our maid last fall in Rockingham County." She produced a slip of sale from the small buffet and held it out, without allowing the man to take it from her. "Best investment we ever made for our daughter."

The man perused the document, and with a slow nod, he looked up at Mama, then at her. Mari's stomach shrank.

"She the only slave you have here, Miss?"

Mari rose from the chair and straightened her skirts about her before answering. "Tilly is my maid and companion, Mr. uh, Mr. Silsby, is it?" She confirmed with a prim nod. "Papa hopes to acquire a stable boy, but with this late unpleasantness, the timing hasn't been entirely right. She is our only servant at this time."

Tilly returned with the man's hat and overcoat. He took them abruptly.

"If there is nothing else, Mr. Silsby, I'll bid you good day." Mama strode toward the door with a smile that could light a lantern. Sufficiently cajoled, the man followed, and as the door shut behind him, the household was done with the imposition.

Aaron and Papa waited for Mama to rejoin them in the dining room.

"He'll be back with others." Papa seemed apologetic in his tone. "That's always the way of it."

"How did you know to leave work today?"

"Got a tip from a friend. I met Silsby's carriage on the road not a mile from here. And not a moment too soon."

Mama pressed the small of her corseted waist. "Thank the Lord, Levi. It's a comfort that you were here."

"I hope our new president has the courage to do away with that wretched Fugitive Slave Law." Aaron barely glanced up at Papa from a preoccupation with the cookie tray on the table. He selected one of the round molasses treats and chewed thoughtfully.

"I wish I could promise that, but even Henry—Senator Seward—feels it would be a provocation to the border states if we don't tone down the anti-slavery rhetoric. Preserving the Union must be our chief objective for now."

Mari's breath whooshed with crushing disappointment. "B-but isn't there any hope that the new administration will champion the cause?"

"I remain hopeful. With the Vice-presidential pick being an abolitionist from Maine, and our esteemed Secretary of State having ties to the Underground Railroad in New York—"

Aaron interrupted. "Has Seward accepted the position, then?"

"Unofficially, of course." Papa nodded. "And I needn't remind you that the news doesn't leave this house."

"Yes, Papa." The pressure in Mari's chest relaxed. So, her hopes might still be realized.

"What precipitated this bounty hunter's visit, Levi?" Mama's hushed tone held unease.

“I don't know. Let us hope our guests from Virginia don't prove to be the source.”

Mari shook her head. “No, Papa. Surely not Ethan.”

“When was the last time you received a letter from him?”

“Just last month. And I've returned one to him wishing him and his family a Merry Christmas and a Happy New Year.”

Papa regarded her in silence and his smile failed to light his tired eyes. He turned to Mama and patted her hand, and they exchanged a lingering look at one another. Mama didn't look at all pleased.

Chapter 11

Bridgewater, Virginia
February 1861

Ethan could hardly keep up with the new sovereign states filling the map. Mississippi, Florida, and Alabama had joined South Carolina's secession from the Union early in the new month. Then Georgia and Louisiana joined the ranks as well. But the more Ethan tried to catch secesh fever, the more he realized he was immune.

Prospective troopers appeared daily to eye their horses. With local militia mustering, plenty of them would pay a premium to ride to war on a good mount. Ethan studied his father's technique, inviting them inside the parlor and filling the guests' glasses with his best brandy until his sales objective was secured.

On this day a banker from Lexington, as liberal with his opinions as his father was with his liquor, led the discussion. "Virginia will have to leave the Union. She has far more in common with her gentleman planter neighbors to the south than those dirty industrialists to the north."

"Here, here," Mr. Thompson agreed. "All of my business associates in the Valley stand with Virginia should she secede."

The banker scanned the room. "How can we live in unity with people who canonized that devil, Brown?"

Devon held a glass of brandy, showing no compunction among his father's colleagues. "They believe their wage-slavery more holy. Filling their factories with children, and paying men starvation wages, they dare call us the chattel mongers."

Half a dozen men raised voices of outrage and agreement.

A dull ache thrummed at Ethan's temples.

Devon continued. "I saw for myself in a Washington cathedral how they use the church to indoctrinate."

Teeth set on edge, Ethan considered the hypocrisy—hadn't Reverend White endlessly sermonized on secession from his own pulpit?

A merchant from Leesburg weighed in. "Those meddling abolitionists should be flogged alongside the slaves they abscond with."

The gathering talked all at once, and Ethan tuned out. He would rather trade the overheated climate of the parlor for the cool welcome outdoors. With Devon holding sway, no one would miss him. They were all too busy maligning people he cared about. People like Marietta.

He embraced solitude, taking brisk strides across the snow-covered lawn. Drawing in the crisp air, his inner turmoil quieted as a revelation came. None of them *liked* slavery, as much as they decried so-called Northern hypocrisy. They might still be swayed. But he found no sense taking on the whole pack of dogs at once. There would be time to influence the ones who mattered.

Ethan rejected what those secessionists had spewed about Marietta's kind. *His* kind. What had happened to him in the Hamilton's carriage house was too personal to be a political manipulation. Why, then, hadn't he found the words to defend it? To explain his encounter with God to Devon? It had been three months since their return from Washington and he was no closer to broaching the subject.

He moved higher up the foothill, and as the sun sank low over the western pasture, he chose a deer trail along the eastern ridge. This was as remote as the property would take him from the smoke and bluster of the old county boors. He'd have to return by and by, but the smallness of the activity down there from this vantage helped him put it into perspective.

The herds moved through the dappled sunlight in the meadow below, and it all looked like someone else's life, a pleasant bucolic scene. Someday, he would build his house and raise his children in the shelter of that little valley. But would it, too, be built on compromise, deception, and corruption?

Ethan sat down on a log at the crest of the hill where the bare trees permitted the best view. Prayer came unrehearsed, springing from deep wells within.

"God, have your way in this place, and in me. And Lord, Devon… open his eyes and his heart. Bring him to the truth, no matter what it takes. Amen."

Energized after the prayer, he made his descent home along the quickest route. Surely the guests would have begun their trek home by now, and a winter's evening by the fire beckoned. Maybe he'd read or partake in a game of cards if his brothers were sporting. Looking homeward, he missed his footing. His boot snagged on a protruding rock. He stumbled and slid to the edge of a ravine. Scrambling to recover, he could gain no purchase on the ice. Over the precipice he hurled in a free-fall. The jagged wall of bedrock grazed his head just before impact. Though he landed in a drift, fiery pain ignited his skull. He touched above his ear, and the last thing he recalled was the startling sight of blood at his fingertips. Then all went cold and still.

☙❧

"Anyone seen where Ethan's gone?" Devon paused at the back door, stomping snow from his boots. A tour of his brother's favorite hiding places proved fruitless. "I can't find him anywhere."

Ben joined Devon in the kitchen. "I saw him leave a while ago. He snuck out whiles ya'all were plannin' to invade Washington."

Devon was about to pull off his gauntlet but stopped. "Which way did he set off?"

"I dunno."

"Did he take his horse?"

"Dunno."

Devon frowned. "Probably off writing to Marietta. Don't know why he still bothers with those people." It vexed him like a hornet in his cap that Ethan should disappear now. He had gossip about rivalries over the horse militia. If anyone should get a placement, it ought to be them. He tromped through the house in his snowy boots, calling up the stairs.

"Ethan?" His voice echoed down the corridor leading to his father's study.

The old man stuck his head out of the den like a bear roused from hibernation. "Shut your saucebox, Devon! I'm trying to balance the books."

One warning was sufficient. He took his search and his mouth elsewhere.

A short time later, and Ethan hadn't returned for dinner. His father and Ben sat down and ate, but Devon hardly touched his plate. He rehearsed the events from the time he last saw his brother. The conversation with their company had turned to war talk. Nothing new. What would cause him to leave so abruptly? All that rhetoric about northern religion, perhaps? And where would he go? On foot, no less. Something didn't feel right.

"Did Ethan say anything about going to Walt's?" his father asked.

"No, but I'll go see." Devon rose from the table and shrugged back into his coat.

Ben jumped up after him. "Should we bring lanterns?"

Their father nodded, turning to Devon. "And a gun. I've been hearing coyotes last few nights."

Devon had seldom seen the old man worried, but this was one of those occasions. It struck an uncomfortable chord in him. "I'll saddle up. You coming?"

Sharpe rose to join them. "I'll have Ezra stay in case he

returns."

ଔ଼ଓ

Peering up from the bottom of a pit, Ethan tracked moonlit clouds blowing across the night sky. Any warmth of the day had quickly radiated off into the darkness, while melting ice trickled over the jagged drop. His right eye had swollen shut, and the left barely opened. But the worst was the blinding headache which shot from his temple down into his neck with every movement.

The only way out of this ravine was to scale a twelve-foot sheer. Even if he could force his body to make the climb, he was still about a mile from the house. He rubbed ice water against his better eye, and it numbed the pain enough for now. Snow lay in deep drifts all around him. Fallen trees stuck up at odd angles, some still anchored by their roots at the top of the precipice. It was a miracle he hadn't impaled himself on a broken limb. He grasped a thick branch and pulled himself to his feet. The throbbing at his temple left him sick at his stomach, but he held on while the rock walls around him spun. He looked up, determined to climb. Each movement produced a pressure in his head like to blow it clear off his shoulders, but he continued up the ladder of branches toward the top. Spiked twigs dug fresh lacerations in his face, but he pressed on until his head and shoulders crested the top.

His hopes of seeing the house lights below evaporated into the thinning air. Kicking against loose stone, he heaved the rest of his body over the precipice and lay gasping for several minutes. His nose filled with the scent of damp wool and the tang of blood. A faint whistle sounded on each exhale. With continued exertion he'd be facing a full-blown asthma attack, so he measured his movements.

Did anyone even know he was missing?

Ethan's damp clothing quickly stiffened on the wind-swept heights. He climbed to unsteady feet, tucking his face into his collar to draw warmer air. Slow and steady strides gained ground until he cleared a dark line of trees where the view expanded. Below, several torches and lanterns milled about like sparks carried on the breeze. Voices called to him. The wheezing in his chest deepened. Expending his breath on shouting was too great a risk. *But they were within earshot.* He cried out, and his voice startled him, harsh, shrill, and weak. Coughing a fit, he staggered to a standstill. Oh, how his head ached. He could barely force air through tightening lungs. He doubled over, bracing hands on knees.

"Lord, send help."

ଔଓ

Devon pulled his black colt Cinder up short of the back porch. The Thompsons hadn't seen Ethan all day, and Devon was out of ideas. The last spasms of color reflected over the western fields, setting the snow ablaze. Devon's keen eyes scanned the grounds for any movement. Just the usual stirrings—horses, blackbirds, and servants crossing from barn to paddock. Devon fastened his attention on a figure leaving the tack barn and entering the granary.

"Jonesy! Hold up!" Devon spurred the colt into a canter. The ice on the path crunched beneath his stride. "You seen my brother?"

The two had become inseparable since Ethan had taken over the boy's training.

"No, suh, I ain't seen Marse Ethan since Marse Sam's comp'ny come."

"Ask around."

"Yessuh. I sho' will, suh."

Ben and the hounds worked the fields. They hadn't picked up the right trail, but instead ran chaos over worn paths. Likewise, the slaves wandered about the grounds, showing just enough effort to keep Devon from taking a switch to them. Jonesy alone had taken up a torch and headed up the slope beyond the barns.

Devon shadowed him from the cover of trees, reining Cinder to a stealthy walk.

Jonesy trudged through the snow into the upper pastures, his torch flickering through the woods. The eastern end had been barricaded to prevent horses from falling into a deep ravine up there. Devon squinted in suspicion. Where was the boy going?

Jonesy stooped over the ground as though studying something.

Devon emerged from the thicket and urged Cinder into a canter up the hill toward Jonesy.

"Hey! What're you doing up here?"

Jonesy turned about. "I felt to look up here."

A crackling sound reached Devon's ears, like tread through dried leaves. Devon swung his lantern, illuminating bales of composting hay and twisted tree branches taking sinister shapes under the flickering light—and just beyond, a half-frozen figure crawling through the snow.

"Ethan!"

His breath hitched. Even in the weak light, it was evident a bright red streak burned a path down the side of his brother's face.

Jonesy ran toward him, but Devon cut Cinder into his path. "Go tell my father we found him. Hurry!"

Devon leapt off his horse. He reached under his brother's arms and lifted him to his feet.

"What happened?" Devon panted, laboring to lift him into the saddle. Ethan crawled onto Cid's back, and Devon held him in place descending the hill.

His father caught up with them halfway to the house. Ethan's ragged breath came rapid and shallow, and Devon wrung the reins in his hands, fretting. The old man reached up and examined the gash at Ethan's scalp.

"That'll need stitches," he reported. "I want all the servants assembled to give an account for the last couple hours."

Devon's coursing blood suddenly chilled. His father had validated his suspicion that his brother had been the target of foul play. Ethan flirted with danger, cultivating imprudent relationships. Just the other day the old man had complained of missing supplies. A coat, some shoes. Perhaps an extra set of traveling clothes, should a slave be hatching an escape plan.

Devon gripped beneath one of Ethan's arms, and his father the other, and they helped him off the horse and up to the house. Ethan's body quaked with shivering, and they set him in a chair beside the fireside. Ezra brought warm, brandied coffee, and Devon took it and set it to his brother's lips.

As the slave departed again, Father's voice sounded from the doorway. "Ezra, take the sleigh and fetch Doc Sterling."

Devon's hands shook, and Ethan sputtered out his coffee. "Sorry, E. Here, now. Easy."

Slowly, between shivers and groans, his brother's wheezing subsided. His father propped Ethan's head with an old blanket but blood already covered the horsehair-upholstered chair. When the old man produced a bottle and a rag, a whiff of iodine burned Devon's nose and eyes. He winced, knowing well how that would feel on a fresh wound.

Ethan thrashed like a senseless beast with one touch of the astringent on blood-matted hair. Devon recoiled, his gut cinching.

"Give me a hand!" Sharpe snapped.

Devon shook off his shock and pinned his brother's arms against his chest, apologizing in a low voice.

His brother fixed his one good eye on him, the other as round as a peach and bruised, besides. A chill coursed through Devon. Ethan's vacant focus passed through him, unseeing. Then he shuttered his lids, rolled his head back, and passed out.

Devon crouched at his brother's side and traced the injury with the lightest touch. The gash began at Ethan's right brow and ripped into his hairline above his ear. It was a good three inches long, and uncertain yet how deep.

His father nudged his shoulder. "Let me tend to the wound, son."

He stepped aside, and his father cut away at his brother's hair. The iodine spilled freely onto the jagged cut now. The sharp odor hit Devon's nostrils the way he imagined its sting bit into Ethan's flesh. He gagged. Thank God Ethan slept through that.

At last his father cut a strip of linen and bound the wound.

Gripping his brother's hand which lay slack in his lap, Devon felt a cold shock. Chunks of ice still clung to cuffs and collar. "Reckon we ought to get him out of these clothes."

His father nodded, and they tugged off Ethan's boots and shirt.

After the old man exited the room, Devon fetched a quilt from the rack and tucked it around his brother's shoulders, then shoved the chair closer to the fire. Still not satisfied, he stoked the blaze and before long, he stood back, satisfied as color returned to Ethan's cheeks. But his worries were far from over. Ethan hadn't stirred a muscle.

He settled in for a long wait for the doctor.

Sharpe returned from the other room and set a bottle of whiskey down next to Ethan's chair. He bent to examine him again, a frown creasing his weathered face. Straightening, he turned aside and threw the bloodied iodine rag into the flames. "What do you suppose he was doing up there?"

Devon swallowed. "Don't know. But *Jonesy* knew where to look."

The old man stroked his goatee with tapping fingertips. "See anything unusual up there?"

"No, not in the dark."

"Let's see what the workers have to say for themselves. Someone's bound to know something."

Devon followed his father to the back door, but the old man stopped him. "I'll handle this. You stay here and keep an eye on your brother. Give him whiskey for the pain if he wakes up."

As he kept silent vigil by Ethan's side, thoughts darted through his brain like the flicker of firelight on whitewashed walls. It wasn't that long ago wild reports gripped the community about an armed, black mob. Ever since, the specter of slave uprisings kept him awake at night. Overseers had been murdered in remote fields, and owners, burned in their beds. Devon stifled a shudder to think that a murder-festering savage might be lurking in their midst. He knelt beside his brother and pieced together evidence of attack.

Ben breezed into the room, still wearing his overcoat and flushed cheeks. He gathered in to see the spectacle for himself. "Hope Ezra hurries with Doc Sterling."

"What's going on out there? Is Daddy calling a meeting?"

"Looks like. Do you really suppose one of 'em could'a done this?"

"We'll find out. Can't put it past any one of 'em, once those freedom shriekers put ideas in their heads. I ever tell you about Nat Turner? He was a slave just like any of ours, until—"

A groan and a stir stopped Devon in mid-sentence. "Ethan? You awake?"

A nod.

"What happened?"

Ethan fought to sit up. "Rock. Hit head."

"What?"

"Jonesy." He rubbed his temple and groaned.

The hairs on Devon's neck stood on end. That's all he needed to hear.

"I'll be back." He dashed away to tell his father.

ঙ৪ঌ

The front door slammed after Devon's hasty retreat. Ethan winced as wakefulness brought back a flood of pain. He put a hand to his temple. "Where's he going?"

"Jehoshophat, Ethan!" Ben exclaimed. "How did it happen?"

"Fell. On the ice."

"Is that when Jonesy hit you?"

"What?"

"You just said someone hit your head with a rock."

"Huh?" Ethan rubbed his eyes with his palms.

"Jonesy. He attacked you, didn't he?"

Ethan lowered his hands and sucked a gulp of air. "*No.*"

"But you just said—"

"Jonesy found me. He helped me."

Ben jumped up. "I'll be right back."

Ethan gathered leaden feet beneath him and heaved himself forward. With staggering steps, he followed his younger brother out the back door. Ben had dashed over the field already and stood near the row of torches where a lineup gathered at the shanties. Ethan clutched the blanket around himself and hugged the porch railing before he threw up or fell down.

Devon's yelling carried over the field back to him.

His father seized Devon by the shoulders. "Didn't I tell you to let me handle this?"

"It was Jonesy! He did it!"

Sam shoved him aside. "Go back inside *now*."

"No! Ethan's awake. He told me everything!"

Ethan's pulse lobbed behind his eye sockets, but he had to clarify the misunderstanding. Holding his hand out, he shuffled down the front porch steps.

"No, Dev. Wait!"

Chapter 12

Marietta had sent Tilly to mail her latest letter. The winter sun slanted low over the front of the house, and the trees in the lawn cast long shadows with their bare branches nearly tapping the window where she sat. How she wished for some diversion for these lonesome days with Papa gone even more than before. Aaron accompanied Papa now, too—every day—until she could almost count the rosettes in the wall paper in her boredom. If only Tilly would return with a letter for her. Surely with Virginia remaining loyal to the Union there would be no disruption in the mail service between her and Ethan. But what else could explain his silence of late? She whispered another prayer for him, one of perhaps a hundred already that day.

Mama's stirring from upstairs caught her attention presently. A seamstress had come to measure her for a new gown. Papa and she had been invited to the Inaugural Ball on the Fourth of March. A small stirring of envy rose within Mari. If she had made her debut, she might have attended with them. But Mama's strictures seemed more pronounced than ever. Their social standing had been elevated considerably with Papa's rising career. She would have Mari properly debuted—no escaping that now. Papa was too busy to intervene as he had in the past. Her options were narrowing. She forced it from her mind for the moment, hoping for some good news as a diversion.

A movement at the window drew her attention back to the road. Tilly walked up the drive with letters in hand.

Mari flounced to the door to meet her. "*Please* tell me there's a letter in there for me."

The maid ascended the steps and entered the house, removing her wrap. "Yes'm."

Tilly's expression was inscrutable as she handed over the stack. Mari shuffled through them. Predictably, most of the envelopes were addressed to Papa. And then, in unfamiliar pen, she saw her name. Tilly exchanged a long, sober look with her. Though the young woman couldn't have deciphered the script, written in French, she would have inferred the meaning of the return address. Paris.

ଔ

Church service had gone on without him for the first time in three months. Nothing could compel Ethan to movement this morning. Nothing, that is, except a strong suspicion that his father and brothers would be bringing company back with them. The thought scared him enough to leave his sick bed. Groaning, he rolled his legs over the side and heaved himself upright. The blood rushed to his head and shrouded his vision. He put a hand to his forehead, and a few gasps later, he steadied himself on his feet.

Ethan punched into the sleeves of a loose shirt, leaving the buttons unfastened at the collar and the bottom loose over his trousers. He smoothed his hair with a splash of water, cringing as his fingers neared the stitches at his temple.

Settling in the chair that he'd occupied the night of the accident, he took up a newspaper and awaited the group's arrival. One attempt at reading the blurry print left him in earnest regret. He laid his pounding head back and closed his eyes. It wasn't long before he heard the jangle of harness and Ezra's deep voice. "Whoa, hoss."

Devon's boot-steps and the girls' chatter approached the back door. Ethan folded his paper over the armrest just as they spilled into the room—Ellen White in a pretty buff-colored coat with white fur cuffs and collar, and her sister on Devon's arm. Ben shuffled in behind them.

"Oh, Ethan!" Ellen rushed to his side. "How are you feeling? Can I get you anything? a pillow, perhaps?"

Ethan smiled, warmth flooding him at the attention. "No, I'm feeling fine now."

"Whatever compelled you to go up to that ridge?"

Casting a dubious look at Devon, Ethan obliged her. "A herd of old boors crowding the parlor."

Devon folded his arms, a half-grin twisting his mouth. "All that war-talk must have upset his sensitivities."

"I'll show you sensitivities!" He pushed from the chair, and both girls cajoled him to sit.

Ben chuckled. "Might want to save your fight for the regiment Thompson's starting up."

"What regiment?" Ethan flashed his focus to Devon.

His brother's eyes were black embers of excitement. "Better get well quick. We're mustering this week."

Ellen tugged on Ethan's arm. "And Daddy has volunteered to be chaplain."

Ethan blinked away his shock.

Devon clapped his shoulder. "Don't worry, E. Since you're still recuperating, I've reserved you a spot with me. Can't have you busting your head open again—least not until you're well."

"You *will* take care of yourself, won't you?" Ellen leaned in and touched the bandage at his temple.

He flinched, but Ellen's attentions only intensified.

Devon winked at his brother, giving him a knowing smile. He offered his arm to the other Miss White. "Why don't I take you to see the new foals?"

Once the couple left with Ben, Ellen stroked Ethan's sleeve. "I didn't mean to hurt you, Ethan."

"You didn't."

"Someone should put you back to bed."

He couldn't resist a teasing smile. "Why, Miss Ellen…."

She huffed. "You're incorrigible! Really, you must take care of yourself."

"Reckon you care enough for both of us."

"I wish you'd let me." She traced a scratch on his hand with the lightest of touches.

Ellen's gesture invoked mixed reactions. Despite involuntary tingles of pleasure, he couldn't ignore a sinking feeling in the pit of his stomach. He wished it could be another young woman's touch imbuing him with tenderness. But that seemed hopeless now, with war on the way.

He tensed as Ellen met his gaze.

Her expression turned to puzzlement. "What is it, Ethan?"

"Nothing."

She turned her head away. The muscles in her throat tightened and he wondered if she swallowed back tears.

"Are you unhappy with me?"

The question left him confused. "No, Ellen. I'm not cross with you."

"That's not what I meant. You never say you like my dress, or the way I fix my hair." She batted dewy lashes. "Devon told me there's another girl."

He clenched a fist. What was Devon up to now? "Don't pay any heed to—"

"How could you, Ethan? I mean, a Yankee?" Her tears suspended, awaiting his reply.

Great balls of fire. Now what was he supposed to say? "You're pretty enough to catch any beau you choose."

"If she's not prettier, then what is it about her?"

"She…." He paused as the voices in the yard neared.

Ellen leaned in, her head cocked like a spaniel's begging for a morsel.

"Marietta and I share certain convictions."

"What convictions, Ethan?" She drew closer, tossing her ringlets over her shoulder.

He sighed, already regretting the conversation. “I don't think you’d understand.”

Her pout wrapped around his heart with the gossamer strength of spider silk. “You know you can tell me anything.”

“…views you might find controversial.”

She plied her spaniel eyes on him. “I hope they're not dangerous?”

He rubbed the area where the stitches pulled at his hairline, recalling the discussion among his father's guests the other day. “Ideas are, these days.”

She slipped her arm into his. “There’s no secret I wouldn't keep for you, Ethan.”

The door in the other room burst open. Blustery air blew in as Devon, Ben, and Adelaide escaped the wintry afternoon.

Devon led the way. “Here come the chaperones! I hope you two are being-have.”

Ethan sought Ellen’s expression for any hint of betrayal.

Devon winked and smiled. “Don’t worry, Miss Ellen. Your sweetheart will come back to you after a month of Yankee-chasing. Meanwhile, he’ll be in good hands.”

Devon leaned over Ethan’s chair and gave him a smothering hug. Ethan pummeled him away.

“See? Why, I reckon he’s feeling better already!”

ঔ

Marietta folded another frippery and laid it into her trunk. She would soon run out of space in this one, even as she ran out of time. In a few short weeks she would be crossing the Atlantic and leaving her girlhood home behind. Preparations had been dizzying, with her mother laying out the best of her wardrobe, only to beckon milliners and seamstresses to the house to create more. Gone was her envy for Mama’s new ball gown. As beautiful as each new hat, dress and petticoat were, she would gladly donate every last piece to charity, if only she could stay.

Tilly seemed to share her grief. The young woman’s typical

industry seemed listless as she passed a warm iron over yards of satin brocade. She hummed a low tune that Mari recognized as a spiritual song, but the slow cadence and deep alto notes lent more the feeling of a dirge.

Per Mama's arrangement, Tilly would accompany Mari to Paris, leaving behind all hope of reunion with her son. It seemed like a death sentence handed down to the poor woman. But the selfless maid had agreed to the trip when Mama asked.

Tilly, with her steady companionship, was the only true friend Mari had these days. The girls her age had already made their debuts or had been sent away to the salons last year. But even had they been available, Mari would prefer this young woman's warm and loyal attendance over any one of the pampered daughters of Washington's aristocracy.

Consumed with her preparations, she hardly noticed the stray ribbon that slipped between her fingers as she cleared out another drawer. Its silky length drew her curious inspection. It corded a small bundle of letters. Her heart ached at the symbolic contact with Ethan. Weeks had passed since he'd sent his last letter. Perhaps that missive at Christmas sharing her beliefs on slavery had been too much. Maybe she had gone ahead of God. Yet again.

"Tilly, I've been thinking. I want you to return to Washington with my mother once I'm settled."

"But Miss Mari, we done been over this."

"Yes. And I can't be so selfish." She dropped the bundle into her trunk and fixed her gaze on the young woman. Brown eyes the hue of richest coffee studied her. "I can't help but believe that somehow, God will answer your prayers. I know it must seem hopeless. But just because I'm leaving doesn't mean you should, too. Stay here and wait. A miracle might come yet."

"But Miss Mari, it take my mind off my worries lookin' after you. What am I gon' do without you?"

"Mama can use your help here. You'll find plenty to occupy yourself."

"But who gonna take care of you?"

Mari smiled, a lump forming in her throat at the maid's devotion. "The Good Lord will."

"But when you reads me yo' letters from Mr. Ethan, I know my boy be all right."

Mari swallowed back the emotion that now choked her voice. "There won't be any more letters from Mr. Ethan, Tilly." She rued the tears that formed over her lashes, and she batted them away. "I'm so sorry I failed you."

Tilly was at her side in an instant, and Mari took the maid's steadying hand in hers.

"I was wrong to interfere. As much as it pains me to admit, I was wrong to think I could rescue you and your son. Only the Lord can do that." She clenched her teeth tightly, denying the anguished sob that sought release. "We must trust Him now to do what I cannot."

"Miss Mari, if you won't let me go with you, then I pray the good Lord don't make you go neither. Maybe Mist' Ethan come back for you with my boy hisself."

Her heart cinched at those words. As winsome as it was to see faith arise in Tilly's heart, surely that was too much to believe for. She must bury her heart across a thousand miles of ocean and embrace the truth. She had seen the last of Ethan Sharpe.

Chapter 13

Devon returned home in the last hour of sunlight, the close of the week bringing a warming spring thaw. He had so much to tell Ethan. Boys had come out in droves to answer their call to arms.

Though their father had insisted Ethan keep to the house until fully recovered, a quick search indoors proved fruitless. Devon fought down a brewing frustration—all day he'd waited to talk, and now his brother had disappeared.

What was Ethan doing?

Since their trip to Washington last fall, Ethan had withdrawn from him, become secretive. There had been no outgoing letters to Marietta Hamilton lately—of that he'd made sure. Were more nefarious influences at play?

He trudged from barn to barn, concern over his brother's injuries weighing on him. Ethan insisted there had been no attempt on him that day, but Devon wasn't so easily assuaged. Jonesy took up more of Ethan's time than anything—even him. He didn't cotton to being replaced by a slave.

The sounds of singing drew Devon toward the stable. He paused outside, straining to pick out individual voices.

"No mo' weepin' and a wailin', I'm gone to live with God."

Devon recognized Jonesy's adolescent baritone. He pushed through the door and all melody ceased. Achingly slow, he patrolled the aisle, inspecting every polished hoof as he passed. He stopped at the last stall, where Jonesy worked. Planting himself in the entry, he braced his arms across the opening.

"That horse wasn't brushed out well the other day. Got the beginnings of a saddle sore."

Jonesy lowered his gaze. "Yassuh."

Devon wasn't satisfied just yet. "Who told you to skip that one's feed?"

"Marse Ethan say this'un eat better after I's done wid him."

"Marse Ethan say?"

"Yassuh."

"Marse Ethan's been spending a lot of time with you, hasn't he?" Devon narrowed his eyes.

Jonesy curried faster. The animal jerked its head and whinnied, and Jonesy held its nose to calm it.

"Funny how my brother's got no time for me."

The horse tossed its head again and kicked the side of the stall. Jonesy took the colt's lead rope to turn him around in the box stall. The animal swung suddenly, upsetting a bucket by the aisle. Water splashed upward, slapping Devon full in the face. The shock of it took him aback.

Devon wiped a sleeve slowly across his eyes, glaring at the slave.

Jonesy flattened against the wall, his complexion turned ashen.

Devon's fists clenched, and he stalked in after the boy.

A hand clasped his shoulder. "There you are, Devon! I've been looking for you."

Devon turned and caught his breath, the anger ebbing away with the sight of his twin. "'Bout time you showed up. Where you been hiding, E?"

☙❧

Looked like Ethan had come just in time. He steered Devon around and they walked out of the barn together. "How's recruiting?"

"Lawdy, E. Walt and I had all we could do to keep up, once

the handbills started circulating. Our ad in the paper starts tomorrow, not to mention posters on every lamppost in the county. Every coon-treein', rabbit-huntin', good-ol'-boy will be signed up by the end of the week."

"And needing a good horse." Ethan laughed.

It sure was nice to see Devon in a sporting humor. It lit the wick of Ethan's hopes. Perhaps it was finally time to share matters of a more consequential nature. The state of Devon's soul weighed on him more than impending war. Maybe because of impending war. He drew a breath, ready to speak.

Before he could, Devon asked, "So, when're you gonna recruit with us?"

Ethan's confidence stuttered with the shift in momentum. "I don't know. Business is booming here."

"Sooner or later, the old man has to manage without us. And your stitches look healed up." He chucked Ethan on the jaw. "You're practically a veteran already!"

Slinging an arm around Ethan's shoulder, Devon led him down the avenue between paddocks.

"Why don't we hang the rest of the day and head over to Walt's?"

Ethan shrugged out of his hold. "You and Walt seem happy handling affairs without me."

Devon slowed, turned. "Why, I declare. Is that jealousy?"

Ethan opened his mouth, but the words stalled. He took a step away from his brother and they both stood still, silent for several seconds. "I think we need to talk."

"Tell me about it. I'm beginning to forget what you look like."

Ethan smiled despite the tightening in his chest. "I'm the good-looking one, remember?"

"No argument there." Devon leaned against the nearby fence, breaking the confrontational stance. "That's why we need you." He winked. "You'll attract the girls. Which in turn will gather the boys."

Ethan released a chuckle. "I think it's your turn to gather a few. For the cause."

Devon fixed his collar and smoothed his hair. "Reckon I'm doing my part. So, are you game? We can talk all we want there. No girls. Just us men. I hear they'll be assigning rank, and they'll be decorating the officers, if you know what I mean." Devon tipped an imaginary flask, a contagious gleam in his eye.

Maybe the talk could wait. It had been ages since they'd kicked back and had a good time together. He cast aside what he had been about to say and found himself matching strides with Devon across the pasture, west to the Thompson's cattle farm.

Devon led through the side entrance, which opened into the drawing room. Young men pressed around a billiard table with the loud talk of drink.

Walt held up a bottle, handed off two glasses to Devon, and poured. "My star cavalrymen."

The others gathered in to shake hands and toast, the aroma of whiskey and perspiration thick in the paneled room. Though appreciating their celebrity, somehow Ethan felt less than celebratory. He hung behind his brother, his libation languishing in his hand.

Devon lifted his voice in the latest chorus.

We are a band of brothers and native to the soil.
Fighting for the property we gained by honest toil
and when our rights were threatened,
the cry rose near and far
Hurrah for the Bonnie Blue Flag that Bears a Single star

Walt approached Ethan, lifting the bottle, which he drank out of straight. "See what you've been missing?"

Ethan nodded in greeting.

"Haven't seen much of you lately, Ethan. You been avoiding us?"

"I don't get around much anymore, with our oldest brother gone. Too much work to do."

Walt's grin spread beneath his blond mustache. "Reckon all

that'll change soon."

Ethan tried to return the smile, but he couldn't make it convincing. "Guess so."

"Speaking of Gideon, I hear he's getting married soon."

"That's the word. Second Saturday in April, to our cousin Leigh Anne."

"Well, good for Gideon. Did very well for himself. She's an absolute angel."

"You've met?"

Walt nodded. "She came to Lexington a few years back with your Uncle Fourreax. They'd come to fetch Gideon and take him back with them to Charleston over Christmas break. We all fell in love before she left. Even that scoundrel Aaron Hamilton."

"Aaron Hamilton?" Marietta's brother. He recalled hearing he'd attended college in Lexington—at Washington College. "Were you friends?"

"We all were. That was before, of course, when it was still possible to look beyond politics. I guess they call that magnanimity. But I just don't see the point of keeping ties with those people now."

"Not everyone's a firebrand, Thompson." Ethan had lost his smile.

"Now, Ethan, I know you don't mean that." He put an arm around his shoulder, turning him around to a quieter corner of the room. "You and I both know by now war's pretty inevitable. And we're all friends here, all loyal Virginians."

"What are you saying?"

"I'm just suggesting if *your brother* had difficulty choosing allegiances, folks might talk." Walt laughed and thumped Ethan on the back. "But we both know there's no fear of that. The Sharpes are the toast of Rockingham County. We all admire your family. I couldn't imagine a reason not to." The light in Walt's blue eyes lent them the look of cold steel.

Ethan returned Walt's friendly pretense. "If Gideon were to choose friendship over a fool's fight, I reckon that's his affair."

"Surely by now even Gideon must have changed his mind. And I'm sure you're not callin' anyone here a fool, Ethan."

Ethan thrust his chin up. What bristled worse than his neighbor's smugness was the certainty of yet another of Devon's treacheries. His interest in Marietta was nobody's business, least of all this braggart.

"You calling me out, Thompson?"

Devon whipped around, buzzing like a bee to its troubled hive. He took Ethan's arm and steered him aside. "What's gotten into you? You know Walt's father is sponsoring the new regiment."

"He insulted Gideon," he said through clenched teeth.

"You're mistaken."

The gathering circled to see if anything would come of it.

Ethan tried to push past Devon's restraint. "You know exactly what I'm talking about."

Devon held on and ground out a whisper into Ethan's ear. "Don't insult our host. I'm hoping for a placement."

"Fine." Ethan shook off Devon's hold, but stood his ground. He squared his shoulders and held out his hand to Walt. "Perhaps I misunderstood you."

Thompson accepted his gesture with an extra force of grip. "Well of course, ol' neighbor. It's your injury that's got you all turned around. I know you'd never be linin' up with any of that Lincoln rabble." He winked and pumped his hand one last time. "You stick with your friends here and we'll make sure you're pointed in the right direction."

☙❧

Maryland on the Potomac
April 10, 1861

Mari couldn't remember a time when Papa looked so tired. Mama bustled about to serve him dinner, keeping conversation and bother to a minimum. She and Aaron were told to speak only if spoken to. Clearly, he had much on his mind and Mama would have him experience a peaceful sanctuary in his own home.

Tableware clinked together, creating the only sounds throughout the first course of the meal. Marietta picked at her dinner roll, dipping pieces into her beef broth absently until the freshly baked flakes swelled up and floated on the surface, uneaten.

Papa cleared his throat. She looked up to find him studying her, dark circles ringing both of his concerned eyes. “You must try and eat, Mari.”

She looked down at her plate, seeing for the first time the wasteful mess she had created. “I'm sorry Papa.”

He drew a ponderous breath and exhaled. “You know your Mother and I only want the best for you.”

She fluttered her lids up and tried to meet his gaze, but she just couldn't without tears springing to her eyes. “Yes, Papa.”

“Mama feels Europe may be your safest option for the time being. With all this unrest here, it's uncertain whether we shall lose Virginia, too. Some believe even Maryland could secede. If that were the case. . .” He looked at Mama, who returned his adoring look with a steadfast fixation. Strength emanated from their exchange. The quavering in Mari's lip stilled, taking in the bigger picture fully for perhaps the first time. Mr. Lincoln's Union was dissolving, and it fell to men like the president, and Secretary Seward, and Papa to figure out how to avoid civil war.

“If it means we must leave this house, if Maryland should secede, the Lord will provide.”

Mama let out a soft gasp but nodded her agreement. Her eyes closed while silent prayers fluttered on her lips. Mari reached across the table and took her hand. Mama looked up and met her gaze with a faint smile.

Aaron shifted in his seat. “Shouldn’t we know where France and England stand regarding the Confederacy before we send Mari abroad? Will they stay neutral, or will they defend their trade with the South?”

Papa tapped his water glass with his thumb, nodding. “You make a valid point, son.”

Her dormant hopes fluttered to life. What if there were a way out of going? Lately Tilly showed more faith than she, that it could still all work out for good. That maybe the Lord would provide an eleventh-hour miracle. Whatever happened had better happen quickly. Her *bon voyage* was only days away.

Chapter 14

April rain swelled creek beds descending the Shenandoah foothills. The tumultuous waters churning even into the placid green valley foreshadowed what Ethan heard in the news: Fort Sumter had erupted. War had come.

Militia drills were immediately canceled. All order vanished in the celebrations that ensued. Devon and Walt had ridden for town hours ago, leaving Ethan back to enlist any recruits that might stumble in.

As twilight descended, Ethan set out to meet Jonesy in their clandestine spot. This would be the last Bible study—Jonesy's last reading lesson. It had become too risky. Making excuses to Devon had surely raised suspicion.

When he arrived, the boy was there waiting inside the tack room. They opened the book together, and Jonesy lead the reading, bolstered by Ethan's pronunciation of difficult King James verbiage.

After a short time, he set the book aside, and Ethan looked him in the eyes. "You've accomplished much in a short time. You should be proud of yourself."

Jonesy looked down. Probably no one had ever complimented his intelligence. Of course, that simply wasn't done, certainly not among Ethan's peers, regarding a slave.

"I reckon this was my way of trying to balance the scales a little."

"I wish more folks was like you, Marse Ethan."

Guilt lanced his ribs. He didn't deserve the boy's praise. "Well, I reckon I've taught you all I can. After tonight, we're done." There was so much more he could do, if things were different. But the evil system seemed anchored in the bedrock, unmoving.

Ethan rose, and Jonesy stood with him. He reached out and shook the boy's hand, and a rush of words spilled from his heart to his mouth. "Things may not always be the way they are, Jonesy. I hope our prayers bring change."

But more likely the boy would grow up like generations before him. He'd serve thirty-odd years, forty if he were lucky, before succumbing to the effects of poor nutrition and endless labor under the blazing southern sun. Ethan swallowed a bitter taste in his throat. What good was reading when denied the right to pursue education and a better life?

Turning aside, Ethan secured Marietta's letters into the binding of his Bible where he kept them safe, and he departed with the book tucked under his arm. Tomorrow was a big day, April 17—his and Devon's birthday. He'd best get some sleep.

ଔଓ

Ethan dispatched his morning chores, eager to celebrate his eighteenth birthday with his twin, who had not yet returned from the previous night. Events were happening with such rapidity that he knew he needed to have that heart to heart talk with Devon and wait no longer. But even before Devon returned, news reached the house in the afternoon that the State Congress of Virginia had called a secession delegation, voting in favor of leaving the Union. Just yesterday the fall of Fort Sumter, and today, Virginia joined the new Confederacy. Time was indeed accelerating.

Devon's arrival added to the whirlwind with reports that their local cavalry company had adopted a flag and a uniform, and tomorrow they would mobilize toward Richmond for official state recognition. Ethan accepted the news, anticipating leaving all his misgivings behind. The eve of their departure for war promised a grand celebration, in fact. Walt's father raised the best beef in Rockingham County and Ethan could smell barbecue smoke when the wind shifted just right. There'd be music and dancing, fireworks, a bonfire. They were sure to enjoy a proper send-off. But before their father released them to go, they'd have to stop by the house.

Ethan led the way in from the fields. "I'll wager the streets in Richmond are filling with boys in uniform already."

Devon nodded. "Walt says the trains are arriving in the city every hour. Reckon all of Virginia is like' to turn out for the reviews."

"What reviews?" Ben asked.

Ethan held the back door open for his younger brother. "The new troops march through the streets and show off their colors. All the citizens of the capital come out and cheer the volunteers and wish them well."

Their father was waiting for them at the table. "Can we go to Richmond, too?" Ben asked, his auburn lashes blinking an eager beat.

Sharpe scowled, and Ben dropped his gaze to his boots.

Devon challenged the old man's petulance with one of his grins. "Bet you wish you were younger. We've got a fifty-year-old in our militia just waitin' to brandish his Mexican sword again."

Ethan cast a wary gaze, ready to come to his twin's defense.

Sharpe leveled Devon with one stern look. "It's a big waste of horses if you ask me. But if these fools want to pay top dollar for a chance to get themselves killed, I'll take their money. Shame they've got to take my hard work with them."

Devon turned to Ethan with a grin. "Reckon he's talking about us?"

Ethan snorted back a chuckle. "Naw. He knows we'd take a bullet for his horses."

Sharpe wheeled about in his chair. "You both know what I mean. Only thing sets you apart from those bushwhackers is they're paying customers."

Devon busted into a laugh, even if it was partly at his own expense. "We'll repay you handsomely when we return with the spoils of war. But since I'm already in your debt, can you see your way clear to loan me a pinch of tobacco? I'm out." He ducked from his father's threatened backhand, laughing even harder. "It's all right, Daddy. You don't have to tell us. We already know you're proud of us!"

Devon scurried out the door.

Ethan hustled after him. "You think he's too sore to come to the party?"

Their laughter rose ahead of them, competing with the sound of crickets and spring frogs on the evening air.

"He's always sore about something. He'll get over it. In ninety days, when this hullabaloo is settled, we'll win some races for him, and things'll be back to normal."

They strode out through the back gate and came to settle along the fenced avenue leading to the barns.

"So, what'd ya get me?" Ethan asked.

Devon's brows furrowed. "Get you?"

"You know. For our birthday?"

"Can't wait till later, huh?" Devon feigned a scowl.

Ethan shrugged. "Later on, everyone'll be milling around. I'd rather do it now."

"It's back at the house."

"Well, so's yours. But I'll tell you, if you tell me."

Devon sighed. "Oh, all right. I found something in town I know you'll like. Cost me those silver spurs I've been wanting, but you're worth it. I got you a bowie knife. Real nice. Got a carved handle and engraving on the blade. Just wait till you see it."

"Dog, Dev. That sounds fine." He shook his head in appreciation, picturing it in his mind's eye.

"There you go again. Off in another world. Is God speaking again?"

Ethan grinned. "He's always speaking, Dev."

"Well?"

"You want to know what He said?"

"No, I want to know what you got me!"

He chuckled. "Oh, yeah. Well, it's not as fancy as what you went and done. But I reckon it's something you need more than you realize."

"Well, what is it?"

"You'll need divine help when the enemy overtakes you. I got you your spurs." He grinned from ear to ear, waiting for Devon to take a swing at him for the crack about his slower horse.

"Really? My spurs?"

Devon was elated. Or was it relieved? Maybe both—Ethan couldn't tell.

"For a minute, I'd swear you were going to say you got me a Bible!"

Ethan's humor evaporated in a flush of anger. "Well, what would be so funny if I did?"

"Oh, come, now. A Bible?" Devon's hoots echoed off the barn wall.

The hair on the back of Ethan's neck bristled, and he clenched his fists. "If you don't want a Bible, fine Devon. But it might save more than just your neck."

Ethan stalked back toward the house. He'd rather brave his father's temper than endure Devon's mockery. Always a joke with Devon. One of these days, his impulses would get him into real trouble.

"I'm sorry, E! Don't be sore. If you got me a Bible, that's fine. Really…."

Ethan picked up his pace, and Devon's voice faded at last.

Arriving at the house, Ethan found the kitchen empty, the room dark. On the table lay a birthday cake all ready for the Thompson's party. Ethan swiped a finger-full of frosting and continued on through the house. He scuffed through the adjoining room where the hearth lay cold, also deserted. The hallway leading to his father's room showed a faint glow, and an aromatic vapor wafted, thicker the closer he drew.

"Daddy?"

The smell of dust and the tang of whiskey drifted all about the room, mingling with the thin blue curl of cigar smoke ascending over his father's silhouette. Seated at his desk, the old man nodded in greeting, and motioned for him to take a seat in one of his leather chairs. Ethan counted the handful of times that he'd been invited to one of these seats, typically reserved for businessmen or other important figures. On those rare occasions, it'd usually been due to some infraction serious enough for a conference with the old man, and Devon was sure to share in whatever consequences awaited. It felt odd to be seated there alone, where awe and dread made a tangible presence. Except that he'd done nothing wrong. He just wanted to say a proper goodbye before tomorrow's departure.

His father's eyelids hung in the twilight filtering through shutters on the room's western exposure. The bottle on the desk was already down a quarter of its contents, the loose wrapping revealing its recent christening. Ethan was glad he hadn't waited until later to say goodbye. His father had only moments of coherency left of the day. But old Sharpe's focus hadn't shifted since he'd sat—he remained staring at him without blinking.

"Did you hear what Devon got me? A bowie knife."

"I saw it. Nice piece—got an ivory inlay."

"Pretty extravagant."

"I helped him. I figure you'll watch out for each other." His father exhaled and shifted in his seat. "Sure gonna miss your help."

"Yeah, but Ben's coming up on our heels. He'll be another Gideon to you."

The old man nodded, extinguishing his cigar. Taking another quaff of his whiskey, his father spoke with a vague slur. "So, Devon's volunteered you?"

Ethan caught his heartbeat before it launched up into his

throat. Could his father discern his reluctance to leave for war? Or did he refer to the party tonight?

"I can't back out after that present. Must have cost a mint."

Sharpe's expression sobered. "So, what are you going to do?"

Follow Devon's prescription for the rest of my life, probably. He forced a smile. "I'll go."

"He can be persuasive, but he can't live your life for you. Do what you have to."

The chimes from the hall clock sounded seven. Ethan was brought into account of the time. Best he gathered his belongings for the morning since it looked to be a late night. Jogging upstairs to his room, he found his present for Devon—the one he knew would be received, the spurs—and placed them in a pocket for later.

He'd save the Bible he'd bought him for another occasion. Setting it on the nightstand, he paused. Had he packed his own? It had fallen on the floor after he'd dozed off reading late into the night. He bent to scoop it up, and it opened to the place where he'd tucked Marietta's letters. He lifted the most recent one. It had been months since he'd heard from her. As if closing that chapter of his life, he determined to close the book over its bittersweet sight but found he couldn't just yet. He carried the opened bible toward his packed bag, and several of the letters wafted loose from the binding. He scrambled after them, finding all but the leaflet with the quote by Matthew Henry. It must have blown out, too, but his eyes hadn't followed it.

He scanned the small room, ducking under furniture. But the incriminating abolitionist publication was *nowhere to be found.*

ଔ

Pounding on the front door disrupted a pleasant afternoon tea. Marietta looked out the dining room window at the drive, and suddenly pulled the curtains closed.

"Mr. Silsby has returned."

Just as Papa predicted. This time, he brought two riders with him. Papa was at work, and Aaron had gone with him. She and

Mama and Tilly had to face them alone.

Mari jumped up from the table, but Mama's calm voice instructed. “Matilda, I want you to keep to the kitchen and allow Miss Mari and I to handle this. Mari, go to the door but do not invite them in.”

Mari swallowed though her mouth had gone completely dry. She took slow, deliberate steps toward the front door while Mama retreated into Papa's study, holding the key to his gun cabinet.

“Good day, Miss. You may recall my recent visit. Gordon Silsby.” He doffed his hat. “And this is Silas Cooper, United States Marshal out of Baltimore, and Mr. William Dupree, a private businessman from Harrisonburg, Virginia.”

“Good afternoon, gentlemen. I’m afraid Father is not at home, and therefore I regret—”

“This ain’t no social call, Missy.” Mr. Dupree gazed at her through squinting eyes. He mopped back the few strings of hair remaining on his pate, disturbed when he removed his faded felt hat. “I've come to investigate a report of stolen property.” He clapped his hat back on, mercifully. “My client believes you may be hiding a person or persons on your property, and I have a warrant to search the premises.”

Mama pressed in behind her. Mari stood her ground at the door, deferring to her mother to reply.

“I'll have that warrant, sir.” Mama commanded obedience even from a trio of slave patrollers. Looking over the document, she lifted her brows. “And may I ask by what authority we are bound to honor a warrant in Maryland, written and signed in Virginia three days ago?”

“Obviously, three days ago, Virginia had not yet seceded. However, nothing has changed in Federal Law.” Marshal Cooper, the youngest of the three and neatly presented in dress uniform, replied. “I am still bound by both state and federal jurisdiction to pursue this matter. With apologies to you, Ma'am.”

“Apologies indeed. You may keep your sentiments, sir. As

you and I are well-aware, we are a country at war, and I have no intention of permitting strange men into my home in my husband's absence. You may return with your warrant when he arrives."

She swung the door, but Mr. Silsby's scuffed boot thrust over the threshold, preventing her from closing it.

"We will have our look around, Mrs. Hamilton. You have nothing to fear from us unless you have indeed broken the law." They pushed past Mari and her mother, and entered the house, going in three separate directions.

Mama followed Dupree into the dining area, and Mari continued straight to Tilly and stood by her side. The maid was visibly frightened, though she held her head high and tried not to show it. Mari prayed under her breath from the ninety-first psalm. "If you make the Most High your dwelling, no harm will come to you, no disaster shall come nigh thy tent."

"Where's that gal's papers, Ma'am?"

"I showed Mr. Silsby on his last visit. But if you must see them, I have them here." Mama walked to the small buffet in the corner and opened the drawer. Dupree shoved her aside and thrust his hands into the drawer, pulling out all the documents. He heaped them on the dining table and rifled through them despite Mama's protests.

"Those have nothing to do with you or your warrant, sir. I will report this to the Attorney General. I'll have you know my husband works for Secretary Seward…."

"That abolitionist rabble rouser?" He grunted, and Mari thought she heard him mutter an oath.

"This is not to be borne! Mind you there will be consequences for your conduct, sir."

Dupree laughed. Marshal Cooper entered the room and approached the slave patroller. "These ladies are in compliance. There's no need to treat them with belligerence."

Dupree seized on a particular document. "What's this? Letter of Manumission. 'Matilda Jones, aged twenty and three in the year of our Lord 1860.' Hey, Silsby. I thought you said this woman was their slave?"

Mr. Silsby emerged from Papa's office, the sound of papers falling in his wake onto the wood floor creating an image in Mari's mind of a hurricane.

"I was shown her purchase receipt. They said nothing of manumission."

"So, it seems our source may have been correct." Dupree withdrew something from his pocket and popped it between his teeth; he chewed on the stump of an unlit cigar. "How many others have you purchased and set free, Mrs. Hamilton?"

"We have never… Matilda is the only."

"That's right, because you never bothered to pay money before, did you? You just 'ferried poor souls to freedom' without considering the financial hardship you created by stealing others' property. Isn't that right?"

"I will ask you again to leave my house at once. You have searched and have found no evidence of any illegal activity here. Now go."

Cooper nodded, and herded Silsby and Dupree to the door.

Silsby turned before exiting. "We'll be watching. Best hope there's no reason for us to return, Mrs. Hamilton."

The lock clicked as Mama sealed the door behind them. Mari watched out the dining room window as the riders cantered down the drive and onto the road. Her knees shook beneath her skirt, and tears of outrage scalded at her lashes. Closing the curtain, she turned into the room at Mama's approach.

Mama stood blinking at the dining room table. She remained silent, surveying the papers left in disarray over the surface. Mari despised the violation, and yet felt too paralyzed to begin cleanup.

Tilly stepped to Mama's side. "I'll warm the tea, Mrs. Hamilton. Today be a good day to dust the drawers and wash the doilies and curtains. What they intend for evil, we turn around for good, ma'am."

Mama reached out and embraced the maid. Then, releasing

her, she wiped each eye exactly once. "Yes, dear Matilda. You're as wise as you are good."

Chapter 15

Devon paced between the barn and the tack room, waiting for his brother's return. What was holding Ethan back? Just a few minutes ago he'd heard the jingle of spurs and the pounding of hooves on the road. The boys were already gathering at Thompson's. If he were to saddle the horses, perhaps that would hurry things along. And the gesture might make up for his most recent of many offenses. The Bible remark was nothing compared to the trip he'd made into Harrisonburg to the office of a Mr. Dupree. But Ethan would never find out about that.

Most everything he'd done was for Ethan's own good. Where would his brother be without someone looking out for him? Someone had to put an end to that Hamilton girl's influence, once and for all. One day, his brother would thank him.

The barn loomed dark inside, the pale twilight dimming inside the double doors. Devon struck a Lucifer match and lit the lantern in the entry. Though he could navigate the familiar space blindfolded, the light was more for the sake of Ethan's gray horse, Nimbus, who wasn't accustomed to Devon handling him. Nevertheless, he would saddle the gray first as a courtesy, or perhaps as a penance. And he intended to take the Bible Ethan had no doubt bought him, too. He figured he'd better try to patch things up any way he could before the party.

Nimbus thrust his dappled head over the half door of his stall and snorted at his approach. Devon balanced the saddle in one arm and extended the other to the gelding, murmuring greeting. The charcoal ears pricked forward, and the long muzzle nudged him as Devon slipped into the stall. A flicker near the doorway caught his peripheral sight. Someone had followed him in.

"Hello?"

A figure in the shadows approached. "I heard you was jinin' the cavalry tomorrow, Marse Ethan, and I got somethin' I wants to ask before you go."

Jonesy.

And the boy had called him Ethan. Devon let the horse's body conceal him, securing the girth strap around the horse's belly, tense with expectation as the boy approached and stood outside the stall.

"I would'a got him ready for you, if'n I knew you was gwan tonight."

"Thanks. I got it." Devon imitated his brother's jovial tone.

"Marse Devon make Colby saddle his colt, but you isn't so proud."

Devon fumed. The blaze in his eyes would surely give him away. He avoided the boy, trifling with stirrup lengths, sliding the iron footing on its leather strap.

"I sho' gonna miss readin' lessons with you. Anyway, I found this here. It mussa fell out yo' Bible." Jonesy extended a slip of paper in his hand.

Shock tingled over Devon's body. He rose above the sixteen hands of dappled gray withers. For a split second they regarded one another, predator and prey, then Devon clamped down onto Jonesy's wrist with one hand and grabbed the piece of paper with the other.

Nimbus scuttled, leaving them standing face to face.

"What's this? Reading, you say?" He held up the print and skimmed the faded writing. *The North Star*—an abolitionist press. "Where did you get this?" Devon jerked the half-door open and joined Jonesy in the aisle.

"Marse Devon, I-I meant no disrespect, suh."

Devon struck Jonesy on the side of the head. The boy covered his ear with a gasp.

"I asked you a question. Where did you get this?"

Devon lifted the slave by the collar until the boy's feet dangled in the air, bringing him even with his gaze. "Did I hear you right? Did you say you've been *reading* with Ethan?"

Jonesy pressed his lips in a firm line, refusing to speak.

The open defiance sparked a rage that swept over Devon's vision with a colorful aura. Head spinning, Devon contemplated why he shouldn't beat the insolence out of the boy that very moment. But that wouldn't do. Ethan needed to learn a lesson, too. He scrubbed a hand through his hair and took a deep draw of air. His father ought to be made aware of the seditious publication, but it wouldn't do if he learned his brother had been the source. As foolish as Ethan was, Devon still felt the need to protect him.

He released the pent-up breath through clenched teeth. Surely Marietta had bewitched his brother to do this. He was glad he reported her family to the slave patrol. Her influence had done enough harm.

He clutched Jonesy's muslin collar in his fist again. "You're going to forget where you got this, you hear? You mention Ethan to anyone, and I swear I'll have you lynched!"

"Yassuh." Jonesy's voice squeaked under the constriction, and when Devon released him, he coughed a fit.

Devon shoved him through the barn door and drove him to the house, all the while rehearsing how to cover Ethan's foolishness.

☙❧

Ethan overturned the final drawer in his dresser, desperate to find the leaflet. The possibilities churned the beginnings of sickness in his gut. Was there evidence that could link it back to him? Had Marietta written anything on it? Righting the drawer, he pushed it shut.

From out on the lawn, a chorus of hounds arose as if a visitor had come. Walt must've gotten sick of waiting. But then, other noises mingled, the scuffle of boots on the porch and someone bursting through the back door. Dual voices—one cursing, and the tight, breathless cries of another—sent alarm through him. He dashed down the steps before he could comprehend the meaning of the sounds.

A chair crashed over in the kitchen. Ethan arrived at the sight of Devon shoving Jonesy through the house. "Whoa!" He rushed after them. "What's going on?"

Following them to his father's study, his heartbeat in his throat, he considered the nagging probability that the missing paper had just been found.

The old man's torpor interrupted, his displeasure showed in heavy brows and a deep frown. He regarded the group through bloodshot eyes. "What's this, Devon?"

Devon held out the document for his father's perusal, but the old man blinked and winced, the fine print apparently beyond his inebriated focus.

"I caught Jonesy with an abolitionist handbill." Devon thumped the evidence down on the desk.

Ethan craned his neck to see. It was wrinkled, worn; he scarcely recognized it. But it was the same size and shape as the missing leaflet, all right. The bottom of his stomach dropped out like a gallows trap door, and the blood fled from his head.

Jonesy's complexion had turned ashen as well. Ethan grasped the back of the chair for ballast, his pulse pounding.

His father's voice rumbled to clear his throat, and Ethan forced his attention on him. Rather than the anticipated wrath, the old man's expression deteriorated into weariness.

Devon held the accused by the scruff of the neck. "What would you have me do about this?"

Sharpe lifted his empty glass to his mouth and withdrew it again with a disappointed grunt. His movements were halting and clumsy in his attempt to refill. The glass and snifter knocked together with a sharp crack but then the liquid flowed in a mellow gurgle.

"I leave the matter to your discretion, Devon. You'll manage the farm one day, so do as you see fit." He raised his cup in a toast and closed the conference.

Ethan's silent hopes crushed beneath the weight of resignation and apathy. He'd received no guidance from his pastor when he'd needed it, and now, no help from his father. He'd have to find his way himself.

Devon led his prisoner out, Ethan following close behind. The group collided with Ben in the hallway.

"What's happening, Dev?"

Devon shot a withering glare at Ethan before directing his answer back to Ben. "I'm fixing someone's mistake."

Ethan coughed against the rising tightness in his throat. Breathless, he followed the party across the lawn toward the shanties.

Devon paused at the gate. "Ben, I need you to gather the workers."

The youngest ran to carry out the command.

One by one, the slaves emerged from their shanties and stood while Devon showed each the piece of paper.

"Have you seen this before?"

The knot in Ethan's throat tightened. An innocent person was about to pay for his mistake. Too late. Colby flinched under Devon's questioning.

"Jonesy had it in the barn. He say he teach me to read."

Ethan thrust his hands in his pockets. Something pierced him. *Devon's spurs.*

He appealed to his twin. "C'mon, Dev. Let it go. We'll be late for our party…."

Devon's coal-black eyes smoldered. "Ben, search their quarters. Maybe they're hiding more *reading material.*"

Ben set off for the first shanty, his efforts crashing and echoing into the courtyard. Ethan's gut clenched at every sound.

"Colby, come over here." Devon beckoned the young man close.

Ethan inclined his ear to their whispered conference.

"You saw Jonesy in the barn with *this* paper?"

Colby nodded.

"And what did it say?"

"I don't know, suh. He put it away when he see me comin'."

Ethan cleared his throat to keep his voice steady. "'What is it to suffer immortal souls to perish, when our persuasions and example may be the means of preventing it?'"

Devon's searing look could have branded Ethan's bare skin. He stepped toward Ethan, shaking the pamphlet in his face. "You wish to use *your persuasions and example* now? Then take Colby to the woodshed." He snapped the paper away, pointing to the outbuilding behind the carriage house. "A good once-over should teach him about keeping secrets."

Ethan squeezed the shaft of the spurs in his pocket. Devon was forcing a confrontation between them. He wished it hadn't come to this. If only he'd been stronger. If only he'd spoken sooner….

"But Marse Ethan, I didn't do nothin'," Colby cried.

Devon covered the distance between them in three strides. "You should have spoken up, boy! You knew of illegal activity, and you said nothing."

Colby cowered at Devon's approach. Ethan moved in to help, but the boy quailed in fear of him, too.

Ethan threw his hands up in futility.

Just then, Ben's returning footfalls approached. "I didn't find anything, Dev."

Devon scooped up a willow switch from the ground. "All right, then, Ethan. If you won't keep order around here, I will."

Ethan gripped his brother's arm. "Really, Devon. There's no need for that."

His brother jerked loose of him and turned to Jonesy. "Set right there. I'll deal with you next." Devon looked over his shoulder at Ethan. "And you best stay out of my way."

Ethan gripped Devon's arms. He spoke in a low tone meant only for his brother's ears. "Listen, Dev. This is my fault. We can work it out between us. Don't take it out on them."

"Let me *go*." Devon shouldered him hard in the chest. "This isn't up to *you* anymore."

The ice in his twin's voice stabbed into him. There had to be a way to mend the offense. *It was their birthday.* Maybe compromise could assuage his wrath. Ethan rued it, but he let go and stepped back.

Devon grabbed the scruff of Colby's collar and swung the crop with his other hand, making it hiss through the air. With the first loud crack, Colby sucked a gasping breath. The second blow produced a long, strident cry. Ethan paced to steady his breathing. Surely Devon would stop with that. A few more lashes had Colby on the ground, begging for the beating to stop. Ethan swallowed, cursing himself for his ineptitude.

Devon stepped away and spit into his hands, rubbing them together.

Surely this had sated his brother's wrath?

Devon shook his head, pointing the makeshift crop. "One small infraction like this can lead to lawlessness." He paced along the lineup, looking at each of the workers, until he stopped in front of Jonesy.

Ethan approached and took the stick out of his brother's hand.

Devon laughed with incredulity. "Really? All right, then, fine. Ben, fetch me the branding iron."

All eyes turned toward the summer kitchen in the courtyard, to the fire pit where the coals still glowed orange.

Ben's jaw went slack. "The branding iron, Dev? Why?"

"Why do we brand our horses, Ben? So if they run off, everyone'll know who they belong to. Now get moving."

Ben stood immobile, his round-eyes fixed on Ethan.

"No, Ben. Don't."

"How dare you undermine me in front of the slaves." Devon's

words hissed.

"You've proven your point. It's my fault. Take it up with me."

"Step back, Ethan." Devon warned a low growl.

"No. *You* step back." He leaned in until their chests bumped.

Jonesy scrambled to his feet. He and the other slaves made way.

Devon thrust Ethan back with the flat of his palms. "You're hatching rebellion! Is that what you want, Ethan?"

Reaching a hand out to appeal one more time to his brother, he whispered, "You can't maim a man for wanting to learn."

"You'd prefer he maim *us* instead." He spat on the ground. "Teaching freedom, putting dangerous ideas in their heads, Ethan? What were you thinking?"

Ethan shook his head. "It was just the Bible."

Devon grabbed the open flaps of Ethan's coat and shook. "The book of abolition? The gospel of sedition?"

He shoved Devon's hands off him. "True freedom can only come from God. 'He whom the Son sets free is free indeed'."

Devon's eyes narrowed into slits. "You either let me deal with Jonesy right now, or I'll have to deal with you."

Ethan stepped between Jonesy and his brother.

Devon clenched his fists. "I warned you!"

The assault came with such force that Ethan hit the ground. Devon straddled him, pummeling Ethan's raised arms. He scrambled for purchase. Rolling sideways, he barely diverted a blow to his face. Devon didn't miss the second time, a crushing pain exploding against his cheek and teeth. Ethan lodged a booted foot on Devon's chest and flung him backward.

Ethan regained his legs just as his twin lunged at him again. Devon's shoulder caught him in the jaw. His teeth crunched down on his tongue and blood spurted out, splattering them both. Ethan swung, blind with rage, and knocked Devon with several senseless blows.

A slow regrouping followed, Devon panting to catch his breath, circling Ethan, looking for an advantage. A sanguine taste filled Ethan's mouth, and he spat, the sight of the crimson sending spirals of shock through his dizzy head. He dabbed at his mouth with a sleeve, pain hardening over him.

"What's so wrong with my idea, Ethan? A brand would give Jonesy something new to *read.* S-L-A-V-E. What does that spell, Jonesy?"

"I just wanted to give the boy a chance."

"A chance? A chance to what? Destroy your family just to please that Yankee Jezebel?"

Ethan charged head-on into Devon's chest, intent on knocking the words back down his throat. Devon's efforts at fending him off became a tangle of wresting, clawing, and choking limbs while more hateful words spewed out, poisonous and irrevocable. They tore at each other's flesh with hands accustomed to reining in a ton of horseflesh, with no notion of stopping. Suddenly Ethan remembered the spurs. He reached in his pocket and raised one above his head to strike.

Through the tumult came the sounds of hoof beats and Ben shouting. A set of arms wrangled Devon around the neck. Walt Thompson had thrust himself between them and managed to gain purchase about Devon's head and shoulders while Ben pulled at Ethan's belt, reeling him backwards.

The four of them fell on the ground in separate heaps.

Warm sticky blood soaked through Ethan's shirt and matted his hair. The coppery tang of his swollen tongue filled his mouth. Heat radiated from his body into the night air, leaving him shuddering, spent.

His fist lay clenched over the gift he had bought his brother for their birthday. In another moment it would have torn Devon's throat out. Shock and remorse flooded over him.

Ethan sputtered. "Lord. Devon. I'm so sor—"

Devon cut him off, his voice hitching. "You just wait. I'm getting the boys down here to take you into custody."

Ethan studied his twin from just a few yards away. Salty sweat dripped into his eyes and open cuts, but he focused hard for a shred of regret in his twin's expression. It wasn't there.

Devon leaned on Walt's shoulder for help back to the house. He stopped and turned, contempt dripping from his glare. "Just wait 'til Daddy hears what you've done!" Devon swung away and cursed Ethan as he went.

Ethan reeled about, staggering to get to his feet. Ben and Jonesy tried to help, but he shoved their assistance away.

"Yo' father be a'comin'."

"I know, I know. And the militia behind him. Fetch my horse, Ben. We've got to get out of here."

Ben spirited over the field to the barn. Ethan stood on wavering legs. He cast one last look toward the house. Swallowing that lingering lump in his throat at the stark silhouette of his twin in the lantern-light, he could only gaze on his best friend like a stranger until even the shadow of him disappeared from his sight.

In seconds, Nimbus' gallop tore the sod. Ben stopped short and leapt off.

Ethan pulled himself into the saddle and motioned for Jonesy to swing up behind him.

Ben hesitated to hand over the reins. "Where will you go?"

Ethan jerked the leather from his hands. "I don't know. But if we stay, Jonesy'll hang." He reached down and patted Ben's auburn head.

Then he spurred Nimbus onto the road and slipped into the darkness.

Chapter 16

Maryland
April 20, 1861 Early AM

Ethan goaded his balking horse up the carriage house drive. He didn't blame Nimbus—he'd ridden him hard for two days and nights, much of that with a double rider. Frustrated, though, and anxious to find help, he slid down and passed the reins to Jonesy. He staggered up to the main house, his weary body rebelling, and tripped over the uneven cobblestone, bashing his knee and splitting a scab. He grunted and heaved himself up, rubbing fresh blood over filthy trousers. No time to clean up. No hiding his shame from the Hamiltons.

Jonesy nodded encouragement at Ethan, bolstering his resolve. He brought himself to the threshold, raised his hand to the brass knocker, and broke the quiet of the midnight hour. Waiting in the silence that followed, he whispered a fleeting prayer. "Oh, Lord, please…."

"Who's there?"

He tried to force sound, but it came out a rasp. He leaned heavily on the door.

The doorknob turned, and the door gave way. Ethan pitched forward into the room. Levi Hamilton stepped over him in the foyer, his hand still on the latch.

"What's the meaning of this? Aaron, come quickly."

The commotion soon brought another man, lit lantern in hand, to Levi's side, both blurring in Ethan's vision. Two days and nights, fleeing like contraband, slipping through marsh and hollow with little or no sleep or food, had nearly done him in. The click of a cocked gun broke through his haze. He tried to rise but his muscles rebelled.

Nimbus snorted, and the Hamilton men turned toward the sound. The lamplight cast a shadowy image of the horse, and the runaway slave standing next to him. Ethan could only imagine the picture they made.

"Aaron, go see to them." Mr. Hamilton nudged the young man. "Go quickly."

Aaron holstered his pistol and obeyed.

Ethan struggled to rise to his feet, and Mr. Hamilton extended a hand and pulled him up roughly. The man's eyes narrowed. "I wasn't expecting a delivery. Who sent you?"

"I'm sorry. I had nowhere else to go."

"Jehoshaphat!" A muffled oath came from the yard. Aaron stood at Nimbus's flank, running his hand over its near hindquarter. "This animal bears the same brand as our thoroughbred."

Mr. Hamilton gasped. "Bring that boy in here at once!"

Jonesy was ushered inside and told to sit on the hall bench. Ethan's legs gave out, and he slumped beside Jonesy. The light of a second lantern flooded his vision.

Ethan squinted, enduring scrutiny as both men shook their heads in disbelief.

Aaron spoke low into his father's ear. "That double S brand means Sam Sharpe's thoroughbreds, Dad. I'm sure of it."

Mr. Hamilton stroked his chin. "Sharpe? By Jove…."

Ethan struggled to speak, to explain who he was, why he'd come. His voice cracked. "It's me—Ethan."

Levi's brows rose to his hairline. "Ethan Sharpe. Are you all right, son?"

"I don't know." He shook his head. The past two days had

been consumed with fleeing the deadly intent of his own brother. No, he wasn't all right. And he might never be again.

"Aaron, go up and gather blankets, fresh clothes, towels and soap. Wake your mother, too. We'll need her help." Gesturing at Ethan's companion, Levi asked. "Is this the stable boy I offered to purchase? A runaway now?"

Jonesy tensed, as though prepared to bolt.

Mr. Hamilton extended his hands in a disarming way. "Easy. We're trying to help. But first, one of you must tell me what happened. Are you being pursued?"

Ethan lowered his gaze to his blistered and filthy hands. The hands that had almost murdered his twin. He couldn't face anyone after what he'd done.

The elder grasped Ethan's jaw and pulled up, boring a penetrating gaze into his eyes. "You helped this slave escape. That makes you a wanted man."

Ethan couldn't defend the allegation. The dreaded sounds of his father's tirades exploded inside his head, and he braced for the same from this man. He swallowed what felt like a stone lodged in his throat and hardened himself against what must be coming.

Mr. Hamilton didn't release him. "Don't fear, son. We won't turn you in. You must have had good reason. But tell me… where's Devon?"

The grief inside him knotted at the sound of his twin's name. Two hot streams coursed down his cheeks. Ethan jerked from Levi's grasp, and he raised his arms to shield his face.

Jonesy cleared his throat. "Marse Devon fixin' to kill him, suh, on account of me. It ain't Marse Ethan's fault, suh. He done helped me escape a lynchin'."

Just then, Aaron pounded back down the stairs, flanked by the more genteel tread of his mother.

Ethan pawed at his eyes to regain composure.

Levi placed an assuring hand on his shoulder. "The Lord vouchsafed your journey, Ethan. You're out of danger now."

Taking the provisions from his son, Levi asked one more task of Aaron. "Please have Matilda prepare a wash basin for them."

Aaron hesitated for the briefest moment, his face inscrutable as he regarded Ethan. Then he disappeared to carry out his father's bidding.

Mrs. Hamilton gathered at her husband's side. She let out a soft moan, her eyes roaming over Ethan from head to toe. "You must be half-starved. I'll warm the stew."

"Come, boys. You'll want to clean up after your long journey." Mr. Hamilton led them through the kitchen to a small room occupied by a large laundry basin. Tilly brought in a steaming kettle from the woodstove, but before she could pour it, she gasped and nearly dropped it to the floor. Jonesy took it from his mother and set it aside, and the two embraced. Mother beheld her son, and soft sobs rose as she caressed his face and bore him to her again. "My boy. My boy. Thank you, Jesus. My boy."

Ethan turned away, emotion crowding his throat again.

Aaron poured the hot water into the basin, set down clean garments, and beat a hasty retreat.

By and by, the warmth of the wet towel on his face slowed the chaos within. Each immersion restored sense, none of it pleasant. He was a refugee from justice. He had betrayed his family with the one unpardonable sin—choosing a slave over them.

His body ached to the bone. But he continued to scour his body until he could scrub no more.

To anyone else of his upbringing, sharing wash water with a slave should have been humiliating. But that wasn't what drove a knife into his heart. As he shed his filthy shirt and trousers, he felt stripped of everything that had once clothed him. He was no longer the son of a wealthy Shenandoah horse breeder. He was no longer even a Virginian. He didn't know what he was, standing in this strange dressing room, naked and shivering and at the mercy of those who owed him nothing.

A robe wrapped about him. He looked up to meet Tilly's warm, expressive eyes, favoring him with a depth of sentiment he couldn't quite grasp. Gratitude? Admiration? She tugged the robe snug around him the way his Mama used to when he was little.

"Lord knows I'm thankful for what you done, Mister Ethan. You answered my prayers." The young woman's eyes held a radiance beyond the glistening of her tears.

He looked at his feet. He didn't deserve any thanks.

She returned to her son's side as quietly as she had before, fussing over him like a mama cat over her stray kitten. "You's home, Vincent."

Ethan stepped into his borrowed trousers, so tired he could hardly lift a leg. *Vincent?* Jonesy's real name. He'd never considered to ask the boy his name, but had called him after his former owner, as though he were no more than a possession changing hands.

"Mama, where is he?" a feminine voice sounded just outside the closed door.

Panic lit ordnance inside his chest.

Marietta.

"Go back to bed, young lady." Her mother's voice brooked no argument. "We'll discuss it in the morning."

"Mama? Where's Ethan?" The latch jiggled, and Ethan's breath stuttered. Her voice pleaded. "Aaron told me he's here."

"You heard your mother, Marietta." Mr. Hamilton's tone was emphatic, almost sharp. "Go back to bed."

The tramp of her feet protested all the way up the stairs. Ethan exhaled, his breath hitching with relief. Could he be reduced any lower? He wouldn't have her see him like this. His head swam but he forced down the emotion once again.

Other needs crowded in on him: hunger, cold, and exhaustion. Though unaccustomed to privation, he accepted it with submission. He was no better than contraband, now.

He shrugged into the shirt and cracked the door, venturing forward only at Levi Hamilton's beckoning. He accepted a chair at the utility table in the warm, close room where Mrs. Hamilton poured coffee. A platter held thick slices of bread, and a crock offered fresh butter. Beef stew, ladled into deep bowls, steamed up a rich aroma. His hand shook as he reached for the spoon. Mr. Hamilton had barely blessed the repast before he launched himself into it.

Mrs. Hamilton stood at her husband's side, the shame of her pitying gaze prickling over Ethan's neck. He continued to swallow in gulps, not impolitely but with a quiet desperation. He wasn't the same self-assured young man that had visited last November. What did she see now? A refugee? A cast-about, devoid of manners, of breeding, of *family?* A fracture went all the way through him. He kept his head bowed.

After several servings, Mrs. Hamilton broke the hush. "Ethan, is there anything else I can do for you, dear?"

It wasn't so much the words as the tone that she employed which threatened to bust his seems open again. He lifted his head to acknowledge her. He replied in a voice so quiet it surprised him. "No, ma'am. I'm obliged."

Her fingers ran over the satin seam of her robe as if caressing a child's soft locks. "My son will show you where you can rest. I'm sure you're eager for sleep."

Ethan nodded. A deep breath filled his chest, and he braced for another small battle. "I'm sorry to bring this trouble to your door, but I just didn't know where else to turn. Thank you."

ঞ৪ঌ

Dimness stretched across the low places, and the deepening shadows foretold of dusk as Marietta gazed out the dining room window. An entire day slipped away like a freedom seeker into the night. What was taking Ethan so long to come down and join the family? She sat at the table, picking at her plate, the aroma of onions and savory meat hanging on the air, but she had no appetite. Her stomach churned with her questions, her heart raced with her many thoughts.

Aaron pointed his fork at the French doors. "Hey! Look who's awake."

Each voice rose in greeting, her own anxious tone blending in the chorus. Marietta poured over the sight of Ethan, his tousled hair, his ill-fitting clothes borrowed from Aaron, his bent posture and slow, careful movement. She willed him to meet her eager gaze, but he looked away.

He took the seat next to Aaron, and nodded thanks as her mother filled his plate.

"We've already asked the blessing," Mama apologized. "We weren't sure if we should disturb you."

Ethan bowed over his plate for a moment, and then looked up with a sheepish grin. "I'm not even the worst for wear. How is my horse? And Jonesy, er, Vincent?"

Papa stroked his water glass with a thumb. "Your horse is bedded down and fed. As for your friend, I thought it best we act on his behalf immediately. I'm sorry I didn't consult with you, but given the urgency of the matter—"

Ethan straightened in his chair. "Where is he?"

"We have acquaintances who aid those seeking freedom. We prevailed upon them to make connections for him and our maid. We felt it wasn't safe for either of them here, if there's any chance of bounty hunters pursuing you."

"He's gone already?" Ethan shook his head.

"The society will see to his relocation and livelihood. You needn't worry for him."

"I see."

His color deepened, and Mari wondered on his thoughts. Had he not risked life and limb, forsaken family, ridden over many days to save the boy? Her father hadn't even given them a chance to say good-bye.

She could hold back no more. "It was so beautiful to see him reunite with his mother. They will be forever thankful for what you've done. And so will I."

He choked on a sip from his water glass but avoided a single glance in her direction.

Instead, he faced her father, clearing his throat. "Is there a chance your friends could point me in the direction of work, too?"

Aaron stifled a laugh. "What would you want to do *that* for?"

Papa frowned at Aaron. He replied to Ethan, "Mrs. Hamilton and I have discussed a more suitable arrangement for you. We wish to enroll you in college for the fall semester."

"You mean, stay on here?" Ethan's ears reddened, the color spreading over his neck and into his cheeks.

"Yes, if that proves suitable to you, son."

Ethan clenched his jaw.

"Is something wrong?" Papa asked.

Ethan's head lowered, as well as his voice. "I have no way to pay for that, sir."

"Mrs. Hamilton and I wish to cover all expenses."

Ethan folded his napkin over his plate. Looking bewildered, he backed his chair from the table and retreated without a word.

Marietta let her silverware clatter to her plate. "Ethan, wait!" She dashed after him.

Marrietta!" Her mother's shrill voice followed.

"Give them a moment, Cora," Papa said. "Aaron, go with your sister."

At the crest of the steps, Ethan turned to glance back at her before ducking into his room.

Aaron waited discretely in the hall, but Marietta followed Ethan inside.

"They didn't mean any harm." She stood just inside his doorway, the rise and fall of her breath pressing at her neckline. She wanted to rush to his side, but his pacing reminded her of a caged wolf. She chose her approach carefully.

He averted his gaze from her with apparent effort. "I'm no charity case. My father told me nothing in this life is free. If I can't work for it, then I don't want it."

"Why are you so cross, Ethan?" She reached toward him.

He fisted his hands and retreated further into the room.

She followed as far as she dared—the edge of his bed. "Won't you tell me what happened? What sent you to us?"

He finally looked fully at her, and his ebony eyes sparked. Turmoil. And another emotion she was hesitant to identify, but which filled her with a tingling heat from her bared arms to her toes.

"I fear I put an awful burden on you. I wanted so badly to rescue Tilly and her son from slavery… and you did it! You're a hero, you know."

"I'm no hero!"

His intensity made her tremble. Still, she slipped over the remaining distance between them and grasped his hand. "Tell me what happened, and I'll decide."

All the anger in his expression drained away, and sadness lingered in the shadows of his handsome features. "Please don't canonize me, Miss Hamilton. There's nothing noble about being a fugitive."

"Oh, Ethan!" She caressed his hand. "A fugitive? From what?"

"Devon found the pamphlet you sent me. He figured I was spreading it around to the slave population and threatened to punish Jonesy for it. I couldn't let him. We both said things—hateful, ugly things. Before I knew it, we were fighting, nearly killing each other."

That cold, hard place in his expression returned, his eyes smoldering coals.

"So I ran. I took off with Jonesy and fled like a coward."

"No, Ethan. You're no coward. I can think of none braver."

She traced the cuts on his face, and he backed away, but he had nowhere to go. He sank to the edge of the bed, and she sat beside him.

"I never meant to hurt Devon." He clenched his jaw in a hard line and clasped his hands until his knuckled turned white. "But what he did… what he said—"

She drew his hand in both of hers, stroking away the tension until he unfurled his fist. "I shouldn't even be here, you know. I was supposed to be sent to Paris. But when they fired on Fort Sumter, Papa said it was too dangerous to travel. Now I see why the Lord intervened—I got to see you again." She smiled and cocked her head to coax a measure of cheer from him.

The ebb and flow of his breath, volatile, restless, his linen shirt pressing against his broad shoulders and chest, filled her with a sudden longing to caress away his troubles. But she checked herself. And recalled her brother standing chaperon outside in the hallway.

Warmth flooded her as his gaze sought hers. His hands clasped about hers. He leaned his head to the side and sought her kiss.

"My brother." The slightest turn of her face brought him to account.

"I'm sorry." He put distance between them at once, rising and pacing to the door.

"You speak of heroism, Marietta. If I were truly brave, I would have done more, and sooner. What of Colby? What of Jim, and Ezra? Because of my cowardice, they'll die *slaves*."

He spat the word like bitterest medicine.

Marietta waited, hoping he would explain.

"God's plans prevail, Ethan."

He shook his head, his eyes harder now than black marble. "Reckon so."

She took a steadying breath and met his gaze. "You must hold on to the promise."

"What promise? I have *nothing*."

"But you do. You have family."

He flinched when she said the word.

"Scripture promises that whatever you give up for God, he'll give it back, many times over."

He scoffed. "Where does it say that?"

She paced to the bedside table and lifted a bible. He followed her back into the room as she leafed through the pages.

"Matthew 19:29 '*And everyone that hath forsaken houses, or brethren, or father, or mother, or lands, for my name's sake, shall receive an hundredfold, and shall inherit everlasting life.*'

"His promises will comfort you, Ethan."

"I don't understand God's comfort, but I understand yours."

Eyes hooded, he moved in toward her again.

Her heart fluttered as his arms encircled her, and he pressed his lips to hers. Intense warmth infused her—climbed higher as he parted his mouth against hers. She submitted to his kiss, though urgency ignited within her to resist. All her will failed.

Aaron's feet shuffled in the hallway. With a low gasp, she pulled away. "We mustn't…."

He bore the look of a wounded animal and turned away.

She hesitated and touched his arm. "I'm glad you're here."

He covered her hand with his, warm and strong. "Are you?" His expression held such raw emotion, her breath staggered.

"Your home is here, now. We'll be your family. If you'll have us."

He nodded, closing his eyes. A muscle moved in his throat, and she longed to hold him close again, to offer him the comfort he seemed so desperate for.

"Marietta?" Papa called from the landing. "Your mother wants you downstairs right away."

Chapter 17

Ethan sat alone on the back steps of the Hamilton's house, facing southward. An overcast sky lent the Potomac a cold, black hue. He huddled into himself, pondering the choices at his disposal. Since Jonesy was gone, he'd volunteered for the care of the horses. He'd do just about anything to avoid Mrs. Hamilton. She was kind, in a smothering way. He'd just as soon stay out from underfoot.

With Mr. Hamilton at work and Mari committed to her social obligations, Ethan accepted his lonesomeness as penance. His welcome here wouldn't last, at least not any longer than he wanted to stay. Expectations would be foisted, such as attending college as a ward of the esteemed family, paraded as their personal mission to the politicians who would commend them for the noble work they were doing. He hung his chin in the crook of his hand, letting his thoughts wash away with the water flowing out to the sea.

Where was Devon now? Probably surrounded by friends and having the time of his life in Richmond. Surely not giving him a second thought.

What were his prospects now? He couldn't stay here—his daddy hadn't raised him to take charity. He'd have to find his own way. But how?

Behind him, the screen door met the wooden frame with a bang and a rattle on its catch.

Aaron stepped down beside him on the stoop. "Mind if I sit?"

Ethan moved over.

"Having fun out here?" Aaron's grin hinted invitation.

Ethan shrugged. "Fun? What's that?"

"The question is," Aaron said, leaning in, "*where's* that."

"All right then, you tell me."

"I heard General Butler's troops arrived from Massachusetts to quell the rioting along the Maryland border."

Ethan perked up.

"Word is, downtown is full of 'em. They're enlisting boys faster than the ink on their signatures can dry! Must be sportin' to see all those boys parading down Pennsylvania Avenue."

"Downtown?" Any break in the monotony would be welcome.

Aaron nodded. "Interested?"

Ethan was already on his feet. "Let's go."

cssso

Marietta parted the curtain on the dining room window as dusk settled. Dinner had been served and cleared and the coffee had gone cold. Fireflies glimmered over the drive on the late spring air.

Still no sign of them.

She closed the curtain. They hadn't even told anyone they were going. They'd just up and left, without a word. Spontaneity from a couple of colts like them wasn't unexpected, but what troubled her were the infinite possibilities to find trouble.

Her father hadn't said a word at the table, but his frequent glances at their empty chairs hadn't escaped her notice. Her mother had informed him of the boys' impromptu gallop down the drive. That had been mid-morning. Now, half-past eight, there was no clue of their destination, nor word of their return.

Marietta remained silent about her suspicions. She'd overheard her brother talk with a neighbor about the military reviews in the city just this week. She'd seen the gleam in his eye. Would Ethan be the sensible one and talk him out of it? She swallowed down an ironic laugh and quickly whispered a prayer.

Rising from her seat at the window she resolved to take up some embroidery and join her mother, when the cobblestone drive erupted with sound. Thrusting her head through the curtains again, she gasped. A tall gray thoroughbred and her brother's liver bay stood outside while the boys dismounted. She dashed from her perch to the door.

Their laughter carried back to the house. Leading their mounts into the carriage house and stables beyond, the boys passed, unaware of her standing in the doorway. She watched them with hammering chest and tied tongue. Just before they disappeared behind the wide entry, she found her voice.

"Aaron! Ethan! Where have you been?"

Ethan turned to her, and she gasped. He stood there where the lantern light cast a dusky spell over him, and he smiled at her in a way that made her insides flutter.

"We've done nothing unusual, Mari."

That provoked Aaron's laughter again, and they retreated into the barn.

She couldn't stand the suspense a moment longer. She cast off her slippers, gathered her skirts, and ran barefooted out to them. She threw the door of the barn open and stood panting, her boldness failing under their stares.

"Tell me the truth! Did you enlist?" She swallowed, holding her position with one hand at her bosom, the other pressed to the door.

Ethan grinned. "Aaron, your sister is asking you a question."

"Don't you dare patronize me!" she said, her trembling lower lip betraying her.

Ethan regarded her with one raised brow. His jaw slackened, and one side of his mouth lifted in a grin.

Aaron spoke for them. "You're shivering out here, Mari. Why don't you wait inside? We'll talk about our day in the city when we come in."

She wouldn't be moved. Her frustration had turned to hot, quivering tears.

Ethan's gaze softened toward her. "No sense keeping her in suspense, Aaron."

"Aw, Ethan." Aaron tossed down his riding gloves into the litter. "You're not going to tell her, are you?"

"Why not? Isn't like she can undo it." He clucked to the gelding to encourage him into the stall and shut the half-door behind him. His raven hair tucked in waves beneath his hat, and the dirt roads had kicked up a considerable deposit on his clothes. He looked irresistibly rugged, almost wild. Something within her stirred at his reckless masculinity.

She regarded her own presentation with self-consciousness. Her hair hung loose in long strands where it had escaped its combs, and her bare feet stuck to the hay. Trumping all, however, was the stubborn threat of tears she couldn't wipe away.

"Your brother and I joined the cavalry." Ethan's sweeping bow halted, and his pride seemed to crash against the rocks of her displeasure.

She put a hand to her mouth, wincing. "Tell me you didn't!"

"What?"

Aaron groaned. "Told you, genius."

"But Mari, that's good news!"

"How could it be? That would mean that you—that you both are going off to war."

"Yes." He looked to Aaron as if her brother could clarify the obvious.

He irritated her with his devil-may-care daring. Surely disaster lay ahead, already licking its carnivorous chops for them.

Leaving the rest unspoken, she fled. As she exited the barn door, she overheard Ethan say, "You'd think she'd be pleased, like all those other girls we saw today."

"She isn't like those other girls, Sharpe."

"I don't care about them. I just want to know why she can't be happy."

Aaron chuckled. "If you want to grab a cat by the tail, go ask her."

ଔ

Mr. Hamilton stood waiting in the foyer when Ethan and Aaron slipped in under the cover of dark. Heavy brows furrowed, the gentleman put a hand over his jaw as if restraining speech. Mrs. Hamilton, standing beside her husband, made her disapproval a silent, tangible force.

Aaron kissed his mother's cheek. "Sorry we're late for dinner, Mother."

Levi turned to his wife. "Would you bring their plates, dear?"

Mrs. Hamilton obliged without a word.

Levi procured his pocket watch while Ethan stood beside Aaron, hung in suspense.

"Near-on nine o'clock." The man snapped the cover back over the piece and stared. Neither he nor Aaron spoke a word. Ethan shifted his stance.

Mrs. Hamilton announced the food was ready, and Aaron brushed past his father and launched straightaway to the table. Ethan followed close behind.

Taking a seat, Ethan allowed the sights of the day's military review to play out in his mind. He fished in his pocket, producing the receipt for his recruitment photo. A grin stole over him. The Maryland Cavalry would blaze his trail to independence. Would restore his sense of self-respect, allow him to earn his own way. And when his 90 days' enlistment was over, surely justice would have been served on the evils of slavery and those who upheld it, and Ethan would be vindicated.

But the disappointment on the patrician faces at the table dampened his spirits. The hush made him downright uneasy. Ethan almost wished to invite a lecture rather than endure this penetrating vigil. He inhaled to speak, but Levi Hamilton's look froze his tongue.

"I wouldn't deny your right to fight for what you believe in." Mr. Hamilton exchanged a penetrating stare at he and Aaron in turn. "But neither of you have any idea what you're in for."

"Not so, father," Aaron replied. "The Bible is full of men who fought for their beliefs. Like King David, we'll take vengeance on the enemies of God."

His father winced. "Repentance cannot come by force. It is a decision of one's free will. God neither subjugates, nor does He ask us to do so in his name."

"But they've had their chance to repent. Right, Ethan? You're living proof!"

"I agree with Aaron, sir. Their hearts are so hard, they might need to be broken before they change."

Aaron waved his hand. "You see?"

Mr. Hamilton scrubbed his brow and sighed. "If you must go, then go with the proper motives. First, put aside all notions of vengeance."

Ethan cracked his knuckles but would not voice his disagreement at the man's table.

"It is the goodness of God that leads a man to repentance. Seek to love your family and pray for them."

The words nettled Ethan. Did the man presume to know something about Devon that his own twin didn't?

"Will you pray with me?" Mr. Hamilton did not wait for assent but stood and laid a commanding hand on Ethan's neck.

"Gracious Father, I ask that you heal the hurt, the rejection, and the betrayal which this young man has borne in seeking to serve you. Restore all that has been lost. And Lord, help this young man to be baptized in your love toward those who have inflicted this hurt upon him. May he experience a revelation of your divine nature which triumphs over hatred."

The man shifted, conferring his other hand upon his son, holding them both now with a grasp like yokes about their necks.

"'I have called thee by name; thou art mine. When thou passest through the waters I will be with thee; and through the rivers, they shall not overflow thee; when thou walkest through the fire, thou shalt not be burned; neither shall the flame kindle upon thee. For I am the Lord thy God, the Holy One of Israel, thy Savior. Since thou wast precious in my sight, thou hast been honorable, and I have loved thee; therefore, I will give men for thee, and people for thy life. Fear not for I am with thee.'"

Chapter 18

July 20, 1861
Shenandoah Valley, Virginia
Stuart's Cavalry Encampment

Three months—three *months* of drilling, maneuvers, and reconnaissance—had yielded no action. Devon's last nerve chafed in the hush of the crickets' evening song. The screech of rockets would have made a more soothing serenade to him this night. Ever since April when he'd last seen his traitorous brother's face, Devon had found no peace or rest.

Receiving permission to bivouac, he sacked his saddle and tethered Cinder among a line of hundreds of cavalry mounts. Days of maneuvering through mountain gaps and valley trails had passed with a dull sameness, and Devon settled into the forest glade to slake his thirst, to stoke the coals of his burning soul, and prepare for battle.

Whispers about their destination scraped over him like the edge of his bowie knife—the one he was supposed to give Ethan the night of their birthday. That old maxim had proven true: gifting a knife had cut the friendship. He rubbed the leather sheath at his side as though it pained him, and he uttered an oath.

Headed back through camp, he overheard rumors of forces gathering near Manassas. Reports of the Yankee's weak performance at Blackburn's Ford simmered hot satisfaction through him. *Blue bellies, the lot of them.* He couldn't wait to serve up what they deserved.

He hefted a hammer and joined two troopers pitching their four-man tent. "Reckon the battle will be over before we get a chance to fight?"

The shorter of the two looked cross-ways at him. "Just drive the peg in straight, Sharpe."

Devon huffed. "The whole blamed war will be over before they send us in!"

An older trooper, reclining against a nearby tree, looked up from the letter he held. "Simmer down, over there. My wife's words are beginning to sound like your yappin'."

Devon swacked the tent stake with one last blow. "You gonna let us do all the work while you fan yourself over there like a girl?"

The cavalier leveled Devon with a glare. "Come'ere and we'll finish what you couldn't with that brother of yours."

The hairs on Devon's neck bristled and his fist tightened over the tent mallet. He'd bust the man's jaw if he said another word. "You leave *him* out of this, Dempsey."

"Heard all about how your twin turned tail on the eve of mustering. You gonna skeddadle, too?"

Devon lunged at the soldier, raising his hammer to striking position. His two companions restrained him before he could deliver a single, satisfying blow. They shoved him to the picket line and grabbed his weapon.

One shook his fist at him. "Cool off or see if we don't tie you to that apple tree for the night."

The other gripped Devon's shoulder, his frown apologetic. "Don't pay Dempsey any mind. We all know the truth about what happened. It ain't no shame of yours, no matter what your brother went and done."

Devon returned to the campfire in folded-armed, clenched-jawed misery. *Did they all know about Ethan?* The pain, humiliation, and anger seared his innards until Devon burned in his boots. Only a good fight would relieve the foment building within him. Or release the pain crushing him from the inside out, blinding him to all else save the lust for vengeance. How could his brother, his own twin, have turned on him? And over a slave?

Headquarters lay a short distance away, and he set out for Walt Thompson's tent, intent on driving out any battle information he had.

A few men still milled about at the late hour. Devon waited in the shadows, biding his time with a wad of chew until they left Walt's tent. He spit the tobacco out with the juice, and wiping his mouth, he poked his head in.

"Captain?"

"Come in."

Devon saluted as he slipped through the canvas flaps and stood before the makeshift desk of plank and board.

"At ease," Walt said. "How goes it, Devon?"

"Fine, if you'd oblige me with some news."

Walt grinned. "Might have some."

"Don't hold out on me, Thompson."

Walt waved him over and bid him sit on an upturned barrel. "Seems like McDowell's got quite a force building over the Manassas Gap."

"I know that…."

"As we speak, railcars are preparing to transport the infantry out of the valley to join Beauregard and engage the Army of the Potomac. We'll be moving out with them."

"How soon?"

"Any time, now. Maybe tonight."

Devon let out an impetuous whoop.

Walt splayed his hand to silence him. "Shhh! It's not official yet!"

"Never fear, Captain."

"Not a word, Sharpe!"

Devon retreated from the tent, clutching the sheath of his knife. "It's high time."

ଔଌ

Twelve hours later
Manassas, Virginia
Union Cavalry

Nimbus's stride matched thousands of troopers to his right and left, before and behind, but somehow, Ethan felt alone. The last three months, spent in close quarters with restless, battle-hungry men dispelled any notions of righteousness. Riding into battle, even with Aaron at his side, Ethan's confidence fled. To think of this group as God's Army choked up a weak laugh from him now.

The campgrounds ran livid with all manner of vice. Games sprang up on a moment's notice, some played on cards that would make a sailor blush. Bets on horses, rats and even cockroaches duped the naive out of his $12 monthly soldier's pay. And though swift punishment met the use of alcohol, the men had an ingenious resourcefulness for procuring it. Not that Ethan was any prude, but he craved a higher tonic now, facing an enemy twenty thousand strong.

If only Marietta hadn't turned a cold shoulder to him that last night. She hadn't spoken a word to him when he'd attempted to say goodbye. Her quivering chin and fiery look had begged his overture, but she'd retreated into the house rather than give a soldier a proper kiss goodbye. Her lips, set in his mind in their silent pout, tempted him all over again. Mocked him.

So, what if she didn't approve of his enlistment. He couldn't expect a girl to understand the hard sentiment for war, nor the necessity to risk life and limb for the sake of honor. He couldn't blame her if his courage contradicted her fragile nature. In time he would be vindicated. When he returned with the conquering army, then she'd be proud of him.

Ethan rubbed the smooth stock of his Springfield rifle with his thumb. His cavalry unit approached the picket line, then came the order to dismount. He and Aaron stood, looking on what appeared to be a full-scale rout. This was it—the action he'd waited for. Then why did his stomach clench, staring across the field at his former countrymen?

Word was that the Virginians under Thomas Jackson had been delayed in the Valley, engaging Union veteran General Patterson. And Jackson's absence meant Devon's absence. At least his bullets wouldn't spill his own blood.

Suddenly battle exploded to life before him. Soldiers crouched to reload, some scrambling for cover. A few skittered back, but Ethan took a step forward, and then several more. Bullets whizzed, cutting through wood, sod, and men. They were alarmingly close.

From the crest, dark, fleet figures descended like a nest of riled bats. A Confederate cavalry charge took the field. Ethan scrambled for cover. They spread out and kept coming with no end to them. A striking figure in black-plumed hat rallied the troopers with forward-pointed saber.

Ethan turned to Aaron at the precise moment the command came to load their weapons. Tearing his powder bag with his teeth, he spilled its contents down the barrel of his rifle, and with fumbling hands drove the ramrod home over a cone-shaped Minie` ball.

"Ready!"

Ethan dug in his caisson for a percussion cap, and cocking the hammer, he placed the small charge over its nipple.

"Aim…."

Raising the rifle, he adjusted it to his sights. With the butt pressed to his shoulder, he covered the trigger.

His fingers tingled as he took aim.

"Fire!"

☙❧

Devon rode low in the saddle, scanning the enemy line before him. At the call to charge, he spurred his thoroughbred forward, breaking formation to bear down on a single target.

The Union infantry had tried to organize a volley in the seconds before they arrived. Their weak firing-at-will gave way to a fixed-bayonet counter-charge. Devon hardly blinked at the sight of the enemy's bayonets, bristling in the afternoon sun like metal teeth. Rather he rode high and clear, firing his double action revolver at-the-ready.

For a good many of the Yankees, it was too late to run, so they made a pitiful stand. Devon and his troopers were upon them. They scrambled to make their twelve inches of steel count. *Fools!* It wouldn't save them.

His predatory gaze fixed on the color-bearer. Cid reared, trumpeting a shrill cry. The Yankee held up a forearm as though that could fend off a thousand pounds of horseflesh. The sun glinted on Devon's saber as he swung it down.

Men scattered before him; few dared to stand between him and an Old Glory souvenir. The color bearer planted himself, visibly horrified at Devon on his lathered black charger. Devon dispatched him, and the flag staff exchanged hands.

Carrying away his trophy, a force welled up from a primitive place within Devon. A sound, half-scream and half warrior's victory, erupted from his throat, raising the hairs all over his own fevered flesh. Other riders picked up the shrill cry until the whole field was livid with sound.

ঞ

Ethan had seen and heard enough.

He fumbled with shaking hands to fix his finger on the trigger and take aim. He fired. His lead ball struck a cavalry charger bearing down on him. Horse and rider toppled and slid to a halt only yards away. Closing his eyes, he made a blind dash rearward, trusting in the horse's hulking cover. His flesh burned so hot that for a minute he believed he'd been shot. He blinked, still running, and swiped a hand over brass buttons—no blood—though his breath slammed against his ribs.

The retreat turned to a melee. Ethan joined the human herd, ready to run all the way back to Washington, but for thought of his horse.

Passing hundreds of fleeing soldiers, he spied the picketed mounts. A tall gray with the sloping lines and angles of a thoroughbred stood among them. Nimbus tossed his head, fighting his tether to join the stampede to safety. Ethan snatched up his reins and jumped astride.

The entire fighting force had been wiped out by a catching disease—panic. Its crippling effects were everywhere Ethan turned. The wounded lay on red-stained dirt, their hands raised in terror and pleading, while medics fled for their own safety. Carts for the wounded, departing on the only lane serving as a road, clattered away empty in their haste to flee. One Federal soldier punched another that got in his way.

Fear could sure turn good men ugly.

Raw misery grated over Ethan's senses. Heat, sweat and thirst pressed upon him.

The mass casualties seemed innumerable. Nimbus reared and sidestepped as someone shouted at him, hissing warning. Wherever Ethan turned, faces twisted in anguish or in the throes of death. He squeezed his eyes shut and gave Nimbus free rein to navigate over the human ground. Then, a voice rose over the clamor. Its repetition broke through his haze.

"Ethan! *Ethan,* over here."

He opened his eyes. "Aaron." Leaping from the saddle, he ran toward the source. A hand reached up, pressing five black and crimson trails down Ethan's shirt where Aaron's fingers clutched. He recoiled. He scanned the face again and his breath stuck. A jagged line extended from Aaron's cheekbone down through his jaw and into his neck.

Horror must have registered on Ethan's expression, because Aaron covered the wound again with his hand. "I got caught in a volley of grape shot."

Bile rose in Ethan's throat and he forced it back down. "I'll find help."

But if this was the rout Ethan feared, this field of wounded men would be trampled or finished off by the Rebs before they ever found help.

"Can you ride?"

"I'll manage." Aaron motioned for a leg up.

"Where's your horse?"

"Dead."

Ethan lifted Mari's brother onto Nimbus's back. Once secured, Aaron feebly drew on Ethan's canteen. A mix of blood and water ran from his cheek. With a screech, he threw the tin from the height of the saddle as Ethan led Nimbus on the road back toward Washington.

Chapter 19

Marietta felt like a frightened canary scuttling from one end of its cage to another. All afternoon the sound of cannon had groaned in the distance, filling her breast with a tightness that left her short of breath and pacing the parlor. She had never known such desperate, clawing worry, even when the bounty hunters had come. For days, talk had centered on the forces surrounding the capital. Neighbors and colleagues of Papa's had speculated on the possibility of invasion, while others drove carriages with a picnic lunch to view the armies.

Each percussion struck a fiery poker through Marietta's belly with thoughts of the Rebels overrunning the streets of Washington. Would Papa be safe in Washington? Indeed, was their home safe from the rebels?

Mama sat on her rosewood settee, needlework flickering in her busy hands. She barely lifted her head at each startling bombardment, and her serene smile only ceded to an occasional few words, such as when she'd beckoned Mari to sit beside her. Mari couldn't bring herself to cease the track she'd worn over the oak floor. The repetitious movement gave her a sense of control, if only over herself.

"You know, dear, you'd do your brother more good praying for him than fretting."

She scampered to Mama's side. "Oh, Mama, how shall we

bear it?"

Mama held her head up with all the nobility she possessed. "We shall bear what the Lord in His infinite grace allows us to bear. But first,"—she laid aside her embroidery and took Mari's hands—"we shall pray."

ଓଃ

Ethan walked beside his horse, adjusting his grip on Aaron's dead weight so his friend wouldn't fall off Nimbus's back. The continuing push toward the capital kept the army groping along the dark road with no rest in sight. The morning's vainglory had been wasted with their blood back on the shores of Bull Run. His friend bore bravely through that long evening against a universe of agonies, occasionally seething through clenched teeth. As dusk deepened into nightfall, however, his reserve faded with the waning light. Now, Aaron's shock wore off, taking all vanity with it. He no longer fought to muffle his pain-filled cries but let them sail out with every pitch of the horse's gait.

Ethan had expended precious energy imagining what they'd find once they reached Washington. Perhaps the Confederates had arrived ahead of them and burned it down. And if they should have failed at that, perhaps they regrouped from behind for a final slaughter.

Time passed with no sight of commander, flag, or company. The crossroads led in one direction to the capital. But the other direction offered an inviting house, the certainty of food, a bed, and the promise of attendance to Aaron's wounds. Ethan turned Nimbus toward the Hamilton's house.

Sometime later, he forced the door and stumbled in, Aaron's sagging form slung over his shoulder. Boots chafing the floor and the door slamming with a backward kick should have been enough to alert the household, but just for good measure, Ethan paused at the base of the stairs and called up. "Mr. Hamilton? Mrs. Hamilton?"

A shadowy form appeared at the crest of the stairs. "Ethan?" He recognized Marietta's sweet voice, and his gut clenched. He hated to alarm her, but it couldn't be helped.

"Yes. Go wake your parents. Your brother's hurt."

She turned and dashed down the hallway, and soon the creak of floorboards filled the upstairs. Ethan settled Aaron onto a couch in the parlor. Levi assisted his wife down the stairs, and Ethan met them at the landing.

"Oh, blessed mercy!" Mrs. Hamilton pressed a hand over the bodice of her dressing gown. The whiteness of her face rivaled that of the scalloped collar.

Ethan's torn shirtsleeve soaked with Aaron's blood must have done it. Ethan put his hands behind his back.

"Where's Aaron?" Mr. Hamilton asked, pulling the sash of his robe tighter, worry lines deepening over his face.

Ethan backed through the French doors into the parlor, loath to reveal the sight to unprepared eyes.

"He's made it through the long march very bravely. But there were no medics…."

The Hamiltons rushed past him to their boy. He winced at the anguished sound Mrs. Hamilton made. While the family's drama unfolded, he backed up to the wall, wishing he could disappear through it. Once again, his night-time intrusion had shattered the peace of their household.

Mrs. Hamilton hovered over her son without touching him. Tears glistened in her eyes but didn't spill.

Ethan's shame rose in a conflagration inside him. *You don't belong here.* Would they cast the blame of this on him? An outsider, a stranger, a ne'er-do-well whose influence had led their son to harm? He should leave….

Levi lifted Aaron for better examination and uttered an exclamation. The image of his son, flickering in the gas light before him, must have shocked the man to the core. Mrs. Hamilton fled to gather iodine and linen, so she said, and Ethan suspected, to empty her stomach.

The scene brought a peculiar lump to Ethan's throat. He must have been more tired than he realized for the attention over Aaron to affect him so. The loving family, bent with concern over their son, brought grief pounding at the barricade over his heart.

A soft creak from the hallway, and a click in the hardware of the door behind him brought him around.

Marietta emerged, her worry-piqued expression somehow easing his turmoil. Her ivory robe fluttering at her sides, she appeared like an angel. Then, if the sight of her wasn't enough, she turned with the most tender look not to her parents, nor to her brother, but to that blackest void where he stood.

"Oh, Ethan." Before he could refuse, she enfolded him in her arms. "I prayed you'd be safe!" He breathed her floral scent deep into places that had taken in the aroma of death and the sulfur of battle. The contrast lit conflicting sensations through him. He didn't deserve her comfort or grace. And yet he drank it in with insatiable thirst.

He almost pressed her to him, but for the blood soiling him. And her mother's presence in the adjacent room. He took Marietta's hands instead, transfixed with her adoring expression. "Didn't figure you'd be glad to see me."

Her smile flickered as one lone tear trailed down her porcelain cheek. "But Ethan," she said, "your return is all I could pray for today—and Aaron's. How is he?"

He shook his head. "You don't want to see him like this."

ଔ

Mari braced herself against the shudder rattling down her spine. "Take me to him."

Ethan offered his arm, and the blood on his sleeve made her recoil.

"It's not mine." He apologized, motioning toward the sofa. "It's his. Are you sure?"

She swallowed and nodded.

Mama sat beside Aaron and sponged his face and chest with a soft cloth. His protests were weak but poignant, and Papa whispered an appeal for Mama to allow Aaron spirits for the pain.

Mama finally agreed.

Her poor brother held up while Mama finished cleansing the lacerations. Marietta flinched, feeling the wash water in place of him. Ethan firmed his hold on her, and his prayers passed through her more as vibration than intelligible words. She whispered her own between gasps and sighs.

Papa lifted the bottle of medicinal whiskey to Aaron's lips. As the tonic hit his flesh, her brother gave such a frightful shriek that her skin tingled. She closed her eyes and her knees buckled. Ethan held her until she could regain her strength.

Mari trembled in his arms. His warmth infused her with a sensation beyond comfort. He leaned in to whisper consolation in her ear. The gentle sounds of his deep voice teased away her desperation, though the words of the prayer were lost to the noise in her head.

"Levi,"—Mama lifted her gaze to Papa—"our son needs a surgeon."

"They've all gone to assist the army, my dear. We may have to manage by ourselves tonight."

Mama wrung her hands. "Surely in all of Washington there must be *one* doctor to be found?"

"I'll go," Ethan offered.

"I'll telegraph Henry," Papa replied. Mari knew he meant Secretary Seward. "He'll find us one."

ଓଃ

Ethan helped Marietta to the piano bench. His own desperation grew with Aaron's shuddering cries while his parents did what they could to staunch the blood-flow. Ethan rose and paced, vexing at the futility of his prayers. Marietta pressed on, her head bowed. With closed eyes and whispering lips, she was oblivious to Ethan's study of her.

Her countenance rested in smooth lines, and her peaceful expression told Ethan that she had transcended misery and connected with something higher. Her white robe had been ruined with her brother's blood, and Ethan fought the impulse to hunt down the elusive doctor himself. Instead he sat beside her and held her.

Her thick lashes curled atop pink cheeks. Her unbound tresses covered her shoulders and their waves rose and fell with every breath. The incense of her prayer sweetened the room, and as she closed her conversation with an "Amen," Ethan did not think it coincidence that at that moment, the doctor's buggy turned into the drive.

ભ્રષ્ઠ

Had the night passed so swiftly? Hushed ladies' voices from downstairs met Ethan's ears with the clatter of kitchen utensils. In the wee hours, when certain he could do no more to help, he had taken the room he'd used twice before, and fell into a thick sleep. Now, blinking up at the familiar ceiling pattern, he allowed the pleasant domestic sounds to wash over his waking senses. Then another voice distinguished itself, deeper in register. It came from just down the hallway where they'd left Aaron last night. After the doctor attended him, he'd fallen into a stupor of opiates and exhaustion.

It couldn't be past six in the morning, Ethan judged by the heaviness which still clung to his eyelids, and the cooler air streaming through the open window. Could Aaron have awoken already?

Ethan sat up in bed to incline his ear. And there it was—that bass voice, to be sure, and what sounded like… singing. Ethan stole toward the room and paused outside the door.

Aaron stood before a tall dressing mirror, examining himself with such absorption he might have been preparing to go courting. His singing reminded Ethan of those lusty ballads heard at public houses, sung with the slur of inebriation. He recognized the melody, a tribute to someone's sweetheart by the name of Aura Lee, normally full of the wistful sentiment of the homesick soldier. The words, however, had been changed. And judging by Aaron's garbled diction, the surgeon's work couldn't have been promising.

"Who could bear to look at you? Never one that's fair.
You'd be wise to hide behind the cover of your hair!
God in heaven, look at you. No one could forbear
Marrying a monster who resembles such a scare."

A long, low laugh concluded the solo. A chill rushed over Ethan's skin, although the July morning was far from cold. Ethan didn't wait for more. He cleared his throat and entered.

"You're quite the poet."

Aaron regarded Ethan from the mirror with a subtle shake of his head. "Poetry was one of my strong-suits back in Lexington. Always impressed the ladies."

"They must have loved your hyperbole."

"Look at my face and tell me I'm exaggerating." Aaron turned then, revealing a puckered, crimson line slashed over his jaw, black horsehair stitches jutting like quills from his flesh.

Ethan's eyes burned as though looking into the sun. He steadied his voice. "Looks better than I figured. The Doc did a good job."

"The only good thing that doctor did was to medicate me out of my mind. But now, it's the morning, and the world looks different. How's that for a nice cliché?"

Ethan drew a long inhale and came around to Aaron's side of the room. For a moment, they stood side by side in the mirror, their two images a study in contrasts. Ethan always considered without vanity that he and Devon were handsome, with their ebony hair, and eyes so dark brown they too looked black. Strong jaws, straight noses and swarthy skin favored their father's Cherokee blood. Aaron had been what most would consider good looking, also. He had coffee brown hair and Marietta's hazel eyes. His fair complexion marked contrast with the fiery scar, and the tightness of the stitching pulled his intact features to the side. Ethan's stomach twisted with the odd curves.

Aaron had earned a right to grieve. But after a moment, in a voice that was neither intrusive nor apologetic, Ethan attempted again. "Give it time to heal. No one could say for sure what it'll look like once the stitches come out, and the swelling goes down."

Aaron narrowed his eyes and lowered his head. "Go away."

"Sorry, Aaron."

"I don't want your pity."

Ethan nodded, and turned to leave.

He'd gotten two strides away when Aaron called him back. "Ethan?"

He stopped and turned to face Marietta's brother, whom he'd grown to consider a good friend.

Aaron's voice rang sterling in the calmness of the morning. "There's no sense to it. Why'd we get the tar beaten out of us yesterday?" His flashing eyes betrayed the rising emotion within him. "I mean, we're fighting for the right cause, right? Does this seem like the reward of a Benevolent God to you?"

Ethan closed his eyes, rallying the same question heavenward. He had nothing to offer but cheap reassurance, so he kept a firm rein on his tongue. Part of him was glad he'd been spared, truth be told. The next moment, Aaron re-wrapped his face in long, clean strips of linen. If only Ethan's misgivings could be so easily covered.

Chapter 20

Eager to put the encounter with Aaron behind him, Ethan joined Marietta and her parents in the parlor. The sober tones of a conversation already in progress greeted him as he walked into the room. Mr. Hamilton related a neighbor's story, whose afternoon buggy ride had provided a birds' eye view of the battle. By all accounts, it had been a disastrous loss for the Union. Ethan shared no details, though he certainly could have. Between the neighbor's observations and the papers, a common theme arose—it was time for President Lincoln to assign a new commander for the Army of the Potomac. Ethan couldn't agree more.

The table grew silent and Ethan's thoughts drifted along another track. He strained to recall what fever had so infected his mind that he'd ever volunteered a day, much less ninety, to this madness. He was ready to admit his folly, even at the cost of swallowing his pride. He turned to speak and came face to face with Marietta's intense study.

Could she see the turmoil behind his eyes? His ninety days would soon be up. So soon, in fact, that if he wasn't going to reenlist he might just as well quit now. Levi Hamilton would vouch for his absence for Aaron's sake. Autumn school enrollments would be just around the corner.

Mrs. Hamilton rose from her seat. "Levi, would you help me carry a tray to Aaron?"

Ethan's heart thrummed in gratitude for the unexpected

opportunity. He and Marietta would have a moment alone.

He met her gaze and tried to smile, but he knew it didn't reach his eyes. "I'll be going back today."

"I know."

"Will you miss me?"

"I do already." Her hazel eyes silently pleaded with him to find another way.

A spark ignited something within him. Ethan couldn't maintain eye contact and say what he needed to, so he studied the broken skin on his thumb and forefinger where they had rubbed a hundred times over the same spot yesterday. Loading his rifle. Firing….

"Your father was right about our impetuosity." He glanced up to catch her biting her lower lip. "And so were you."

"Oh. Ethan, I don't care who was right or wrong. I just want you to be safe. I want—" She closed her eyes, her chin quivering.

"What? What do you want, Mari?" He gathered her trembling hands in his. The gesture made things worse. Now her whole body trembled.

A single tear slipped down and trailed her perfect cheek. What he wouldn't give to caress it away.

"You must come back to me."

Ethan's hopes soared. Had she truly said it? Had she declared her heart as more than the simple affection of a sister, or a friend?

"Come back to you? I will." For her, he'd promise anything

She closed her eyes, and the ends of her lashes glistened. The pale, creamy skin on her throat moved as she swallowed. Ethan restrained the impulses that rose in him. For her sake, for the sake of them both, he risked no censure.

"And Ethan? I was the one who was wrong. What you've done is noble. I couldn't see it because I was selfish."

"Selfish? You?"

She nodded. "If you believe God called you to this, how dare I or anyone else say otherwise. If it is God who has led you, then He will keep you. The center of His will is the safest place to be."

Admiration filled him. The feeling transcended mere romance; she inspired courage and conviction in him. Could there be any more compelling mixture of virtue and beauty in a creature? He longed to gather her in his arms, but instead he contented himself with thoughts of her pressed in his arms, her lips offered up to his kiss. If he didn't capitalize on his resolve at that moment, he feared he might take liberties that weren't his. He forced himself to do what he knew he must. He fished in his pocket for his carte de visite portrait, the one he'd sat for in that Washington studio three months ago, and he set it before her. Then he stood and placed a gentle kiss on each of her hands, the soft floral scent of her soap invading his senses.

Without a backward glance, he gathered his gear and left for war.

*

"I forbid it!" The ripples of Mama's outcry still hung on the air.

"I know I heard from the Lord." Certainty anchored Mari's words. Her focus sailed past her mother's frown. Even the yellow-flowered wallpaper of her bedroom gave way to the imagined sight of the hospital down the river, and its influx of soldiers from last week's battle. Aaron recovered there. They had visited him every afternoon since.

"But, Mari, darling! Do you realize the tasks with which you would be involved? It's indecent! How could you breach the innocence of your eyes?"

Her mother's civil bombardment did nothing to move her. She was resolved.

"It's more than a mere regard for your reputation. It is a matter of your very virtue as a young lady. It is out of the question!"

"Virtue, mother?" Mari smiled. "Since when was charity and compassion lacking in virtue?"

Mama sat down on the hope chest at the foot of Marietta's

bed. "Attending strange men of diverse backgrounds—situations that would be uncomfortable for even a seasoned matron—this could not be what God has in mind for my seventeen-year-old! What about finishing school?"

"I realize you only want good things for me. To be the accomplished wife of a respectable Washington reformer like Papa, to enjoy a prosperous life of charitable service. But must I have a ring on my finger before devoting my time to the Lord's work?"

"Would the Lord defy decency and good taste? Would He instruct a young lady to ruin her social standing and challenge her parent's good sense?" Mama's voice had lost its tirade, and now held only pleading.

Marietta took a seat beside Mama, hoping to draw the torment from her brow. "I remember a story about another girl named Mary. I'm sure the virgin birth was difficult to explain to her mother's friends at synagogue. She wasn't primarily concerned with decency and good taste. If she had been, how would God's son have come into the world?"

"But wounded men, Mari! You don't realize…."

She drew her mother's hand in hers. "I think God stretches our understanding of ordinary to accomplish the extraordinary. Since sin entered the world, there will always be a need for ministry. Please, Mama. They're only boys like our Aaron, and Ethan, and Devon, who need help."

"Let the wash-women do the dirty work."

"Would you have Aaron languish because the good girls mustn't soil their clothes?"

"Clothes can wash, Mari, but memories cannot."

Mari swallowed back a sudden surge of emotion and willed her voice steady. "Then pray for my mind, and my eyes, that I may be able to look upon such things with the perspective of Christ."

Mama's searching gaze softened. "You will not leave Washington?"

"I will stay here and do what I can."

A sigh preceded her response. "Your father will have many objections. How shall I ever assuage them all?"

Marietta flung her arms around her mother. "Oh, thank you, Mama! Thank you. I knew you would understand."

"I'm not sure that I do."

ଔ

October 21, 1861
On the Maryland side of the Potomac
Union Army Encampment

The sound of drums woke Ethan, and bugles echoed in the predawn hour. Half-awake men stumbled from tents all around him into the chill air. Torches soon lit the avenues as the camp came alive. Tents were quickly flattened, and all evidence of their presence, save cinders and refuse, disappeared into the waning night.

Ethan had been assigned to this infantry outfit as Nimbus recovered from a temporary lame bout. He listened for orders: crossing the army quickly and quietly over the Potomac. From where he stood at the river's bank and looking across, all appeared serene. He joined the third transport over and arrived as light lapped at the eastern horizon. Murmurings arose amid the ranks, and officers came down the lines, hissing through clenched teeth to shush a hundred voices. The element of surprise was at stake.

He stood at attention, awaiting word from a colonel named Devens to move out and surround the rebel camp which supposedly lay beyond the trees. The mild autumn sunshine of late morning glimmering through the branches boosted spirits. The day promised an easy victory with the added thrill of invading Virginia. After a short while, echoes rippled back that no camp awaited them. A chorus of disappointment erupted from 300 men, but Colonel Devens rallied their spirits with decisive words.

"Well, then, boys, it's on to Leesburg."

Ethan marched, collecting apples and easy pickings of harvest time to fill his haversack along the way. Some distance from the city, the columns' forward progression halted from the quick-step. A detachment went ahead for reconnaissance. Ethan and his fellows remained while commanders determined the best approach into the city. The fall foliage blazed, much like the festivity of McClellan's military reviews recently celebrated along Pennsylvania Avenue. Nothing would do better than a victory to reclaim the pride of the Army of the Potomac after the disappointing summer.

"We'll be camping in Leesburg tonight," one of the men said.

Idle talk stopped with Colonel Devens' sudden return. Faces flushed and discourse urgent, he and his staff snapped out orders.

"Fall in! Rebels ahead!"

Snipers reported from the road with exploding muskets.

Bull Run's massive scale made this minor skirmish seem paltry, and the whiz of bullets almost felt inconsequential. Ethan was back in Virginia, after all. What would his folks think of that? Would Devon be surprised to see him fighting with a blue coat and a belt buckle bearing the stamp of the Union Army? They'd label him a traitor. A turncoat. But Ethan had decided his allegiance the moment he'd fled with Jonesy. He had no regrets. He gritted his teeth, the taste of gunpowder and thirst for action mingling in his mouth.

The first casualties trickled back, and Ethan's bravado vanished. Whether twenty-thousand or one, bullets still possessed the capacity to deliver death.

The Lord is my Shepherd, I shall not want. He makes me lie down in green pastures.

Echoes amplified in the acoustics of the forest and Ethan's ranks fell back. Rifles roared like cannon, bugles blasted like thunder in the mountains. The chaos of battle reverberated against ravines and riverbanks, rippling across waters, lifting in great arcs of sound that pounded at Ethan's ears. All the while, the rebels seemed to come on and on.

He leads me beside the still waters. He restoreth my soul and guides my path in righteousness for his namesake.

Before long, ravines and trenches filled with the fallen. Ethan's unit continued to lose ground, though reinforcements rushed in. The woods impeded them from behind. The Rebels swarmed thick as the underbrush. Ethan's company could retreat no further. A backward glance through thinning trees showed they were forced to the edge of a palisade plunging backward to the river.

Sweat poured down Ethan's collar and under his muslin shirt in the heat of Indian summer. Ahead, whole lines threw down their weapons, or their bodies, refusing to go on. The reinforcements, those last in, were the first to leave, forming a trail which extended past the right flank following the general direction from which they'd come. But a few stout-hearted remained, attempting a counter-attack. His heart pounded in his throat until his breath threatened to close off, but he hunkered down with the few boys remaining.

Men dropped like fumigated flies in the smoke and chaos. In a sudden rush, one man turned on another for the only towpath down the fifty-foot drop called Ball's Bluff. Hundreds stampeded at once, and Ethan was swept in with them. He watched in horror as his comrades hurled over by the dozens, headlong onto rocks and even upturned bayonets.

The scent of blood seemed to intoxicate the pursuing Confederates. The spray of bullets intensified, and men beside him fell, struck from behind, down the palisade to the riverbank below.

Ethan's peace perforated under the hail of piercing lead.

He gasped out a desperate prayer, shut his eyes and dropped to his knees. There, miraculously at his grasp lay an outcrop of root and he held on with a horseman's grip. Just then, the human crush launched him over the precipice.

He hung suspended, clinging for his life.

Body after body fell over him, casting split-second shadows as their free-fall blocked out the sun. He steeled himself against the hideous sounds of screaming and bones cracking, lest they drain him of strength. Booted feet crunched his fingers, their bodies sliding over the edge. The dull thud of a 160-pound body jarred him. He anticipated his imminent fall and glanced down to predetermine his landing.

A shout broke out above, sounding like a yard of geese squawking at full capacity.

"The Rebels are coming!"

Ethan's hold slipped. The air seemed to suck at him, pulling loose flaps of jacket in upward ripples, and flinging his black hair into his face for a breathless second. Then, impact rattled his bones.

He was immobile. Sound waved in and out, as though he bobbed up and down under water. Surrounded by blue, he gasped a breath and realized it was not water, but wool.

"Get off!" A shove vibrated beneath him.

Ethan blinked. Realizing he was impeding someone's escape, he rolled aside. He and the soldier under him toppled down the bank just as rocks and bodies poured down from above, punctuated by bullets. He tucked his feet under him and raced dozens of men to the river, chased by sharpshooters lining the crest. The herd plunged into the icy channel, some trying to retain side-arms, a few assisting the wounded. Here, nobility was rewarded with certain death as the wounded fell with their benefactors, both shot through.

Though I walk through the valley of the shadow of death, I will not fear. Thou art with me.

Ethan cursed his selfishness and dove in, tearing his jacket off to escape its restraint. The chill rushed at him from all angles, and he fought the churning surf, impeded by drowning or dead bodies, struggling to get to that deeper current where the swiftness of the water would carry him to safety. He dove underwater and fought to outdistance the rifles. When he could go no further, he surfaced for breath. The water rained white around him in a hail of bullets. Choking in another breath, he thrashed under the surface and swam hard until suffocation forced him to emerge again. An island loomed ahead.

He coughed. His breathing constricted from the cold and tension. The day had been spent marching and fighting until exhaustion crept into every muscle. Horror tried to paralyze him, as he wrestled his way through a floating graveyard. Still, desperation propelled him forward.

The clay banks of the island rose before him. He lacked the strength to lift himself. A large hand grasped his collar and helped him to his feet. Stumbling over the narrow strip of land, he neared the opposite shore. Turning to thank his benefactor, he saw no one running the gauntlet with him.

Thy rod and thy staff, they comfort me.

Anticipating the water's weightlessness, he fell in again. The burning in his muscles cooled, though his breathing still labored. The current dragged him downstream. Here the channel ran stronger. He fought to keep his head above the surface.

"Jesus…" He called out to that unseen hand. Then water enfolded his head, washing away all light and sound.

ᘓᘐ

Army Hospital at Georgetown
October 23, 1861

Carrying one more pitcher into the ward, Marietta rehearsed the story in her mind of Rebekah, how the Bible heroine had watered camels for her Uncle Abraham's servant. How many camels were there? Ten in a caravan? How many gallons of water did it take to satisfy even one of those thirsty desert creatures? Rebekah had committed herself to hours of exhausting labor by offering to water the traveler's animals. Marietta prayed for the Biblical maiden's strength as she stopped at another bedside in the endless aisle, filling one more tin cup.

How could she not have compassion on these men, weak as boys, stretched out in pain, in strange surroundings so many miles from the caring faces of home? Her brother had been discharged, but she pressed on for those like him, though her arms ached into her neck and down her back. The water pitcher vigil was one tangible thing she could do. There were so many things she could not do, denied the privilege of nursing with the Sanitary Commission. She was too young, too unmarried, and too pretty, according to their requirements. But she could offer a cup of cold water. One Aaron and one Ethan at a time.

The Battle of Ball's Bluff and its influx of wounded had dominated talk the last two days, but the casualty lists left more questions than answers. Ethan's cavalry hadn't engaged, and yet, some wounded bore the butternut stitching and crossed swords of troopers.

Her own thirst parched her as she served others, and she licked dry lips with no relief. Her new pitcher was empty already, so she set it down on a windowsill to catch her breath.

She recalled the first weeks of Aaron's convalescence, how she'd made sure he had the best of medicine for his chronic pain. He still made regular trips to see her and the nurses here. Too bad he hadn't come today. Aaron would be the first to receive information via telegraph at the war department. Her father had secured him a desk position to satisfy his enlistment.

Then, a familiar buggy eased along the iron fence in front of the armory. Had the end of the day come already? A secret thrill awoke her tired limbs, and she bore her empty pitcher across the ward again, this time toward the exit. Shrugging out of her soiled apron and rolling it for the laundress's cauldron, she prayed that another Rebekah would take the night vigil.

And then she heard that voice—Aaron's—engaged in an animated conversation with Papa.

"Of all the bureaucracy!" her brother growled.

"These Habeas Corpus arrests have gotten out of hand." Papa's grave tone made her pause mid-stride.

"So, rather than checking his alibi, they place him under military arrest?"

"You have to figure, Aaron, your regiment was not among

those engaged. His story doesn't corroborate with the evidence."

"Who's story?"

The two swung around to face her. The haggard look on her father's face made her gasp. Aaron hopped out and joined her on the street. "Mari, we were just coming to take you home."

"Military arrest? What's going on?"

"No need for alarm, Mari."

Her father's placating tone made her want to fuss, but she kept her tongue.

"What's this about, Aaron? Tell me."

"The good news is Ethan is alive, and…."

She sank against the door, and Aaron helped her into the carriage. "Sit down. We'll explain everything."

As Aaron slid in beside her, Papa slapped the reins over the horses and they pulled away from the curb.

Her father looked back at her with concern. "Very well. She deserves to know."

"It seems our good friend has been arrested in the aftermath of battle. No formal charges have been filed."

"But why have they arrested him?"

"He was picked up by the border patrol." Aaron attempted a reassuring smile, but it only made her insides turn. "Surely he's been released by now. Surely."

"I don't understand. Why would they do this?"

Aaron shifted in his seat. His mouth puckered more than usual, even with the scar that ran laterally from his upper lip to his ear. "They think he's a spy, Mari."

She lurched forward in her seat and cried over the din of horses, creaking springs, and leather. "A spy?"

Her father slowed the rig and turned to her again. "I've spoken with Secretary Seward, and on my word, he was willing to sign an affidavit attesting to Ethan's loyalty. But Mari, this is my reputation on the line. If the boy isn't who he claims to be...."

Mari's heart clenched so hard in her chest she couldn't

breathe. She grasped Aaron's hand. *Please, Lord. Ethan would never betray us like this. Would he?*

ଔ

Ethan rubbed his eyes and surveyed the enclosure again. Stockade fencing with its imposing walls and sharp peaks drew a bleak picture of imprisonment around him. His body ached in every joint and muscle after the cataclysmic events of the last couple of days. He couldn't scale this height, even if he sprouted wings.

The small yard enclosed a handful of sullen figures with him. A wounded Confederate languished in one corner, his bloody bandages drawing flies and contemptuous looks from the others. Swollen, bruised facial features hinted at the brutality he'd suffered. For a moment, Ethan struggled to remember why he found himself at enmity with his former countrymen.

The jingle of keys drew his attention. The gate open and there stood a Union officer, Levi and Aaron Hamilton behind him.

Ethan rose on shaky legs and strode forward. The provost marshal motioned him through the gate and down a corridor of stockade to another enclosure. The Hamiltons closed rank, their boots drumming over the hard-packed dirt like a military tattoo.

The marshal bid Levi and Aaron to take two of the three campaign chairs situated in the middle of the space, then the man took his seat. Ethan was told to wait in the corner like a stray dog to be claimed.

Levi spoke first. "My son and I can offer character references for your prisoner. We'll vouch for his allegiance to the Union."

"Mr. Hamilton," the officer replied, "you should know it's not that simple. The detainee was apprehended in hostile border territory, carrying no military identification, no side-arms, not even wearing a regulation uniform, as you can see."

Aaron held his hands out as though slowing a runaway horse. "Whoa, now. Weren't there many such casualties after the conflict? With all due respect, sir, it was a rout. It's a miracle he survived at all between battle, the fifty-foot drop from the palisade, and all the reported drownings. Why has my friend been singled out, when others have been restored to their regiment?"

"I'll cut to the chase. Your friend's Virginia dialect sets him apart from our boys. We've had enough of border loyalists turning secesh as soon as our backs are turned. You've no idea! A single spy can cost entire campaigns." The marshal glared side-long at Ethan. "If I were you, I'd think twice before sullying your good name with riff raff."

Ethan's innards burned at the accusation. God knew, that last battle had nearly killed him. He'd served to the last of his strength, and almost drown in the rain-swollen Potomac. Now the Grand Army of the Republic had dismissed him as a traitor.

Levi rose to his full height before the runtish commander. He reached into his waistcoat pocket and produced a paper bearing the State Department letterhead.

"It's a shame that this young man's service these past six months and the witness of two civil servants aren't enough for you. This soldier should be decorated rather than denigrated. Nevertheless, I have a signed document from the Secretary of State releasing your prisoner." Levi produced the document with a snap of paper. "You can either release this prisoner, or face court martial. What will it be?"

The marshal read the order for himself, and nearly stumbled backward on his cocked chair. He fumbled to right himself. "Very well. I'll have him restored to his regiment right away, sir."

Levi flashed a smile. "We'll see to that. You need only sign his release."

Ethan straightened, fixed his rumpled clothing, and followed them out of the garrison without a backward glance. It wasn't until they were out of earshot of the guards that Levi paused to look Ethan over. "Were you mistreated in any way, son?"

"No, sir." Indignity heated Ethan's face as they emerged into the afternoon sun. But one glance ahead at the carriage and its occupant told him his humiliations had just begun.

Ethan approached the vehicle, avoiding contact with the fair gaze peering from the window. He skirted the conveyance door and climbed aboard at the rear baggage compartment. From the corner of his eye he noticed Marietta turn in her seat to follow his movement. A quick self-assessment only strengthened his resolve. Mud saturated his clothing, and as he ran his fingers through his hair, they tangled on silt and leaves. He must have been a sight. He folded his arms over his chest, covering the bruised remnants of his pride.

Mr. Hamilton snapped the reins and it seemed an eternity passed as they drove along the military boulevard.

Aaron, seated directly behind him, opened the canvas flap between them. "You must be famished."

Mr. Hamilton raised his voice over the street noise. "Why don't you have dinner with us?"

Ethan turned around to face them. "No, sir. Thank you. I'd best report for duty."

He stole a glance at Marietta, and she quickly cast her eyes down. Ethan turned back around, too, and watched the road churn up a cloud of dust behind them.

This wasn't the romantic scene she must have envisioned when next they should see each other. And he certainly wasn't the hero she deserved, hunched over and covered in nothing but a common undershirt, suspenders, and torn uniform pants. Two days' growth of stubble covered his normally clean-shaven jaw. He must make the perfect picture of a scoundrel.

But a traitor? A ruse?

His blood chilled like the river water that had nearly claimed him. Could they believe that about him? That he would use her family to sell military secrets to the Confederates? Lonesomeness beat a slow thrum through his chest. The Hamiltons were the only semblance of family he had left. If they were to lose faith in him now....

The Union encampment surrounded the road on either side of the carriage. Tethered horses as far as the eye could see foretold the cavalry divisions. Soon enough Aaron pointed out their regimental flag, and the carriage rolled to a stop. Ethan let himself fall from the baggage board. His body ached as if he had fallen over a cliff. But then, he had. He tried to hide his aching muscles and halting gait from Marietta. He'd rather suffer untold agonies than let her regard him as weak. He wasted no effort on lengthy goodbyes but forced a smile with his handshake and thanks to the Hamilton men, and a slow nod at Mari. Then he trudged along to report to duty.

He'd moved halfway down the avenue of tent rows toward headquarters, when he heard a slight commotion behind him. A faint voice cried out.

"Ethan? Please, wait."

He turned his head, though he kept moving away with determined strides. Marietta gathered her skirts, padding her little feet in swift succession to meet him. Behind her, Aaron ambled toward him, likely sent as chaperon. Ethan stopped and let her overtake him, still uncertain of her intent. His throat constricted on the hope that welled up within him, but he couldn't trust what his heart longed for. After all, if Devon—his own flesh and blood—had believed the worst of him, why wouldn't she? He pressed his lips in a firm line and braced himself.

When she caught up to him, her arms enfolded him, and her breath gasped against his chest, launching waves of astonishment through him. How could she still care for him? He closed his eyes and returned her embrace, knowing he was a thief to partake of affections he didn't deserve. For that blissful moment, he savored her sweet scent and warm nearness. He cast a glance at Aaron, who'd stayed at a distance to grant them privacy.

"Ethan, please, won't you come back with us? The army can do without you for a night, surely."

"I reckon they can," he shook his head. "But I can't do without them. This army's all I've got. I'm determined to stick it out, even if it kills me."

"Don't say that!" She touched his lips as though she could catch the omen before it sprouted black wings. "You're *not* going to die!"

He searched her face, still distrustful that she should waste such sentiment on him. Her sincerity blasted away at his cynicism, one glistening tear at a time slipping down her pale cheek. He answered her the only way he knew how.

"Pray for me, Mari."

He squeezed her hand and let her slip from his grasp. Hollow, aching, empty, he turned from her and resumed his march toward the tent line.

Deliberate footsteps forewarned Ethan of her dogged pursuit. He braced himself again, this time clenching his teeth against her tenderness. Her hand slipped into his, turning him around to face her. His vulnerability could not be hidden from her this time, and he rued his boyish weakness. This was what he'd feared, and he seemed helpless to thwart the emotion rising in him that her affection had unleashed.

Gazing into her eyes, he longed to claim her as his own. But she was too fine for him, too cultured. She belonged to a class he could never attain to now, without his father's largess. He was a common soldier, not even an officer. Maybe if he rose in rank?

"I love you, Marietta."

Had he said it? Her nearness set his heart pounding in his ears, and those eyes, gazing at him so longingly, so full of trust and hope.... He couldn't fight it anymore. Right there, regardless of the army surrounding them, and even her brother watching, he kissed her. It was a desperate exchange, his quaking and volatile passions erupting past his reserve. Her silken locks gave way beneath his urgent stroking, he, pressing her soft face to his. She returned his kiss until they both broke away gasping for breath, for words.

"I know I've no right to stake a claim on you, Mari. I have no fortunes to offer you."

He tried to rein in his desperation but could sooner stop a herd of charging horses. "I know I've no right to ask, but tell me, Mari.

Will you still wait for me?"

He waited for a terrifying eternity to see if his impetuous sentiments were mutual.

She threw her head on his chest, her arms pulling him nearer. He buried his face in the piles of her locks, savoring the sweet scent of lavender sachet. His heart soared.

She released her hold on him and stepped back. "You mustn't idolize me so."

He winced at her words. "I-I understand."

"I will wait for you, Ethan, however long it takes. My heart is yours."

Calm strength returned to him at her words, the pride of hard-won ground bolstering him.

Had she seen the change in him, then? He'd grown from the unproven youth of last spring until he stood before her, a man. Her response to him indicated that she, too, had matured.

"You're beautiful," he said, tracing the exposed skin on her shoulder to the back of her neck, wishing he could press finery and gemstones there. He vowed to himself that he would. She would have engagement jewels if it took a month of Sundays to save for it.

She blushed and bowed her head, peering up sweetly at his attentions.

"I wish this wasn't goodbye." His hand nestled in the hair at the nape of her neck, and he pulled her face to him, whispering in her ear, "May I kiss you again?"

She lifted her chin and received his goodbye kiss.

Her lips' silky press still sent pulses of liquid fire through him, long after he left her standing there waving after him on the dirt road.

ઊ

Aaron gave her a dubious look when she joined him near the carriage. Marietta's head swam, and she barely registered anything beyond the masculine smell which still clung to her of the trooper she already missed. Before she could step up into the carriage, her father drew up alongside her. She turned to him and met with his scowl. The swirls of pleasure surrounding her went instantly still.

"I see you said your farewells."

She wondered if Papa could hear her quaking pulse, it beat so loud in her ears. She maintained a calm tone in her reply. "We did, yes."

His nose quirked as though an insect had stung him, but nothing else moved on his solid, stalwart frame. She resisted the urge to swallow and met his gaze evenly, though not unblinking.

"That was quite a *generous* farewell."

Then she swallowed. Just to be sure her voice wouldn't waver in her reply. "As he returns to battle, I wanted to be sure he carries the assurance of my full support."

"I see." Her father folded his hands behind his back. "Is this your custom with every soldier leaving for war?" One brow quirked up, but there was no hint of droll teasing in it.

Mari wanted to drop her gaze, but she couldn't tear herself from the glimmer of restrained wrath in her father's coffee-brown eyes. She started to defend herself, but he cut her off.

"Because if it is, you are done *ministering* at the hospital. And you are overdue at finishing school, young lady."

She wanted with all her heart to assure her Papa of her compliance, and almost gushed out a promise. But she stopped, convicted by the lie before it left her lips. Instead, she spoke her heart with quiet force.

"I give my heart to whom it chooses, Papa. And all of the schools and disciplines you can throw at me will not change that."

A muscle twitched in his cheek, and his eyes turned umber. Was it sadness that colored them darker? He helped her into the carriage without another word and closed the door after her.

Chapter 21

Mama and Papa had given Marietta a choice. If she put away her volunteer work at the hospital, they would be willing to negotiate finishing school. They'd finally agreed that perhaps she needn't cross an ocean. After all, there were opportunities opening to young ladies of breeding and character right here in the states. Female Seminaries such as Oberlin welcomed girls of her station. But beyond a cloistered environment and a strict moral standard, what Mari longed for most was a chance to use her influence to help others. An education equal to that offered to men might be the perfect solution.

And only one institution offered a lady that chance.

Elmira Female College in New York State had become the talk among the more progressive of Papa's acquaintances. Once again, the Senator from New York, an Auburn man himself, proved a divine acquaintance. He had spoken well to Papa of the institution. Their abolitionist ties had made them closer allies than mere political cronies. "Henry" as William Seward's closest friends called him, offered to pen a letter of introduction for Marietta. She thanked Providence to have such a powerful ally as Lincoln's Secretary of State. Her parents warmed to the notion of Marietta earning an education, most likely in hopes of tempering her strong-willed ways.

The day arrived when she received a letter from Dr. Augustus

Cowles, Elmira College's President. Her hopes deflated when she learned that she would have to pass a rigorous exam before enrollment. Not to be defeated, she asked Papa for a tutor. And Papa, most likely at her mother's suggestion, arranged for Mr. Hastings, Aaron's accomplished musician friend, to fit the bill. His recent return from abroad made convenient timing.

To pass a long winter's evening, Mr. Hastings escorted her to the opera, also no doubt at Mama's suggestion. Mari had managed to keep her smile in place while the bookish young man lectured on about the act's history and recitative. Keeping her from enjoying the actual performance, his monotone overshadowed all. If only Ethan had accompanied her, all would have been divine.

As Hastings drove her home, a dark wave washed over her, only compounded by the dim alleys passing by the window of the coach. The deep shadows and ragged pedestrians gripped her heart with inexplicable sorrow.

Mr. Hastings could offer her many things—a fine house, the polished life of the gentry, lavish evening wear, glittering jewels. And nights out on the town like this had been, sheltered inside his carriage, insulated from the poor and underprivileged who filled the streets. Before she had volunteered at the soldier's hospital, the theater had been her only destination past seven o'clock in the evening. But now, with the cries of wounded men still ringing in her ears, she grasped to know to which world she belonged.

Ethan filled her thoughts with his less-than-polished presentation. His rough charm. His unassuming heroism. He'd done the impossible in returning her dear maid's son. How she missed Tilly. How she longed for Ethan. He could offer her so much more than mere material comforts. He would surely support and advance her desire to champion those of lesser privilege in this world. For it seemed his passion, as well.

Hastings's carriage ascended the road, and her house now in sight, she warmed at the sight of the lamp glowing on the porch, lit for her. The coach slowed and rolled to a stop, and the footman took his time getting to the door. Her escort shifted in his seat beside her, his hand finding hers in the close interior. His touch felt clammy, and she cringed.

"Miss Hamilton—Marietta—we've been spending many wonderful occasions in one another's company, and-and I would be pleased if…" He moved closer to her, his narrow shoulders forming a barricade blocking the door. Her stomach shrank as he leaned in for a kiss.

"Mari?" A most fortunate intrusion hailed from outside. *Aaron.* Thank God. Hastings flung the door open and stepped down, offering his arm to help her alight. She took Aaron's proffered hand instead. Nodding a prim good night to her tutor, she drew herself up the stairs and slipped in through the door.

"Looks like I came out just in time."

Mari nodded. "Thank you."

Wasting no time on explanations that wouldn't change her parent's decree, she turned and ascended to her room where she prepared for bed. Tilly's companionship had given her comfort through the loneliness of many a winter evening. For a moment, she wished Mama would come and tuck her in tonight like when she was a little girl. But she was no longer a little girl.

Splashing floral scented wash water over her face, she prayed. Anguished words spilled out, and in return, a sense of calm settled on her. After toweling off, she slipped into her chemise, and peace like mist surrounded her again.

A few moments of reading her Bible fed her hungry soul. But her heart yearned for something more still. She may have assented to Hastings as a tutor, but she hadn't promised to stop writing to the one who owned her heart. Her letter to Ethan would have been fraught with the thistles of worn flesh if not for the help of scripture. The words she longed to share at last formulated on the tablet of her mind.

My Dearest Ethan,

I pray daily for your safety, while I long for an end to this war. I thank our Lord for answers thus far, counting ourselves blessed to be spared the ravages all around us. I consider that rather than my hand holding yours, it is One more powerful. Rather than My adoring eye beholding you, it is the ever-watchful Master who attends you.

With this I choose to comfort myself. But it is your comfort which consumes me. What can I say to encourage you in these times? This world is passing. The Word stands when all else fails, so I offer the only comfort I have found. Remain in Him, Ethan. He will keep you hidden under the shadow of His wings.

"But we had the sentence of death, that we should not trust in ourselves, but in God which raiseth the dead." II Corinthians 1:9

We have been chosen to share in His kingdom which has no end, no death and no decay. He offers us this inheritance through His resurrection. We cannot fail!

My prayer for you is that you would be encouraged by the hope that is in us, Christ Himself, the Hope of Glory!

With all devotion,
Your Marietta

 css&

Army of Northern Virginia
Spring 1862

Devon sat alone on a shady knoll outside J.E.B. Stuart's headquarters, slumped against the trunk of a massive white pine, his latest vexation jabbing at any hope of peace. He rubbed his eyes and inhaled the sweet scent of the pine needles carpeting the ground but refused to give in to sleep.

Stuart had abandoned the Shenandoah, leaving its defense to General Jackson. Federal armies even now threatened to pick clean the bread basket of the Confederacy.

Of course, Stuart had his orders to scout for General Johnston on the Peninsula in defense of the Confederate capital. Besides, destroying that Yankee supply train at Manassas Gap Railroad *had* been a grand escapade. Consuming the supplies and burning what remained served fitting retribution on the Yankees for invading his Valley. His blanket rolls bulging with delicacies, Devon conceded that riding to Hades itself with General Stuart might prove profitable.

Now with battle lines drawn all around the James River, Devon faced another year of war. Though the Federals had come within twenty miles of Richmond, Jackson's victories held the Valley. *They'd whip the Yanks before they had a chance to pluck so much as a blade of grass back home.*

Home. His mind retraced the acres, the barns, the paths. Old times, happier days when he'd had the constant companionship of his closest friend.

At last his thoughts found rest, and Devon succumbed to the dull, heavy fleece overtaking him. His chin sagged to his chest, and his eyelids grew darker, heavier.

A bugle blast jolted him. Before he was fully awake he was on his feet and had found his mount. Mechanically, he began the routine of saddling up alongside hundreds of cavaliers.

He nudged the trooper beside him. "Where to now?"

"The devil knows. Maybe reconnoitering Abe's privy."

Cid protested as Devon led him out of his tie. Devon swung up and joined the swarm of riders forming double columns. He spied Walt Thompson and rode up on his heels.

Walt spun around, his brows twisted. "Oh, it's you, Dev. Word is, we're moving out."

"Retreating?"

"No. Johnston's been bad-hurt. President Davis just instated a new leader, Bobby Lee, to assume field command."

"So, where's Jeb taking us?"

"Your guess is as good as mine." Walt shrugged, and spurred away. Ahead, orders came straight from the lips of Stuart himself.

The monotonous landscape took him past wooded roads that smelled of bog, drenched in the humidity of early June. Each pitch of Cid's gait rocked him like a cradle. It brought him back to square rays of sun, pouring through the latticework of Mama's rose trellis. He hadn't been truly sleeping then, or he wouldn't have remembered the blissful scene, or her soft hand soothing the hair over his brow. She'd rocked him slowly on her lap in the porch rocker. Her gentle humming floated on the air, reminding him of birdsong, sunshine, joy. The rhythm of her swinging held a pleasant cadence that seemed to go on forever, back and forth, without interruption. He relaxed his guard and abandoned himself to its comfort.

Cid stumbled over a rock on the road, and her arms gave way beneath him. He landed on his back, the impact knocking the wind out of him.

Devon fought for breath, panic burning in his lungs, while tall equine legs stepped over him, just missing his body, his face. Panting, he caught his breath and sat up. A hand extended, and he took it. The dizzy ascent brought his recollection back.

Mama had gathered him up with her beside Ethan, one hand about his shoulders, the other under his knees. She'd stifled his protests with maternal cooing. "There, now. All better." And his twin had patted him on the arm, echoing their mama's words.

He blinked, and his surroundings came back together. He stood beside his horse in the middle of a field as hundreds of cavaliers trotted past him. One of his gauntleted hands clutched mane, the other gripped reins and pommel, ready to pull himself up. No mother, no twin, no familiarity or comfort. Even the helping hand had passed indistinguishable into the forms dashing past. He was alone. By God, he was completely alone. He had taken for granted that Ethan would always be there.

His eyes burned.

Why had his brother left him? It wasn't for a slave, as he had so often accused, or even for a girl. Rather, Ethan had drawn allegiances with an invisible God when his own flesh and blood lay bleeding in a field, alone.

His best friend in the world had broken his trust and his heart. Right up to the night of his betrayal, a year ago on their last birthday, he believed Ethan would come to his senses. But it was too late.

Fixing his face like flint, he climbed onto his steed's back and sat tall as the road slipped beneath them. If he was to be alone, so be it. Never again would he allow another's disloyalty to pierce him, for he needed nothing and no one.

ଓଃ

Late Summer 1862
Union encampment

It was now late summer, and Ethan had been at war for over a year. Politics replaced the failed peninsula campaign in the newspapers as the Union army pursued Lee ever northward in clever maneuvers leading them away from Richmond. Victory had slipped from them again with the first hint of a cool evening breeze.

Marietta's letter had provided weeks of succor to one homesick soldier. He read and reread her words while others received news from mother, father or brother. Hers was his sole correspondence. On this August evening, upon a rare occasion when the troopers were given a few hours respite, Ethan settled himself beside a quiet stream, half in sunlight, half in shade, and produced a bottle of ink and a nib from his pack. A soft wind rustled the paper laid across his Bible. He leaned against the broad white pine at his back and pondered his response.

Beyond, the drilling infantry plowed the field, their lines crisp and angular. The snap of regimental flags stroked the scene with color, drawing his eye to their fluid movement. In battle his heart would skip a beat at its sight. It rallied him but invoked a shudder as well.

Heaven and Earth shall pass away....

The past year's defeats raised serious questions. Far and away, the rebels were whipping them in every major contest. The Seven Days' Battle was one more instance of Union commanders' ineptitude against brilliant southern strategists. It could shake his theology if he allowed it.

Defending the downtrodden, releasing the captive,

proclaiming liberty had assured him of victory no less than an Old Testament epic. Oh, how the fervor of those misguided sentiments ached in his chest now.

Did God cast lots in war? Jeff Davis could profess Christ as much as Lincoln. In fact, Ethan recalled Thomas Jackson's religious zeal from school days, and had heard of the pious reputation of the new Confederate commander Robert E. Lee, too.

The North had General Ben Butler who offered escaped slaves "sanctuary" by putting them to work digging trenches.

Ethan fought to free the slaves, or so he had believed, even when no one had made that declaration official to date. But did Moses wage war with Pharaoh to emancipate the Israelites? Did Nehemiah organize a coup to overthrow the captivity? Did Jesus resort to insurrection with Barabbas to free Israel from Roman tyranny? Bearing the right arm of the flesh against their enemies didn't jibe with the examples given in scripture. Even David, a man after God's own heart but a man of war, was denied the privilege of building God's house because of his bloody hands. The battle—the *real* warfare was in the heavenlies.

The pen rested heavy in his hand while his mind wrestled for words to say. Should he feign encouragement in return for her sincerity? Might he find a way of expressing his heart without imposing his human shortcomings?

Dear Marietta,

I have long contemplated a reply worthy of your last letter. Your courage inspires my admiration. Please think no less of me if I share my misgivings. I entrust them to you and God alone.

I have no more love for the systems of this fallen world, North, South, Union or Confederacy. All are the filthy rags of man's righteousness. Does God call us to fight for rights on this earth, or is it better to be wronged? Thanks to you I have taken a stand on slavery. But to kill over it? Do you think I am treading upon something far more sacred in bearing arms against some child's father, some woman's son, for the cause of liberty?

I know I was impetuous to enlist. But I am here for the

duration, or until the Lord sees fit.

As I write to you, I watch a field of men in martial review, and what a spectacle it is! Can I describe the swell of my heart, my affection for these impossible heroes? I used to think I could win you by my courage or vainglory. Now I wish that we were both still unaffected and naive to the hardships of war, and I grow impatient with these circumstances which keep our courtship at bay. I wonder why you go on when yours is a choice of the will, and mine, a duty-bound lot. I wish you would find insulation from this mess as you deserve. I long for the day when I can reward your patience in a manner worthy of you.

Until that day I am devotedly yours,
Ethan

Chapter 22

Maryland on the Potomac
August 28, 1862

Marietta's studies passed before unseeing eyes, while an increasing sense of urgency drew her focus. The movement of armies toward the capital had built a slow tension over days and weeks, almost dulling her to the approach of battle. She left her book open on the secretary desk and went to the front door, seeking news, perhaps a mid-day edition of the paper. Instead, the mail arrived.

One envelope bore a military stamp and Ethan's familiar script. She carried it through the house and up to her room, all her faculties resting on his words though she should have been applying herself to her studies. Reverberations in the distance lent an eerie immediacy to his words. At the climax of the letter, a deep bass percussion rattled the window panes. Reaching to inspect the glass, she scanned the horizon southward toward the sound of the storm. Puffy white cumulus clouds filled the sky—a perfect summer afternoon. The parchment trembled in her hand. More indistinct rumbling. A groan as though the heavens cried out.

The letter dangling, she confronted the evidence. This was no storm. Those were guns, and close by.

Fire lit through her. She scurried down the stairs and stumbled over the last step. "Saints spare us!"

A vision of Ethan clutching his side, doubled over in his

saddle, invaded her thoughts.

Her breath hitched. “Mama!” She made her way to the sewing parlor and staggered in, holding the letter pressed tight to her ribs. Her mother’s eyes widened, and her brow drew lines of concern. The pane rattled again at the window, sending Mari scuffling to her mother’s side.

Setting aside her needlework, Mama studied her.

“This is more than a poor grade on Mr. Hastings’ latest exam.” Mama’s hand reached for the paper, but Mari jerked it back.

“Young lady, I’ll have that, *now*.”

Mari surrendered, praying Mama wouldn't tear it, or her heart, to pieces. Mama’s eyes scanned the pages, her blue gaze widening. At last, she set the script down.

A thousand terrors tortured Mari's mind, searching Mama's inscrutable face.

“You love him, don’t you?”

Her mother’s words stunned her terrors silent for a moment. Mari nodded.

Mama shook her head. “He’s why you volunteered at the hospital, isn’t he? It was never about your brother.”

She looked down at her hands folded in her lap. The stifling summer air burned in her cheeks, her bodice, her very being. But she didn’t deny the truth. Instead, she braced for the verdict, all the while thinking she wouldn’t change a thing she’d done.

Mama considered her with a long perusal. “Look at you. You aren’t eating properly. You’re sick with worry. What are your father and I to do?”

Marietta could hold back no longer. A sob caught in her throat. “Why don’t you approve of him?”

Her mother cupped her face in firm but tender hands. “This is not about him, Marietta. This is about you. Your father and I have not conducted this season of your life with wisdom.”

Her tears wouldn’t be restrained but ran down her cheeks and nose. "What would you have me to do, mother? Put social standing in higher regard than my convictions?"

"Marietta, when a woman marries, her role is to be supportive of her husband. His leadership, his convictions. You must get used to sacrificing your high ideals."

"Ethan loves me because of my ideals."

Her mother's eyes flashed. "Oh, so he loves you, too, does he?"

"Yes, he does," Mari replied, caressing the letter with her thumb.

Mama's sigh hinted of weariness, or—dare Marietta hope—capitulation? "You'll probably do as you please regardless of what your father and I tell you. But it will be to your ruination."

Mama grasped the hand holding the letter, her contact soft and unexpectedly comforting. "Before we consider where this infatuation is going, first we must be sure he survives. Let us pray."

The two bowed their heads together even as the sound of cannon blasted its way into their parlor.

Marietta clutched her free arm about her middle. Her throat constricted, making prayer impossible. It became too much to bear, staving off calamities with the seeming futility of mere words.

"He's going to die, mother! And it's all my fault, because I've gone against your will."

"Hush, child," Mama soothed the hair trailing down Mari's cheek, wet from tears, her voice serene and her own eyes moist. "It's not your fault. The passion of war would sweep any girl into its whirlwind. And I suppose you could do much worse than Ethan Sharpe."

Hope settled into places where only a tender mother and a wise, merciful Father could reach. At that moment the din of the battle settled into a curious silence. It was as though an acoustic shadow had passed over their home.

September 1862

Confederate Cavalry

Devon rode with Lee's advance guard two days out of Chantilly and into Frederick, Maryland, before he fully knew his commander's intentions. High from victory again at Second Manassas and crossing the Potomac under the light of a romantic moon, Devon contemplated amid the cool Northern waters that the impossible could indeed come true. The strategy which had spared Richmond from siege suggested forces providential. The laugh was on Ethan now, and on all those who supposed they fought a holy crusade for the North. By all accounts, God seemed to be fighting—and winning—on Devon's side.

The first stop on their moonlight invasion was a town called Urbana. His cavalry division officers called for assembly in an old schoolhouse. Devon expected tables with unfurled maps and men bent in somber discussions of strategy. Instead, he was taken under the spell of sights and sounds quite apart from protocol. At his approach he was greeted by a regimental band's departure from martial mien to a more secular air. Couples gracing a makeshift dance floor swirled past the windows. He and Walt Thompson tethered their mounts outside and joined the party in progress.

Watching these imperious officers transform under the influence of the fair sex merited a good laugh. But the spectacle soon provoked Devon to participation.

The Maryland ladies appeared fair enough for all their misguided loyalties. Politics certainly hadn't spoiled their beauty any. He stood off to the side to survey the field with Walt and used the moment for a glimpse into his shaving mirror. A douse of pocket pomade fixed the ebony hair falling over his eyes, swiping it to the side. Devon then eschewed his saber and pistol for a more potent side-arm—his silver flask—and imbibed liquid boldness. Letting it wash in a slow burn down his throat, he contemplated the field of wallflowers gathered near the musicians. And then, two ladies stepped in from the torrid September evening, unescorted. Despite the myriad flags and banners on display, providence had directed this tall redhead and her brunette companion to step beneath theirs. No doubt a sign. Devon gave Walt a grin and a nod, and with another swig, the lieutenant led the captain into the charge.

Devon swaggered past the young ladies, and with his most beguiling grin, he stopped beside them, lingering so close that they couldn't ignore him.

"You ladies seem unruffled by invasion."

Blushes colored the two fair faces. The taller one with the red locks cast a gaze at him so direct Devon's own cheeks warmed.

"If you're as daring as they say, why have you waited so long?"

Impressed at once, Devon focused on this sassy-tongued creature. Her curls rolled about her shoulders as she wagged her head at him, seemingly daring him to come up with a retort. Devon would not disappoint.

"Our reputation precedes us, Captain." He grinned at Walt. The girl's animated expression sent a rise through him like Champagne bubbles in a glass. "You can believe every word, it's all true."

"Ah, so Stuart's horses fly, and breathe fire?"

The redhead's demure friend covered her mouth to stifle a chortle.

Devon quirked a brow. Contending with a woman of considerable height and sharp wit, a lesser man would have been intimidated. But Devon didn't flinch.

"No, that's all fancy. The truth is, we're immortal."

"Invincible," Walt corrected him with a nudge and straight face.

"Deity." Devon gave a nod of finality.

The brunette giggled and raised her eyes to meet the emboldened gaze of Walt Thompson. He offered his hand and led her to the dance floor as introductions were voiced breathlessly over a lively reel. But Devon didn't ask his companion to dance. He had other ideas.

"What brought you out tonight?" He stood so close to her that she had to look straight up at him, even from her impressive stature. He was one of few men in the room taller than she, and he wanted her to take in the fact. He pressed in, using the crowded floor as an excuse. "Are you a sympathizer?"

She turned her chin away with a sly smile. "I sympathize with whoever suits me."

"Do I suit you tonight?"

She narrowed her jade eyes and took a step away. "I haven't decided."

"I'll help make up your mind." He gathered her in his arms. "And not just for a dance. I'll have you taking the oath before I'm through with you." He allowed a hint of amusement to show through quirked lips. And he could tell she was not immune, despite her cool veneer. The essence of leather, pomade, and liquor surrounded him, and he figured if his wit failed to intoxicate her senses, then he would win her with his other masculine charms. One glance into her mesmerized gaze and Devon could tell it was working.

"Shall we?" He looked toward the dance floor as a waltz had just begun.

She fluttered coy lashes and nodded. "This doesn't mean I'm a Bonnie Belle yet."

"It's only a dance."

Leading her into the triplet rhythm of the music, their movements melded together with fluid grace, and the contact set his blood ablaze. Every direction he turned her brought visual reminders of his army's invading presence. The rustle of air upturned by dancing feet set the rows of flags and banners to motion. Sabers hanging beside them anchored the rippling cloth with steel. Proud officers surrounded them in long tunics with flashing brass buttons, yellow sashes defining trim waists tapering from broad shoulders and deep chests. Devon knew he cut such a figure and aimed to use his considerable appeal to every advantage.

The height of the band's pitch swelled to contemporary tunes well played.

Devon led the young lady through each lively step until her breath rose and fell like a doe under the hounds. She appraised him without the fluttering lashes or coquettish smiles of her peers. Her expression was enigmatic, with the slightest curve of her lips. The mystery of her inclinations intrigued him.

The fact that they had not yet introduced themselves only occurred to him as another song drew to an end.

Then, before he could lead her to the refreshment table and speak more than an offer of a cool drink, a sound erupted. Distance-muted artillery checked the altitude of the climbing festivities. Closer rifles picked up the call to arms until all music ceased to a sound more infectious than the fair sigh of dismay at arm's length.

Officers departed in a dash for their side-arms while the bewildered ladies looked on.

Devon bowed, hurried out the door, and retrieved his horse. Mounting, he was apprehended by an urge to look back before spurring his thoroughbred to flight. The red-haired girl was standing off to one side, away from the trampling hooves, her expression earnest and beseeching as she waved to him. Devon reined over and extended his hand to hers.

"What is your name?" he asked over the terrific din of horsemen riding off to battle.

She hesitated, but threw her other hand in his, lest he leave. "Gwen--Gwendolyn May Harris. Will I see you again, Lieutenant…?"

"Lieutenant Sharpe—Devon. Yes, I believe directly, if I know Stuart. He never leaves a party without dancing with all the pretty girls. You'd better hide from him, because your card is filled tonight, Miss Harris."

He tipped his hat and galloped off, rueful that Cid blew dust on her lovely rust-colored dress.

A hundred riders thundered beside him in the direction of the battle, appetites whetted by the sounds of skirmishing. Upon discovering that there was no enemy left to engage, one by one he and his fellow troopers returned to a ballroom suspended on baited breath. Walt resumed with his brunette, but Devon nearly ruptured a blood vessel hunting down his spirited auburn companion. *Miss Gwendolyn May Harris.*

Dismay set in to think that she'd given up on his return. And then, he found her occupied by a senior staff officer. She returned his fawning with polite attention. Devon sauntered right up and juxtaposed himself between them. Her relief to see him was unmistakable. Devon grinned.

"I see you've met my Gwen," Devon said, lifting her hand to his lips. "Thank you for entertaining her in my absence."

The officer's protests followed them as they rushed toward the door. He led on until they'd slipped through clusters of cavaliers regaling ladies with exaggerated tales of battle. He didn't stop until they caught their breath outside in the mild night air. Her hand clutching his trembled, and Devon shed his cavalry coat. He placed it over her slender shoulders, drawing the collar snug about her milky white neck. Her jade eyes glowed at him.

"I told you I'd be back," he said softly. "You haven't sworn the oath yet."

Her musical laughter filled him with wonder. How could it be that she had followed him out into the lawn where the crickets' song climbed in contrast to the distancing sound of the party? Where torches glimmered, illuminating a line of sycamore trees at the perimeter of the schoolyard. It was all too fine to be real. And yet there she was, on his arm, gazing at him with those gem-like eyes. Devon ambled toward the dappled white tree-line. And she followed without the slightest hesitation to where other girls would shrink back.

They came to settle beneath one of the pale trees with a trunk-span wider than the two of them standing side by side. It would completely conceal them, if he was of the mind to want privacy. For the moment, he took her hand, and stood before her, committing the contours of her face to memory.

Her study bathed him in unexpected sentiment, placing on hold the kiss he had been ready to steal. No girl had ever looked at him like that. Nobody had ever let him that close. Except for his twin. And then, even Ethan had chosen to leave.

For a wavering moment, rejection taunted him. *She'll leave you, too. Just wait and see. She may want you now, but it won't last. It never does.*

The spark of passion filled her gaze as she looked into his eyes, then lowered them to his lips. What did this lovely creature see in him? A cavalier at the zenith of his youth, a conquering hero at the height of a grand moment in history? Or an empty young man, longing to be filled with love and tenderness. He swallowed, drawn to her despite the protest of caution in his aching heart.

Gwen's lashes batted like flags of surrender. Devon leaned in, first absorbing her warm, sweet breath before engaging. Then he tasted her lips, her savor fiery like whiskey. He did not stop at the first taste. An ache swelled in his breast with this sweet connection to another. It hadn't been since Ethan left that he'd allowed another into the hard circle of his heart. Devon struggled for a moment with his desperate loneliness, and almost considered letting her go. He gazed deeply into her eyes. They were beautifully formed and held a substance he'd never seen in the gaze of a girl. He'd cement a claim on her. Make her swear to it.

"Take my vow." All teasing had vanished from him.

She regarded him, her mouth a circle of curiosity. Still, she nodded consent to his conceit.

"Say 'I, Gwendolyn May Harris, do solemnly swear'. . ."

She laughed. "I do solemnly swear. It's a terrible habit, but redheads have legendary tempers."

He sobered her with a steely look. "…that I shall never avow my allegiance…."

She shook her head and frowned but repeated his words.

"—with any personal interest other than…."

"Must I really take a pledge?"

No matter how she might laugh, he didn't budge. He'd have that promise, to know she wouldn't leave him.

"Say, 'I pledge to Devon Sharpe, and his allegiances, as long as I shall live.'"

She smiled with more than amusement. "I don't remember all of that."

His hands encompassing her waist, he squeezed. "Just say you will."

She danced under his tickling touch. "Okay! I will." The words rolled from her tongue with the languid diction of pleasure.

He kissed her then, until she grew slack in his embrace. He relented, and she gazed at him under hooded eyes, her head sagging onto his shoulder.

Sweeping her neck with a caress of lips, he withdrew inches from her ear. "I will not disrespect you, Gwen."

He held her up against the silvery bark between kisses that were as firm as his grip about her. "May I have the privilege of calling on you properly, and courting you, Gwendolyn May Harris? I want to go to your father and mother, and—"

"No, Devon." She held her hand to his chest and pushed him away. "You can't do that."

"The devil, I can't!" He nearly hit the tree with his fist. "Why not?" A boyish susceptibility stole over his voice, and he rued it, but he had to know.

"They're not southern-minded. They wouldn't approve."

Disappointment pierced him for a full second, but he fought past it. "They wouldn't approve? I guess they wouldn't approve of this either." He pressed his lean body against hers with more intention than before. She neither flinched nor resisted but received his advances with a trembling openness.

He shook himself out of his trance of desire. "I'm sorry."

"No need," she whispered, and returned his kiss in the same

manner.

Chapter 23

Sharpsburg, Maryland
Union Encampment
September 17, 1862

Sunset filled the Maryland sky, igniting swirls of smoke into fiery vortexes above the fields of Sharpsburg. Antietam Creek ran like a red ribbon through fields of harvest, making Ethan question the disposition of its color. Was it a reflection of the sky in its last spasms of light, or did it derive its blush from more nefarious sources? Before Ethan followed the question to its conclusion, darkness mercifully closed over the land. Twilight performed what had in effect happened to his mind hours ago, the dimming, the numbness, and the camouflaging of too many unthinkable realities on this godforsaken field.

Soldiers turned in beside cheerless firesides. They lay on the grass, under trees, and beside fences, and it was hard to discern who merely slept from those who would never again rise. Others stood alone like him, looking on wide-eyed at the world of shadow. Lanterns swung in the distance, the chip and grind of shovels indicating the burial detail's business even at this hour. Death did not rest here.

Ethan shut his eyes for the first time in many moments and their dryness burned. Exhaustion hit him with a thousand tiny blows, his cramped muscles protesting under the weight of saddle blanket and riding gear. He had just finished tending Nimbus and settled his tack on its rail. He then headed out to find relief in the form of a cool drink or a warm blanket. Before rest could come to his body, he'd pray. After a minute of wandering, with silent prayers streaming through his mind, he stopped and stood in a remote place, staring about. Who could have survived such a day?

Had his brothers?

Or had Ethan's good favor finally run out?

Urgency prodded him like a poker stirring embers within him. *Search the field.* He set out at once to obey the impulse. The dew of human sacrifice clung to his boots and wove up his pant-legs with each step. He shrugged off a shudder and trudged onward.

Beyond, a rebel cavalry unit had met with Federal artillery earlier in the day. Swollen masses of equine wreckage littered the ground. Covering his nose and mouth with a sleeve, he scanned through the dark to determine colors. Dirt-colored roan, dust-hued duns, browns and bays blended into the darkness. A great sickle could not have mowed them down any more efficiently.

A scrap of Confederate regimental banner lay in shreds next to its bearer. Both held the colorless quality of the night. He passed a dry tongue over even dryer lips without aid.

He'd heard about Stuart's heavy casualties. If death had struck him a personal blow, it would surely be here in this hellish place. His gut twisted in a knot. The medics had already combed through these parts. The rest lie in the domain of the undertakers. But he needed to be certain. What if one of these fallen men still clung to life?

He stepped into gusting wind and uncertain light. A chill rose up his neck. Ahead of him lay a dark horse, its hip and girth rising above the ground. A saddle looped in twisted shreds above it. Its rider had met a similar fate, bent around the carcass in impossible contortions. Beneath the cavalry hat was a lock of dark, maybe black hair. The form compelled him near—nearer.

An involuntary moan escaped him.

Standing over the fallen charger, he studied a scar marking its black flank where his father branded his horses.

Palsy overtook his limbs until he fell to his knees beside the hulking mass. He rushed around the lifeless forms with clumsy desperation, clambering around the long neck of the horse to get to its rider. The cavalier lay under the animal, difficult to access, pinning vital areas of identification. He tore at the tangle with his bare hands to uncover the rider's face. It was too dark; he couldn't see details. The syllables of the name got stuck between his dry tongue and the roof of his mouth.

"Please, Lord. Not Devon?" *God, spare my brother.*

He rolled the head toward him. Its dull features and large, rounded nose, its heavy brow at once clarified the dead soldier as a stranger. A flood of relief thawed his frozen blood. No. No, thank God. Devon was not here.

Holding the body of a stranger in his arms Ethan was brought back to his senses, and he recoiled. Crawling a few feet away, his stomach constricted so hard he vomited into the grass.

Clutching his empty, aching middle, he gasped out a plea like the retching of his soul. "Lord, please—don't take Devon before he makes his peace with you. And with me."

Needing to find better air, he rose and shook off inertia, ambling toward his encampment. His breath came easier on higher ground. This place marked the first major Union victory in the east, and it occurred to him that his prayers were being answered. But to trust that God would save his family? He just couldn't summon that much faith.

"Lord, I believe. Help my unbelief."

ઉ૪ઈ

Somewhere in Northern Virginia
Confederate encampment

An autumn forest passed unseen before Devon. As the evening wind blew in beds of clover or whispered through tall, fragrant grass, it seemed a benevolent presence hovered. Birds exchanged their evening benediction to the crickets' nocturne. Amber campfires breathed warmth while twilight ceded to darkest night.

The small band of cavalry bedded down in the clearing, and he hunkered in for the night with a blanket roll and his silver flask. The Army of Northern Virginia's first major defeat rested bitter on his tongue, and Devon imbibed to drown the gall of it. He closed his eyes, inviting the darkness to claim him.

His hair stirred in the breeze and he blinked. Stars shone above in a twinkling array, and something moved deep within him gazing at the heavens. He recalled a night, almost two years ago, sitting with Ethan and looking up at those same stars together.

Forgive.

A shiver cascaded over his skin, raising the hairs on his arms. Still he would not acknowledge the calm voice resonating inside him.

Come, Devon. Lay down your burden.

He tossed on his blanket roll, nudging his hard shoulder into the mossy earth, and turned his mind elsewhere. The introduction of the mystifying Miss Harris only two nights prior had awakened an appetite in him that only fed frustration. Her charms were as distant tonight as those cold points of light in the sky. But even if she were near, he told himself he needed nothing, and no one. He could not risk needing anyone ever again.

Other forces, if they existed, held nothing for him, either. Whether God or devil, good spirits or bad, he scoffed at those superstitious fools with their weak-minded need for guardian angels or other rabbit's-foot-caliber charms. Friends had long since ceased to invite him to their tent meetings, drawing his inevitable, cynical response.

The nagging reminder of *God* never seemed to leave him alone. Just beyond, someone whispered solemn words by fireside vigil.

"Yea, though I walk through the valley of the shadow of death, I will fear no evil: for thou art with me; thy rod and thy staff comfort me. Thou preparest a table before me in the presence of mine enemies: thou anointest my head with oil; my cup runneth over.

"Surely goodness and mercy shall follow me all the days of my life: and I will dwell in the house of the Lord forever."

Silence settled in again, and he was glad of it.

Then, a notion percolated to the surface. *I, even I, am He who comforts you.*

Gentle warmth spread over his skin through his linen shirt. It felt like someone had touched him, embraced him. But how could that be? There was no one. *No one.*

His weary bones crunched as he sat up, hunched over, resting forehead in his palm. The ache in his middle, a consuming emptiness, threatened to swallow him whole. His breath came in sudden gasps. Two large, hot tears welled over and stole down his face. He swabbed them with his gray sleeve to destroy any evidence of importunity.

Was he no more than a little pawn in the hands of an omnipotent player? One little lead soldier among thousands? If a child could have favorite playthings, then God the Great Strategist must have His favorites, too. And He'd chosen Ethan over him.

Jacob have I loved, Esau have I hated. Twins, too. God had chosen to bless one and take the other's birthright. Jacob the supplanter. Jacob the manipulator. The betrayer. If God had chosen Jacob, er Ethan, then Devon would endure the butchery and defeat of a hundred more Sharpsburgs rather than resign himself to a God of arbitrary favoritism.

೧೪೧

Washington City
September 22, 1862

Days after the battle at Antietam, word of a proclamation to free the slaves reached Ethan's ears. On his first day of furlough, he rode Nimbus down Constitution Avenue, hoping to call on Aaron Hamilton at the War Department to confirm the rumor. If true, the decree held the power to validate all he had sacrificed and fought for. And it would give him one more reason to celebrate.

Cradling a ring box in his hand, he dismounted and tied Nimbus. Once inside the building, he scanned the marquee for Aaron's name. He shoved the box back into his coat pocket and crossed the hallway to the proper office. With a smile he recognized the familiar face of his friend.

"Your brother Gideon's been wounded. He's on the casualty list from Second Bull Run."

Aaron blatted the news so abruptly it compounded the impact. As Ethan recovered his breath, he thought it might have been a sumptuous cut of meat the way Aaron relished it on his tongue. Dumbfounded, Ethan stood in the doorway.

"Did you hear me, Sharpe?"

"I heard you," Ethan replied, still trying to pry his spine loose from the jolt. "How bad?"

"It reads: 'Major Sharpe, Gideon C., Second South Carolina Battalion, wounded." Aaron glanced up from the page. "The Secesh government doesn't publish details."

Ethan bit his bottom lip and warned himself that he couldn't punch a man with the stamp of war hero stitched across his face. He'd exit before his temper won over his good judgment. "All right, Aaron. Thanks for the news. I'm headed to your parents now to see Marietta."

"Wait, I'll go with you!" Aaron grabbed his Federal blue frock coat on the way out.

Ethan mopped a hand over his face and ducked out the doorway.

Aaron flanked his steps. "What do you think about Lincoln freeing the slaves? A real beaut', ain't it? How convenient he waited for the army's first major victory to unleash that dog."

Ethan spun on his heel and faced him. "So it's true? I thought you of all people would be happy. Your parent's sacrifices have finally paid off."

"How they waste their time is their misfortune. But you're a fool to think Lincoln cares a whit about the cause unless it benefits him."

"How is it self-serving to free the slaves?"

"If it keeps England from trading weapons for slave cotton, then hurrah for freedom."

Ethan turned away, shamed by Aaron's ugliness. Worse than the jagged scar running laterally across his face was his inexplicable malice. Ethan hurried to his tethered horse but couldn't shake Aaron's dogged pursuit.

"You seem determined to pick a fight today."

"Keep fighting this lousy, miserable excuse for a war, and spend your youth on the agendas of rich old men playing you like a chess piece if you want. But when you wake up without an arm, a leg, or a face, you'll remember I told you so."

Ethan loosened Nimbus' reins from the post. "You're talking like a bitter young man."

"Bitter or wizened? I've discovered a more excellent way. What are you saving yourself for? Drink, cheat, and be merry, for tomorrow we all die. Grab a bottle, or a gal, or both, and join me!" He pulled the flap of Ethan's jacket.

He wrenched away and studied Aaron's glazed eyes. This was not his friend. Something had taken over his personality. He stepped away and swung up onto Nimbus' back. "I don't understand what's gotten into you, Aaron. But whatever it is, I'll be praying you get over it." He spurred Nimbus and galloped off. Even as the vision of Marietta's face filled his mind, doubts swirled like carrion crows over his hopes.

Would she marry him? In the heat of emotion, they had exchanged promises, but now that time and distance had cooled her passion, she might have changed her mind. What did he have to offer her beside a ring and more uncertainty? With no holdings, rank or status, her family was certain to refuse his suit. Was it worth risking his dignity like he daily risked life and limb for *their* cause?

Maybe Aaron was right. Accommodation was his for the

taking if female company was all he desired. A superficial dalliance came cheap enough. Maybe that was all his affection was worth.

He traced the ring box in his pocket, spirals of pain sinking from his leaden heart down to his gut. He clenched his teeth, trying to rally himself from this sudden attack of doubt. He was already invested well beyond turning back now. Nothing short of her yes would satisfy him. The chance of her exclusive love trounced the promise of a meaningless embrace with some company gal. He whispered a prayer for favor, and rising with the crest of the road, he met the sight of sunlight on brick.

The smoke of native wood curled up from the chimney, its distinct aroma promising welcome. He hastened up the cobblestone drive and settled Nimbus inside stable.

Before he ascended the porch steps, she appeared in the doorway. Her smile trembled, and he feared his did, too. He sprang over the few paces remaining and she met him on the cobblestone. Marietta's arms enfolded his, entwining him like a tendril. He lifted her off her feet and spun her, her gown trailing and billowing like a beautiful victory banner. Speaking her name in a whisper, he slowed his movement while his yearning grew. He set her down, maintaining a burning stare, thinking of all he longed to say to her. She lifted her face to meet his, inviting his kiss.

"Wait. Let me look at you." He caressed her cheek with his fingertips, igniting a desire he could no longer deny. "All right. I've waited long enough." Tempering a grin, he found her with his kiss. She shivered at his touch, and he sought to warm her with his embrace.

Her parents approached at the back porch, their shadows darkening them. Mari shimmied out of his grasp. He took a shuddering breath and followed her up the steps.

Levi and Cora Hamilton received him with hospitality. Eyes sparkling and greetings chattering, they ushered their homecoming soldier through the threshold. Mari's hold on his arm relinquished just long enough, only reclaiming him when they were done. Hand in hand they made their way to the dining room table where another setting was quickly laid.

"What brings you home, dear?" Mrs. Hamilton asked. "Are the armies making their winter encampments so soon?"

Ethan withheld his purpose for the moment. "I was issued leave. I do apologize. My letter notifying you of my arrival will, in all likelihood, come after I've gone."

Levi grinned. "Always good to see you, Ethan."

Mari regrouped her hold on his arm. "He looks well, doesn't he Papa?" She blushed a lovely shade of rose.

Mrs. Hamilton raised a brow, consulting her husband.

"See to it that this boy eats enough to get through an army winter." Levi heaped another slice of roast beef on his plate and passed the platter of potatoes.

Basking in the reception, Ethan found the opportunity he'd waited for. His free hand dipped into the pocket of his coat and clasped the velvet box.

The sound of hooves erupted from outside, and all heads turned to the window. A sorrel horse and a uniformed rider appeared.

Marietta stood from her seat. "Aaron!"

Ethan's fist clenched at the interruption, and maybe a bit at the one interrupting as well.

Mrs. Hamilton bustled to the doorway. "You're just in time for dinner, son."

He brushed off his mother's kiss and approached the table. Aaron's grin broadened seeing Ethan. "I wouldn't miss it, Mother."

The domestic scene with hearth crackling and the aroma of warm food was so unlike the universe of battle, of the roving life of the cavalry, that Ethan basked in its pleasures, forgiving Aaron's earlier antagonisms. Marietta represented all things sweet, pleasant—and permanent—to Ethan. Tracing the box again, he pictured sliding the ring over her slender finger. He'd speak as soon as the chance availed itself.

Mrs. Hamilton quickly added another plate. "Aaron, you're so thin and pale. Are you well?"

"I'm fine, Mother."

She hovered over him. "What you need is someone to look after you."

"Oh, you know," he said, glancing at Ethan. "I get 'looked after' when I can."

Ethan frowned, wanting to call him out, but it was best the family didn't know of Aaron's scandalous allusion.

Mrs. Hamilton went on. "You must dress warmer. I was knitting woolens for the bazaar, but I'm giving them to you instead."

Aaron smirked. "She still thinks I'm eight years old. So, Ethan, what's the feeling on Lee's first big defeat?"

Ethan squeezed the velvet ring box in clenched fingers. "I reckon he's as tough to beat as Johnston was, if not tougher. But we might've found his Achilles heel."

Aaron laughed. "That's what I love about you, Ethan. Ever so upbeat despite two years of defeat."

Mr. Hamilton interjected. "The Lord's ways take time, son."

"Oh, sure. God takes time, while Lincoln takes men. A hundred thousand dead, so far. And how many commanders has it been, now? Four for the Army of the Potomac, and only two for the South? Let's see, we've had Scott, McClellan, Burnside…."

"Aaron, eat your dinner before it gets cold, dear."

"I'm not hungry, Mother. I ate in town. All I'm saying is that the South has no shortage of brilliance, while we struggle to find one competent leader. Johnston wasn't fired like ours were—he was injured. Does this frustrate anyone else here, or is all of Washington pretending to see the Emperor's clothing?"

Ethan glanced between father and son and bit his tongue. Mr. Hamilton remained silent, too.

"At least eat your greens, Aaron. You must have your vegetables."

Aaron shooed his mother off with a patronizing smile and targeted Ethan with a pointed finger. “This naive thinking has to end. Delusions of moral superiority don’t win battles. Stop throwing our boys at them like they’re a cheap commodity, for god-sake, and hit the South where it hurts! I mean, letting Lee escape after Antietam?”

Levi arose from his chair. “Son let’s take this into the parlor—”

“Does Lincoln honestly think that freeing the slaves is going to rally tired troops? Half of the boys wouldn’t care whether the slaves were freed or shipped off to her Majesty’s royal zoo!”

“*Aaron Hamilton!*” Mrs. Hamilton’s reserve snapped like twig.

He hardly skipped a beat. “Does Lincoln think God’s going to smite the enemy for us?”

Mr. Hamilton moved to stand beside Aaron’s chair. “Son, you’re tired. Why don’t we take our coffee into the parlor?”

“I *am* tired, Father.” His heightened pitch reverberating off the dining room walls made Marietta huddle in closer to Ethan’s side. “I’m tired of incompetence and antiquated thinking. I’m tired of impotent religion....”

“All right, son.” Levi reached out to herd his eldest into the other room. His gentle-but-firm tone, coupled with his size and authority at last brooked no argument. “Cora, would you bring strong coffee, please?”

With Aaron’s compliance, and Mrs. Hamilton’s retreat into the kitchen, Ethan found himself alone with Mari. “Your brother’s sure got an ax to grind.”

“He’s been like this for months. Mother and Father are beside themselves.”

“It’s his injury. It’s turned inward.”

“Oh, it’s worse, Ethan. Before I left the hospital, he came in every afternoon. I thought it was to see me, but it was for the morphine.” Her face fell under shadow.

"It's not your fault, sweetheart."

"We pray and pray! We don't know what else to do."

"I'll pray, too," he said quietly. He caressed her fingers, holding each one at a time in his rough hands. He paused at her ring finger.

"You're chapped." Her concern poured over him in a warm wave.

He was a fool for her adulation. "Don't you worry about me, Mari." He gathered her little hands between his, to feel her nearness and confer his warmth. "I'm immune to the elements." He grinned.

"Oh, but I do worry! Every time it rains I worry that you're out in it."

"Thoughts of you keep me warm."

She turned to receive a kiss, but he looked aside.

"Ethan?"

"I must ask you something." He gathered her left hand.

Her hazel eyes searched him, and he tempered the intensity of his stare.

"Marietta, God brought you into my life at a crucial time. You showed me the truth. You represent everything dear to me in this world. I want to share my life with you, for as long as God permits." He sank to one knee, sealing his intent.

She gasped.

He placed the box in her upturned hand.

He lifted the cover from the box and seated the opal-jeweled ring at the tip of her finger, poised to place it further, should she consent. "Marietta Hamilton, will you marry me?"

Heat pulsed through him as he looked deep into her eyes misting with tears.

At last, she broke her silence, and responded. "Yes, darling. I will."

She pressed her hand in his, and he moved the band upon her finger. The fire of the cabochon opal shifted from lightest blue to emerald green, then sparkled in candle-lit hues of yellow, flashing orange, and deepest ruby. She kissed him, but suddenly pulled away.

"I can't wait to show Mama and Papa!"

Jehoshaphat! Her parents. He'd intended to seek their blessing. Sobered, he grasped her elbow. "Wait, Mari. Let me go in and talk to your father. I'll be right back."

Ethan took the few strides into the parlor and met a sight.

Aaron paced over the floor, yammering something about his medicine. He wiped at his rheumy nose and eyes. "Go ask Mari if she remembered my medicine. I hope she remembered!" He crossed his arms over his chest, his hands chafing his upper arms. His mother draped a blanket about his shoulders, but he cast it off with a growl.

"See here, Aaron. Your mother is only trying to help." Mr. Hamilton's tone hinted of desperation. "Oh Ethan, beg your pardon. Aaron's just experiencing a touch of soldier sickness. It'll soon pass, once we give him his dose."

Ethan chewed the inside of his cheek, watching as Mr. Hamilton opened a small leather case. Its velvet interior revealed a hypodermic needle and a vial of liquid. Levi measured out the dose, while his son fidgeted and sniffled.

"Sir? I've seen this cured. At the tent prayer meetings." Ethan hesitated, knowing he tread a delicate path. He'd come in to ask for their daughter's hand, and what he was about to say would not endear him to them. "The Morphine isn't the antidote to soldier's sickness. It's causing it."

Mrs. Hamilton placed her hand over her heart, mouth agape. "Why my dear boy, our son is in pain. Surely you can see that."

Mr. Hamilton narrowed his eyes. "What are you saying, Ethan?"

"With all due respect, sir," Ethan whispered. "You'd be better off praying him through this, and not giving into his cravings."

Mr. Hamilton held the measured dose in his hand, consulting his wife with an expression of doubt. She returned her husband's look with raised brow. Ethan's stomach dropped. He knew from seeing this in camp. It wouldn't be pretty if they withheld the medicine. But it was the best thing they could do if they hoped to deliver him once and for all.

Aaron stalked across the floor, bound in Ethan's direction. "What are you discussing over here?"

"Ethan says we should help you without the use of this." Mr. Hamilton withdrew the medical apparatus behind his back, squaring his stance.

Aaron scratched a claw-like hand through his unkempt hair. "Are you going to take his word over mine? Your own son?" He cast a venomous gaze at Ethan. "I think he's interfered in our family long enough."

Mrs. Hamilton straightened her flagging shoulders. "Perhaps Aaron's right, Levi. I feel it would be best if we left this between fami—"

"Mother!"

Mari stood in the entryway.

"Ethan *is* family."

Ethan's gut tightened into a sphere of lead as she raised her left hand up for their inspection, the incriminating ring glaring on her finger for all to see. She finished off his last hope of salvaging the mess as she said, "We're getting married."

Mrs. Hamilton fairly shook, and her eyes hardened into bits of grape shot. "Your father and I will discuss this with you privately."

Chapter 24

December 1862
Fredericksburg, Virginia
Stuart's Cavalry

The winter winds portended more than snow. Devon felt a keen sense of impending combat on the chilled air. Along the banks of the Rappahannock River, his squadron had been dispatched to survey the outlay of the town of Fredericksburg. Federal occupation had amassed in the area, and Lee called on his best scouts to give a report.

The town's bridges had fallen to the Federals, except those that had been destroyed by the Virginia home guard. The morning hung still as an icicle. The frost rising from Devon's breath suspended on the frigid air while a dog's distant barking pierced the quiet. Even the river's roar had been muted by a shield of ice. Frozen clay muffled his party's approach.

Devon obeyed his commander's hand signals to spread out into two details, a forward and rear guard. He led the higher while Walt took the lower band of scouts. The bluffs over the riverbank afforded a view of the city below and uncovered the first glimpse of Union engineers slapping together a pontoon bridge.

Devon's calculating eyes measured the breadth of the bridge the Yankees planned to cross. Looked to him like a full-scale invasion was imminent. He relayed the conclusion back to Walt, stationed below. They exchanged knowing looks, and held up fingers communicating their guess, settling on four columns of infantry or two columns of cavalry. In the service of the army for eighteen months now, Devon had a well-honed intuition. Though he couldn't see far, he felt them. The enemy presence was strong. And close.

Horses tossed bridled heads and men shifted gazes over every inch of woods. Fear filled in the gap between each drifting snowflake, stealing its way through the fabric of Devon's uniform until it threatened to sink its clutches into his heart.

Walt shifted his position and Devon lost his visual on him. A courier ran liaison between them as Devon gave positions of Yankee sharpshooters he had spied along the bank. Devon adjusted his position and tried to read the Captain's expression, but the brim of Walt's hat cast a shadow over his weathered face.

Walt's mouth formed words. It looked like he'd said, "This'll be the death of me."

Rendezvous with their camp lay beyond the Federal gauntlet. They'd have to ride right through enemy lines. Devon's signature audacity would be put to good use today.

He swallowed, waiting for Walt's response. The Captain raised his field glasses toward the opposite banks. He signaled a number, confirming Devon's count of engineering corps concealed in the woods.

Devon contemplated their advantages: dry land, and speed. These were impervious factors to an airborne bullet, of course. He scratched his head underneath his cavalry hat and sat statuesque until many minutes had passed, formulating a plan. Then he moved down through the handful of troopers to consult with his Captain. Walt met him halfway at the courier's signal. They agreed that a headlong gallop with their pistols ready would be the best way. The Yankees along the water's edge wouldn't know what to do with a sudden appearance of cavalry; most had tools in hand instead of weapons.

Devon gave Walt his best cock-sure grin. “They ain't half the shots we are, Captain. I could take half of 'em out before they even knew what hit 'em.”

“Ain’t no firing unless fired upon, Sharpe. Get past those boys as quick as possible. Understand?”

Walt's stern directive chafed Devon, but he deferred. “Sure, Captain. Whatever you say.”

They were decided. The subordinate scouts crowded in to hear the plan, and with the exhale of pent-up tension, a dozen riders wheeled around and spurred across the flat.

They raced like a wild herd, onward, faster, further with each stride. Devon fought to the front while bullets ricocheted through the woods. Cinder bore him to a sheltered outcropping first and Devon looked back over his shoulder for the riders behind him. The balance of the pack thundered up and joined him. His heart skipped a beat when two riderless horses brought up the rear—Walt’s among them.

He thrust his weight about, swerving Cid with a violent tug on the reins. He dug his spurs into the stallion's flanks, charging back into the woods. He couldn’t yet see his pursuers, but he could hear them, their guns dislodging even as Devon drew a visual on a hapless figure crawling for cover on the icy bank. The Captain's bars on a gray and butternut coat confirmed Walt's identity. Devon drove Cid directly into the line of fire and scooped his fallen friend from the ground. He threw himself in the saddle as he spurred Cid around once more toward safety.

He held Walt across his lap, and once he reached his troopers, found a covert spot to examine his friend’s wounds. The sun retreated behind a pine shroud and deep darkness enclosed the party. He dispatched a rider for help while the others gathered around. Upon his first good look at Walt, he knew help wouldn’t matter. His friend clutched at his collar, strangling sounds crowding his throat, a wild-eyed stare his only communication. Devon sliced the collar open with his Bowie knife, hoping that would help Walt breathe. Instead, the neck wound gushed unhindered now. Walt was dying before his eyes.

Hardening himself to the reality, still Devon found it difficult to grasp. Beyond the anguish of losing a friend, fright fastened about his heart, tugging like a heavy chain down a long, dark well.

How quickly would death come? Would Walt fall into a peaceful sleep? Or would he continue to claw with desperate hands, as if to wrest the very breath from Devon to save himself? He wanted to draw back, convinced the condemned would drag him wherever he was going. Eerie shadows took on forms in the winter light. A flicker of dark, winged things flitted in the hanging branches, and Devon had all he could do to combat full-out panic. Walt's fingers latched about Devon's collar, his legs thrashed in the dirt, and his eyes pitched and rolled back in his head. The mounted troopers around him shifted and shied. Devon half-expected the Yankees to emerge from the woods at any second. One of his boys dismounted and approached Devon's side, presumably to hurry him back into the saddle. Instead, the cavalier grasped Walt's hand.

"Cap'n! You need to make right with the Lord. I'll pray, 'cause I know you cain't make no words. Lord Jesus, receive this man into your arms this hour. Forgive him his sins and give his soul peace. Amen."

At once, Walt's fingers released Devon's collar, and his arms fell slack at his sides. The tight lines of his white face smoothed. His legs fell still, sprawled where they lay, and his eyes no longer stared wild, but seemed to drift off to sights more sublime.

Devon stumbled backward. He reached for something solid and found his horse standing like a wall behind him. Unable to tear away from the sight of Walt's flayed throat, he grasped the leathers of Cid's bridle and pressed the animal's head to him like he might have embraced a brother.

"Take him up," he ordered a subordinate, shutting his eyes on the scene.

With a movement of controlled terror, he leapt into his saddle and let his horse carry him away. It took many miles before the sensation of Walt's grip fell away from Devon's throat, even after he swiped there repeatedly with his gauntlet. He dismissed his trembling as the cold when he and his men arrived to give report. But no mere temperature could have chilled him to the bone as the sight of a friend narrowly escaping hell.

ꕥ

Army of the Potomac Winter Camp
January 1863

Ethan sat by a campfire amid ten thousand soldiers hunkered down in winter quarters, and still he felt alone. He had pulled a pen nib and paper from his saddle bag, but he couldn't bring himself to write the letter. The same letter he'd been mulling for four months.

If Marietta's parents believed him unworthy of their daughter after all he'd done to prove himself, then more than likely they would intercept any attempts he made to contact her. It had been a lonely Christmas spent in frozen desolation. Fredericksburg's horrors were still freshly etched on his mind, scraping his heart dry of any notion of holiday merriment. The New Year promised nothing to alleviate his present situation. Marietta hadn't written. His brothers were a war front away. His home. . . His home was a tent on an icy patch on the banks of the cold Potomac. And God was silent on all counts.

If he thought there was any way to reach Marietta, he might have told her not to wait for him anymore. But like the guttering flame inside his lantern, he held a stubborn hope that maybe somehow, some way, he might yet find a way to make good on his promise to come to her. Perhaps the war would end this year. Perhaps he could reconcile with his family and prove worthy of Marietta's hand through his share of his father's substantial estate. Was it really money the Hamiltons esteemed? Land? He'd have had a better chance at winning her if he'd stayed in Virginia.

They apparently didn't value his service to the Federal army, or the fact that he found himself on the wrong side of the river from his family. All because he sought to protect Jonesy, a slave they'd offered to buy.

Would he do it again?

He'd thought long and hard on the question since that April day, almost two years ago. Given the situation, how the boy faced disfigurement or worse at Devon's hands, and being unable to prevent it any other way than by fleeing, he figured he'd do nothing different. It was just the timing. The blamed timing of it all had made the action irrevocable. But how was he to know that then? That the courses of their lives—he and his very twin—would forever be severed because of it.

Yeah, he reckoned he'd do it again, given what he knew then, and not knowing the consequences. But what it would take to measure up to her family, he didn't know. He prayed to the same God they claimed and gave himself to the same causes they espoused.

If it weren't for this war yawning before him with the gaping maw of eternity, he might be able to distinguish himself in business or some other affair.

Wrapping the wool blanket tighter about his shoulders, not unlike the saddle blanket Jonesy had worn after sacrificing his coat for his enemy, he let his head fall to his huddled knees, nodding off into a fitful sleep. Perhaps if he could make rank…. Yes, perhaps with one more battle, if he wasn't killed, he might be able to win her parent's respect with a promotion and an officer's commission.

It was his last shot, and he'd have to give it all he had.

ঔ

May 2, 1863
Maryland on the Potomac

Marietta dared not close her eyes. The dream had come again. Ethan's horse ran riderless through charred, smoke-filled woods. Broken branches with smoldering ends gave way to the frantic gray war horse, while trumpets and shouts and blasts echoed in the background.

Each time she dreamed it in more vivid detail. This time the saddle was riddled with holes which streamed fresh blood. In all the visions Ethan was never there, but the smear of his crimson hand print on leather pommel showed where he'd fallen.

She lit the lamp by the side of her bed to read the clock face. She wouldn't return to sleep, though it was not yet four in the morning. Exhausted, she rolled back over, leaving the flickering candle lit. Her Bible lay open where she had nodded off reading. Even the comfort and promise of Psalms couldn't dispel her gnawing intuition that something was terribly wrong, that Ethan was in imminent danger. She fought the urge to flee to her parent's room and ask them one more time to reconsider. If only she could see him again, she was certain her restless heart would find peace. But she held there, repeating the same wildly whispered supplication.

"Oh, God! Please keep Ethan safe."

The warm air offered no relief even in the slightest tousle of a river breeze. Night insects grew loud outside her window, marking the cadence of her prayer vigil. Her words after a short time had turned to repetitious sounds, losing all meaning, as her anguished heart crumbled to futility. The armies had converged along the Rappahannock River, Lee challenging General Hooker's bid to advance on Richmond. For two days, another bloody battle like Fredericksburg raged. And no doubt, Ethan was there.

She couldn't know his fate unless new casualty lists were posted. Aaron couldn't be more obliging with the latest news from the War Department, after she had blamed him for destroying Ethan's and her chances at happiness. Lately, Aaron had been a changed man. But all his penitence wouldn't bring Ethan back.

Sighing transformed to tears which whispered at first, then grew into sobs that echoed down the hallway, consumed as she was with grief over the one for whom she longed. He could die not knowing she still cared.

Her parents' footfalls announced their approach.

While Papa hung in the doorway rubbing his eyes, Mama entered.

"Your father and I heard you crying."

Marietta regained her breath and composure, but words would not come.

Papa approached. "Come now, Mari. How can we ease your mind?"

She wiped her face with the handkerchief Papa handed her. What could she possibly say to her parents? After their cruel send off, it was clear why Ethan hadn't written. Why did they pretend they cared when they were the reason her heart was breaking?

"We know these battles are hard on you."

She took measured breaths to command control over her suffocating fear. Her mother sighed and tried again to comfort, but Mari's attention shifted to her father. He could do better than offer paltry consolations. He could make everything right.

"He could die, Papa. Don't you care at all what happens to him?"

"Ah, sweetheart." He stood beside her mother, the glow of the bedside lamp illuminating the worry-creases on his brow. "I know you're afraid. We all worry for him. But he's in the Lord's hands. And you'll be enrolling at Elmira College in the fall."

"Papa, please...." *I love him so much.*

"Come, now. Don't cry."

"I saw it in a dream. It was so real. His blood. The saddle was covered—"

Heart-wrenching sobs overtook her again.

"Listen, Mari. Stop crying. You can't go on like this." Papa waited for her to calm. "You might as well know, I'm looking into the matter. The War Department won't give Ethan a full discharge, but they might grant a transfer. Now, it's not official yet, but it looks like I might be able to secure a post for him away from the front."

Her chest stopped heaving. "Away from battle?"

"Yes, sweetheart," Mama replied. "Your father has been working on it since news of this latest confrontation. We weren't going to tell you until we knew for sure—and we're still not sure yet."

"If you can, then Ethan will be safe?" Sniffling, Marietta wrapped her arms around her pillow and pulled it to her. "You would do that for him?"

"Now, this doesn't mean your father and I have changed our minds about your betrothal, Mari. We just want to ease your worries."

Mari shook her head, wiping the last of her tears away. "I know." If she couldn't get them to change their minds, at least she might know that he was safe. After ruining his life, she owed him that at the very least.

Chapter 25

Gettysburg, Pennsylvania
July 4, 1863

Ethan stood on the bluff of Cemetery Ridge. A victory celebration fifty-thousand strong pealed in fireworks, music and gunfire salute, all while corps of black soldiers gathered the dead from the field. The air hung heavy with residual smoke and the threat of rain in places like Little Round Top, Devil's Den, and Seminary Hill, bearing the same acrid reminder of a dozen other battlefields over the past two years—the pungent aroma of smoldering grass and singed wood, of fevered flesh, and the bright tang of blood. He looked skyward and whispered a prayer for cleansing rain to renew the face of the earth.

In truth, the sight of carnage no longer haunted him. At least not to the point anymore that tore at him. For that he was almost sorry. Was this battle-hardness? If so, it was merciful. He prayed that it would not harden him to the good. The North had won, and that *was* great cause for rejoicing.

His army's victory yesterday coincided with the surrender at Vicksburg, opening the Mississippi to Yankee control. If that wasn't enough, that the Confederacy had been divided in two, cut from East to West, and that Lee had been stopped from invading the North, and was even now retreating into the bosom of Virginia, then the date alone should have produced a swell of patriotism. It was Independence Day. Enough to make any American proud. But Ethan stood alone, silent among the revelers.

The past three days of conflict had tried both sides to their limits. But the victors had emerged, and he was counted among their survivors. The miracle of it still escaped his full grasp.

He turned in his hand a letter, freshly delivered from his commander. His courage in battle—or, he thought ruefully, the fact that he'd survived, and given the shortage of officers—had led them to offer him a field promotion to First Lieutenant. An officer's commission. The honor wasn't lost on him. But looking out on the ripped fabric of the farmland where so many had perished, he could only drop his head in a moment of silence.

The letter rustled with the first pelting of rain, and Ethan considered the offer again. He'd waited for this moment. Prayed for it. Surely God was rewarding his patience. He'd humbled himself, and didn't the Word say before honor came humility? He would be an officer. Maybe now Marietta's parents would see him as worthy of their daughter's hand.

He would write and request an audience with Mr. Hamilton, presenting his case man to man. Perhaps now he would convince him at last.

Stuart's Cavalry
Several hours later

Devon's mind wandered in the manner of the sleep deprived. The events leading up to the battle at Gettysburg replayed in his mind, as though recalling them could make sense of Lee's astonishing loss.

He'd taken liberties. A month ago he'd attempted to locate Gwendolyn May Harris. Stuart's orders to protect the mountain gaps into the Valley while Lee pushed North had placed him dangerously close to the Maryland border. Temptation had simply overcome him. Instead of finding her, he'd found truancy from a major cavalry clash. Not until the conclusion of the battle of

Brandy Station had he rejoined his company in the Virginia countryside. Skirmishing at Aldie, Middleberg and Upperville only whet Devon's appetite for a bigger contest. And he was soon satisfied.

General Lee in giving Stuart discrepancy to harass and demoralize the enemy, to gather supplies and learn of enemy strength, had inadvertently set Stuart out on a daring ride around the Union army. And Devon, eager to drown personal disappointments over a failed rendezvous, had been an eager accomplice.

Miss Harris. Her image eluded him while a host of vexations intruded upon his thoughts.

Storm clouds overhead opened in a deluge. Devon pulled the brim of his hat low over his face and hunkered down in the saddle. The roads would soon be a mire, with many miles to cover in their retreat.

Devon prided himself a top-notch scout. How then had he failed to locate Miss Harris in Urbana? Was she a ghost? He should've known she'd prove a false fix to his chronic solitude. He should never have allowed himself to hope for anything more.

Seems he'd never learn on that score. Another infatuation of sorts had claimed him, this time with General Stuart's fearlessness. Exploiting and embarrassing the Yanks with raids on supply trains and wagon caravans through Virginia and Maryland had done wonders for Devon's wounded pride. Scouting parties in Westminster and Hanover had been a lark, and such stuff they had gotten way with at Rockville! Food and stores of which Devon could only dream, after months of privation. Stuart was a genius at pioneering the sort of adventure that could rally boys like him.

Devon fancied Stuart a veritable Robin Hood, stealing from the rich stores of the North to give to the loyal citizens who had shown them support. And not just the necessities to keep alive, but luxuries like imported brandy, supposedly the personal property of a Yankee general. Thus armed, Stuart's boys rode into

Pennsylvania giddy to present gifts to their beloved commander "Marse Robert" Lee.

What heights of anticipation Devon had felt presenting Lee with the stolen Yankee treasures. With the increasing likelihood of battle, he considered this his army's shining moment. At no other time had the reason for his existence come into clearer focus. Finally, he had regained a belief, a purpose so long in returning, a trust in another person so hard-won, culminating in this moment. Every satisfaction could be had, striking a blow on enemy territory.

The sequence of events since then forced his mind back to Gwen's hair. Such a ready escape, worthy of a weary cavalier's imagination. Cinder's gallop substituted for the meter of the dance, the sensation of another warm, near form moving with him. Even the silk of his horse's neck conjured up the memory of her skin. His thoughts reclaimed what his eyes, hands and body had been privy to that night in Urbana. He drew his lids down on the march of defeat all about him and welcomed the carnal memory to help him escape.

Thunder groaned overhead, and the universe of battle exploded, jarring him wide eyed. The nightmare came of more than just exhaustion. This defeat went all the way through. How could it have happened? The Marble Man—Lee—the one who could not fail, had failed. And the guilt lay squarely on a marauding band of cavaliers pirating the countryside. Stuart larked when he ought to have been giving reports on the enemy. In those critical hours, could Stuart have misread his purpose more? The eyes and ears of Lee's army, folly had blinded them all.

That moment Stuart presented the wagon train loaded with supplies and prisoners, Marse Robert had answered with searing rebuke. Devon had never seen dejection upon the countenance of a man as he'd seen on Stuart then. He felt it himself, down to his core. Perhaps it was that moment which had thrown the battle. Devon had always fancied the cavalry the heart and soul of the

Army of Northern Virginia, if not the Confederacy herself. They were the pride, the toast, the bravado, the barometer. If they, the cavalry, hadn't performed up to par, how could the rest? They couldn't even wrestle free to help General Ewell at Culp's Hill on that last abysmal day.

Now their gay ostrich plumes mocked them from the crest of their hats. Devon snatched his rain soaked hat from his head and wrenched the foolish feather out, casting it away to be trampled in the mud.

☙

Maryland on the Potomac
July 10, 1863

Marietta read and reread the Gettysburg casualties. Ethan had somehow come through unscathed, according to the latest lists. Many a prayer of thanksgiving spilled from her lips, but still a voice inside her troubled the waters. How could she be sure? No casualty list could describe the condition of his heart. Only a letter—no, only seeing him in person could possibly remedy what her soul cried out for. But that wasn't going to happen.

She reasoned that if she could keep herself occupied, this unbearable angst would pass. But the days had turned to a week, and the remedy of busyness failed to bring relief. He might as well have perished in battle for the heartache she carried.

Grief surfaced at the most inconvenient times. It overtook her at the wash basin, with soapy rag and dish in hand, or even seated at the dinner table. Paralyzing anxiety overtook her, a weight so heavy she could barely hold herself up, until Mama bade her lie down and rest.

Her father had departed several days ago on a business trip. He had neither indicated where he was bound, nor when he would return. Her mother seemed too comfortable with the mystery, and Marietta suspected her mother knew full-well where he was going. Indulging in fantasy, she imagined her father retrieving Ethan from the battlefield. That he would come, and they'd be married at once, and all would be well. But right now, she would content herself just knowing he lived. And still cared for her.

Her thoughts tumbled one after another until they tangled together, and nothing but escape would free her. She strolled out to the lower garden where the river flowed past the property, and the moving air cleared her head. A storm gathered from the west. Slanting rays of sun pouring through indigo clouds bathed the boathouse and shimmered over the water. Perhaps the storm would hold off until evening. If the rains did come, she cared little, for the linens on the clothes line would benefit from another rinse, and her roses, lilies and bachelor buttons here in the back garden needed a drink. As she pinched off faded blue seed-heads, she was compelled to linger. Spears of light transformed the colors on the river into brilliant jewel tones of emerald, sapphire and peridot so breathtaking that she drew her right hand up to admire her ring—the one she was forbidden to wear on her left. *Oh, Ethan.* Without warning the sky split with a fork of lightening and poured down sheets of rain.

She made a dash for the boathouse, but not before her blouse soaked through. When the cloudburst passed, and rain-laden limbs dripped about the garden, she emerged, carrying her slippers on swinging arm. She rounded the house and approached the front where the post-shower dripping seemed to grow louder. The steady rhythm transformed into the cadence of hooves on the road. She paused. Whoever it was must be in a hurry. Mari turned and strolled up the side yard to the edge of the road.

Standing where their drive branched from the main road, she lifted a hand over her brow. Those hooves churned more briskly than carriage horses' hooves. She cocked her head to the wind. Was that the boisterous laughter of men? They appeared over the crest, two riders on fleet horses, both in Federal blue. Their speed conveyed an ominous message to her, a young lady alone and unprotected. Yankee or not, strange soldiers invoked caution.

Then the lead horse stretched into a ground-swallowing run. Ice coursed through her veins. She gathered her sodden skirts and made haste to the front door. Heavy and cumbersome with the soaking, her trappings resisted all speed. She clambered up the slippery grass slope toward the house.

The soldier's rough voice goaded his beast until hooves pounded behind her. The doorstep still eluded reach.

"Wait!" the man called to her. She thought she heard her name, too, but the roar in her ears muffled the sound. The soldier drew up and dismounted so close the animal's breath steamed her skin.

Large, rough hands enfolded her arm just as she reached the steps. She shrieked as the man spun her about. Her heart leapt into her throat, squeezing out her cry for help. She fought as the soldier forced her to look up into his face. Laughter, gentle and full, enveloped her and she scarcely resisted a swoon. The soldier's smiling countenance came into focus and all dread dispelled. Hazy cognizance of kisses enthralled her. Ethan's mouth pressed hers until she couldn't breathe, renewing her half-hearted struggle against his benign ravages. He would not relent, clutching her in his arms, drinking in her nearness. Her gasps and cries seemed to whet his appetite all the more. Not until the second rider arrived did he grant her reprieve. Ethan set her aside as Aaron rode up the drive. Leaning on her beloved, she allowed him to walk her to the door.

"Enjoy your reunion while you can," Aaron warned. "Papa's carriage is coming any minute.

☙❧

Ethan ignored the pall cast by Aaron's words. Right now, he intended to soak in nothing but purest happiness with Mari in his arms. He walked her through the foyer and over the parlor to the same sofa where he had brought her wounded brother two years prior and reluctantly set her down. He sat beside her, his eyes caressing her even as he longed to with tender fingertips. But first, he must take no untoward liberties. He leaned in to whisper in her ear, and a blush lit her cheeks. He smiled and averted his eyes as she drew her arms about herself in a shiver of modesty. He placed his coat over her shoulders to cover her blouse, made translucent by the rain so that her corset lines were defined. Then he lifted his hand to tuck a curl of her damp hair behind her ear. He filled his chest with a shuddering breath and whispered, “I've missed you so much.”

She returned a caress, her sweet, soft fingers rasping against his unshaven cheek. “Why have you come?”

Before he could answer, the front door opened, and Mr. Hamilton's tread crossed the threshold.

Mari looked down at herself and quickly took her leave. As Ethan stood, shrugging back into his uniform coat, Mr. Hamilton, standing a few paces away, shook his head.

Ethan planted his feet and folded his arms across his chest. “Reckon I startled her. She certainly wasn't expecting me.”

Levi raised his brows but said nothing.

Surely the man couldn’t find fault with his riding ahead to see her, not after he'd come all the way to headquarters to fetch Ethan. Explaining that he asked for the sake of the girl they both loved, Levi had requested that Ethan come at once. He’d brought a signed furlough, no doubt a favor from one if his political cronies. Having gone to such trouble, Ethan figured the man wouldn’t begrudge him one kiss.

Perhaps he would finally give his permission for them to wed. He hadn't negotiated yet, but rather had leapt at the chance to see Mari again. With a week’s furlough, perhaps they’d be married by week’s end. Ethan lingered under Mr. Hamilton’s stare.

Levi spoke at last. “Oh, I don’t think you startled her. I'm thinking she ran, knowing it was you.” The twinkle of jest sported in the elder’s eye.

“You saw everything?”

“Indeed, I did.”

He would not apologize. His intentions toward the girl he loved were honorable, if the man would just acknowledge them. "We have much to discuss—"

Marietta made her grand re-entry, this time in a frock of mariner green. Its full-hooped skirt tapered to her slender waist, and its hue brought out the green in her hazel eyes. Ethan was struck speechless. How had he been able to leave her in the past? Maybe after this week he'd never have to leave her again.

Her father's eyes burned hot on him as he took her hand. The man would have him self-conscious. Wind-blown hair, rain-drenched uniform and road dust all testified against him. But when he learned of Ethan's new officer's rank, he'd be sure to forgive his appearance.

"You must be wondering why I brought you here, Ethan."

Marietta's eyes shone with eagerness. "Yes, Papa. Do tell."

Ethan tightened his hold on her hand for a second as a thrill passed between them.

"I'll get right to the point. I've learned of an opportunity that I hope you will agree to, a perfect fit for a battle veteran like you. Lincoln's Conscription Act has created an influx of soldiers in need of training. I've secured a position with the cavalry unit, should you agree. You would be quite a distance from the front, to ease my daughter's worry."

A chill iced his fingers, and Ethan released Marietta's hand. "Away from battle, sir?"

"Yes, Ethan. You would be sent immediately."

He clenched his fists, and the momentary chill melted to liquid fire coursing through his blood. His ambitions had been trumped by this man's substantial influence and persuasion. "All the details are arranged, then." It wasn't a question. Just like with Jonesy, the man had decided Ethan's fate without consulting him.

"It only awaits your signature, son. If you only knew what a relief it would bring to Mari. She neither sleeps nor eats but worries ceaselessly for you. If you truly care for her, you will surely want to relieve her state."

"But Papa, how far away is it?" she cried.

"All I know is they call it Camp Chemung, and it's far enough north that you can be sure no army will ever attempt to invade. Ethan will be quite safe. And," he continued, directing his commanding gaze back at Ethan. "It would be a promotion from your enlisted rank. They'll take you on as a sergeant."

Ethan battled a tightening sense of strangulation. Mari's eyes swept over him, large and beseeching, pleading with him to affirm her father's offer. The carefully constructed noose enclosed him. There was no way out.

She loves me. She longs for my safety. I owe her that peace of mind.

But could he just leave everything he had worked so hard for? Give up his officer's commission? Should he? One look at Mr. Hamilton's expression, as though he had played every ace in the deck, was all Ethan needed to understand the man's motivation. Mr. Hamilton was getting rid of the nuisance he posed, once and for all.

Leaving would be the end of him and Mari.

She slipped her hand back into his and pressed herself beside him, peering up at him so earnestly that a pang shot through him.

"Oh, please Ethan. Won't you say yes?" Her frail body shuddered against his and he drew his arm about her. But before words of assurance could form, Mr. Hamilton spoke.

"Surely you can see how much it means to her, Ethan. If indeed you are the unselfish, honorable young man I believe you to be, you won't think twice." He folded his arms across his chest, his mouth set in a firm line.

Ethan's heart crumbled like rain-soaked earthworks. He took a slip of her damp chocolate tresses between his fingers, knowing it would be the last time he would enjoy her nearness, sense her warm perfume, touch the silken strands of her hair. He commanded breath through the crushing heaviness and cleared his throat, suddenly crowded with emotion. He knew he must protect her at all costs.

"When does my train depart, sir?"

"In twelve-hundred hours, Sergeant." Mr. Hamilton clapped Ethan on the shoulder and beamed a smile that seemed too bright in the face of his darkest misery.

Chapter 26

July 1863
Northern Central Railroad

An unyielding oak bench bore Ethan over many rough-hewn miles through the heart of Pennsylvania. A whole day passed on his military transport car as the tracks twisted and turned, rose and retreated over the Allegheny Mountains. Here the land protested taming like a half-broke horse. At the window, he noted settlements a century old, straddling the Susquehanna River, not unlike his home back in the Shenandoah Valley. His heart ached with a singular thought. He should have been heading south, not north. This iron horse bore him further and further from the promise he once believed. That God could somehow reunite him with his twin, and he could yet settle down with the girl he loved and build a happy life.

Soon, the pristine wild tempered with cultivated hollows and the sedate dwellings of South-Central New York. There the Chemung River wove a silver band through the middle of the town, dividing it north from south. His destination would be the north side of town. As the train pulled into Erie Depot, he knew now that his fate had been sealed, and there was no turning back.

Signs advertised The New York and Erie Rail lines west to Chicago and east to New York City, while yet another, the Elmira, Canandaigua, and Niagara ran north to Canada. But this was where his journey ended. With a sigh and a hefting of his bag, he rose from his seat and walked stiffly down the aisle.

Stepping into the evening air, Ethan looked down from the platform at the town. At first glance, he perceived Elmira an affluent community. Several church spires rose over the skyline to greet him as he walked the boardwalk back to the livestock car to retrieve Nimbus. The gelding seemed eager to be rid of the stale confines and nickered at him. Ethan led him, saddled, down the gangplank and out onto the street. Pedestrian and equestrian traffic set a brisk pace even at the twilight hour. Ethan hailed a livery cab for his luggage and asked the driver about lodging. He directed Ethan over the brick-paved Railroad Avenue a few blocks south to Brainard House. Accommodations here would serve for several days until Ethan's furlough ended, and he would muster in with the New York cavalry.

He was in no hurry.

The saddle made a welcome change after the confines of the train. The fresh air upwind from the station felt cooler than in Washington, but humidity still pasted his clothes to his body. The damp scent of the river drifted on the gently moving air, and Ethan rode without incident to the grand brick façade of the five-story hotel.

Though tired, a certain energy tingled over his skin. He'd felt this sensation before, at times in church services. At times in quiet tents with his Bible open, his knees bent. A presence. A comfort. A *promise*. Handing off his horse to the livery driver, he checked into the hotel and ascended to his room alone.

He might have been on his honeymoon had things worked out differently. He should be cherishing the beautiful woman he thought so sure the Lord had reserved for him, the gift he believed awaited his faithfulness these past three years. Now all he had to look forward to was reporting to active duty among strangers in a strange land.

In moments he opened the door with the borrowed key and looked into the furnished room. He set down his bag and sat on the bed. A bed to be sure, and not a rubber army blanket on a hard, often damp and cold ground. But an empty bed, nonetheless.

He hadn't felt a sense of belonging anywhere these past three years. Not since home.

Home. Would he ever have one again? He could have made just about any place with Mari a home. And now, she was gone from his life forever. Oh, she had promised to write, but he knew better. Her parents would intercept—or have her so busy she wouldn't have time, and before long even the inclination, to write.

The jingle of spurs accompanied hoof-beats on the road below his window. Ethan's blood stirred with the call to saddle. He'd considered the nomadic movement of the cavalry his home for the last few years, and his brothers-in-arms, his family. Now all of these were gone, and once again, uncertainty marked his future.

A confluence of circumstance and fate had brought him to this time and place, to a little town called Elmira, New York. It was farther north than he'd ever cared to come. Would it prove his True North, the direction of God in his life? Or was this move another impulse he'd acted upon to make a girl happy? Like he'd done the day he'd left the Valley. He was now further away than ever from reconciliation with his family. With Devon.

His gazed dropped to the street far below, and his heart plummeted from the height as well.

This couldn't be the end of his road, could it? Perhaps this was just one more stop.

He turned back to the bed, to his bag setting on it, and withdrew his Bible. He kneeled beside the bed and turned to a random passage. Genesis. The story of Joseph. That same sensation coursed through him as when he'd stepped off the train, like a harbinger.

He knew Joseph's story. Had lived it. Been exiled from his home, too. Had faithfully served Potiphar's commands, only to be rewarded with a prison sentence. But would God ultimately promote Ethan like He had Joseph, and reunite him with his brothers? Joseph had married among the daughters of his exile, but Ethan had no wife to comfort him in his.

Joseph's son's names, Ephraim and Manasseh, translated "I will be fruitful in the land of my suffering", and "I will forget the trouble of my father's household." Joseph never embraced Egypt as his home—never stopped longing for Canaan—ordering his bones brought back for burial there. If Elmira be his Egypt, Ethan's heart would hold out for his home, too. And reconciliation with his brothers. And Pharaoh's daughter's hand in marriage.

A renewed sense of hope stirred despite the seeming impossibility. With a wry grin, he bowed his head and prayed.

ꕥ

Three weeks later
Prospect Hill
Elmira, New York

"Mr. Hamilton and Miss Hamilton, I presume?"

Mari rose from the hardwood bench and took a step toward the gentleman wearing dark overcoat and sporting white mutton-chop whiskers. His smile was meant to put her at ease, and she feigned confidence though a swarm of dragonflies fluttered in her stomach. Her kid leather boots made no sound over the great octagonal lobby, muffled by her petticoats and the stifling August air, but the clicking of Papa's heals echoed over the cavernous room, marking the thrum of her pulse.

"Levi Hamilton," her father intoned, clasping the shorter man's hand. "My daughter, Marietta."

With a quiet dignity the man said, "I am Dr. Augustus Cowles, and it is my great pleasure to welcome you to Elmira Female College. Please, won't you follow me to my office where I shall conduct our admissions interview?"

Mari proceeded to follow the man. Young ladies passed her in the hallway, carrying books and ledgers, their nods toward their president both cordial and deferential.

Dr. Cowles ushered them down a corridor until he opened a polished walnut door. "Please, come in and be seated." He showed them two Windsor chairs facing his desk.

Mari eased herself into one, letting her moss-colored skirts gather modestly beneath her.

"I've reviewed Miss Hamilton's academic assessment and I am fully satisfied that she will meet the rigors of our classical curriculum to begin her baccalaureate degree. It is always a distinct pleasure to greet a prospective student hailing from as far away as our capital. Please, tell me what aspirations have brought you to our school."

Papa nodded at Mari to answer for herself.

"Thank you, Dr. Cowles. My parents' initial ambitions for me of finishing school and a tour of Europe were, as you can imagine, quite inconvenienced by this late unpleasantness. For the past two years I have taken up studies at home with tutors."

"Very resourceful of you, Miss Hamilton. Please, go on."

"Thank you, sir." Encouraged, she took a steadying breath and continued. "I long to champion those who have no voice, be they the illiterate freedman or woman, the impoverished immigrant, or the widow and orphan of this wretched war. And I am certain that by improving myself with the very best education available, I will be better prepared to help others."

Dr. Cowles' apparent scrutiny broadened into a smile. He turned his attention to her father then, his expression once again sobering. "And you support your daughter's ideals, Mr. Hamilton?"

Papa cleared his throat. "Our family holds the highest regard for these Christian ideals and we're proud that Marietta feels so passionately. Abolitionist work has acquainted me with many good men from New York. Secretary Seward, for one. Through his close association I have had the privilege to meet your school's founder Simeon Benjamin, as well as your town's pillar, Jervis Langdon, all champions of the cause. Knowing that your community boasts men of such impeccable moral character goes a long way to assuage my concerns in sending my daughter so far from home."

"I see." Dr. Cowles steepled his fingers on his desk. "And what are those concerns, Mr. Hamilton? Perhaps I may help to further alleviate them."

Papa shifted in his seat. "The war brings its own concerns, Doctor, chief among them my daughter's safety."

"Let me assure you that our young ladies' activities are closely scheduled and strictly monitored with a matron present at all times. I realize that the confluence of traffic through our railroad and canal town can be perceived as both an asset and a liability. Because of our ample connections, our town benefits from the best cultural and moral fabric, as well as economic prosperity and commerce. But I'm sure you've noticed that our rail hub has also attracted a confluence of military occupation."

"That is precisely what concerns me." Papa drew a deep breath and released it slowly.

Marietta worried her lip. Papa wouldn't dare denigrate the service of these brave enlisted. She listened intently without interruption as they continued.

"With such a population of young men at large, what safeguards have you employed to secure your young ladies' protection and virtue?"

"I appreciate your candid questions, Mr. Hamilton. I can tell you that Colonel Eastman conducts his training camps with the utmost discipline and military mien, but equally as regimented are our young ladies, if not more so. Our objective is to insulate our students from the outward community, and provide them with a nondenominational religious environment, with strict adherence to the propriety becoming of finest society. We allow visits with local residents only by express parental permission and discourage leaving campus altogether except on the rarest occasions."

Mari fought to keep a smile in place, but she couldn't be sure that her eyes didn't betray her as she cast a fleeting glance at Papa. Was he going to come right out and tell the good doctor that she wasn't allowed to consort with common soldiers? As if it were a habit. None could possibly replace the one for whom her heart still yearned.

Papa peered down at her with his most penetrating gaze.

She fluttered innocent lashes back at him and made every effort to make her smile convincingly demure.

"Very well, then, Dr. Cowles," Papa said. "It is our privilege to entrust Marietta to your esteemed institution." He produced his checkbook and Dr. Cowles' pen and signed a check for $120 for the year's tuition, board, and supplies.

ꕥ

At week's end, when the professors' lectures had faded, and the screech of slate pencils stilled, Marietta's homesickness crept in from all corners of her dormitory room. Her roommate, a chatty student named Josie, whose petite frame was packed with as much spark as a Washington Fourth of July, hadn't returned to the room yet. Mari was left alone with her thoughts.

Her father had spoken a name where Ethan was being sent—*Camp Chemung*. Funny, but that name had come up more than once this week. The river here had the same name. And hadn't Dr. Cowles mentioned a military rendezvous while speaking to her father last week? Before she could tie her thoughts together, the door swung open, and Josie and a few others blustered into the room.

"We're going sight-seeing!" Josie swept a brushed-linen-sleeved arm toward the window.

"But how? We're not allowed to leave the grounds."

"Follow me, ladies!" Josie gathered her skirts for dramatic flair and led the procession back through the door. Mari weighed whether to risk trouble, but being the last one left, she followed.

Josie climbed a staircase up to the top of its five stories. There, an octagonal cupola towered at the pinnacle of the building. Like a wreath ensconcing an open room below, the tower could either look down on the gallery within, or the view from its panoramic windows could see in any direction without.

From here, the highest point atop Prospect Hill, and the tallest structure in town, Mari gazed out in the last moments before twilight. Hills fringed the valley to the east, reflecting an amber sunset, and halfway in from those hills echoed the faint calls of canal boatmen. Turning to the south, toward downtown, she spied miniature gentlefolk in finery emerging from banks and shops, and leather-aproned mill workers. Across the road to the west stood the college president's home. Beyond that, more hills framed all within their deep green shadow. And finally, to the north, houses and farms dotted the valley as far as the eye could see. Coming back to center, Mari stood with a sigh. It was a pretty town, even if she'd never get to venture out into it.

"Look girls!" Josie pointed east. "Soldiers!"

Mari rushed to Josie's side and stood on her tiptoes. To the northeast, almost a mile away, a miniature troop of cavalry performed drills on the fairgrounds.

One of the girls brought in a chair from Mrs. Dunlap's botany class and placed it before the tall window.

"Give me a hand up, Mari," Josie said.

"You're not climbing on that, are you?" Her stomach lurched at her friend's hatching such an idea. "You'll lose your balance and topple out the—"

Too late. Josie grasped Mari's arm and Sally Jenkins's on her left and hoisted herself up. The dear, impetuous chit teetered for a second until her skirts ceased swaying. Mari clutched her until her knuckles turned white, and the girl settled like a cat walking a stair rail. "Now, hand me that basket," she commanded with a mischievous tilt of her head.

Lillian Pye scurried to do Josie's bidding.

"Have you ladies any letters?" Josie slanted her mouth in concentration as she threaded a rope through the basket handle.

Alice Schilling wrung her hands. "But Miss Bronson must approve all correspondence."

Sally and Lillian fished in their sewn-in pockets and produced a letter each.

Mari had been duly warned about the school's policies. "But Josie, what are you doing?"

"We have our own way around Miss Bronson's strictures." She took Alice's letter and dropped it into the box, along with the others the girls handed over. Then she lifted the basket up through the opening at the top of the window pane and slipped it through, letting it dangle from her rope. She lowered it down until a dove call signaled that the messenger below received their parcel.

After Josie hauled the basket back, she handed it to Lillian, who untied the rope and returned it to its place in the corner. There were a few return letters which Lillian distributed.

Mari bit her lip. She'd had nothing prepared for Ethan this time, but next time she'd be prepared. If *Camp Chemung* were sufficient enough address. Perhaps add *cavalry division*?

A train whistle blew in the distance. Another shipment of soldiers departed on the Elmira and Williamsport, southbound for the battlefront. Mari looked back toward the horses and riders, catching a fading glimpse of the cavalry encampment by the light of their campfires.

"We must do something for our boys." Josie murmured, practically reading Mari's thoughts. Josie then grasped Mari's shoulder along with Sally's and billowed down from her perch, light as a paper lantern.

"What shall we do?" Alice asked, her expression of earnest exaggerated by her spectacle lenses.

"Housewives!"

"Don't be silly. No one's proposed yet." Lillian waved an unadorned left hand in the air.

"No, I mean *make* housewives—sewing kits." Josie skipped across the wooden floor and flounced her skirts. "We'll see if Mrs. Bronson will allow us to deliver them to the boys as they board the trains. It's the least we can do! And besides"—she winked like a vixen—"no one would mistake our patriotism for silly romantic notions."

ଔଷ

Camp Chemung
Barracks One
September 1863

A pinprick of light shone from Prospect Hill, flickering from the octagonal tower of the Female College. Like a city set on a hill, its light could be seen for miles. Ethan sighed. Was the lamplighter as lonely as he? Did she long for some faraway love, wondering if he gazed on the same moon as she?

Did Mari, wherever she was?

He turned on his army issue rubber blanket, away from the tent opening, and cradled Mari's tintype in his hand. The shadowy light revealed only her basic outline, but his mind filled in the details. She didn't smile, didn't beckon him with come-hither eyes. She only gazed out with firm, tin resolve.

She hadn't replied to any of his letters sent to her Maryland home—and there had been several since he'd left Washington—asking if she might still wait for him, laying out his heart in each line to tell her why he hadn't wanted to leave. Sure, the war had slowed mail, but he'd never had trouble before, not for this long. Perhaps she had taken her parent's advice and forgotten him. Maybe he'd lost her after all.

He climbed to his feet with the stealth of a cavalry scout and retreated from the tent. A pang stirred within him. He'd prayed silently for over an hour, wondering if there was anything to be done about Mari. Though his heart ached like starvation itself, he told himself he had tried his best. He turned his mind to another matter, another relationship that still lay fractured. But in the case of this other one, he knew he hadn't done all he could to mend it.

He slid a paper from his sack and in the pale silver moonlight, he dabbed his nib across it, fighting a tempest of emotions over every word tugged from his heart.

Dear Father,

I'm sorry it's taken me over two years to contact you. Pride comes in many forms, including fear of rejection. I owe you my apology, and to assure you that I am alive and well. I'm sorry for the way I left. I am sorry I brought you shame, worry, or upset. I'm sorry I lacked a cooler head or a braver heart so that things might have worked out differently.

It may satisfy your curiosity to know that my journey took me to the Hamilton's, and from there, to the Maryland Cavalry. I served through Gettysburg unscathed, as God's grace permitted. I have settled in New York since Levi Hamilton arranged a post for me at Camp Chemung, a position training cavalry.

I regard you with the same respect and affection that I always have. I hope that our valley never sees the devastation that other parts have, and that someday our distances would be no more than geography. When this war is over, I look forward to a day when your grandchildren might grace your table and hearthside. Perhaps you might extend a welcome again to me, too.

Please share these sentiments with each of my brothers—Gideon, Benjamin and Devon—as I mean them from my heart. May the Lord bless and protect each of you, as is daily my prayer.
Your devoted son,
Ethan

He slipped the letter into an envelope and prayed it would reach home and bridge a gap that had been left open and aching for too long.

Chapter 27

Stuart's Headquarters,
Autumn 1863

A curious thing happened. Its peculiarity had been so rare that Devon could count its frequency on one hand since he'd joined the army. He'd gotten a letter.

He held the wrinkled, dirty parchment, turning it over and over. How old was it? When had the sender penned it? The edges were frayed and fuzzy. The ink had faded in spots. But the writing itself—it belonged to no one in his family. It was of long, deliberate pen strokes. Even in its weary condition, it was still a pretty thing.

A veteran sergeant sitting at the campfire sliced an apple with his pocket knife and popped it in his mouth. "You gonna open it or kiss it?"

Devon scowled and turned his back to the man. Curiosity spurred him. Who could have sent it? His gauntlets got in the way, so Devon shed them to handle the paper with bare hands, calloused though they were, and not as clean as he preferred. Perhaps he sought the physical contact of another human being.

The dry outer seal peeled away at the touch of his Bowie knife, and he used care not to rough its contents easing the paper out of its sheath. He turned to the last page and found the signature. A flood of warmth flowed to his cheeks. His mind recalled a colorful scene. The name synonymous with that night in

Urbana was written there, and the gala of dance, of music, of banners, and burnished brass buttons replayed before him. The heady fragrance of autumn roses had festooned the hall. Sounds swelled all over again, rippling currents crossing the Potomac and the singing of "Maryland, My Maryland," the laughter of men and ladies together, the plucky fiddles and cornets, and her voice, as if Gwen sat beside him and read the words of her letter.

Dear Devon,

How grand a time I had when you came to Urbana with your general last fall. As much as your cavalry has haunted the minds here with legendary exploits, lately I find that my own mind has been haunted by you. I wonder about your present state; are you well? Have you managed to keep yourself safe thus far? Imaginations can't summon your heart. Is it well? Does it think of me? Or is it engaged with other attachments? You had spoken of none, and you had said that you wished to see me if ever you came this way again.

Sometimes I walk down to where the music and dance brought us together, and I wonder if you have ever tried to find me here, as I have tried many times to recreate the night our paths crossed. Am I foolish to be writing these things, Lieutenant Sharpe? I still recall the words you bid me pledge. Were they the ravings of a love-struck girl? I don't think you found them silly then, and neither do I take back a single word now.

Will we meet again? I write to send you the way to come, should you be so inclined.

With all fondness,

Gwendolyn May Harris

Strange sensations possessed him. A rush of pleasure coursed through his body even to worn fingertips. From his rhythmic breathing to the paper in his hand, details came alive to him. He'd walked the corridor of human experience from death to life and everything in between, but this moment was all new territory.

I write to send you the way to come. She had written a decimating thing. He could not compel himself to put the letter or the notion away. The corrupting blaze of her suggestion had ignited kindling upon his heart, dried out and parched for the slightest indication from fate. If he couldn't see her, he would burn out long before he ever partook of her quenching kisses again. If she only knew that her words had sealed his course. To return to her was only a matter of time.

꧁꧂

Camp Chemung
Autumn 1863

"Private Billings. Corporal Langley. Sergeant Sharpe..."

Ethan paused mid-stride on his way to commissary. He'd ceased lining up for the mail call weeks ago, expecting none and receiving none, but the syllables that the orderly called had sounded so much like his name that he didn't have the heart to tell himself it was only wishful thinking. Again.

The young orderly clutched the mail bag, reading names from envelopes before he relinquished them to eager hands. He'd paused when no one claimed the last one, then resumed, chucking the envelope into a pile of discards.

"Private Todd…."

"Wait!" Ethan jogged over to the cluster of men and shouldered his way through. "I'm Sharpe. You got something for me?"

"Right there," the orderly replied, pointing to the thin stack on the ground. Ethan took the one on top, scattering the parcels in his haste. The envelope bore his name, all right. His heartbeat quickened. He looked for the postmark, expecting Harrisonburg, Virginia—home. But there was none. No stamp, either. Who would have hand-delivered correspondence marked for Camp Chemung? Perhaps it was military—sent from one of the other camps in town. He frowned. The script didn't look official with its freehand and hint of artistry.

He peeled the envelope's seal and fished out its contents. A letter. He unfolded the missive and a floral scent emanated from the handwritten stationery.

"Mari?" he asked aloud. "How can that be?" He looked around to be sure no one had heard him, and hurried toward the only private area of camp, the latrine. No one would bother him there, and he could read what she had to say without interruption.

Dearest Ethan,

You must have thought by now that I've left you to utter neglect. I have not abandoned you, my darling, but have followed the Lord's leading. With my parents' constant urging that I should attend school, I had little choice but to comply. I struck a compromise and here I am, enrolled in Elmira Female College. I'm practically at your doorstep.

Although my preceptress forbids gentleman callers, I can tell you that I will be among a group of girls handing packages to soldiers at Erie Station. Perhaps, if the army can spare you a few minutes following Sunday service, we might chance a meeting there. One adoring look from you would fix the stubborn ailment of my heart. You may write to me, but to keep from raising suspicions, perhaps you could discretely slip it into one of the girls' baskets at the station.

With all my heart's affections,
Your Marietta

Ethan clutched the letter to his chest. Marietta was here? Was it possible? He looked at it again to be certain it wasn't a trick of his homesick mind. But there it was, her signature, and the verification of her words. *How good you are, Lord!*

Sunday he would search her out. To have her near, even for a moment, it was all he dared hope for.

ଓଃ୬

Camp Chemung,
Later that week

A sullen Sunday afternoon yawned before Ethan. A dismal mood settled in with the gray skies blanketing Chemung Valley. He hadn't been able to break away from duty to ride past the depot yet. And it looked as though his captain would have him busy the rest of the day.

He'd written Mari a letter, and patting his breast pocket, assured himself it was still there, awaiting the opportunity that hadn't come. *Lord, how long?*

"Hope deferred maketh the heart sick."

"What's that, Sergeant?" The captain looked up from the papers he perused.

Ethan shook himself out of his daydream and saluted the officer.

Captain Darcy had doubtlessly timed the request today just to toy with him. He fancied himself quite the dandy, with his loose hair waving beneath his broad cavalry hat. He never broke a sweat but looked on as the drill sergeants performed the muddy, cumbersome labors of command. Ethan scarcely contained his contempt. "Nothing, Captain." He resumed scribing the captain's scribble into legible missive.

His prayers for Marietta, though silent, came from the heart. Surrounded by an army by day, he could not intercede as he would like. Sleep and duty consumed all else, except Sundays. This was the one day he should have had an hour of respite.

Bitterness pierced him with jagged edges. His prospects looked more dismal than the storm gathering over East Hill.

After a while his commander concluded his report and dismissed him. Ethan wandered to the picket post where Nimbus chewed his grain. Surely it was too late to try now. If the girls had been to the depot, they were gone by now. Mud soiled his cavalry boots and he stooped to wipe them with his bandana, inadvertently dislodging a spur.

He picked up the object from the ground and held it up for inspection as unexpected emotion welled up. He was going to give these to Devon on their last birthday together. Twenty-nine months ago, now, to be exact. The engraved surface of the silver reflected a split-second image of a young man weathered by flint chisels of anger and resentment. Doubt and unbelief had carved itself onto his very visage.

Lay down your burden, Ethan.

"But Lord, it's too late. I'm never going to see Mari or Devon again."

Do you trust me? Go to her. Now.

Ethan mounted Nimbus and rode south along the canal, battling doubt the whole way.

Moments later, smoke and steam thickened the air at Erie station. Soldiers filed into transport cars similar to the one he had arrived on last month. Beyond their orderly ranks, a small troop on foot approached. Their rustling skirts, colorful shawls and bonnets had already drawn a small crowd. And yet at the center, he could see a sage green dress. Mari. She'd come.

He straightened and sought her gaze. Shining eyes met his, and she mouthed a soundless utterance of his name. She looked right and left and bustled over to him. Then, reaching inside her basket, she held out a sewing kit to him.

He turned the folded fabric over and over in his fingers. He wished it could be her hands, pressed in his.

"For you, Sergeant. Lord bless you." And then she passed him by.

His heart staggered. She'd been so close—how could anyone be nearer without touching?

The dull ache swelling inside his empty heart pierced with sudden sharpness.

Indeed, how could anyone be any dearer, and yet so far away—closer than a twin brother? Closer than the girl he loved? It seemed he could have neither, whether the work of a protective father or a jealous God.

He hung his head and prayed.

Oh, God, it looks impossible. But if you're the God of the impossible, then help me believe that you'll make a way, both with Marietta, and Devon. Whatever it takes.

Before he forgot, he fished in his pocket and dropped the letter he had written for her in the basket of the next girl he blindly passed.

Chapter 28

Elmira Female College
December 1863

"Wake up, Mari!"

Josie shook her bed—it was not yet five o'clock. "Come see—Lillian's beau has written to her in secret code!"

A small entourage of Lil's close friends descended the cellar stairs, their candle lanterns casting an uncertain light over the dank corridors leading to the laundry. Mari stifled a shiver at the winter damp, and she suspected, at more than that.

Josie squealed. "The Major's friend sent a separate letter, instructing her to hold it to the heat to see the hidden message. Isn't that the most romantic—"

"Sh-shh! You'll wake the matron," Lillian scolded.

"Put an iron on the fire, Alice." Josie pointed.

Alice set an iron on the end of a poker and held it to the flame. Then, she set it on a wrought iron firedog to cool the scorching metal.

Lillian slipped open the envelope and spread the letter over her skirt. It appeared to Mari nothing but blank paper with a singed edge and a few lines. She gathered in close enough for the embers in the hearth to heat her cheeks and steam her skirts. Sally took down a bed sheet from the clothesline and folded it into a rectangle twice the width of the foolscap. She set both on a wooden board while Alice wrapped a cloth about her hand and lifted the iron by the handle. She dotted her finger with saliva and touched it to the hot iron bottom, sending a sizzle-pop through the room.

"It's ready," Alice said.

All the girls huddled tight to watch as Alice moved it over the paper. A whiff of lemon and scorched paper filled Mari's nose, and as the iron withdrew, Lillian blew cooler air over the letter with quick breaths. Dark lines formed into letters, and letters into words.

Josie read aloud, Lillian blushing a comely pink.

"Am captured in Libby Prison. Men are packed tight as straw in this old warehouse. Praying for home, and for you. Love you my Lillian.

–Your Silas"

Five sighs erupted, and a lump formed in Mari's throat. "Oh, Lil—we must pray for his release!"

While Sally hugged Lillian, who wept openly, Josie took Alice and Mari aside.

"The Christmas party will cheer her, don't you think?" Alice's plain brown eyes filled with warmth and concern.

Mari patted down a smoking hem that had caught on a live coal. "If Lillian could send her Silas something to ease his plight, she'd set right to work on it, and perhaps that would lend comfort."

"Perhaps she can." Josie tapped her finger to her bottom lip. She spun around and faced the other two girls. "Lillian, listen up! Dry your tears. They don't help our soldiers."

Lillian dabbed her wet lashes with an embroidered handkerchief. "Whatever d-do you mean, Josephine?"

"I mean we shall forego our Christmas party to purchase sundries for our brave young men. They sacrifice so much. Surely we can sacrifice one night of merrymaking for them."

Lillian's spine straightened, though her eyes still glistened with unshed tears. "Yes, Josie. You are quite right. I shall speak to the other girls upstairs and win them to your idea."

❧

Camp Chemung, Cavalry Division
Christmas Eve

Ethan polished Captain Darcy's boots while the young dandy donned a perfectly lint-free federal blue frock coat. Ethan knew it was perfectly lint free because he had brushed it the last hour for the insufferable toad. The man stood before a plate and turned this way and that to admire every conceivable angle of his considerably full self. He had foregone his butternut and blue standard issue cavalry trousers for charcoal pantaloons, and he looked like a French dragoon complete with ridiculous whiskers that would make General Ambrose Burnside jealous.

An ambitious lieutenant grabbed the pair of polished boots from Ethan's hands and presented them. "There you are, Darcy. So burnished you'll be able to see under the ladies' petticoats as you dance."

Ethan bit the inside of his cheek to keep his tongue in check. The captain cracked a riding crop down on the bench beside him.

"Make yourself useful Sharpe and bring me my horse."

"Yes, sir." He charged out into the blustery air to escape. It was the officer's Christmas ball, and he'd fought the devil to keep from feeling sorry for himself that he couldn't go. He'd heard the girls from the college had sacrificed their own Christmas party to purchase a small organ for the military hospital. They would make an appearance at the officer's ball to present it. And Captain Darcy would be there to receive them. Marietta, included.

Breathing in the cold air did nothing to cool the burning in Ethan's gut. The man was a cad. A wastrel. And maybe, just maybe, Ethan was a tad jealous of him.

He led the man's bay thoroughbred out, grudgingly admiring the gelding's lines and angles. Good enough to be of his father's stock. Saddled and readied, all the sooner the animal would carry Darcy off to the Brainard House and begin Ethan's miserable night of waiting.

With a sniff of contempt, the captain took the oiled leather reins from Ethan's hand and swung up. He made the animal prance a bit and in a backward spray of dirty snow, then Darcy and the lieutenant galloped off for their merry night.

Dusting off his frock coat with worn gauntlets, Ethan headed toward the light of a nearby campfire. The aroma of coffee and mellow wood smoke warmed him, and he laid aside his anger in their friendly greeting.

"Hey, Sarge. Pull up a log and warm yourself. We're making Christmas *sloosh*."

"Thanks, boys. Don't mind if I do."

In the background, someone picked at a stringed instrument and a trio sang "Oh come All Ye Faithful."

A stray dog wandered from one campfire to another, partaking of salt pork bits that the soldiers doled out for the pleasure of seeing the mongrel's tail wag. The stray came over to Ethan and set its head on his knee for an ear rub. He obliged, taking his gauntlet off to caress the unkempt fringes of fur.

"Sarge must be missin' someone. Look at him pat that curr as though he's pettin' a pretty gal."

"Who says his gal's prettier'n that dog?" the other replied, and laughter erupted.

Ethan grinned, taking the good-natured ribbing in stride. "Oh, she's pretty all right. Don't you worry about that."

"Sarge got hisself one of them fancy college girls."

A chorus of ooh's and ah's rose. Ethan swung his hat at them, half grinning.

"Why are you settin here, then? You should be at that party with her."

"He cain't—he's only got a stripe, not a bar."

Ethan nodded. "It's for officers only."

"If'n it were me, I'd see if the ladies' entourage needs an escort." The soldier nearest him nudged him and winked.

Ethan rose from his makeshift chair and stood. Slapping his hat back on his head, he turned. "Wish me luck, gentlemen."

Ethan rode out of camp and turned west onto Mill Street. Caroling in the sweet octave of young ladies' voices carried on the frosted air as dozens of young ladies, some holding a lantern wreathed with holly, spruce or ivy, descended the hill from the college bound for town. He tied Nimbus at a hitching post and overtook them at a brisk walk. New warmth suffused Ethan, moving alongside them. His frosted breath rose, joining them in song.

The group parted as he neared, clearing a path to one of its members. Marietta was a sight to behold in her red velvet dress and forest green overcoat. Her cheeks sported a full blush against the downy fur lining her bonnet, and her eyes shone in the halo of lantern light. She pulled one hand from her fur muff to smooth a strand of hair from her face, and something sparkled against her finger. She wore his ring.

"Mari."

She had stopped singing, too, and walked beside him, her chest rising and falling with each frosted breath. The carolers surrounded them, shielding them from the chaperons, and he seized his opportunity.

He took her in his arms and drew her close. Her clothes, her hair, her breath, bore a sweet essence. She was close enough to kiss, and he brought his face down to meet hers.

ଓଃ

Standing in the middle of Union Street, Mari let his warm lips meet hers. The contact ended too quickly. She touched his cheek and stubble bristled against her fingertips. He closed his eyes and sighed at the slightest gesture apparently fighting the same battle that raged within her. She skimmed her fingers over his ear and through his hair. He emitted a moan so low it resonated in her own chest, as he gathered her closer, tightening his hold where strong arms encompassed her shoulders and waist.

His eyelids hooded, he whispered her name, the warm aroma of wood smoke and coffee emanating from him. Snowflakes landed on his uniform coat, and she reached up and brushed them away. He slid his hand up behind her neck and slowly tilted her head back to receive another kiss. The firm yet tender caress of his mouth on hers sent a warm current through her. She went slack in his hold, longing for him to sweep her up into his arms and carry her away. He released her abruptly, dizzily.

The matrons, Miss Bronson and Mrs. Stanley, appeared and she prayed they hadn't seen anything.

"Merry Christmas, Ma'am." Ethan tipped his hat. She could hardly keep her balance or her wits. A group of students gathered in again, and one of them pressed a care package in his hands.

Gratitude filled her at her friends' gesture, protecting them from the chaperons' watchful eyes. Ethan took a step away, and then another, and another until students filled the gap between them and she could no longer touch him if she reached.

"May your fondest prayers be answered in the New Year, Sergeant." She hoped Ethan had heard her as she was swept along by the crowd. She hoped God had heard her, too.

Chapter 29

The Wilderness, Spring 1864
Confederate Cavalry

The muddy Rapidan gurgled along its path beside the road as Devon marked time in the saddle. Singing camp songs, Devon inspired a dozen troopers to join his charismatic renditions.

Come tighten your girth and slacken your rein;
Come buckle your blanket and holster again;
Try the click of your trigger and balance your blade,
For he must ride sure that goes Riding a Raid!

Stuart himself had lent his tenor to the group passing through. Devon would follow his cavalry commander to the very gates of perdition. Today it was in Lee's first line of defense for the Confederate capital.

The federals under General Meade had crossed the river in the thousands in early May. A year prior, this same theater staged the contest at Chancellorsville, and the memories of the bitter fighting still engaged Devon's mind. For miles along Telegraph Road, dense forest disguised the gathering army. A hush fell over their singing as the advance stilled to a halt. Devon's voice traded song to carry orders in the next moments, and the men took position. A few stayed mounted, while others crouched in picket lines, burdened with the task of slowing the Union advance.

Devon and his company picketed their horses and dug escarpment into the thick-rooted ground. Composting leaves and a faint char from fires a year past thickened the air. As one of the troopers hefted a shovelful of dirt over his shoulder, a shred of moldering blue uniform—an arm bone still in it—came up. Several of the boys jumped back, some expelling oaths, others crossing themselves and chanting prayers.

"Aw, that ain't nothing but the boys from Chancellorsville wavin' us on." Devon laughed and kicked a heap of leaves over the sight. "Carry on."

An eruption of sound crested the canopy, filling the air with vibration. A tingle rose over his flesh watching hundreds of birds take flight overhead. The acrid whiff of gunpowder saturated the dense glade. Meade's guns had arrived.

Combat turned the clock to nightfall, while Generals Stuart and Fitzhugh Lee held Grant on the left flank. Word had it that General Longstreet's infantry were due up from Petersburg. In the meanwhile, Devon and his dismounted company huddled in the darkness, surrounded by enemy forces so close that they could hear their taunts.

"Come on out, you Virginia cavalry. We know you're in there." Voices dared them to respond, to give away their position and invite a lead greeting. Hardened veteran or not, prickles crept up Devon's spine.

Then, mingled with the sabre-rattling of their tormentors, came a sound from the deep woods, gathering in around them. Pressing in shoulder to shoulder, the ghosts of Chancellorsville formed ranks that just about set Devon's men fleeing into the woods. Before anyone skedaddled, Longstreet's infantry broke the tension with laughter.

"Thanks for settin' up camp," one man said as he bumped Devon with the barrel of his Springfield rifle. "Now us Tennessee boys can git to the real work!" The cocky assurance of his twang had a calming effect.

One of the Virginians from Fitzhue Lee's division replied. "Sure, step right up and do our clean-up for us!"

As the sun's approach stole over the eastern woods, the long muskets of Devon's new comrades set about their work. Grant's easy push to Richmond halted.

Devon weathered the firestorm all through the early part of the day. Then Federals—sometimes eight men deep—came at them. Even in the face of Lee's artillery guns, these ghouls, instead of recoiling, actually rose up a cheer, volley after gruesome volley.

Reports came in with a scout that Union General Sheridan's cavalry had struck General Robert E. Lee's rear, threatening the line of communication with Richmond, or worse yet, the capital itself. The sight of enemy cavalry bearing down Telegraph Road four abreast, stretching reportedly 13 miles long, stripped Devon of the light of hope.

All day Devon's troopers took a stand against the foe. He and his company had no rest until arriving at Hanover Junction some time after sunset. Exhausted to the point of impairment, the boys waited for permission to fall out. Devon overheard the order. They had until the second watch of the night.

Stuart departed for the nearby home of Dr. Fontaine where his wife and baby waited. A stir of jealousy turned inside Devon. If this battle were to be his last, he'd die without seeing Gwen again. The arbitrary and nonsensical notion lodged in his mind before he fell into a deep sleep.

Hours later, as the boys prepared to move out, Stuart appeared again. He had returned from the respite with a light in his blue eyes that reminded Devon of Thomas Jackson in times past. "Old Blue Light" Jackson. It seemed fitting to rally the boys with the image.

"Stand strong for Richmond and for Old Blue Light."

He led the men on a ride that stretched through the day and into another night. All the while they were pushed to Richmond's doorstep—eight miles outside the city. At mid-morning, they stopped to rest again. They'd arrived ahead of Sheridan's Union cavalry and paused to catch their breath at a little town called Yellow Tavern.

Placing artillery on the left of Telegraph Road under an officer named Lomax, and another on the right under Wickham, and positioning still a third nearby, Stuart ordered his troopers to eschew their lathered horses to the rear and prepare for hand to hand combat.

The morning whittled away with a familiar cold nervousness, but by afternoon, now the third day of fighting, the sun warmed Devon with resolve. This would be the last sight some of his boys would take in this world. He reckoned none of them saw Telegraph Road, but the women they loved, the homes they'd fought for, and the lives they'd left behind. A home-fire wafted smoke again from the old stone chimney, and the last meal he'd shared with his father and brothers returned to Devon's tongue. He imagined being with Gwen, too, as time drifted, awaiting the knoll of Sheridan's spurs to mark his passage into the next world. A cavalier beside him penned a quick note, dated May 11, 1864, to bid mother, wife and children goodbye.

Devon bit into an ancient piece of hardtack, each flex of his jaw an exercise on sore teeth. His keen eyes poured over the extent of the road, but nothing stirred. Glancing over his shoulder, he could just make out the dim silhouette of horses tethered well to the rear. Knowing his Cid would be spared the immediate onslaught made him more accepting of his own fate. He swallowed the salty paste and breathed in the last gulps of fresh air before battle smoke fouled it. The clean aroma of pine and humus filled his senses, and for a few moments, he was relaxed.

If only I could have made peace with Ethan.

An ominous noise arose over the chatter of woodland creatures. A gust swept over the woods, and then, an eerie amplification of swift hooves numbering in the hundreds echoed between trees. His company's horses neighed shrilly at the vast herd approaching. Chaos erupted in the breath of firearms, the roar of cannon, the shriek of animal and man, the clash of metal sabers and the thud of flesh. All tangled together in an acoustic dissonance that rang in Devon's eardrums.

The road filled with the casualties of the first wave, so Devon climbed to find footing. He set his sights on a target and fired his pistol to join the cacophony. Forces pulled at him from all sides, bumping, grabbing, and jostling him, projectiles slurring past him, officers calling an incomprehensible melee of orders. His instinct for survival drove him on.

A Yankee laid on the ground before him, a cartridge box full of ammunition clipped to his belt. Devon stooped to collect the spoils of war, when fingers clenched about his face. The dead Yankee leapt up—very much alive—and toppled Devon, jamming him into a split tree. Devon struggled to reach his Bowie knife tucked in his boot before the Yankee found his pistol. He could hardly breathe as sharp splinters pierced his back.

With a free hand, he staved off the clawing fingers gouging his eyes. He kicked frantically, driving his weight further back into the shredded tree trunk. His homespun shirt snagged with a loud rip. Just when the splinters tore flesh, the Yankee's grip loosened and his eyes rolled up in the back of his head. His attacker sank down at his feet. Devon pulled free of the wooden daggers at his back, leaning over the immobile body. He lifted the munitions caisson from the dead man's belt uncontested now, as well as a revolver, and scampered down Telegraph Road.

Smoldering undergrowth created a smokescreen allowing him to slip close enough to the artillery piece just as it changed hands. The Yanks had stolen their gun, and attempted to discharge its load, when Devon raised both his pistol and the absconded revolver, one in each hand. Firing into the column of blue, he emptied both barrels. When his mind cleared, he had a sickening feeling that even if the gunners were all dead, the fuse on the cannon wasn't. The barrel pointed in his direction.

He dove for cover just before branches, earth, and air fused where he had just stood. Devon sucked in a breath and picked himself up from the pile of debris. Swearing, stumbling, and falling, he ran as the left flank crumbled. No sight of his company, or his horse. He managed to reload in mid-stride and turned to fire intermittent shots in his wake. Finding the road again, he rallied at the sight of Confederate cavalry rushing in around him. He did an about-face and took a stand with them.

To his surprise, the federals were turning back. Sensation returned to his face, and he wiped away a trickle of sweat—or was it blood? The counter-charge won him a moment's time. He moved amid grim-faced companions, and their assault cleared the avenue except for a few straggling Yankee cavaliers leveling off a round or two as they scrambled for cover.

Another shout arose among his ranks—not a cheer but an anguished groan. Devon searched about to determine the source. An officer lay slumped over the back of a frantic horse. Several men rushed to him and struggled to lift the commander from the head-tossing beast. Devon gasped at the insignia on the man's shoulder—three stars inside two laurel wreaths—a Major General. His thick beard could not obscure the grimacing face of Jeb Stuart. The stoic general clutched his side as the men transferred him to a steadier mount.

Stuart's last battlefield command carried on the air to Devon and the other stunned men.

"Keep fighting!"

With that, his beloved commander was spirited away.

Devon tore his eyes back to battle. The federals closed in again. Firing, reloading, time ticked by in a blur. He could not recall how or when, but at length he found himself surrounded by confederate infantry. Their fresh movement quickened around him and soon overtook him. All urgency seeped from his exhausted body, and Devon took inventory for a second. His footsteps wore to a halt. Coughing and wiping smoke from his eyes, he blinked in the dim light.

For the first time since Yellow Tavern had erupted, the immediacy of battle had distanced from him. He stood motionless for several seconds.

Stuart was gone. His hero. His reason to keep fighting. His last reason to resist Gwen's arms.

He cast one last look down the road at the remnants of the Virginia cavalry. He spied a group of tethered horses, and then, as if possessed of a will of their own, his feet took over. Each step overcame numb inertia, until he ran to retrieve his horse. Swinging astride, he reined about, then spurred Cid hard into a flat-out run, away from Yellow Tavern, away from the fray, away from his army, unfettered up Telegraph Road.

ଔ

Urbana, Maryland
Summer 1864

A sliver of a moon lit the midnight garden. Devon moved through the shadows where a rose trellis peaked above crumbling sections of low stone wall. The rendezvous Gwen had described in her letter appeared before him as though it were a dream. Despite the dangers lurking, he ventured forward, his anticipation rising within him like the tangle of foliage climbing the arbor.

He tied Cinder beyond the stone perimeter. It had taken him days to skirt the army through the thickest of the enemy's presence between Richmond and the Potomac before he could cross into Maryland. He could have been detected, shot, or captured at any moment along the way, and even now. But personal safety faded, overpowered by Gwen's invitation.

The wood-framed farmhouse lay dark and still, no lantern lit at this late hour. But she had described which upper window belonged to her. He scooped a handful of acorns littering the yard and judiciously pelted the black panes of glass. Somehow beneath the romance of a summer moon, the war, the years, all cares slipped away to a sweeter time, and he was just a young man in love, and she....

The window slid up on its sash and a face framed in tumbling auburn curls peered out. His breath hitched.

Gwen.

Even bathed in shadow, her smile fell on him brighter than the celestial lights. She retreated into the dark interior, and he fell back into the dense foliage to await her.

In three years riding with the Army of Northern Virginia, never in all the peril could he recall having such a time steeling his nerves. Trembling anticipation heightened every sense until the night became livid with the stirring of his horse, the warm air thick with wild honeysuckle, the coursing of his own blood. And just beyond, the click of a door closing softly, and light tread of feet.

The breeze shifted, carrying a new flora to him. He turned his head but paused before stepping out. His pulse quickened. Drawing a deep breath of this perfume, he closed his eyes and savored its sweet nearness. All his memories of her sprang to life. Then, fixing his eyes on the object of all that summoned him, he stepped from the cover of the arbor into the moonlight.

Nothing about her had been exaggerated by memory. Auburn curls dipped across one shoulder, her sashay rippled the dark fabric of her hoop-less skirt, and her enigmatic expression came into focus, provoking him to tease a smile from her. And if the sight of her failed to awaken him, her embrace engulfed his body like kindling thrown into the fire.

He pressed into her soft warmth, his caresses seeking out the places where he ended and she began. And then he kissed her, gently, fearing he'd shatter his dream world if he pressed too hard. She wrapped her arms about his shoulders and drew him to her.

He broke contact, searing a look into her hooded eyes.

"I've come to give my oath to you this time, Gwen."

Her smile flickered, quickly replaced by a pierced look. "How long do we have?"

"My time is yours, now." He cupped her cheek in his hand. "But you?"

"I won't be missed until morning." She took his hand, turned, and led him into the stable. Breathless, he drew the door closed. Inside, the moonlight dimmed, and he had to navigate by touch.

She gasped and seized his wandering hands. He felt her mischievous grin as she brushed her lips against his.

"I'm right here," she said, stepping just out of his reach.

He caught her wrists with a rough grip. "Don't tease me, Gwen." He kissed her again, communicating his urgency, drawing her against him.

She stilled. "Oh, Devon." Her murmur tickled his ear, shooting sparks over his skin.

"Gwen, I don't want to wait for you anymore. Please, honey, don't make me."

She sighed, her breath ruffling the hair about his collar. She grew slack and passive in his arms. But she didn't respond to his demands with spoken assent.

"In your letters you promised yourself to me." He pushed the words against her neck near her ear, restraining himself—barely.

She snapped out of her swoon, retaliating with a vigor of words. "And what about you? You've made no promises to me! What you're asking, demanding, isn't right."

He dropped to one knee before her, drawing her down with him. "Marry me now, Gwendolyn Harris." He gathered her right hand to his chest and his lips grazed her ear. "Don't deny me, darlin'."

She moved ever so slightly under the pressure he exerted on her. "What of your oath to me?"

He hunkered down in the straw on both knees and drew her to him. "I pledge my heart and my unyielding loyalties. My lifelong pursuit—"

She placed a finger over his mouth and shushed him. Then, placing her lips where her finger had just been, she pressed a kiss, signaling the yielding for which he longed.

Chapter 30

Cavalry training barracks
Camp Chemung
June 1864

The Sunday morning *Elmira Advertiser* sat on Captain Darcy's desk, drawing Ethan's notice while the officers enjoyed their clandestine card game. Ethan had been ordered to keep watch, lest Major Colt catch Darcy and his staff passing around the brandy. Sipping black coffee, Ethan read of Grant suspending all prisoner exchange. This policy promised to swell prison populations beyond already burgeoning numbers.

Interest in that story faded as he moved on to read about the ongoing campaign in the Shenandoah. Just a few weeks ago, Major General Franz Sigel had lost the battle of New Market, fighting Confederate General John Breckenridge and cadets from Virginia Military Institute. So close to home. The coffee soured in his stomach. Sigel had subsequently been replaced by Major General David Hunter, who launched an offensive toward Staunton. Ethan closed his eyes temporarily, wishing he had gone to the tent meeting instead of being relegated to picket post for these reprobate officers. Shaking himself out of his souring mood, he turned the page back to the previous article.

Overcrowding in Point Lookout, Fort Douglas, Rock Island, and Belle Isle begged for a solution. Rumors hung in the air of possible sites for a new prison camp. Secretary of War Edwin

Stanton, replacing Simon Cameron, had Elmira in his crosshairs. Stanton's policies had reportedly taken a shrewd turn.

The paper cited Elmira's rail connections while regional policymakers touted the town's experience housing army populations. Lumber abounded to make modifications to the existing forts. But Ethan guessed the biggest factor in Elmira's favor was its political climate. *The Advertiser and Republican*, sympathetic to the Lincoln administration, would raise no objection to such a proposal. It was ordered, then, that Barracks No. 3 on the Chemung River be vacated of recruits and prepared for the arrival of Confederate prisoners.

Ethan closed the paper and slapped it back onto the desk. His disgust was suddenly eclipsed by the card players' outburst as one of them laid down a winning hand.

Darcy voiced his contempt in a growl and tossed paper bills toward the winner. He rose from the table and his eyes met Ethan's. "Sharpe, if you're going to just sit around, why don't you go make yourself useful. I have a message for you to deliver to Camp Rathbun."

Ethan stood and saluted. "Yes, sir." He hoped he had fixed his own poker face sufficiently. No sense letting the man know how much he despised him.

After a cleansing two-mile ride, he arrived at Camp Rathbun and tethered Nimbus at a post near the gate. The camp measured over thirty acres at the western end of the city. The barracks abutted the Chemung River. Additional wooden housing and a twelve-foot stockade fence imposed the first tangible changes on the grassy banks. A pile of lumber lay to the east, foretelling of more construction to come.

Ethan delivered the dispatch to its party and rode back through camp, but not before he'd glanced at its message. Colonel Eastman's recommended capacity of 5,000 prisoners had been doubled by Quartermaster General Meigs. The first Confederates were due to arrive in the coming weeks.

Ethan clenched his teeth. Of all the places in the North, why had he been sent here? Why did he have to witness this? Was this his personal punishment from God for failing to reach his family while he still had the chance? Surely it was too late to reach them now. It seemed he was consigned to watch passively as the punishment he and Aaron had foretold came and consumed the land he had once called home.

ᏅᏅ

As a token of appreciation from the freshman class, Marietta and Josie had been chosen to deliver a peach pie to Dr. and Mrs. Cowles' home. Always glad to escape the ever-watchful eyes of their dormitory marm, Mari tempered the skip in her stride to a more ladylike stroll. It was near the end of term, and Mari's parents would be arriving on the train in a week to bring her home.

"I'm going to miss you this summer, Josie."

"It isn't summer quite yet, Mari. And besides, we have this lovely day together to stroll the town."

Mari shouldn't have been shocked by another of Josie's propositions, but she raised her brows with a hint of amusement anyway. "Josephine Fowler, you're going to get us both expelled."

"Are you saying you don't want to go find that handsome sergeant of yours?" Josie's eyes danced with merry daring, and Mari found she couldn't resist.

They rapped on the president's door and the maid answered. "Won't you please step in, girls?"

While Mari and Josie waited in the foyer, male voices from the drawing room carried to Mari's ears.

"As soon as Colonel Hoffman sends word, they're going to start sending them."

"Yes. Seems Washington is very determined to make this town a prison fort."

"I've seen pictures of those human skeletons from Andersonville, Georgia. Very bad business, these camps. I mean, do we really need that here?"

"Ladies," greeted Mrs. Cowles. "Thank you for sending over the pie. How thoughtful of you!"

Josie curtsied. "The freshman class sends its warmest regards, ma'am."

Mari smiled. "Thank you for the countless things you and Dr. Cowles have done for us. It's been a wonderful year."

As they departed, Josie took Mari's hand and spirited her around the corner of West Union Street to Mill Street, where they slipped out of sight. Breathless, Mari clutched her middle. "We've forgotten our parasols!"

"Never you mind, Marietta Hamilton! We're going to have fun today."

"And what do we tell Miss Bronson?"

"Simply that Mrs. Cowles had us for tea—all afternoon."

Tittering, she and Josie clasped hands and strolled up the avenue. The pounding hooves of a horse and rider caused them both to turn. Some bewhiskered dandy passed too closely and splashed mud on Marietta's blue brocade tea dress.

The captain reined to an abrupt halt and swung from the saddle, turning back to them. "I do beg your pardon, misses." He proffered his handkerchief to Marietta with a bow.

She was slow to accept the token, her smile refusing to relax from clenched formality.

"You see, miss.... Uh, Miss?

"Hamilton." She dabbed at the mud on her dress, but it only smudged deeper into the fabric.

"You see, Miss Hamilton, I have vital dispatches from Washington, and I was so absorbed in urgency, I failed to stop in time. I do hope you'll pardon me for intruding on your pleasant afternoon."

His breath released a hint of spirits and an abundance of cheroot. Mari squinted and held her prim smile. "Then pray do not let me detain you, Captain"

"Darcy, ma'am. Captain Darcy at your service." He doffed his hat, revealing a quaff of auburn hair which had been no doubt pomaded in anticipation of such a moment.

"Good day, Captain Darcy." Marietta nodded and moved along, dragging a bewildered Josie along with her.

Taking two strides to Mari's one, Josie struggled to keep up. "What on earth is the matter with you? You might have at least introduced me!"

"Are you ladies in need of escort? Where are you going this fine afternoon?"

He certainly is persistent.

Josie's pleading eyes wore down her reservations. Outnumbered, Mari sighed. "My friend Miss Josie Fowler and I were merely taking a stroll."

"How do you do, Captain?" Josie slipped the captain's handkerchief from Mari's hand and held it out to him.

"Good afternoon." He left Josie dangling the soiled white square.

"Actually, we were on our way to deliver a message to a soldier." Josie stroked the ribbons of her bonnet and batted her eyes.

"Oh? Perhaps I know the man. What's his name?"

Mari clenched her teeth and glared at her impetuous friend.

"He's Mari's beau, but no one is supposed to know that."

"I see." He placed his cavalier's hat back on the top of his head and walked along, leading his lathered horse behind him. "Your secret is safe with me, ladies. But how will you find him unless you have help?"

The man's shameless flirtation inspired Mari's pity. And besides, surely a cavalry captain would know where to find Ethan. She desperately wanted to say goodbye before she left for the summer. "Well, I…."

"Please, allow me to assist you in delivering your urgent message." He winked, which she was sure made Josie's silly heart throb. "The gentleman's name?"

Mari's ice finally melted. "Ethan Sharpe."

The captain's boot kicked a stone and sent it skittering across the street. Did she imagine that his brown eyes just turned a shade of green? "Oh, I know the sergeant quite well. He's my personal adjutant."

He looked away, and a muscle in his jaw pulsed. "Allow me to fetch him for you. I'll be but a moment." The man mounted his steed and galloped off.

Josie waved his hankie after him. "Thank you, Captain!"

Uneasiness riffled through Mari's stomach, and she whispered a prayer that she hadn't just opened Pandora's box.

ଔ

"Sharpe!"

Ethan glanced up from drills to see Darcy riding across the fairgrounds toward him. "Sergeant, I'd like a word with you."

Ethan relegated command to his corporal and guided Nimbus toward Darcy. He stiffened his spine, waiting for the customary upbraiding. What would the man accuse him of today? Neglecting to submit the captain's weekly report to headquarters? Leaving the granary unlocked? All the usual things the undisciplined peacock was responsible for himself.

"Yes, Captain?"

"I've just been made aware of your clandestine activities with the ladies of the town."

He blinked, and laughter welled up at the ridiculous notion, but he stifled it, looking into the man's spiteful eyes. "What?"

"I have just spoken to a woman brazenly walking the street without a parasol or a chaperon. She asked for you by name."

He shook his head and bit back a derisive laugh. Joke or not, this man had sunk to a new low trumping up a charge of that magnitude against him. Was it because the recruits favored him and despised Darcy? Because Ethan had served in active battle, as compared to his untested, political appointment? Or was he just that insecure of his position, fearing Ethan would rise in rank and expose him for the do-nothing that he was?

The man was an insufferable liar and Ethan called his bluff. "You don't say? And where is this brazen tart of which you speak?"

"Why don't you come see for yourself?"

Darcy commanded him to follow and spurred his horse toward the street. In a moment they rode along Mill Street toward the college. Ethan's gut twisted. In the distance he spied two young ladies. Marietta, and her petite friend. *She* was the one of whom he spoke?

He passed the captain's horse, but Darcy slapped the steed's flank and initiated a race.

They thundered down the avenue until they neared the girls at a dead heat. Ethan pulled up short, Nimbus sliding to a halt. Darcy's thoroughbred proved more than the man could contain and charged past.

"Mari." he dismounted and stepped to her side.

"Ethan, I had to see you. Papa will be coming for me next week. I won't return until the fall term, and I—"

He took her hand but was rudely interrupted.

"So, this is your girl, Sharpe?" Darcy pressed his horse too close, his face burnished like a glowing coal. "You should have told me you had yourself such a pretty thing instead of sneaking around to see her."

Ethan's fists clenched as he faced Darcy. "Mari, I'm afraid you'd better go. Leave us now."

She backed away, a look of confusion spreading over her face. Darcy dismounted, and caught her by the arm. "Allow me to escort you, Miss Hamilton. No gentleman would allow a lady to walk the streets alone."

"Take your hands off her." Ethan pushed them apart and stood between them, squaring off with his captain. He prayed Mari would take his advice and leave before things escalated.

"Fine pretense, after saying such sullying things. What was it again you called her? A brazen tart?" Darcy whistled.

Ethan gave her an apologetic look, shaking his head. He turned once more toward the captain. "I told you to leave the lady alone. She's out of your league, Darcy."

"Ethan, please. It's not worth it." Marietta tugged at his arm.

Darcy swung at him. Distracted, Ethan caught the blow to the jaw. Mari's friend shrieked.

Ethan shook it off and regrouped. The captain made another move, but Ethan dodged. He shoved Darcy up against his horse, holding the captain's arms in a bear grip. He could easily flatten the scoundrel, except Darcy would levy charges against him. And he couldn't afford notoriety if he held any hope with Mari's parents. Darcy wrested free and swung. Again, and again Ethan blocked Darcy's advances and parried his blows but refrained from delivering the come-uppance he itched to serve. He kept the man at bay long enough for Mari and her friend to spirit away.

Once assured she was safe, Ethan held his hands out from his sides and backed away. "Enough, Darcy. Let's both forgo the provost marshal, shall we?" He turned to retrieve his horse.

"Don't think I'm finished with you, Sharpe. This isn't over."

࿇

Mari's world seemed to have switched up for down. Why had Ethan told her to go home? Turned his back on her? Called her those unspeakable names? It couldn't be true.

"Mari, wait!" The gray thoroughbred thundered after her as she approached Prospect Hill from the east.

Josie looked at her with doe eyes. "Should I summon Miss Bronson?"

"No, wait with me," she replied, and faced the approaching cavalier.

"Mari, did I hear you correctly?" he said as he dismounted. He held a hand out to her and though she wanted to take it, instead she shrank back.

He stopped. Leaned in, whispered, "You're leaving. Is it true?"

Footsteps clicked, windows slid open, and doors creaked behind her. She sensed an audience gathering. Her words caught in her throat.

"You're leaving for good, then?"

Ethan's eyes were black wells of pain. Clarity began to drip back into her mind, but the feet behind her shuffled nearer and the whispers grew louder, and she knew she didn't have much time. If he didn't care for her, surely he wouldn't look so wounded. She longed to reassure him.

Ethan ran a hand through his thick, dark hair. "If this is goodbye, then at least have the courage to tell me." His voice crowded with such harshness, she retreated another step away from him.

He bowed his head, his eyes wincing at her. Was it anger, or hurt?

"I—"

"Miss Hamilton, what is the meaning of this? Come inside at once!"

Marietta swung about but didn't budge. She glanced back at Ethan, ready to declare her love to the great cloud of witnesses surrounding them. If only he would give her a sign.

"If you don't come this instant, Miss Hamilton, I will report your conduct."

Pricking tears formed, and she bit her lip. What was the use? Her father would never allow them to marry in any event.

"Good bye, Ethan."

She turned and fled up the steps.

Chapter 31

Camp Chemung, Elmira
Cavalry Training Rendezvous
July 1864

Darcy had made good on his promise. He was indeed not finished with Ethan, and his grudge wasn't over. Hundreds of horses on the cavalry training grounds created no shortage of waste, and that problem suddenly fell to him. After a long day of drills with the recruits, he oversaw the task of raking, shoveling and loading a ton of manure onto wagons and carting it off to local farmers. The insult held a certain vindictive genius, the more Ethan considered it.

But no punishment that Darcy doled out even approached the open wound left in Ethan's chest after Mari had ripped out his heart. Even if he'd had the foolish notion to see her off, his duties kept him too busy to get near the depot. A hardness had formed over the scars left of his hopes, few things penetrating the cloak of protective indifference he had drawn about himself.

And if Mari's leaving weren't enough, captured Confederates were already arriving to fill the camp on the other side of town. Townspeople approached the concept of the prison camp with a mixture of morbid curiosity and entrepreneurial spirit. Water Street along the Chemung River saw a business boom. Sutler wagons appeared, peddling goods to the prison population. And to mitigate the twelve-foot perimeter for spectators, a tower arose. For a nickel apiece, thrill-seekers could climb Mears Brothers' Observatory and view the corralled southerners like the next best spectacle to P.T. Barnum's museum of curiosities.

These developments pressed on Ethan's oldest wounds, now three years festering. *His people*—Virginians, Carolinians, boys like him with the misfortune of hailing from below the Mason-Dixon Line—languished in captivity and utter scorn of this community. Ethan pushed down his regrets, grieving a past as dead as his hopes of reconciliation with it.

This place, where the hills framed the narrow valley as if encasing it from fresh air and winds of hope, had taken a toll on his faith. It was just so hard to trust in a God of redemption when all seemed beyond all reconciling.

ঔঌ

Urbana, Maryland

"Gwendolyn May Harris, where did that animal come from?"

Devon flinched awake. The woman's hollering set pigeons to flight around him in the loft, and he turned slightly to peer down through the rafters. It wasn't the first time Gwen's mother had come close to discovering him. But it was the first Devon had sensed true danger in the woman's tirade.

"My horse," Devon whispered. He held his breath, hoping Gwen would come up with a plausible cover. For her sake.

While the home guard kept diligent watch, folks had been imprisoned for the slightest evidence of aiding the enemy. Gwen faced too great a risk harboring him.

Gwen entered the barn, hefting a water pale. "I found him in the woods, mother," her sweet voice replied. "We can use a good cart pony to carry father's wares to town."

"That's no cart pony! That's a war horse, and a rebel one at that. If you're aiming to catch trouble, go on and harbor that beast."

"No, mother. I'll set him loose after dark."

Devon's gut clenched. He had a decision to make. Neither completely having Gwen nor wanting to leave her, he hung suspended between the two. And for her part, she was either explaining her frequent absences to her mother or to him, relaying how her father, Jentezen Harris, hovered just above the threshold of death. His condition kept her busy with his care, and she had to sneak away to Devon when she could. All of this placed her in a terrible position.

Truth was, Devon's thoughts had turned to another mistress across the divide, the Shenandoah. Grant had launched the worst campaign yet against the South, raiding the bread basket of the Confederacy, scorching his beloved Valley. As July saturated the land with humidity and haze, so too, the woods teemed with blue scouts. How long could Devon continue to lay low, foraging for subsistence just to borrow time with Gwen while his home lay imperiled? These stolen moments together would destroy them both.

He knew what he had to do.

Gwen's mother slammed the barn door, muttering all the way to the house. In a moment Gwen climbed the ladder to the loft, her braided hair cresting the bales of hay. He helped her up and she snuggled down in his arms. "False alarm. She's gone back inside to tend Daddy."

He studied her as she rested against him, sorry he had nothing to offer her in his present state. Weighing his options, he concluded he couldn't return to Fitz Lee's cavalry now that Stuart was dead, and he'd deserted. Perhaps he could take up with John Mosby in these parts. Mosby's Raiders would be sure to defend the Valley, whether or not they offered a wage to send home to a soldier's wife.

Before he did anything, he'd ride home to collect one of his mama's rings. Once it rested safely on Gwen's hand, then he would join Mosby for the duration of the war, come what may. As soon as darkness covered his departure, he'd be gone.

He stirred, and mercifully, she did not wake. She rested in complete and utter trust next to him on the army blanket they shared as a sham marriage bed.

She would wake up alone. But he would make it up to her.

He sighed into the air. "God, Gwen, you ain't making this easy, are you?"

Her eyelids fluttered and rested again. He would have to do this now. Slipping his arm from beneath her head, he turned his end of the cover about her and slid away. He shrugged into his shell jacket, but withheld donning his boots, belt, or scabbard for the noise they would make. After gathering his possessions, he took one last, devastating look at her and descended the ladder.

Cinder waited in the stall for him, saddle and trappings within reach. With deft hands he cinched the girth strap without so much as the creak of leather. Securing saddlebags, he would have been mounted in seconds. A hiccup gave him pause. He turned, and there she was, the betrayed expression on her face shaming him.

He returned her accusing gaze with a smile, his voice robust despite the guilt gnawing his insides. "I wasn't leaving for good, darlin'. I *will* come back. . ." He swaggered as he came to her and scooped up her sagging shoulders.

Her hot breath penetrated his shirt where her face pressed against his chest.

He buried his face into her hair and whispered. "You *will* be my wife."

Though she wasn't given to tears like other females, he guessed she resisted them now, her muscles tensing under his hold.

Suddenly she wriggled out of his arms, her green eyes glinting. "Who says I'd marry you if you *do* return? Were you going to sneak off and leave us now? Now that I…" The heat of her fury melted the ice in her eyes into large, cascading tears. She flung his arms from her and wrapped herself in her own embrace. Her head hung, and sobs came.

"Gwen, honey? What do you mean 'leave *us*'?" He stroked the fire from her with caressing words and touch. "And now that you're *what?*"

"Why don't you guess, Lieutenant Sharpe?"

He took her hand and placed both his and hers over her stomach. "You mean y-you might be…?" Sentiment overtook him, and he gathered her to him again. She beat her arms at his chest, but he pressed her closer, wrestled her sparks and barbs away until she clung, subdued in his arms.

"Yes." She sniffed. "I am with child. And now you're leaving."

"Oh, sugar, you knew I couldn't stay here forever with the war pressing in."

"The war? I thought you had come to your senses about that. Pledge your loyalty to the Union and stay here with us."

He caressed her. "You know I can't."

She hung in his embrace, and her protest left a trailing lament. "Why, Devon? Why?"

"Do you believe me, Gwen? You're my cause, now."

"Then stay!"

"Honey, I've got to do this." He cupped her head against his shoulder, fighting emotion as he assuaged hers. He leaned in to kiss her.

She gripped his neck in one hand and withdrew her other, bringing it with all her might in a sudden slap across his cheek. Then, her whole body went limp. He caught her before she swooned, and he lifted her in his arms, cradling her to him. Her angry flush had receded to a sallow complexion, complete with fluttering eyelids.

He stroked her face with his thumb. "Gwen, I'm sorry."

His apology didn't change his intentions, of course. The lines of her expression hardened as soon as she opened her eyes. She collected herself on shaky feet and turned for the door.

"Gwen?" He stood by his saddled horse.

She blinked hollow eyes as though anticipating his goodbye.

"Wait!" He strode to her. "I'll marry you today. Who can perform the ceremony?"

She sighed. "You don't have to feel trapped, Devon."

He grasped her arms, forcing her to look at him. "It's not like that! I *don't* feel trapped. Don't you understand? I *want* to marry you. I just wanted to do it right, with a ring, and vows."

"It's a little late for that, isn't it?" She shook her head and laughed.

"I was going—well, it doesn't matter now. I want our baby to know he has a daddy, in any event. In case something happens."

"Oh, Devon, come back to us. *You will,* won't you? But you don't have to go! Do you really have to go now?"

"Awe, Gwen, this ain't easy for me, either. I don't want you to bear this alone. That's why you must marry me now, before I leave. Who'll recite our vows with us?"

"I know a minister in Frederick who won't report you to the home guard. My parents will stand up for us. Oh, Devon, I wish it weren't happening like this."

"I'm sorry, Gwen. It's all my blame. But after the war, I swear I'll make it up to you. We'll have a big wedding, and you can have the most extravagant honeymoon money can buy."

Her smile was brave and sad. "No, Devon. I just want you."

❧

Bridgewater, Virginia
Shenandoah Valley

Sleep engulfed Devon. It seemed days, though only hours had passed on a real bed of feather ticking, sheets and quilts. Home. Before he ever opened his eyes, he brought his heavy arm up to shield against the glare of the sun. His focus came slow and bleary and his stomach rolled in queasy waves. How had he arrived? Hallucinations of the night before left him unnerved. Fleeing a squadron of pursuing Yankees, taking a grazing blow to his shoulder. He placed a hand there and winced at the tenderness.

"Dad?" The hoarse voice startled him—his own. "Ben?" His mouth was so dry that the back of his throat pinched. Coughing racked him until his skull would burst. Moaning, he lay still on the pillow, waiting for the aura in his eyes to dispel. Then, he attempted again.

"I'm a'comin' Devon. Hold on!" a young man's voice replied in an unfamiliar register.

When Benjamin appeared, Devon whistled. "Be darned if you ain't sprouted!"

"I'm as big as you, now. And I'm the one's gonna help you down the stairs, so you might as well get over yourself." Ben's sturdy hands helped him out of bed.

"Don't sass yer elder." Devon hung on to his dignity, which seemed to amuse Ben all the more.

"Where's yer father?"

"Oh, he's out in the barn taking care of Cinder. You both came in mighty banged up last night. Daddy says you had a scrape with Yankees."

Devon stopped short. "Is Cid hurt?"

"Naw, not bad hurt. Just stressed." Ben released his rib-hold on him as they came to the bottom of the stairs, and Devon regained his bearings. "Don't worry, Devon. Daddy'll have him race-ready in a few days."

"I should take after his care. Ain't no need for the Old Man to be trifling when he's got the whole farm to run."

Ben gazed at his feet. "Ain't much to do 'round here these days, Devon. First Jackson's army cleaned us out, then the Yanks. What wasn't worth riding, they ett."

Ben's words stabbed him through. Could this be true? Herds numbering in the hundreds, gone?

"See for yourself." Ben said, as if reading his mind.

Devon followed the familiar old path out to the barn. The pleasure that should have accompanied him treading the home grounds turned sour. Sure enough, the fence posts stood sentinel to fields of weeds. The emptiness of the acres broke his heart. Where had it all gone, his memory of robust mares dotting the hillocks as far as the eye could see? He nearly lost his strength halfway out to the barn and leaned over the top rail along the avenue of fence. Ben offered him a hand.

"You sure you're up to…?"

"I'm fine!" he swatted his brother's arm away. "I want to see my horse. And Daddy." His tone softened.

Ben fixed a hand on the door latch and sighed. "If you insist." The double door opened and ushered the afternoon sun in with them. Familiar aromas engulfed him, as powerful on his emotions as the sight of the pastures had been. Even if chaos ruled without, inside the barn was as neat and well-attended as ever. Leather, manure, and liniment mingled into one of the sweetest perfumes Devon ever breathed—home. He stood immobile, basking in the rays of sunlight catching motes of dust from the loft. In that time, his father disengaged from bandaging Cid's leg, and strode over to greet him. His embrace surprised Devon, but he returned it.

"You're a sight for sore eyes," the old man said.

"You, too," Devon replied.

"When you stopped writing, and we heard of all the casualties around Richmond, and about Stuart, we feared the worst. But when you stumbled in last night, I reckoned there must be a resurrection of the dead."

"Well, I'm no ghost. Ghosts don't eat, and I'm starved!"

They laughed. "Sure enough," his father said, scratching his unshaven jaw. "We still have stores hidden. The Yanks ain't managed to steal all that yet."

As the trio left the barn, Devon inquired about his horse. "How bad is Cid?"

"He needs a day or two off. If I weren't so glad to see you, I'd lay a riding crop to your backside for letting his legs go lame like that!"

Devon shrugged. "War gives rest to neither man nor beast."

"Nevertheless, you're both to rest until further notice."

Devon wasn't about to contradict his father's orders.

The evening found Devon in an uproarious tale of stealing a Yankee's ham dinner, over a table spread with more humble offerings—a couple of stewed rabbits and turnip greens.

"Got news of a more personal nature," Devon announced. "I tied the knot. And my wife and I are fixin' to have a baby."

His father stood from his chair and reached to clasp Devon's shoulder. "Congratulations, son." The old man fumbled in his pocket and produced a small pouch of tobacco, just enough to fill the pipe that sat on the table. "Well, I warrant. . . What's next, taking Washington?"

Turning up the wick on the lantern, he lit the end and took a drag of the sweet smoke, offering the pipe to Devon. "You haven't told us your bride's name yet."

"Her name's Gwen. Gwendolyn May Harris. Well, Sharpe, now." A proud smile tugged at his lips.

Ben nodded his approval, and his father raised his brows. "And tell us about your Mrs."

A flush warmed his cheeks. "She's a red-haired gal, and pretty as a Shenandoah sunrise. Fiery as one, too."

"Reckon she'd need to be to put up with the likes of you," Ben replied with an ornery grin.

Devon slugged him in the arm. "You're turn's a'comin'. You'll see."

ঔ

The next morning Devon and his father spied a rotted rail in the near paddock where Cinder grazed with two ancient, toothless mares. Lifting the old beam out, they had another ready to take its place. The morning was already alive with buzzing insects in the sweltering July air.

"Got a favor to ask you."

The old man swiped the perspiration rolling down his forehead. "What is it, Devon?"

The creases in his father's brow had deepened since he'd last seen him, and gray had overtaken his goatee and spread from his temples into a silver-lined crown. At forty-seven, his father was still strong, but cares had carved lines of worry in his swarthy face that were now indelible. Living in the shadow of imminent invasion had taken a toll. Devon wavered before asking his favor. After all, how could he take one more thing from the man? His mother's jewels were perhaps all he had left.

"Gwen and I want to settle here after the war. I'll help rebuild this place to what it was."

"One rail at a time, son."

Devon smiled. "I can't stay long now, but when I return, you'll have my untiring service."

"Exactly how long are you at liberty to stay?"

"At liberty?" A shrug came with the implication of his father's question. "I am at my own liberty these days."

The old man leaned on the adjacent rail.

Devon figured they were in for a conversation, now. He wiped his hands on his pants. The dirt and sweat streaked the front of the worn grays down to the fringes at the knee. His bare upper body glistened with streams of sweat, and he took his homespun from around his shoulders and swathed it over his face and chest.

"I'm on indefinite furlough."

His father winced. "You deserted."

"That's your word, not mine."

"What else would you call it, Devon?" He shook his silver head. "Last I knew they hung deserters."

A cavalier laugh escaped him. "That's only if they catch 'em."

"What do you plan to do next?"

"I'll go back to Gwen. I was hoping to give her a ring when we got married, but wedding rings are hard to come by these days. I wanted her to have it before I return to active duty."

His father squinted. "Back to active duty?"

Devon bit his bottom lip. "I'm gonna join up with Mosby. I'm bound to defend home with whatever army'll have me."

"A bit of advice, Devon? Watch yourself."

"Yes, sir. I will."

"And about that favor," his father raised a brow. "I'll see if there's something left among your mother's rings for your blushing bride."

Devon laughed again, rekindling a light-hearted mood. "Thanks, Daddy. You know me too well."

When the insect hum overtook them in their silence once again, his father hefted his side of the rail. "I got a letter from your brother, Devon."

A cramp cinched his gut. He knew by the inflection in his father's tone *exactly* which brother he meant. He looked up and then back at the rail, the heat of the summer sun beating down on him with every thrum of pulse.

"He asks forgiveness. From me, from all of us. Says he's well. Wants to come back home after the war."

Devon spat into the weeds growing up the post. Forgiveness? His chest was a void. He felt no forgiveness. But neither did the hardness of hatred press there anymore. "Should have thought of that three years ago." He said it in a mutter, not expecting his father to hear.

"High time you mended real fences, Devon."

He straightened, letting the rail slip from his hands. "I'm bound away in the morning. Reckon you'll have to finish mending this one yourself."

Chapter 32

Camp Chemung, Elmira
Cavalry Training Rendezvous

Ethan held the leather lead, pacing a young horse around the perimeter. The cavalry rendezvous had received a shipment of mounts for the recruits, and most of them were badly in need of breaking to saddle. Dust rose from each strike on the parched earth, mingling with the swelter to leave a film on him. He ran a bandanna over his face.

As the animal completed neat arcs, Ethan contemplated the many times he had performed the task back home.

His father had not returned his letter. In all these months, the man might have attempted. If engineers had spanned the chasm at Harper's Ferry, why was it so hard for a father to bridge a gap to his son?

He dropped the tension on the line and issued the final order for the day. "Fall out with your mount, private. You're dismissed."

Drills were over for the evening, and all he cared about was getting some food and rest.

His habitual gaze drifted to the college, towering over the city's respectable homesteads—neat clapboard structures with shaded lawns, and carriage houses with sloping roofs and cupolas. His heart compressed in a familiar ache. He was still unable to offer Mari any of these things. In his most wistful dreams, he would bring her back to the Shenandoah. In his mind, he rode along the Valley Turnpike, each stop in a row of houses the home of a Sharpe. His father Sam. Gideon, Devon, Benjamin, himself. But unless the Lord sent some indication that he might one day reconcile with his kin, he might remain a stranger in a strange land the rest of his days, alone.

Lately the papers boasted of Grant's campaign in Petersburg, and traced the recent developments of Sherman in Georgia, and Sheridan in the Valley. As much as raiding the Shenandoah was a tactical necessity for Lincoln, he was glad he wasn't the one doing it. Maybe God knew what he was doing by sending him away from the front. Ethan primed the well pump then splashed the sweat and grime from his neck and face. Maybe God truly was watching over him.

The sound of singing eclipsed his thoughts. The voices of many men carried a hymn through the open tent. Deeper stirrings than hunger beckoned him, and he moved toward the sound.

Before he crossed the threshold, a soldier named Hicks approached. "Did you hear, Sergeant? There's been a terrible train wreck in Pennsylvania. They were sending another shipment of prisoners up here, and it collided with an oncoming locomotive."

Ethan's mood deflated, and he didn't respond. Maybe Hicks expected him to say something, but nothing came to mind. Another senseless tragedy of the war. He was glad he hadn't bothered with his evening meal now, his stomach gone sour.

"They're still sorting through the wreckage."

Could have been one of your brothers on that train.

A dark wave crested inside him. "What do you expect me to do?"

The soldier's eyes widened, and he shrugged. "You were heading into chapel, and I reckon you'd want to pray, is all, Sarge. Survivors are arriving as we speak."

He stood in silence, exhaustion overtaking him between breaths. His disillusionment smoldered inside him until he turned away from the trooper with a scowl.

What do you want, God? This is war. I haven't fought in a dozen battles and killed men to cosset enemy prisoners.

Hicks shifted uncomfortably beside him. "Would you go with me down to the hospital and pray with them?"

Ethan turned back, eyeing him askance.

"I'm sorry, Sarge. I just reckon that since they're *your* people, you might want to do something."

Lord, you're asking too much. "My people." He shook his head, losing all malice to the abandon of apathy. "I can't help them now, even if they were. Salt in the wound, Hicks. That's all I'd be to them."

From inside the tent meeting, scripture interjected into his conversation. "Let us not be weary in well doing, for in due season we shall reap, if we faint not."

He fisted his right hand. *My family couldn't even acknowledge my apology.* "I've done all I know to do."

He turned away from the tent meeting, back through camp. He still had shovel duty to perform, but at least he had found farmers who'd help with the cleanup and transport. He moved toward that end of camp, where the wheelbarrows dumped the compost, and where the wagons lined up to carry it away. The sound of hymns rose again on the evening air. His soul was too burdened for a sermon, but music was a balm. Hot swirls of anger subsided by and by, and his breathing slowed. *God, help those recovering from wounds, physical and otherwise. And if I never see my loved ones again in this life, please let us be reconciled in the next.*

ꕤ

Shenandoah Valley Turnpike

Dawn hadn't yet come when Devon rode Cid along the valley turnpike. Mist shrouded the road, muffling their hard gallop. By and by, they diverted from the path, he reining Cid down to the river. There he breathed in the scent of pine needles and crystal mountain water. Sunrise over the Blue Ridge Mountains almost made him sorry he was leaving the valley.

But Gwen would be so pleased to receive the parcel he had sewn into the seam of his coat pocket. He had no second thoughts. His hand went there, tracing the contours of the ring. He was determined that she have this token to legitimize their marriage. She deserved what little he could offer her, no matter the risk to himself. After Cinder drank his fill, he goaded him back up the bank and commenced the long road to Maryland.

In the afternoon he stopped along the riverbank to water again, and to dip into his haversack for lunch. Reining Cid down the slope, he rode to the water's edge until the horse's front hooves stood in the clear stream and the steed's nose quivered just above the cool surface. Cid's breath snorted ripples over the water with a low rumble, and then he quaffed. They hid from the intense heat under a copse of fir trees and Devon chewed his dry biscuits, speculating how far they'd come.

His own canteen was well-nigh full, so he remained in the saddle, letting the swishing boughs and the sound of the water lull him. Cid lifted his muzzle from the water and turned his head toward the opposite bank. A dribble fell from his whiskered chin, and his black ears flicked a time or two in the same direction. Devon took casual notice. He lifted his canteen to his lips and imbibed a cool bath down his throat. Cid's shrill whinny across the stream snapped Devon to attention.

Shadows moved under the trees. He wheeled Cid up into the thicket, pulling his pistol from its holster. The stud's hooves slipped on the pine needle carpet and Devon urged him on, deciding on flight rather than fight. He holstered his weapon and, once on the road, spurred hard. Cid responded with fleet gallop. The jingle of spurs and the splashing of many hooves echoed behind them, but the glade had made forms indistinguishable. At least three riders, he guessed. They slipped around a bend, and the first discharge of a pistol sounded. He hovered low over Cid's neck and goaded him into his longest stride. The second and third gunshots reverberated through the trees. The reach in Cid's stride tightened in the next quarter of a mile, but they still outdistanced their pursuers.

Good thing, since that gunfire would summon more attention, and fast.

Cid's nostrils heaved, and veins like black ribbons rose over his neck. Devon dug his heels into his flanks, urging more, pleading for his stallion's best. His strides lengthened again, but the animal's breathing labored. Devon's neck-hairs bristled. Something was wrong. His thoroughbred would normally be able to go for miles like this. Before Devon could assess the problem, Cid stumbled and veered off the road.

Bramble and tall grass thrashed at his face as his horse plunged down an embankment. If it had been a thicket they might have sought shelter, but the open terrain offered nowhere to hide. "Come on, Cid! Let's get out of here!"

The horse swung about and circled in the middle of the field. Devon tried to compel the animal with kicks and shouts, but no effort could make the horse obey. Oblivious to the oncoming Yankees, his steed continued to circle and bite at his side until they toppled into the tall grass.

Devon rolled clear to avoid the animal's weight. High-pitched screams sounded like a woman under assault as the stallion threw his legs in the air in a desperate attempt to rid himself of whatever torment lay beneath his saddle. Blood foamed over the saddle blanket and the lathered black coat.

Devon approached Cinder, speaking low assurances. The stricken animal lashed at its left side, all the while broadcasting dissonant squeals. Lips and teeth shone bright crimson under the afternoon sun.

Devon's voice calmed the animal for a few seconds. Quivering muzzle sniffed the air. Then, after a few explosive efforts to regain his feet, the horse settled with a foundering sound. Devon gathered in by Cid's head and, pulling his muzzle up into his lap, he stroked his forelock smooth between terrified eyes. Disbelief addled Devon's senses, making him oblivious to his surroundings and the enemy who even now gathered. He couldn't let his horse suffer. His hand withdrew to his holster.

The Yankee scout party rounded the bend. Devon trained the pistol toward the road, waiting for a clear shot. Seconds remained to formulate his defense. He opened his chamber: one bullet. His munitions caisson emptied where he had fallen, yards away. Thunder from the small army bore down on him. *One last bullet.*

He could either deal retribution to these Yankees or put Cid out of his misery. *Or take the easy way out....*

Swallowing bile, he placed the cold circle of steel in the cross between Cid's eyes and ears. But before he squeezed the trigger, another discharge knocked the gun out of his hand.

The Yankees surrounded him. Except for his Bowie knife, he was defenseless. But he hesitated to retrieve it from his boot yet. At last one of the riders came near. Devon blinked at him, and the Yankee aimed his revolver square at his chest. Three more joined, all training weapons at him.

One of them spoke. "Get up, Reb."

He lunged with drawn knife at the nearest soldier, and a booted foot crunched into his side. He swung wildly and made contact at least once before they overpowered him. They rammed him again and again with the stocks of rifles, boots, and fists but he wouldn't go down. Jostled and stumbling, he tried to wage one last attack. He lunged again, and they grounded him, beating him until somewhere in the struggle he dropped his knife.

The sky above spun. Devon looked to the heavens for help, but all he could see was Ethan, handing him over to these Yankees in waves of brutality. They tore at his uniform, his hair, his face, and all he could comprehend was that he had no more desire to fight his brother.

Vomit burst from the depths of his stomach, and his vision turned red.

ଔ

Maryland on the Potomac

Summer 1864

Marietta looked out at the cobble drive and wondered why Ethan hadn't attempted to write. She'd been home for over a month now—nearly two—and no word had come, no indication that he still desired to court her. If it weren't for Josie making her swear to return to Elmira in the fall, she would beg her parents to stay home.

She'd failed at yet another thing she'd attempted to do for God. What would have happened if she'd just obeyed Mama and gone to finishing school? She'd made such a mess of things trying to impose her own solutions to life's injustices.

Maybe she should accept her mother's prescription and agree to a suit with some accomplished Washington politician or banker and put away her notions of ridding the world of evil. Perhaps Mr. Hastings was as good a match as she could hope to get. What had her meddling ever accomplished for anyone, anyway?

But then, a fleeting memory of Tilly hugging her estranged son in their kitchen replayed in her mind's eye. If Mari hadn't intervened, the auction would have separated Tilly from her son forever.

"Mari, are you busy?"

She turned with a start from her familiar old perch by the window, unaware anyone entered the room. "No, Aaron. Not too busy for you." She offered him a smile as he sat down near her on the window seat.

"Since you've been home, I've been meaning to tell you something. It's about that day when Ethan proposed."

"Yes?"

"I know I'm to blame for the way things turned out."

She tilted her head to the side. "We've talked about this, and all is forgiven."

Her brother rubbed his palms together as though trying to scrub away invisible dirt. "No, you deserve to know. It wasn't just my sickness that made me do what I did that day." He turned to face out the window, catching the last dying rays of the sunset on his fiery scar.

"It was jealousy. All I knew was that Ethan was going to marry the girl he loved, and I… I felt that if I couldn't have anyone, then neither should he."

Mari's throat constricted as emotion crowded. Though her brother had made a full and miraculous recovery from his addiction, his scar still left him unable to look a pretty lady in the eye. Her heart twisted in deep compassion for him, but another part of her wanted to shake him for his selfishness.

"I know I hurt you. I'm willing to do anything to help you both, if you still want to be together. I'm powerful sorry, Mari. Please forgive me."

Tears pricked the backs of her eyes. How could she hold malice toward her dear brother? She threw her arms about his shoulders. "Of course, I forgive you. And you're so wrong, Aaron. You *will* find a woman to love you. You will!"

He turned away again toward the twilit window and she released him.

"I'll go speak to father and see if I can convince him to reconsider. After all, it was Ethan who helped me believe the Lord for deliverance from the morphine. And it was him who carried me from Bull Run. He's been more a brother to me than if he'd been born to our family."

"Thank you, Aaron. I'll pray Papa listens."

"Oh, and I reckon its only right you have these." Aaron withdrew a stack of envelopes from a cigar box. "Seems as though someone has been keeping Ethan's letters from you for quite some time."

She gasped, lifting the bundle bound with twine, thumbing the edges and counting ten. . .fifteen . . .twenty-three. "Why would Mama and Papa do this?" She shook her head.

He bowed in penitence. "It wasn't them, Mari. It was me."

࿇

Sheridan's Union encampment
Shenandoah Valley, Summer 1864

Devon awakened to unfathomable pain, though his thoughts lagged behind his senses. He heard the buzzing of insects, felt their biting, and smelled the stench of raw wounds. His eyes? They had swollen shut and he couldn't see. Nevertheless, an image had been burned into his brain.

Cid, his beloved horse, had taken a bullet for him.

A flurry of wings fanned near his ear and the sharp squeeze of talons dug into his shoulder—a bird lighting, no doubt attracted by carrion.

"Git!" A Yankee soldier fired his pistol off before it could pick Devon's wounds. He started at the report of gunpowder, suddenly fully awake.

Crusted blood stiffened Devon's face. He tried to reach up, but his hands were bound behind him. Something hard at his back propped him in a sitting position, and his neck crooked forward, unable to support the weight of his head. His side creaked with each breath until a sharp pop lanced his ribs. He would have cried out, but it took too much strength.

Men conversed at the outer range of his hearing.

"Sheridan ordered all Mosby's boys hanged."

"Like the ones they caught the other day? They let one go to tell the tale. Guess we should' a finished 'um off then."

"What're they gonna do with this one?"

"Dunno. Don't seem worth it to stretch that scrawny neck. He'll be dead before they question him."

Devon tried to contain his pain, but he couldn't help the low groaning in the back of his throat. He hoped they were right—maybe death was imminent. But then, he remembered the small parcel in his pocket. Gwen would never get his ring if he died now. His baby would grow up without a daddy. He grimaced, kicking to sit up against the pole at his back. It alleviated the pressure in his rib.

He called out. "You, there. Yank?"

They grew quiet as though the dead had spoken.

"Got water?"

"I s'pose even a condemned man deserves a last request."

A canteen pressed to his split lips, and he gasped down a few swallows. "Don't suppose you could loosen these ties?"

They laughed, and their jabs and jests jumbled together.

"Sure, and set you up on a fresh horse, too."

"With a full haversack and munitions to skedaddle back to your raiders."

And yet, to his surprise, a notch of tightness slipped, allowing him to settle into a better position. "Obliged."

"You got ten guns pointing at you, Reb. Don't get any ideas."

"Don't matter anyhow. You're a dead man tomorrow."

If a soldier had good in his heart to give water to a condemned man, he might be worth more. Devon had no other ideas. "That so? Seems a shame, 'cause I was bringing something to my girl."

"Sure, you were, Reb. Like spy reports?"

"See for yourself. It's in my coat pocket here, on the left."

"They already searched you. Ain't nothin' in your pocket."

"It's sewn in, small. They wouldn't 'a seen it 'less they knew where to look."

One of them reached in, and Devon waited for him to feel the metal circle.

"Well, I'll be. What is it, Reb?"

"If someone's gonna steal it, might as well be you."

The Yankee ripped Devon's pocket out. A low, appraising whistle proved he'd found the treasure.

"It was my mother's," Devon said with quiet dignity. He had succeeded to weave a thread of sympathy. He capitalized. "I wanted my wife to have it. It's all I got for her. And our baby."

For a moment, Devon wondered if he'd lost his audience while they absconded with his family heirloom. He ventured with faltering breath.

"Her name's Gwendolyn Harris Sharpe. She lives in Urbana, Maryland. A Union loyalist."

"Well, Reb, it's your lucky day. The Harris's are my cousins."

Chapter 33

Elmira Cavalry Barracks

Ethan's teamster, the one he relied on to load the compost wagon, had failed to arrive with the mule train. Of all the sweltering days. The lack of rain had everyone ornery, especially the biting flies. The temptation to cuss hadn't been this strong in many a day. He'd have to hunt down a replacement at this late hour. Across town on the northwest end, a freedman kept a tidy farm parcel, and Ethan was sure he could find help there. John W. Jones was an enterprising soul, with a crew who worked for him at the cemetery abutting his land. Perhaps Ethan might borrow a man and a cart if the burial detail could spare them. He rode Nimbus along a westerly road directly to the Jones property.

The workmen sang in a familiar, steady cadence. A tug of homesickness rose and quickly passed. Resisting the temptation of self-pity, a scripture quickened to his mind, spoken by Marietta the night he'd fled to her home with Jonesy.

Verily I say unto you, There is no man that hath left house, or parents, or brethren, or wife, or children, for the kingdom of God's sake, who shall not receive manifold more in this present time, and in the world to come.

In *this* present time? That was the part that always stopped him. He could readily believe in rewards hereafter. But restoration and redemption in this *present* life?

Nimbus neighed to the approaching horses pulling a flat cart. A freedman dressed in plaid cotton sat in the driver's box. Two others nearby bent broad backs over a tree stump, one with a shovel and one with an ax.

"I'm looking for some help moving compost from the barracks. Could you use another load of fertilizer for the farm?"

The older man set his tool aside and straightened his back, stretching out the stiffness. "That's the work of the Lord, now, ain't it, Sergeant? He take a pile of ol' manure and grow a fine new thing up from it."

Ethan ran a hand over his chin. "You know, it is at that. Yes, it surely is." He laughed and the men around them laughed, too.

"I'll send the wagon directly, suh. You over at the cav'ry depot?"

"That's right. And I sure am obliged." Ethan tipped the brim of his cavalry hat and turned Nimbus back toward the road. Before he spurred, a tenor voice called out.

"I'd know dat hoss anywhere."

Ethan tightened his hold on the reins as the other workman at the tree stump set down his ax and strode forward, advancing right up to hold Nimbus's cheek strap. Ethan looked down into the matured face of a boy he hadn't seen in three years.

Jonesy—Vincent Jones, rather—stood as tall as he, head and shoulders. Heart swelling with disbelief, Ethan swung down from the saddle and embraced the former stable boy.

"Look at you. You're the full measure of a man, as sure as I stand here. And a sight for sore eyes!"

"Yassuh, Mister Ethan, you is, too. I been prayin' ever' day the Lord bless and keep you, suh. Good to see this war ain't done you in. You, nor your hoss."

Ethan gripped the young man's shoulder and looked him in the eye. "That means a great deal more than you know, my friend. Thank you."

"Come up to the house when you gets a chance, Mist' Ethan. I been working with my Mama's cousin John Jones, here. We livin' in town. She workin' for a lady from the Congregational Church. You come set a spell and Mama fix us some sweet tea, and we'll share all our news."

Ethan nodded, almost speechless with wonder. "I'd be pleased to."

ଓଃ

Union prisoner transport
Northern Central Railway

A whine of brakes and the desolate echo of steam whistled against the Pennsylvania mountainside. The locomotive's clacking wheels beat out a tattoo not unlike martial drumming at an execution. Devon listened from a corner of the livestock car, trying to catch what little sleep he could before the train delivered him to his fate. He'd already forgotten the name of his destination. It seemed a forgettable place, and he wished he could as easily forget its implications. Every mile took him away from his future, holding Gwen's hand, walking the pastures back home, anticipating the arrival of his child. Would he live to see those days?

After a time of fruitless interrogation, his captors had canceled his execution and consigned him to export. Perhaps his bribe had helped, though it was a shame that a Yankee ended up with Mama's ring instead of Gwen. Though, who knew? Maybe the man told the truth. Maybe his relation to Gwen had spared Devon's life.

Regardless, by all accounts his destination promised worse. His mind circled many versions of what awaited him, his senses dulled from chronic pain. Now hunger, a parched throat, and sickness added to his list of miseries. His rib fractures restricted him to shallow gasps, but a developing cough worked new vexations. The crowded transport car broiled in the summer heat. Delirium worked tricks on him, blurred reality.

History lessons, professors with droning voices, lectured on conquering warriors, breathing life to scenes straight out of dusty texts. Shouts and trumpets summoned to war, while drums and fifes marked the triumphal entry of returning armies under great arches. City gates admitted a host of broken men in chains.

Having spoiled principalities and powers, he made a show of them openly, triumphing over them.

Devon blinked his one good eye open. The train had stopped.

No movement now but the door sliding open. Super-heated air swelled from the idling locomotive engine, the overwhelming smell of sulfur stealing what breath he could gasp. Devon clutched his ribs with one hand and pushed up with the other, joining the exodus from the cattle car.

In the outer reaches, through the smoke, an unfriendly dialect spoke. "Welcome to hell, boys."

Just beyond, the sun blazed without mercy, like a brimstone fixed in the sky. Hell, indeed. Then he remembered the name of the town. It sounded like that nefarious assignment. *Hellmira.*

The engine belched steam sinking and cascading across the brick road. Heat lightning sent thunder like mocking laughter across the valley, offering the false promise of rain. There would be no relief on this dry and weary land. Not twenty steps from the platform, and rivulets of sweat ran through his clothes and down his skin. What he wouldn't give for some alleviation to his baked tongue. The smell of confinement rising from his clothes made him retch, and instead of rain, he swallowed back vomit. He steeled his wits—best to conceal any weakness here, a prisoner in the land of the enemy.

Marching in a double column, the prisoners moved across town. Curious onlookers peered from shuttered storefront windows. What did they hope to see? Oddities clad in Confederate gray? Monsters to thrill them at the end of tethers, safe for the spectators who had never beheld a genuine hatchling south of the Mason-Dixon Line?

Devon dropped his gaze and followed the procession. How long would it take for his bandages to run red in his dripping sweat? That'd give them something to talk about over their lemonade. Five years ago, any one of these prisoners might have alighted from the train and strolled down the avenue as a guest, a tourist, a countryman. Now, they were regarded with titillation and sanctimonious delight.

A man in a carriage spoke to another. "Marched their slaves in shackles just like that. Serves them right."

Little boys pointed stick-muskets at Devon and his fellow prisoners and shouted "bang!" while jeers erupted from children and adults alike.

Devon met the eyes of a little girl who clung to her mother's skirts.

"Are they going to kill them, mama?"

Devon couldn't help but listen for the answer, too.

"It's men like that who shot your daddy. No. Killing's too good for them."

Their hostility stung him like the swarm of gnats gathered around his face. Not lethal, but unrelenting in torment.

About a mile up the road to the west, tall posts of a long stockade wall rose above the heat waves, and a wood frame building protruded perpendicular to the fence line. Guards milled about the area, outfitted in crisp, blue frock coats or shell jackets and clean kepis. And above, pickets stood sentinel armed with Spencer repeating rifles, stationed on elevated platforms split by a double gate. In that courtyard, river silt churned to airborne powder by the tread of a thousand men led into the yawning maw of the prison. Set apart from the rag tag southerners, an officer stood with clipboard and pen, collecting name, rank and regiment from each prisoner passing through. Flanking him, an orderly issued a rubber blanket, soap, and a tin cup to each prisoner once the officer verified information. Then, the line ambled away, disappearing into the enclosure beyond.

"Devon Sharpe. First Virginia Cavalry." His own sound startled him, the rough hoarseness of his voice. The orderly handed him his bundle and looked past him to the next soldier. Devon shuffled forward.

Long wooden barracks spread to the left and to the right for a considerable expanse, but he was not directed toward them. Rather he was steered down an avenue beyond the wood structures, deeper into the camp, toward the bright sound of hammer hitting stakes. The flapping of canvas marked a tent line. He followed the human train into the farthest reaches of the prison fort.

A scrubby blond figure walked up beside him. "Jamie Truax. Tennessee Infantry. Come up from Point Lookout. You?"

The man's head barely reached Devon's chest. His blue eyes had a cagey look, though not sinister. He seemed to size Devon up too, inch for inch.

He tipped his hat. "Name's Devon Sharpe. Here on holiday."

Jamie grinned, flashing rows of uneven teeth. "You look fresh from the front. How were ya captured?"

"Keeping Mrs. Lincoln company." Devon raised a brow. "You?"

That earned him a chuckle.

"Been tossed 'round Yankee prisons since Chattanooga." He leaned in closer, as if in confidence. "But I learned a thing or two, Devon. Fixin' to get one them tents by the fence. Stick with me an' I'll show you 'round."

The man led the way more briskly than Devon could comfortably follow, but he didn't let on. He bit his lip and sucked each breath painfully to match Jamie's pace.

"When do we eat?"

"Git two rations a day, but I reckon we missed both today. Better not be late for roll in the AM. Best soup gits served first; got real beans, and maybe a bit of pork. Nothing but broth later, if you call hot water broth. And mind these vultures don't steal yer bread. Always thieves in these places."

Batting at mosquitoes they neared the work crew pounding in tent stakes. Devon slowed and fell into line. Jamie took his hand

and pumped it. “I’ll bunk with you, if you got no objections. You got an honest face.”

Devon shrugged. “If the river mire don’t bury the lot of us first.”

Once issued a tent, Jamie spread his rubber blanket over the spongy ground on the river bank. Devon all but collapsed, his weak coughing disclosing his condition now.

“You sick?” Jamie approached cautiously.

“Injured,” Devon said. “Ribs are broken. Don’t reckon it’s catching.”

“First thing, Devon. Let yer folks know you’re here, so’s they can send you help. You don’t want to go to no hospital.” Jamie unpacked his paltry belongings, darting his weasel eyes about. “Look here, Devon.” He held up a benign-looking vessel. “This here’s illegal. But it’s worth twice its weight in gold. Here. To medicinal purposes.”

Devon took the flask and swallowed the liquid fire, just once. One swallow was enough. It rushed through his chest and rose straight to his head. What in blazes had he just imbibed? Gasping, he nodded thanks with a satisfied wipe of his cracked lips. “So, there are pleasures, even in hell and mire?”

Jamie laughed, and took a swig himself. “To Hellmira! Devon, you an’ me are gonna git along just fine.”

Chapter 34

Elmira Rail Depot
September 1864

Marietta's return for the fall term promised the sort of busyness she welcomed. As much as it had been a pleasant summer at home, she missed the little canal town, the rigors of academia and the distraction of her lively friends. Josie and the girls' society would offer the perfect cure to her lonesomeness for Ethan. His letters had told her of his continuing devotion, and her longing for him had only grown, reading his tender, lovelorn words. But her parents had shown no signs of relenting. She determined to pray and accept whatever the Lord decided, though her heart ached.

Presently, Papa hailed a livery while she stood on the train platform waiting for a baggage handler to retrieve her trunk. Stepping down from a separate car, one of her classmates was just arriving on the Canandaigua line.

"Annabelle Taylor."

"Marietta! How was your summer?"

They embraced, and carried their chatter up the boardwalk, catching up over the noise of traffic. Papa signaled the porter to carry her trunk to his rented conveyance, and Mari invited her friend to join them.

"How kind. I'm meeting Hattie Langdon and her uncle for dinner. Perhaps I could sit with you until they arrive."

“Yes, let's!” Mari led her down the ramp toward Papa, and he helped them both aboard the open cabriolet.

“The newspapers back home in Watkins Glen have talked about nothing all summer long but the drought and the Confederate prison. Why, Mari, there are more southern soldiers here than our own these days.”

“Have they arrived already?” Mari fanned her neck with a silver and blue silk fan pulled from her reticule.

“Oh, indeed. And the talk isn't at all favorable. It's scandalous, how we must waste our precious resources on those traitors, while our own boys go off to war with scarce enough to face another winter on the front. But my mother would be positively appalled if she were to hear me speak of such, so I do beg your pardon. Oh, look, there is Hattie's Uncle's carriage now.”

She waved her own lace and tortoise shell fan at them.

Papa stepped out to meet the Langdon’s, tipping his hat.

The driver drew his handsome pair of horses into alignment with theirs. He secured the brake and stepped down from the driver's platform. “Levi Hamilton.” The gentleman clasped Papa's hand. “How providential to see you. Is Cora with you?”

“And you, Jervis,” Papa doffed his hat with a deferential greeting. “No, I'm afraid she stayed behind this time. I'm here to see my daughter off for her second year at college.”

“Yes, my niece is attending this year as well. You know, I was just telling my wife how grand it would be to have you both to dinner while you're in town. Are you staying for a few days?”

“Yes, at the Brainard. I believe I will stay on through the week, to help Marietta get settled.”

“Splendid. Then you must join us for Sunday service and the evening repast before you return to Washington.”

“I have some business Sunday morning, but if you'd be so kind as to take Mari to church, I'd be pleased to join you later in the afternoon. Thank you.”

Marietta smiled and nodded to the gentleman and his niece as her friend alighted, joining their party. But a disconcerted feeling swirled through her at Annabelle's words. Would she find such a lack of charity among her other friends here? Were the prisoners at Camp Chemung so very unlike Ethan and his brothers? With Sherman capturing Atlanta and Grant wearing Lee out in Virginia, no one expected the war to drag on much longer. The South was finally coming to its knees. Would not reconciliation work the Lord's will better than humiliation?

ଔ

Mari settled into her room and second year classes with the ease of a veteran. Carrying a fresh cause with her into the new semester, she proposed the girls' charitable efforts focus on the camp on the west end of town. Winning Josie to her side, Mari and she soon convinced Hattie Langdon, too, citing how Reverend Beecher himself led church services for the prisoners. Some reacted to their notions of collecting food, writing material, and knitted goods with opprobrium. And many of the girls felt that donating their Christmas funds for the Union soldiers' hospital last winter had been quite enough. Aiding enemy soldiers was a step too far.

But opposition only served to forge Mari's determination in steel, and before the week's end, preparations were underway. Sewing and baking, she and her close-knit sorority found ways to extend Christian charity to souls in need, no matter what color their uniform or flag. Mari would bring their donations with her on Sunday and hope the church would see to delivery.

Early Sunday preparations for church were made, donning her best day dress, keeping at bay her rogue imaginings of slipping her host and hostess's watchful eyes for a few stolen moments. If only she could see Ethan. It had been so long, now. But she must be on her best behavior. After all, the Langdons were one of Papa's abolitionist associations, and quite influential in town. Indeed, they were the family to whom to appeal if a girl hoped to bend the strictures of the college on a matter such as charitable work.

A strong September sun radiated through wide-open windowsills. Marietta pushed back her homemade curtains drifting in and out on the streaming air, anticipating the carriage's approach. But Hattie sounded the announcement.

"They're here, Mari."

Josie scurried to gather the baked goods and blankets they had made for the prisoners. "Take these with you." She winked. "For the church mission."

Hattie Langdon led the way out and down the hall. She looked back at Marietta and offered her an encouraging smile. "Uncle Jervis can't say no to both of us."

ଔ

Elmira Cavalry Training Rendezvous

Ethan couldn't believe his fortune. Darcy had called off his weekly card game, and by some miracle, hadn't said a word about Ethan staying behind this morning. He'd left early, too early even to order him to shine his boots. This would mark the first Sunday since arriving in Elmira that he was free to attend church in the community. Coincidentally, the college girls had just returned for their fall term. Would it be too much to hope that a certain young lady attended the Congregational Church? And that he might steal a moment with her either before or after service?

"Lord, please allow our paths to cross somehow today. Show me one way or the other if I... if she is to be...." He sighed. Somewhere in the actual asking he lost his nerve. If the Lord hadn't answered by now, would one more prayer matter? "Your will, Lord. Not mine. But can you at least take this ache away?"

What if I've allowed you to carry these burdens for a reason? Have you given them fully to me?

He had no answer to that, so he donned his best linen shirt and frock coat, wishing he'd had the time to brush out the wool like he always did for Darcy. He performed a quick shave, a spit polish on his cavalry boots, and shined his spurs. He hated to be vain, but a quick dab of the captain's pomade wouldn't hurt, and the peacock would never miss it. Lastly, before he ducked out of his tent, he grabbed his bible and tucked it under his arm, whistling a jaunty tune as he headed for the row of tethered horses.

If Mari *were* there, would she be surprised to see him? "Lord, I give you my hopes and my longings. For Mari, for my estranged father, for this war, and for Devon. I place them all in your hands."

A little more than a mile's ride later, Ethan settled into a seat toward the back of the Independent Congregational Church, fortunate to find an opening among the filled pews. Reverend Beecher asked his congregation to open to Matthew 25:36. The significance of the passage slipped his notice, searching for a certain pretty face among the assembly. Beecher soon brought him back to the sermon, expounding on the Christian duty to visit prisoners in their captivity and suffering.

"*I was in prison and you came to me.* Jesus identifies with the captive, even he that wears Confederate gray."

Ethan's wool coat began to itch, and the burden of sitting still burned in every coiled muscle. Hicks' lecture on aiding his countrymen buzzed in his ears like a June bug until he wanted to vacate, except there was no escape. Hemmed in by people on every side, he was anchored to his seat.

Beecher finished up by inviting volunteers to accompany him on an outreach into the prison camp immediately following service. The air seemed super-heated. Ethan tugged at his shirt and he shifted on the pew. The Lord was speaking to him, and he thought of another time and place where he'd been the captive audience of a preacher. Then as now, he squirmed under the uncomfortable conviction from the pulpit. Then as now he'd come with an objective in mind. To see Mari. That preacher in Washington had singled him out from among the entire gathering. Ethan hid his gaze lest Beecher make eye contact with him, and once the benediction was prayed he barely refrained from bolting through the crowd.

On the way out, he caught his breath and craned his neck over the congregants to spy for a certain college girl. Hadn't she come?

All summer he had asked the Lord to show him a sign. Was he to forget her and move on? He didn't know if he could. Or would God answer his fervent prayer that she might still be his? He'd hear it from her lips before believing one way or another.

The last of the people filed out after service. A tall man in a top hat brushed past him, and two young ladies trailed behind, chattering and clutching bibles to their chests. The essence of a floral sachet circled in their wake—Marietta's fragrance. He looked up in time to recognize her familiar silhouette before she passed through the door.

An icy jolt struck him. Had she not seen him? Taller than most, and in uniform, he didn't exactly blend in. Had she passed him with complete indifference? He charged after her, nearly colliding with an elderly lady before he stopped short with a "beg pardon" and navigated around her.

"Marietta? Mari—wait!"

ଓଃ

Mari's heart stuttered at the familiar voice, and she locked her sights on the impossibly handsome sight of Ethan in his dress uniform. Unable to contain her smile, she clutched her bible, silently thanking the Lord for fulfilling her fondest wish.

"Do you know this man, Miss Hamilton?" Her chaperon approached.

"Oh, yes I do, Mr. Langdon. This is Sergeant Ethan Sharpe. He's a dear family friend." Her lashes fluttered involuntarily, still bewildered at his sudden appearance.

"Very well, Sergeant. Say your piece, but with all haste, if you please. I prefer not to keep supper waiting."

"Yes, sir. Pleased to meet you, sir." Ethan shuffled his Bible and papers, looking uncertain when Mr. Langdon didn't shake his hand. "I—I was just hoping to.... "

Mari tried to ignore the insecurities clamoring like fire bells inside her. Surely Ethan hadn't come all this way to lose her now.

"I was hoping to speak to Miss Mari, sir, if you would permit."

"If you wish an audience with the young lady, I will allow you a moment. Pray I have no reason to regret it."

Ethan nodded his thanks, and removed his hat and leaned in, capturing her in his warm, ebony eyes. He'd grown even more robust over the summer, if it were possible. A deep tan bronzed his features, and hard work had chiseled every muscle outlined under his coat. "Did you receive my letters, Mari? I wrote you several since you left."

A pang shot through her. "I just recently became aware of your letters, Sergeant." She swallowed, ruing the formality forced upon her in the company of Papa's esteemed acquaintances. She wished she could declare how she had savored each letter. How much they had meant to her. "I hope you received mine as well?"

"I'm afraid not." His smile fell, but quickly lit his face again. "Let's never mind that, now. I hope all is well at home?" His eyes seemed to communicate some urgency.

"Of course." The horses snorted and shook the bits in their mouths. Her host was eager to be off, and Mari's thoughts raced, desperately reaching for a way to extend their time, but coming up with nothing

"I wish to call on you in person, if it can be arranged."

"Are you joining the entourage accompanying Reverend Beecher? Because I have these parcels." It was all she could think to say to prolong their conversation. And the donations *did* need a way to the prisoners.

He stroked a hand through his black hair, turning from her to the gathering spilling out from the church and onto the lawn, each volunteer holding a basket or parcel designated for the outreach. Mari held up her basket with the loaves and blankets. She pleaded with her most earnest gaze. "Perhaps you could give us a report on the mission afterwards?"

Her escort consulted his time piece. "I won't have Miss Hamilton break school policy on my watch, Sergeant. Now if you please—"

"Mr. Langdon," Mari interjected. "Permit me to share my favorite exhortation with Sergeant Sharpe before he ventures on the church mission. 'If a man know that his neighbor is in danger by any unjust proceeding, he is bound to do all in his power to deliver him. And what is it to suffer immortal souls to perish, when our persuasions and example may be the means of preventing it?"

Mari still held out the bundles that she and the girls had assembled for the prisoners. He reached for them, and his hands brushed hers in the exchange, a charge passing between them. Their gazes communicated something beyond his recognition of those words, deeper than their longing for one another. It was a spiritual understanding, a oneness of purpose.

"I'm greatly obliged to you, Ethan, that you would see these distributed."

Her handsome soldier bowed, replacing his hat back on his head, and shifted the parcels in his hands with his Bible. "Anything for you, Marietta." His gaze was so intense, she thought the autumn air had ignited. How she loved this man, who championed her every cause.

"Godspeed, Ethan. My prayers go with you."

Mr. Langdon reached down from the driver's box to shake Ethan's hand. "I should like very much to hear that report on the outreach when you are done, Sergeant. Please come by our home later. You see it there, the large gray house across the street? My wife and I would be pleased if you'd stay for dinner."

Ethan straightened, his bearing lending inches onto his height. "Thank you, sir. It would be an honor."

*

Ethan's heart clenched at those words, *unjust proceedings* and *delivering immortal souls.* The Matthew Henry quote had now returned to bring him conviction and confirmation once again of the Lord's will. Hicks's words about the Shohola train wreck and reaching out to his countrymen. The Reverend's exhortation to visit those imprisoned. All were part of God's plan. He mustn't resist the call any longer.

Lord, forgive me. For not trusting you with this burden sooner.

Armed with three loaves of bread, a few blankets, and Mari's resolve, Ethan stepped alongside the mercy mission. He straightened his tunic over his shoulders and marched, all the while wrestling with what he was about to face inside those walls. Reverend Beecher led the way along Water Street with brisk stride, and Ethan fell in. The western edge of the city stretched before them until, almost a mile distant, a grand white structure on the right—the Foster House—came into view. On the left, a wall of twelve-foot tall stockade, abutted by the guard house.

Ethan's stomach tightened as they approached the guard shack, and Beecher spoke with one of the officers. With a few shouted orders, the main gate swung open for them, revealing an ocean of humanity beyond. As Reverend Beecher moved forward, soldiers in both blue and gray parted before him. Ethan followed the pilgrimage, clutching his paltry offerings like a shield over the misgivings twisting in his chest.

In moments they reached a clearing, and Beecher took his place. A sizable crowd gathered in, and "ushers" in Federal blue flanked the congregation, holding rifles. Ethan surveyed the crowd, the perimeter of which stretched to the line of wooden barracks. How far would Beecher's words reach? Standing near, he took in the sermon, while doubt gnawed at the tender shoots of his faith. Beecher's voice carried well over the distance, but would it penetrate stony hearts?

Ethan reviewed the story of the prodigal son with the minister, having heard the words so often that they'd almost lost their immediacy. Beecher invited broken souls to come home to a father who ran to meet them, to a home that was never so willing as now to restore their standing, a country poised to receive their allegiance.

Ethan examined his surroundings. The green boards of the shoddy board and batten barracks had begun to warp. A foul smell arose from the river. The men themselves, dressed in tattered clothing, defied the whitewashed accounts depicted in the *Elmira Advertiser* of the “pleasant” camp conditions. Ethan tallied sunken cheeks, gaunt visages, overgrown, scraggly hair, and bare feet. The evidence of privations wrote an indicting story which the hirelings at the papers wouldn't. Indignation burned within him.

He looked down at the loaves and blankets in his hand. This shallow outreach could never cover the needs. A few words and morsels, scattered in the face of abject need, only patronized these seasoned veterans, stripping them of their dignity. Even for the Master, a few loaves had not sufficed without the miracle of multiplication.

Deep down he wanted to believe. If the efforts here were but seeds, at least they might take root and sprout something able to bear the weight of the burden. He sighed out the heaviness bearing down on his heart.

The need was just too great.

Chapter 35

Mr. Langdon's conveyance bore Mari around the corner from the church to the main thoroughfare, and turning left, passed one city block north to the carriage lane behind the Langdon home. Viewing the home from three angles she took in its scope, consuming the entire city block across from the church. Her host stopped at a carriage house covered in a wall of vines. After handing off his team to a stable keeper, Mr. Langdon helped Hattie and Mari down from the carriage, and led through a latticed garden fence. She continued to survey the expansive home from this more intimate perspective. A four-story affair, including a widow's walk cupola, the mansion was undergoing expansion. Parts of the exterior hung with scaffolding for which her host apologized, explaining he had purchased the property two years prior and his architects and builders still had a way to go in completing his vision.

What she viewed was indeed grand. An orchard, greenhouses, gardens both formal and informal with a pond and fountains, boxwood hedges forming a maze, flowers, potted tropical plants on slate patios, wrought iron benches with canopy, a bird cage with exotic tropical species.... the property offered more than her eyes could take in. And that was just the exterior.

On the porch, a young lady lounged in a hammock, book in hand. She perked up as Mari arrived with Mr. Langdon's guest entourage.

"Livy, may I present Marietta Hamilton. Miss Marietta, my daughter Olivia."

The girl did not rise, but her smile was warm and engaging. Drawing nearer, Mari noted her unusually pale complexion. "How do you do, Miss Langdon?"

"Pleased to meet you, Miss Hamilton. My dear cousin Hattie has told me wonderful stories of your crusading."

Heat flooded Mari's cheeks. "Dear me. I'm afraid our dear Hattie has mistaken me for someone of genuine importance."

"I do so admire your spirit. I think we should become fast friends." Livy's smile twinkled with a vitality seeming at odds with her general health.

Mari smiled then, shaking her head modestly. "The honor of your acquaintance is mine." The book in Livy's hands caught her eye. *Uncle Tom's Cabin.* An older novel now, but certainly an important one. "Harriet Beecher Stowe. Now that's a crusader."

"Ms. Beecher Stowe happens to be our Reverend's sister."

A maid emerged through the wooden screened door, carrying a tray of sweet tea. Mari reached for one of them, and when she looked up to thank the woman, she almost dropped the glass.

"Miss Mari?" The same delighted astonishment stealing over Mari spoke in the breathless voice of her dear Tilly. The maid set the tray down on a marble and brass table and the two embraced.

"You know one another?" Livy straightened from her reclining position.

"Yes, Miss Livy." Tilly still held Mari's hands pressed between hers, patting them with affection. "This my Miss Mari I been telling you about. Her Mist' Ethan the one who help my boy."

"Remarkable." Miss Langdon set her book down. "Harriet Beecher Stowe has nothing on you, Miss Hamilton. You will simply have to regale Mother and Father with your story."

Mr. Langdon emerged from the house with a missive. "I've just received word that your father's enterprises this morning have delayed him a bit longer. We'll hold supper until his arrival."

ଔ

Camp Rathbun
Less than a mile away

The sun dipped lower in the west, sending harsh rays sloping through the opening of Devon's tent. Coupled with the day's oppressive mugginess, his burning fever became unbearable. Flies dogged his every move, hovering his eyes and nose. He raised a listless hand to bat them away and gathered himself to rise.

Nagging thirst drove him to seek the nearest well. The way passed close by Foster's Pond, an inlet from the river with no outlet. Devon turned his back on the thick, sluggish water, befouled by leaching from the latrines of ten thousand men. Choking on the foul air, he wished he could turn his back on the implications of his water source's proximity, but the nearby well offered the only accessible relief to his cracked lips and parched throat. Devon tried to force the unpleasant notions of typhoid, cholera and dysentery from his mind, and tightened the tatters of his wrap about his ribs as he shuffled toward the well.

The spinning in his head threatened to topple him, and he narrowly avoided colliding with another soldier hustling toward the front gate. Devon staggered sideways a few paces bracing for impact, and it was then he noticed the large gathering. Too early for evening roll call, and too late for meal line-up, the assembly's purpose puzzled Devon until the preacher's words reached his ears.

"For this, thy brother was dead, and is now alive; was lost, and is found again."

An image filled his mind of Ethan, standing before him, a hand reaching out in reconciliation. The sun scorched his eyes, tearless. If only the vision were real, but he knew he didn't deserve such a mercy. He set his jaw and turned, regaining the ground he had lost.

"Devon," a familiar voice came up behind him.

"Jamie." He cracked a smile. "Where've you been lately?"

"Here and there." Jamie looked him up and down, stroking a hand over his mouth. "How've you been?"

"I'm managing." Devon lied. He hadn't been to mess hall today—too weak to fight the scavengers or to wait in long lines and take his meal at the standing tables.

Jamie leaned in to tell him a confidence. "A group of us boys are fixin' to get out. We're tunneling, Devon. Might be our ticket out of here."

Devon swayed under the blazing September sun. He stood to benefit in no way from Jamie's news. As sick as he was, he'd never make it. "Hope it works out for you."

"I'll know soon. Wish me luck." Jamie waved as he departed.

So that was it. Jamie had taken up with fellows with better offerings. He couldn't blame him, of course, but seeing Jamie's side of it didn't help his own dismal prospects.

Turning back to the well, Devon reeled the crank to lift the bucket. His arms shook from the effort, and crushing pain radiated from his ribs into his back. Gasping for breath, he imagined the crystal mountain streams of home instead of this putrid brew. He closed his eyes and drank from his tin cup. A fit of coughing brought most of it back up.

Beads of sweat rolled from his overgrown hairline down his neck. "Oh, Lord," he moaned, pressing an arm to his ribs. The stunted prayer was heartfelt. He had no pride left to deny his need of God's help.

The church service closed in on him again, a call to prayer marshaling all within earshot. His body ached. He was *so tired.* Tired of sickness, tired of fever, tired of running from the Lord. If he were dying, he'd better make peace the way Walt had. He sank his head down until his chin hit his chest and he closed his eyes.

God, are you willing to hear the prayer of a prodigal?

His throat constricted from the taste of the well water, or at least that's what he told himself. He held a hand against the hammering in his head.

Lord, I got nothing to offer you but this weight of sin. But I got people depending on me, now. Please forgive me ....

He couldn't finish the prayer until the dizzying emotion dissipated.

I need your help. Please, God, let me live. Send a miracle.

Nothing. No immediate sense of relief enjoined his supplication. No burst of hope, no deliverance from pain or hunger manifested. With the dejection of scorned humility, he collected his legs beneath himself and made his agonizing way back to his tent.

ଓ୪ଌ

A pathetic scarecrow of a soldier held Ethan's gaze, moving toward the distant tent line. The figure did not exactly ambulate in a limp; it was more a lifeless shuffle. He'd seen the ragged condition of Confederate soldiers before, but these specimens exceeded his worst imaginings. That one was tied together as if the straw stuffing about his mid-seam was about to spill out. Then, stepping into his view directly before him, another of those scarecrows appeared, his blue eyes expectant as though waiting for something. Ethan blinked for a few seconds before it registered that others were handing out their packages to the prisoners. He extended a loaf of bread to him, a blanket to the one behind him, and the last of Marietta's parcels to another. In seconds, his hands were empty, and he wished he'd had a thousand more packages to distribute. Nodding their thanks, the men departed, and the rest left empty-handed after standing an hour in the blazing sun.

Ethan shifted where he stood, searching his heart for any hope. *Oh, God, where are you? Where will their help come from?*

ଓ୪ଌ

Devon arrived at his tent with the last bit of his strength. As he lowered himself to his mat, three others paused outside and peered through the open flaps, a parcel tucked under each arm.

"That was good preachin' wa'nt it?" The man unfolded the brown paper and tore a hunk of bread, popping it into his mouth.

"I reckon it were." Another man replied.

"It was sure worth it for these fine loaves," the third said.

As Devon settled painfully down, they stepped into his tent.

"S'cuse me. Didn't know this tent were occupied."

Devon waved them in. "Always room for more."

They broke the three loaves and held a portion out to him. Devon downed his unexpected meal, one miraculous bite at a time. Its crunchy crust and soft, doughy center melted on his tongue and hardly pained his brittle teeth or his sore mouth. By and by, his stomach gurgled with the first real fill he had experienced in months. Overwhelmed to the brink of tears, he closed his eyes in gratitude.

God had heard his prayer after all.

ଓଃ

Ethan followed Reverend Beecher's assembly back toward the gates. The preacher lingered at the rear, collecting the last stragglers, people like himself Ethan supposed—curious and appalled at what they'd just experienced, and reluctant to depart.

Roll call sounded, and the gray ghosts who had gathered for the camp meeting now formed rank on the open parade grounds.

A guard pushed through the crowd and signaled Ethan. "Sergeant, we need an extra hand."

Ethan cast a consulting gaze at the reverend, hoping Beecher would somehow absolve him. He'd seen and done enough here, suddenly wishing to put as much distance from this haunting place as possible. Beecher gave a paternal nod and smile. "I'm sure you can find your way back when you're done, son. Thank you for coming out with us."

The guards led Ethan into the heart of the camp, moving south along a dirt avenue past the barracks. Everywhere he walked, he felt eyes on him. He shook off a shudder and quickened his pace to keep up with the guard.

A trio of Confederates stood outside one of the tents. The tallest of them flagged Ethan and the guard. The man pointed. "In here."

The prison guard paused outside the open tent flap and peered in. Covering his face with the sleeve of his jacket, he turned away. The disgusted look on his face told of conditions more unpleasant than the filth in the nearby pond.

"This one's fit for the Trans-Mississippi Ward." The guard gestured to the tent city across the pond.

"What's that? Ethan asked.

"Where they put the hopeless cases," he answered flippantly, stepping away from the tent and letting the flap fall.

The tall Confederate standing off to the side muttered to the other. "They gonna just leave him there to die?"

Ethan took a step in their direction. One held a blanket rolled up under his arm, and the taller man half a loaf of bread, the third, nothing left but crumbs on his homespun shirt. Ethan dismissed the fleeting thought that maybe these three had been the same scarecrows who'd taken Mari's supplies. Out of nine-thousand prisoners, what were the odds?

"What's the problem, gentlemen?" Ethan met the taller man's gaze.

A flicker and a squint passed over the man's startlingly blue eyes. The prisoner then turned to his companions and they exchanged inscrutable looks and whispers.

Unease roiled in Ethan's stomach, imagining they'd noticed his southern dialect, and how that must sound, coming from a Yankee. He clenched his teeth, soldiering past a wave of shame. He thought he overheard a stitch of their conference. "Identical, I'd say."

"Even sound alike."

This was what he'd feared in coming here. He'd never faced his countrymen since joining the Federal war effort three years ago, except on the battlefield. He couldn't stomach their disdain. It figured that he'd pay for his crimes of rejecting the south and betraying his family now that he'd come to ease their suffering.

"Someone ought to get that man to a doctor." The tall Confederate with those unnaturally blue eyes gave Ethan a pointed look. "Reckon you're the one."

Ethan nodded and sidestepped as the tall one lifted the tent flap for him. No sign of life stirred within except the buzz of insects. Ethan forged in, head-first. One breath of the foul air took Ethan aback. He would have retreated, but the lanky Confederate braced him with an arm at his back.

Ethan cleared his throat and stepped in, letting his eyes adjust to the dim interior. A form lay on the ground in the corner. Flies crawled and fought over the real estate of arms crossed over chest, a face frozen in a grimace. Ethan looked back at the tent opening to see if anyone was going to help him lift this dying or dead man, but the rebel was gone.

The guard looked in, a sneer etched over his weathered face. "Confounded Rebs will let each other rot before they report 'em dead! I'd better alert the burial detail."

Ethan turned back and squatted beside the man, covering his nose with the flap of his jacket to mitigate the smell of fever and refuse. A swirl of flies rose and circled above the man's open eyes. They blinked.

Ethan started.

The man's dark pupils slid in their sockets to focus back at him. The man was alive, but barely.

Ethan stooped over the emaciated face, surveying a wave of black hair and several days' growth of beard. "Cancel that burial detail. This one needs a stretch—"

"E-e—" A soft rasp rose from the man's throat.

An inexplicable jolt stroked through him, and his heart hammered an erratic beat. That face. Ethan narrowed his gaze, scanning features again. Letting go of his wool lapel, he bent in, nearer.

It simply couldn't be.

The nose, although reduced by starvation, was the same. The jaw line, the cheekbones, and brow wore on Ethan's sight like a distorted reflection in a mirror. But the eyes. A chill coursed through him despite the oppressive heat. Ethan registered in one disbelieving look. They were his own. And they looked back at him in the same incredulous survey.

"Ee-e?"

His gut constricted as though he'd been punched, and he clutched his stomach. Sinking to his knees, he reached out a tentative hand to the figure before him.

Devon?

He touched the tips of his fingers to cold skin. Recoiling, he steadied himself and rested his right hand over hands the same scale as his. And they rose and fell on his chest in a shallow breath.

Oh, Jesus.

"By God, Devon. Yes, it's me. Ethan."

Trembling overtook him, first in his knees, and then all over his body. He took a firmer hold of the hands beneath his and bent over his brother's ear.

"It's Ethan," he whispered. "Can you hear me?"

His voice faltered, and tears stung the backs of his eyes. He warded away the flies and smoothed the straggled hair out of his brother's face. Clawing desperation seized his throat. Devon *had* to know he was here.

A feeble hand reached up and wiry fingers curled around his. Emotions welled painfully inside Ethan's chest, stealing his breath until he choked. He swallowed to keep his voice from breaking. "Hold on, Devon. I'm here."

He lifted the dear head from the ground and cradled it to his own. His brother's fevered skin seared his brow. Two teardrops rolled from his eyes and fell into his brother's hair and he squeezed his streaming eyes closed.

Ethan gathered him up into his arms. Devon was so weak that his arms hung limp. A rasp intoned his name in a voice he hadn't heard since his eighteenth birthday.

"E-e-than?" The searching in Devon's eyes gutted him.

"Yes, I'm here." He fought through the emotion to speak. "And I'm going to get you out of here. Hold on. I'm going to carry you." He lifted Devon from the ground, and though he was every bit as tall as himself, his brother couldn't have weighed much more than a newborn foal. Ethan's stomach sickened with more than just the overwhelming smell. How had his brave, proud brother come to this?

He emerged from the tent carrying his burden, and met the same blue eyes of the Confederate who had directed him in.

"So, it's true," the man said, looking between Ethan and Devon. He pulled a tattered gray slouch hat off his head. "Brothers."

"Twins."

Ethan bowed his head and moved slowly past. Devon's head rocked back into Ethan's chest with every stride, but for all he surely suffered, his brother did not cry out.

"I'm here, Devon. It's okay, I'm here." Once the light hit Devon's eyes, he emitted a low moan and buried his face deeper into Ethan's chest. He could go no further in the knowledge of the pain he inflicted on the fever and sore-ridden body in his arms. "Lord, show me what to do." Beside him the three prisoners, keeping silent vigil with him, bowed their heads and prayed too.

"Over yonder's the hospital," the blue-eyed one said, pointing. "Be his best chance."

Ethan nodded and moved in that direction.

Ethan's tears had dried on his face in a stiff trail. Such a long trail, he reflected, that had led him here to this place, this moment. If he hadn't agreed to Levi Hamilton's demands banishing him to this miserable military rendezvous, if he hadn't been given a day off to go to church today, if he hadn't obeyed the prompting of the Lord to come to the prison outreach—so many if's—he never would have found his brother. Yet, gazing down on the form laying slack in his arms, doubt crept through him with a dark fluttering.

Was he too late?

He entered the hospital and an orderly directed him to an empty cot. Ethan laid Devon down, holding his breath against the likelihood of his brother's pain.

"Skin and bones. Dehydrated bad." The man bent in examination. He wore Confederate jacket and trousers, apparently an aide recruited from the prison. "Help me turn him," the man said, pushing back the blanket Ethan had carried him in.

Devon cried out when they rolled him on the cot. The aide stripped off his filthy shirt, and convulsions shook Devon's body at the sudden change in temperature. Ethan shuddered in sympathy, squatting by his brother's bedside. Goose-flesh rose over Devon's skin, and the ribs on his right side curved inward, misshapen. Weak cries protested when the orderly ran wash-water over his many sores. Ethan took his brother's hand, crouching low to his ear, and repeated assurances.

The orderly gave him a sideways glance, placed the soiled clothes in a pile, and gathered a blanket from a supply shelf. "You can cover him if you're of a mind."

Ethan took the folded blanket with a nod of thanks, and shook it out over his brother, tucking it gently around him.

Devon opened his mouth to speak. The sound was so faint, Ethan had to lean in to hear it. "I prayed, E. I prayed, and you came."

The lump in his throat tightened and his breath staggered in a sob. He recovered and looked steadily down into Devon's eyes. "God answered us both, then."

"How... did you know?"

Ethan shrugged. "God knew."

Devon's teeth chattered until Ethan strafed the blanket over his shoulders, then his brother's eyes rolled back. Slow, rhythmic breathing told Ethan he had succumbed to something akin to sleep. When he rallied after a minute, he sought out Ethan's face, as though to assure himself he was still there. He struggled to speak again. The aide returned with warm broth, interrupting Devon's efforts. After the first spoon, the aide could not keep up with Devon's voracious appetite.

Watching this brought the tears back to Ethan's eyes. He dabbed them with his sleeve and sunk to the dirt floor beside the cot.

The aide spooned the last of the broth, all the while giving Ethan furtive glances.

"What are his chances?"

"He's gonna need good food, strong medicine, and constant care. Not like' to get that here."

Devon reached out for him, his fingers extending until Ethan met them with his own. They were so cold. He searched his mind for someone who might be able to help. The image of Marietta came to him immediately.

"Devon, I have to go."

Wildness lit Devon's eyes. "You're leaving me again?"

Ethan firmed his hold on Devon's hand, steeling himself against the shame trying to crumble his resolve from within. "There's something I must do. I'll be back directly."

Chapter 36

Foster House lay roughly 300 yards from the main gate, housing the officers who presided over the military training rendezvous as well as the prison camp. Ethan covered the distance faster than his thoroughbred could have carried him. As he ascended the porch steps, boots tromped up behind him.

"Sergeant Sharpe. What are you doing away from your post?"

Darcy.

Ethan turned slowly.

"Who gave you permission to gad about town all day?"

"I received no specific orders to stay or otherwise, Captain."

Folding his arms over his chest, the man laughed. "For once, you've saved me the bother of reporting you derelict. Major Colt has noted it himself."

Ethan ground his boot into the step and mopped the back of his neck. He wished the officer were bluffing, but he could see by the vindictive glitter in his eyes he was not. Ethan stood his ground, searching his mind for a diversion—Devon's very life counted on it. "Requesting emergency furlough, sir."

"*Denied.* I told you things weren't over between us, Sharpe."

The Captain's smug grin danced in Ethan's enraged sights. He curled his fingers into a tight fist, coiled it back, and....

The front door swung open, and out stepped Major Colt, followed by an older civilian gentleman in a long coat and top hat.

“Ethan? My goodness. Providence must have brought you here.”

He unclenched his fist and shook out the tension. He blinked to focus, but again the image of Levi Hamilton stood there beside the officer.

“Sergeant.” Colt barked.

“Sir.” Ethan saluted.

“Step inside. You too, Darcy.”

Ethan obeyed at once, gritting his teeth. How could he possibly parlay this meeting to Devon's aid now? *Lord, go before me.*

Mr. Hamilton remained outside, where Darcy had been. Ethan stood at attention.

“At ease, Sharpe.”

He exhaled and met the Major's piercing gaze.

“I've just been made aware of an incident involving you and Captain Darcy in June of this year, outside the ladies’ college.”

Darcy sent him a withering look.

Ethan's breath fled. Darcy was surely behind this.

“I have civilian witnesses saying that Captain Darcy initiated a fight with you. That he struck you in the face, and that you attempted to break up the fight and refused to retaliate. Is that correct?”

Ethan let out a cough of pent up air.

Darcy's face blazed crimson.

“Are these all the pertinent facts, Sergeant?”

“Yes, sir. Yes, I refrained from engaging with my superior officer, sir.”

“Is it also true that the captain publicly harassed two of the college students?”

“Harassed, sir?”

“Made untoward advances and used unflattering speech in their presence? Insults?”

Ethan searched his conscience. It would be too easy to shovel dirt on Darcy's coffin. "I'm not sure, sir."

"What precipitated the incident?"

"Captain Darcy summoned me from drills that day, sir. Said there were women walking the streets, asking for me by name. He accused me of consorting with them."

"Mr. Hamilton tells me you are engaged to his daughter Marietta, one of the young ladies in question."

Engaged? Ethan thought he'd already been numbed to the core by the day's events. But a soft breeze could have bowled him over. *Engaged.* He looked out the window where Mr. Hamilton's silhouette stood, and a flood of gratitude—and wonder—filled his heart.

"Sergeant?" Major Colt demanded a reply.

"Mr. Hamilton wouldn't say that if it weren't true," Ethan replied, as much to himself as to Colt.

"You are aware of the college's strictures? Students are not to fraternize with soldiers, or anyone else without the express permission and supervision of college staff."

"Yes, sir, I...."

"Thank you, Sergeant, but I was talking to Darcy."

Darcy snapped his boots together. "Yes, Major, sir."

"Then why did you stop them on the street, when you carried dispatch from Colonel Eastman for the telegraph office?"

Darcy worried the flap of his holster with a subtle movement of his fingers. Ethan could feel the heat emanating from him, the fury, nerves as frayed as the leather he stroked.

"Captain, you can surely appreciate the delicate position you have placed me in. I must uphold a standard for my men and strike a balance with the other institutions of this city, particularly where the ladies of the college are concerned. You have jeopardized the reputation of the military command here. I have no choice but to charge you with conduct unbecoming an officer. Your bars will be taken, and you will be demoted to Staff Sergeant, where you will teach—and relearn—order and discipline."

"What? That's an outrage! My father will hear of this, Major." A series of oaths sputtered from Darcy's mouth, and two guards from the provost marshal's detail stepped up to take him into their custody.

While Darcy made his dramatic exit, Ethan stood, waiting to be disciplined in kind. How would he broach the subject of his brother, who even now languished on his death bed?

"Sergeant Sharpe, your future father-in-law tells me you gave up a field promotion to come here."

"Sir?"

"Can you tell me why you would do so, after serving meritoriously through three campaigns with the Army of the Potomac?"

Accusations crowded Ethan's mind. *Traitor. Coward. Shirker. Ne'er-do-well.*

"I felt it my duty, sir. To pay a personal debt of honor."

"I understand it is because your betrothed's father persuaded you to take the transfer. You laid down your career, a promising one, to serve those who mattered to you most."

Ethan blinked at his commander. How did Major Colt know any of this? And where was this going?

"I've been looking into your record, Sergeant. The recruits admire you, and you work well with them. You know first-hand what battle preparedness entails. What's more, you're a man of principle. You've served with distinction under unscrupulous circumstances. Don't think I haven't seen what Darcy's been up to with his poker games and drinking. I've let him have enough rope to hang himself. Sharpe, I'm recommending you for promotion. I'd like to offer you Darcy's command."

His head swam. He clenched his toes so tightly in his boots it almost set him off balance. "Sir, I don't know what to say. I—I'm honored."

"You may commence with your new command after a three-day furlough, effective immediately."

Ethan saluted, and it was returned. But before he would be dismissed, before he would even allow himself to process what had just happened, he had to help Devon.

"Sir, permission to speak freely."

"Granted."

"Sir, I am a loyalist from a secession state, as you are probably aware. My family is from the Shenandoah Valley. I have three brothers, two of whom I know serve the Confederacy. Sir, it has come to my awareness just today that my brother—my twin brother—is incarcerated in barracks three. In very grave condition. Can you advise what can be done to—"

"Off the record, Captain? I would advise you to find a private citizen to see to his care, to visit him in the camp hospital. For the record, I cannot sign off on any prisoner's discharge *unless* they take an oath of loyalty and are deemed no threat to the Union. Furthermore, I must caution you that it would be extremely unwise for you to make a conspicuous presence inside that camp."

Ethan's interview over, he exited onto the avenue, mulling Colt's advice. He took several hurried strides before he sighted Mr. Hamilton.

Marietta's father joined him.

"Major Colt used a curious phrase, sir. He said you referred to me as your future *son-in-law.*"

"It seems I've been unduly hard on you, Ethan." The man walked with head down and his hands folded behind his back. "Aaron contacted your former commander, and he told him of your meritorious service at Gettysburg. The officer mentioned that you'd been given a field commission as lieutenant. Considering the choice I put to you last year, I see I am to blame for your coming here. I realize now how badly I've misjudged you, son. I ask that you forgive me and accept my blessing on your union with my daughter."

Ethan halted. "No, sir. The Lord paved my road here. I see now that if I hadn't come, I wouldn't have found my brother. He's starving, Mr. Hamilton. In the camp. I just left his bedside."

Levi's grave expression registered his words. Motioning to the livery he had waiting, he invited Ethan to join him to the Langdon home. "Perhaps we may find help there."

Along the way, Ethan related the whole story of finding his brother, and ended just as the coach parked before the mansion on Union Street.

Ethan's nerves buzzed. He had so much to tell Marietta, he was sure to burst before they were likely to find a moment alone.

ঙ

Expecting Papa to arrive at any moment, Marietta tried to focus, but the words of her hostess turned to tinkling bells in her ears. They'd held back dinner twenty minutes now waiting for him. And what of Ethan? Surely, he would keep his promise and come. How long did the church outreach last? She had so much to tell him. How providence had reunited her with her dear friend Tilly, and how she had found kinship with the Langdons, people who shared their convictions deeply. And how they'd listened raptly to her retelling of Ethan's selfless rescue of Tilly's son. And then, there were those little particulars between lovers—how she'd missed the feel of his hand in hers, and those brooding eyes gazing into hers, the gentle intonation of her name on his lips.... But she would have to settle for a staid and proper account of the church outreach while her insides ignited, and her hands strafed inside her gloves from wringing them in her lap.

When the servant announced two guests, she only heard one—Ethan Sharpe. But a full second later, the name Mr. Levi Hamilton followed. It seemed fitting that they had arrived together. Marietta rose from her chair, her hand pressed to her heart to settle its flight. Papa led the way into the room, and her host stood, welcoming both the men she loved.

The Langdons received Ethan next. When at last he turned to her, Ethan's face bore a concern that haunted his handsome features. A boyish vulnerability wore on him so raw that her breath staggered. She mouthed the words, "What is it?"

He took the seat nearest her, and leaned in to her ear. "Devon. He's here. In the prison camp."

She shook her head, willing his words to be true, and yet not true, at the same time. "How is he?"

He glanced between her, her father, their hosts, and back. He squeezed her hand. "Not good. Please pray."

She stroked his hand in hers, sensing desperation in his touch. She closed her eyes to offer the only prayer she could muster. *Help, Lord.*

"We're all eager to hear of your afternoon at the prison camp," Hattie Langdon's Uncle Jervis said, nodding at Ethan. "While our servants adjust the seating in the dining room, won't you regale us on Reverend Beecher's excursion?"

Ethan cleared his throat and met the man's friendly inquiry. "I made a startling and rather personal discovery while there, sir. I...."

Mari squeezed his fingers and willed strength to him.

"It seems, Mr. Langdon, I have family there. A brother. In fact, my twin." His voice lowered, and he paused a moment before he carried on. "He is, like many there, undernourished, sick, and in desperate need of help. The overcrowding, poor air quality, and insufficient housing—it is a pitiable place, sir. A blight on this city."

Ethan rose and released Mari's hand with a look of regret aimed first at her, and then at his hosts. "I pray your forgiveness, but I must decline your invitation to dine this evening. Arrangements for my brother must be made immediately. I came only to let you know."

"Wait, Ethan."

Marietta turned her attention to her father who had spoken.

"The work Mr. Langdon and I shared for many years united us in the cause of freedom. My daughter's betrothed," Papa's eyes twinkled at her before refocusing on Langdon, "has sacrificed much for the same cause. A Virginian by birth, he's forsaken home, family, inheritance, and reputation to fight for our cause. It seems fitting to me now to aid him in his cause—freeing his captive brother. What can be done to help?"

"Yes," Langdon replied. "Your daughter has told us this young man's compelling story. Just this week I have heard plans to release sick prisoners. The ones so sick that survival over the winter seems unlikely." He turned to Ethan. "Do you believe your brother fit enough to last transport to Baltimore?"

"No. I mean, not without a miracle, sir."

"When the time comes we have connections with a railroad man who will see to your brother's accommodations. Until then, he must be able to make the selection."

"If he survives." His voice thickened. Marietta clasped his hand. "He'll need immediate help. Food, medicine. And someone to go into the camp and see to all of this."

"I'll go."

Ethan and Mari both turned their heads to the entry where Tilly stood.

"I'll see he get well, Mr. Ethan. My boy and I—he go in to that camp with Mr. Jones evr' day with the burial detail. We gladly help for what you done for us."

Mari burst with gratitude. In the course of a day, the Lord had answered all of her fondest prayers.

"I'm greatly obliged, Tilly." His hat in his hand, Ethan bowed to the woman. "I regret the imposition, but we must go at once."

"By all means," Mr. Langdon replied. "Tilly, send for your boy to drive you all in my carriage. I believe he is presently with George Jones across the street cleaning the church. And Mrs. Langdon," he turned to his wife, "please have the cook prepare a basket of provisions for Sergeant Sharpe's brother."

Mari prayed a silent thank you. Ethan cleared his throat, she suspected, to master the emotion from stealing over his voice.

"God bless you, sir. I'll gladly repay you for your kindness."

"Not at all, son. Would the Lord have us do any less? You have our prayers, and anything else you may require."

"Will you walk me to the door, Mari?"

Her father nodded consent, and she slipped into the vestibule with Ethan. He lifted her hand to his lips. "Have you heard? Your father has consented to our marriage."

Mari's tears breached their dam. She swallowed and nodded. "I only wish I could accompany you."

"I covet your prayers." He drew her to him, and his kiss came suddenly, taking her completely off center. She hung in his arms, suspended by the need they both felt—for comfort, for assurance, jubilation at having their marriage blessing at long last. She broke away first.

"I will leave school. My place is with you now. Besides, you'll need a nurse for him, won't you?"

He trailed his fingers over her cheek, sending new sensations through her. "You would do that for me? and for Devon?"

No glimmer of doubt lingered in her decision. "All I've ever wanted was to make a difference in the lives of others. If I can't serve the ones dearest to me, then my devotion is in vain."

"I'm a blessed man. But let's wait and see what comes of this transport first. Make no decisions just yet." He lifted his gaze to the threshold of the foyer where Tilly waited. "Are you ready?"

She nodded and stepped toward the front door carrying Mrs. Langdon's provisions.

"God go with you both. I'll wait for your return."

ଓଃ୫୨

Ethan knelt at his brother's bedside. He tucked his hand beneath the cover, feeling Devon's chest for the warmth or breath that would assure him he yet lived. Finding scant evidence of either, he pealed back the blanket to examine him. Was he truly only sleeping?

"Devon?" He nudged him gently. "Devon, I've brought help."

Slits of lids opened, and the twilight of a soul peered out. Ethan gasped a prayer. "Jesus, help us to help him."

Thoughts of Mari's prayers bolstered him. Of her lovely countenance, so rosy and healthy, compared to Devon's colorless complexion. His brother had become a fraction, a wraith. But was this unto death?

"We must pray, Devon. If God sees fit to keep you alive, I can get you home."

This moment where life and death hung suspended like his baited breath required the greater agreement of two or three gathered in faith. Tilly and her son were Devon's angels, come to offer answers to his prayers.

Vincent retrieved a Bible from a nearby patient's bedside and opened it. He cleared his throat and read the words in his rich voice.

"'How can I give you up, Ephraim? How can I hand you over, Israel? My heart is changed within me; all my compassion is aroused. I will not carry out my fierce anger, nor devastate Ephraim again. For I am God and not man, the Holy One among you. I will not come again in wrath."

Ethan's focus on his brother blurred, and he wiped his eyes again and again. Hadn't he meditated on Joseph's son Ephraim when he had first come to this seemingly forsaken city? Surely God was here.

He searched his brother's face as their former slave, now a voice of authority, continued reading: "They will follow the Lord; his children will come. They will come like birds from Egypt, like doves from Assyria. And I will settle them in their homes,' declares the Lord."

Vincent concluded the passage and closed the book.

Ethan pressed his face against his brother's chest, barely able to hold back from weeping. Such a promise. God would settle them back in their home, together. Mari and he would be married at last, and they and their children would build a homestead alongside Devon's one day.

Mari. How he loved her. She had played a vital part of this miracle with her sustaining loaves and offerings, leading them to this moment.

Ethan returned his focus on his brother. "That's God's promise, Dev. He's going to bring us home—both of us. Our story isn't over."

Devon blinked, and a spark lit his eye. "And our children. I'm going to be a daddy."

Rounds of toasts might have been shared on such a momentous occasion, but Ethan contented himself with his brother's weak hand clasp.

"Can't wait to meet your wife."

"Gwen." Devon's thin smile suddenly sobered. His expression intensified. "Pa told me you'd asked forgiveness, Ethan, but I'm the one needs yours."

"No," Ethan replied. "You've always had it."

Devon nodded and closed his eyes. In a moment, he murmured again. "What about you? Married yet?"

"I've been waiting for my best man before I marry my sweetheart."

"Mari?"

"Yep."

The faint smile returned, and a twinkle in his brother's eyes with it. "By God."

One by one, the worries and sorrows which had arrested Ethan's faith fled away with the truth his brother had just spoken. By God, who had indeed answered all of his prayers.

And they would all go home again. Together.

Epilogue

Bridgewater, Virginia
One year later

The sound of hammering brought Ethan around the corner of the barn. His father held a mouthful of nails, and at Ethan's approach he paused for a moment from driving one into the new pine board Devon held in place.

"Mari sent me out. She and Gwen are setting the supper plates. Reckon that means we'd better wash up."

His father spit the iron nails into his free hand and tucked them into the front of his leather apron. "Far be it from me to argue with a lady."

"Let's finish this last board first," Devon said. "I'm fixin' to starve, and I can smell Gwen's biscuits and gravy from here."

Ethan couldn't help shuddering at Devon's choice of words. His brother had come from the very brink of starvation, taking months to recover. But that was Devon, making jest of something as serious as that. He shook his head and stepped into his father's place, balancing the board in one hand, hefting the hammer in the other.

"Where's that scalawag Ben hiding?" their father asked, as though he'd just noticed that his youngest was missing.

"He's in with little Levi and Jentezen, keeping them company." Ethan replied.

"Both of you had boys, and not one Samuel between them." The old man didn't miss an opportunity to faze them about it.

Devon snorted a laugh. "You sure dug yerself a hole with that." He chucked Ethan on the shoulder.

"What about you? Yours came first. You could have named him after your Pa instead of Gwen's, you know."

"After Gwen's father passed, it gave her Ma plenty of comfort to know his name would be remembered."

Sobered, Ethan nodded. But his grin broke through in a minute. "I had to butter up Marietta's father, since I had to decline a captain's commission. But how else could I have come home? I've given enough years to the army."

"Captain, eh?" Devon raised his brows. He nudged their father. "Reckon we're worthy of the honor of a Captain at our table?"

The old man finished his coffee and wiped his mouth. "It's his table, too, don't forget. Now let's get inside before Ben beats us to that table." He clapped both boys on the shoulder. "Sure is nice to have two ladies cooking. A man can get used to that."

"And we'll have all the fences mended before you know it." Ethan added. "Somehow those two new colts are the spitten image of your Cinder. Reckon they're gonna need room to run."

Devon looked out at the small paddock where the farm's last two mares suckled black colts, and then turned back to Ethan with a grin.

"We'll mend as many fences as it takes."

"Yep. One board at a time, Dev."

The End

Kathleen L. Maher has had an infatuation with books and fictional heroes ever since her preschool crush, Peter Rabbit. She has a novella releasing with BARBOUR in the 2018 *Victorian Christmas Brides* collection, featuring her hometown of Elmira, New York. Her debut historical, *Bachelor Buttons*, blends her Irish heritage and love of the American Civil War. She won the American Christian Fiction Writers Genesis contest in 2012 for this novel under the title *Closer than a Brother*. Kathleen shares an old farmhouse in upstate New York with her husband, children, and a small zoo of rescued animals.

If you enjoyed reading *The Abolitionist's Daughter*, one of the best ways to let me know and say "thank you" is to write a favorable review on Amazon as well as other sites. Thank you so much!

I love hearing from my readers. If you have any comments or questions please feel free to contact me at kathleenleemaher@gmail.com

Follow me

- on the group history blog I contribute to the 8th of every month: https://www.hhhistory.com/
- on Facebook: https://www.facebook.com/mahereenie
- on Twitter: https://twitter.com/Mahereenie
- and on Amazon https://www.amazon.com/author/kathleenlmaher

Editorial Notes

Great care has been taken to represent the historical accuracy of real people, places and events mentioned in this book. But certain artistic liberties have been used, for example, where the exact dates were difficult to pinpoint, ie the timing of Jervis Langdon and his family occupying The Langdon Mansion across from the Congregational Church. Some sources have them living there at the end of the Civil War, whereas other sources indicate the purchase of the property following the end of the war.

Made in the USA
Middletown, DE
19 April 2019